HIDDEN
WINGS

FROM BESTSELLING AUTHOR
CAMEO RENAE

This is a work of fiction. All characters and events portrayed in this novel are fictitious and are products of the author's imagination and any resemblance to actual events, or locales or persons, living or dead are entirely coincidental.

Cover by Mae I Design and Photography
Edited by Crimson Tide Editorial
Book design by Inkstain Interior Book Designing
HIDDEN WINGS POETRY by Amber McCallister

Published by
Crushing Hearts and Black Butterfly Publishing, LLC.

To my GRAMMY.
A firecracker, in her eighties, who reads every single day.
She was the very one who instilled a love of reading into me at a
young age, and has been so proud and supportive of my journey.
She's my hero, an amazing role model, and an inspiration.
If I have an ounce of her inner strength—
I'll be fine, and make it in this life.
I love you, Grammy!

xoxo

ACKNOWLEDGEMENTS

To my awesome publisher, SJ DAVIS, who believed
in my stories and published them.

To my kick-butt editor, VICTORIA RAE SCHMITZ. Thank you
for helping to bring Hidden Wings up to par. You rock!

To my magical cover designer, REGINA WAMBA,
who took my vision and turned it into a reality.

To my book designer, NADÈGE RICHARDS,
who makes my words look pretty.

To ALL OF THE AWESOME BOOK PAGES, who
promote authors and help the world to notice us.

WHAT HAPPENS WHEN DARKNESS AND LIGHT COLLIDE?

HIDDEN
WINGS

ONE

M Y EYES SNAPPED OPEN. I was on my back, disoriented. Strangers surrounded me.

"Seventeen. She's fading in and out," a short-winded voice briefed the others.

A red sign glowed as we passed through a set of double doors.

EMERGENCY

What the hell happened?

My heart pounded furiously against my chest. There was excruciating pain, but I couldn't pinpoint it. It was everywhere. I tried to raise my right arm, but it was fastened to some kind of board, and twisted at an abnormal angle. Strong hands held me down as I tried to sit up.

"Just stay still," a low voice instructed.

Hot tears streamed from my burning, swollen eyes. With every breath, sharp pains shot through my chest, and every beat of my heart sent throbbing pulses through the rest of my body.

I was pulled into a small room and carefully lifted onto a bed, where warm blankets quickly replaced the cold, bloodied ones. A bright light blaring down on me made my eyes ache. Faces in white and blue masks scrambled all around me. I tried to speak, but my voice was too weak.

"She's lost a lot of blood."

Where are my parents?

I focused on the faces surrounding me, but none were familiar.

"We need to start a transfusion, *ASAP,*" someone instructed from a hidden corner.

I felt a prick on my left arm.

"Blood type?" a nurse asked.

"AB negative," another answered.

"AB negative?" a distressed voice countered. He was hushed and the voices became muffled.

"It's alright sweetheart. You'll be just fine," a female voice whispered from behind her white mask. Her bright, blue eyes fixed on mine, offering a glimmer of hope.

A mask was placed over my nose and mouth just as the pain started to numb. Voices soon trailed of, and I faded into darkness.

Before my eyes opened I felt pain, and slowly peeled my lids back to reveal a hazy world. My right arm was casted, and places I never thought existed, ached. My head throbbed and acid raced through my stomach, making me nauseated. The scents of bleach didn't help much.

I was in an unfamiliar room. The walls were painted in light pink, with a thin strip of pastel wallpaper lining the top. A TV hung from the wall, and to the side, was a large bay window with white blinds pulled halfway shut. Wires attached to my arms and face, were connected to a machine next to my bedside.

I glanced around, but there were no signs of my parents. Maybe they'd stepped out for a while, or went to get a bite to eat.

Something happened. Something horrible. But I couldn't remember. My mind was dark and blank, like a fresh canvas waiting to be painted on.

"Knock-knock," a voice called from the doorway. "Is it alright if I come in?"

A tall, blonde woman with hair pulled back into a long ponytail, dressed in a black, pin-striped suit stood in the doorway. Her face was warm, donning wide, green eyes.

I nodded, returning a weak smile.

She stepped into the room and pulled a stray chair from the corner, setting it next to my bedside. After placing her leather briefcase on the floor she reached over and laid her soft, warm hand over mine.

"Hello. My name is Abigail Reed. I'm a social worker assigned to you by the state of California. I'm here to help you."

Social worker? Assigned to me? Shouldn't she be talking with my parents?

"Can you tell me your name?" she asked, gently squeezing my hand.

"Emma," my voice exited in a whisper. At least I remembered that much.

"Do you remember anything about the accident?"

"Accident?" I questioned, shaking my head. "I can't... I don't remember anything. Where are my parents?" My mother would usually be glued to me if I was hurt or sick, and my dad was always a glancing distance away.

Miss Reed's eyes flitted downward.

"Emma," she started, then paused. Her brow furrowed. "I'm so sorry, Emma. There's no easy way to tell you—"

"Where are my parents?" I demanded.

A pang of fear surged through me. My heart constricted and doubt rushed over me like a tidal wave. What if they were injured? I needed to know. I needed to see them. *Now.*

She took in a deep breath and slowly exhaled. "Emma... your parents were killed in the accident."

It took a few moments for my brain to absorb her information. *Your parents were killed.*

The horrifying words echoed, over and over, through my mind. And then it slammed me... shattering pain, quickly spreading like a brush fire. My body trembled, as hot tears of horror and panic sprang from my eyes.

"No. It's not true. It can't be true," I cried, shaking my head. This had to be a nightmare.

"You're going to be alright, Emma," Miss Reed said in a calming voice, gently rubbing my hand.

"How will I *ever* be alright?"

I suddenly realized I was alone; an only child – no aunts, no uncles, no grandparents, no surviving kin.

My world spiraled uncontrollably, and my mind became completely numb. "How... how did it happen?" I sobbed, looking at her for answers.

"Well, it seems the car you were in, swerved off an embankment and hit a tree, while traveling at a very high speed. There were no other cars involved, so the police are running an investigation. They think it could've been an animal, but they aren't certain. If it's any consolation, your parents didn't suffer. It was a complete miracle that you survived," she said softly.

I couldn't think. I could barely hear anything above my loud sobbing sounds.

"So what now? What happens to me?" I asked, swiping the tears from my soaked face. Would I be placed in foster care? I was too old for adoption and would never let that happen anyway.

Maybe my friends would take me in. In a year, I'd be eighteen anyway, and could technically take care of myself. But the mere thought of being alone sent my burning acid to my stomach.

Abigail cleared her throat. "Well, Emma. We've been contacted by a woman," she said cautiously. "Her name is Alaine Gray, and she's asked the courts to appoint her full guardianship."

"Alaine Gray? I've never heard of her." I tried to think of my parents' acquaintances, and couldn't recall anyone named Alaine Gray. I was sure this was the first time I'd heard that name.

"She is your aunt."

"Aunt?" I shrieked. "There's no way she can be my aunt. I don't have any living relatives... Well, not anymore."

She paused and glanced down to her briefcase on the floor, but didn't say anything.

"Well, I hope the courts have looked into this. I hope they're looking out for my interests, and not just sending me away to some stranger because it's the easiest thing to do. What if this lady is a *kook*? Has anyone done any research on her... checked her background?"

I was angry, my words were trembling, and new tears flooded my eyes.

"Emma," she said, leaning forward. "I've personally looked into this matter, and have undoubtedly confirmed that Alaine Gray is your mother's half-sister. She is positively a blood relative and genuinely wants to take care of you. I spoke to her on the phone, and she has already prepared a room for you."

"Why haven't I ever heard of her? My mother never mentioned she had a half-sister. Not once. Why would she hide a relative from me?"

"I don't know, sweetheart. Maybe your mother had a good reason. Sometimes things in life are better kept secret."

Great. Family secrets. I never thought my family would have any secrets. We were a seemingly normal family. A happy family.

I needed my mom. I needed her to hug me and tell me everything was going to be alright. I wanted my dad to kiss me on the forehead, and give me some encouraging words. At this moment, I wished I'd died with them in the accident because the thought of living without them was too much to bear.

I turned away from Ms. Reed, as hot tears poured from my eyes. She placed her warm hand on my back.

"Your Aunt Alaine is widowed. Her husband passed away a few years ago from some sort of illness, but he left her with a sizeable inheritance. She has a beautiful home in Alaska."

"Alaska?" *God, wake me from this nightmare!*

I kept my back to her and wept. This couldn't be happening to me. The once beautifully, quilted fabric of my life was quickly unraveling into one giant, tangled mess.

"What if I don't want to go?" I sobbed. Maybe there was a better way. There had to be another way to get out of this.

"Because your parents hadn't appointed a guardian for you, the court has granted full custody to Mrs. Gray. It's only until you're eighteen, Emma," she sympathized. "One year is really not that long. It will come and go before you know it."

There was another long pause, and just when I thought she was done, she spoke again.

"Your Aunt will be working closely with the state and your parent's lawyers to take care of all the details. She is also sending an escort to take you to your new home tomorrow. I know it's soon, but she insisted, assuring us you'll be given the greatest care. Don't worry, Emma. Everything will be alright," she expressed in an optimistic tone.

Yeah, right. How could she know? She was getting paid for delivering news like this to who-knows-how-many countless kids. Miss Reed paused and then the warmth of her hand left my back. A few moments later, footsteps exited the room.

I couldn't think. My brain hurt too much, throbbing to the brink of explosion. I was glad she left. I wanted to be alone. I wanted everything around me to completely disappear.

"Mom. Dad," I whispered to myself. Muscles in my stomach tightened as I gripped my pillow and pulled it to my face to muffle the uncontrollable cries. My world was quaking beneath me, opening up, sending me falling into a dark, endless abyss.

For the first time in my life I felt completely and utterly alone. Helpless. Abandoned. Lost.

Why were my parents taken from me? Why did I survive? Unanswered questions pierced my already fragile heart. I hoped this was all just a nightmare. I prayed that when I opened my eyes again, everything would be back to the way it was.

I pulled the blanket up, covering my face and cried so hard it hurt.

I must have fallen asleep for a while, and woke to whispers at the door. I heard tidbits from people astonished and baffled that I had survived; that *anyone* could have survived such a horrific crash. But here I was…a medical marvel, with lacerations that seemed to be healing remarkably fast, and one broken arm. No head injuries, no internal bleeding, no major damage. A complete and total miracle.

I kept silent and still, hoping they'd think I was still asleep, and leave me alone.

But my mind was wide awake and wondering how the crash happened. I tried to think back, but my mind was blank. I couldn't seem to remember anything beyond my seventeenth birthday, so I went there. I went back to that happy place, and pulled the memory from the depths of my mind.

We were all at home, a beautiful home near the beach. My parents were in real estate and made their first purchase together.

My mother adored throwing parties, and had decorated our pool area with hundreds of twinkle lights. Floating candles bobbed in the water, and everything was decorated in lime green, pink, and turquoise. There were balloons, streamers, tables filled with fancy cupcakes, a chocolate fountain with an assortment of fruits, colorful candies in iridescent bags, sorbet punch, and a spread of make-your-own sandwiches.

Dad hung a huge banner which read: HAPPY SWEET SEVENTEEN, EMMA! with swirls of the matching décor colors around it.

My parents had invited my friends, along with some of their closest friends, as well. I had two friends, to be precise…Jeremy Needles and Lia Ling.

Everyone sang 'Happy Birthday', I blew out the seventeen candles flaming atop my strawberry-cream cake, and then opened my gifts.

The adults gave me envelopes filled with cash or gift cards, which was the safest gift for a teenager these days. Lia gave me a bright-pink digital camera, with a matching pink case and scrapbooking kit, and Jeremy got me an electronic reader.

"It's a touch-screen," he said with excited eyes.

He even managed to download all of his favorite books onto it. Wonderful. A lifetime worth of Jeremy Needle's lit-picks. Just what I always wanted.

They slept over that night and we watched the whole Lord of the Rings trilogy, ate popcorn, and drank Dr. Pepper, until four in the morning.

Two years prior to that day, we were living in an apartment in the middle of Los Angeles. It was close to my parent's office, but mom started second-guessing me attending high school in the city. I'd gotten into some trouble with friends. You know... the friends who weren't really friends; preppy, wannabe bitches who used and abused everyone around them, thinking they were better than everyone else.

Well, a few of them started a cat fight in the bathroom with some gothic chicks. The goth girls kicked their butts which I was secretly happy to witness, but everyone involved was dragged into the Principal's office. I wasn't a bad kid, just guilty by association, and therefore, suspended for a week.

That's when the desperate search for a new high school began. My mom chose a religious, stuffy academy; a total one-eighty from my previous school. No one stood out there because everyone looked the same. The dress code was navy blue, no-more-than-one-inch-above-the-knee skirts, white blouses, mid-calf socks and covered shoes for girls; and khaki pants with navy polo-shirts for the boys.

It was hard starting a new school without any friends. Everyone had settled into their own cliques, and I was suddenly the outsider.

I remember that first day in the cafeteria, standing alone with my tray in hand, searching for a place to fit. As I did a quick scan of the tables filled with students talking, laughing, teasing, and staring; two smiling faces, sitting all alone at the back corner of the cafeteria, caught my glance. They waved for me to come and join them, and so I did, every day since for the past three years.

Lia Ling was a shy, sweet, Asian girl. She was short and thin, with long, stick-straight, black, shiny hair, and slightly pudgy cheeks under pink-rimmed glasses. Her mother made her homemade lunches, which she carried in a tin Care Bear lunchbox.

Then there was Jeremy Needles, our nerdy sidekick, AKA the Nerdmeister. Even a makeover wouldn't work for this guy. Nerdiness was too deeply embedded into his genetic makeup. He was tall, stick-thin, and his only noticeable muscle was his brain, which was covered with untamable, curly-brown hair. Every day he wore his bright orange, coke-bottle glasses on a large, pointy nose, and had barely-there lips. His true loves were his books, and anything electronic.

Because of them, I remained an outsider with the other cliques. But, I didn't care. I actually liked the fact that I was flying under the radar in the new school. I had no pressure to please, and a chance to breathe and have some fun.

The accident must have been directly after my birthday because there was nothing but darkness after that.

Regret started to seep into the cracks of my shattered heart. Did I tell my parents I loved them enough? Did they really know how much I appreciated them? I think they did. At least…I hoped they did.

And then, I heard my mother's voice speaking softly in the recesses of my mind. "*Don't dwell on the negative,*" she'd say. "*Always look on the positive side of things. It's a lot brighter there, and easier to find your way."* A tear escaped my eye as my thoughts lingered on her.

My future looked grim, but then, even in the darkness, there was the tiniest glimmer of hope. I had a relative still living on this God forsaken earth, who had a part of my blood flowing through her veins. And more than that, she actually wanted me. Which should count for something.

The fact she was related to my mom, the kindest, most beautiful person who ever walked the face of the earth, was definitely a plus.

I missed my mom and the thought of her sent a piercing pain straight through the middle my heart. I wished the pain of losing my parents would go away, but I knew every time I opened my eyes, it would be there in some form, haunting me for the rest of my life.

I was exhausted, and my eyes were still heavy and swollen. So, I closed them and faded back into a deep, needed sleep.

TWO

THE NEXT MORNING THE DOCTOR gave me the all-clear, and signed my release forms. I sat on the edge of the bed, waiting for Lia and Jeremy to arrive. I was still wrapped in a dark cloud of pain and sadness, but I didn't want Jeremy and Lia to see me falling apart. I was always the strong one. I needed to reassure them I'd be okay, no matter what.

I'd called Lia to let her know where I was and what had happened, but she'd already heard the news and sobbed through our entire conversation, apologizing after nearly every word. She was glad I was alive, but devastated about my parents. She and Jeremy had grown very close to them over the past three years.

I asked her to complete one, final, *humongous* favor for me; to swing by my house and grab a few of my things. And not to forget the picture of my parents on my nightstand.

She already knew the key to the front door was hidden under

one of the potted plants on the porch, and although she was a little freaked out by going in, she agreed to do it...as long as Jeremy went along.

I instructed her to grab my warmest clothes, even though I wasn't sure if the warm stuff I had was sufficient for Alaska. Everything I had was "wimpy" warm - for California cold. I knew I'd have to update my wardrobe before winter, or I'd freeze to death. It was still fall, so I had some time. Hopefully they had malls wherever I was going.

The thought of moving to a new place, with an unknown relative, was awkward and unnerving. I didn't know what I'd be walking into, and it was the unexpected that scared me.

Voices carried down the hallway, and I instantly recognized one of them. Jeremy had such a distinct, goofy laugh. As soon as they rounded the corner my heart felt a little lighter and the room suddenly became a little brighter. I didn't realize how much it helped to see their familiar faces.

"Hey Emma," Lia said, dashing over and giving me a big, warm hug. I winced in pain.

"Oh my gosh. I'm *so* sorry," she gasped, backing up with her hands in the air.

"Don't worry about it. I'm alright. Just a few bumps and bruises is all."

"Are you sure you're alright? How are you...really?" Lia was a worry-wart, a trait she'd picked up from her mother. Even though she didn't want to admit it, they were a lot alike.

"Alive," I answered. There wasn't much more to add to that.

"Emma, we're so sorry about your parents. I hope you'll always remember that Jeremy and I will be here for you. Always."

I nodded, trying to hold back tears, but they started to flow as soon as Lia's did. She plopped down next to me, and wrapped her arm around my shoulder... carefully this time.

"Yeah, Emma. We're always just a phone call away," Jeremy said, sitting on my other side, carefully placing his hand over mine.

Jeremy was like my nerdy brother, and this gesture was most sincere because he wasn't a touchy-feely kind of guy.

"Thanks. You guys are the best," I said, wiping my face dry. Lia popped off the bed and headed towards the tissue box in the bathroom.

Jeremy cleared his throat. "We brought your things," he said, shuffling to get my suitcase.

He was wearing long beige shorts, a brightly colored Hawaiian shirt, knee-high tube socks, and bright-orange Converse shoes. His curly hair was matted and unkempt. Typical Jeremy.

"Oh yeah...and I think you'll need this," Lia said, handing over a plastic bag.

I reached in and pulled out some clothes. My traveling clothes, and they all matched. Typical Lia.

"Oh. And your make-up bag, toothbrush, panties, and bra are in there too," Lia whispered.

"Too much info," Jeremy protested, scrunching his face.

"Oh please, Jeremy. You were the one who reminded me to make sure they were in the bag," Lia scolded.

His face turned a bright shade of red. "I did not."

"*What-ever,* Jeremy," she huffed, holding her hand up in his face.

"That's it... I'm gonna go change. You guys can sort out your differences while I'm gone."

I smiled, bundling everything into my good arm and headed for the bathroom. As soon as the door snapped shut, I heard them grumbling, and then the TV blared on.

I tried not to think about my parents, even though they were constantly on my mind. I needed to look strong while my friends were here. They needed to know I'd be alright, and that they didn't have to worry about me. But the thought of being brave and alone, made me feel so weak. This would be the most difficult task I'd ever have to face.

I slipped out of my hospital garment, noticing the countless cuts and bruises all over my body. I sighed, staring at my reflection in the mirror, carefully tracing an inch-long gash on my left cheek. It had been much worse the night before, but it seemed to be healing very quickly. I hoped it wouldn't leave a scar. At least it was near my hairline, so I could conceal it with my hair.

Getting dressed with a casted arm was a crazy task. My head looked like it had a scraggly, brown, birds-nest perched on top of it. I sighed and grabbed the brush. *Another major problem.* My right hand—the dominant one—was in the cast.

I'd never tried applying makeup, or brushing my hair with my left hand, and now I knew why. But after it was all said and done, I managed to pull it off, and somehow looked halfway decent.

Who cared anyway? I was going to Alaska, for heaven's sake. I'd never heard of any hotties from Alaska. All I pictured were big, scruffy men in red flannels with plenty of facial hair.

Well, this is it.

I gave myself one last glance. "Are you ready?" I whispered to myself.

Nope. I wasn't. How could I ever prepare for something like this? I sighed and exited the bathroom.

Jeremy hollered, "*Finally.*" He was sprawled out on the bed with the remote in hand. Lia sat on a chair in the corner of the room fiddling with her new cell phone.

I mustered a fake smile. "Sheeze. I'm a bit busted up here. Give me a break."

I noticed Lia wasn't wearing her favorite pink-framed glasses.

"New glasses?" I asked.

"Oh, yeah," she said, tucking her hair behind her ears to show me. "My dad accidentally sat on my pink ones; so I decided it was time to change it up."

"Well, the turquoise frames look really nice on you," I commented.

"Thank you," she chimed. "And you look nice too."

"Nice try, but thanks anyway. And thanks so much...you know, for grabbing my stuff. You guys truly are the best friends ever."

"Well, you totally add the coolness factor to our group," Jeremy chuckled, flicking off the TV.

"Hardly," I croaked.

"It's true," Lia admitted. "We were the terrible two. No one even gave us a second glance until you showed up."

"Yeah, and then we became the terrible three," Jeremy howled and snorted, holding his stomach. I'm glad he thought it was funny, because Lia and I didn't. We both rolled our eyes and shook our heads.

After humoring himself, Jeremy finally pointed to my bulging right arm. "So what's up with that?"

"Oh," I said, attempting to tug the long sleeve up, revealing the bulky, white cast. "It's broken, but the doctor said it can come off in a few weeks."

"Oh. Can we sign it?" he asked with a gleam in his eye.

"I guess. Why not?"

"I'm first!" Jeremy exclaimed, excited like a little kid.

Lia inhaled sharply and I turned to watch her dig through her purse, pulling out a bright-pink pencil case. She unzipped it and sifted through the pile, picking out all of her multi-colored sharpie pens. She held them up, fanning them out to Jeremy.

Jeremy plucked the black and orange from her grasp, his favorite colors.

I grinned and shook my head. "Go ahead Michelangelo. Create your masterpiece. But you only have about ten minutes to do it, or at least until my *escort* arrives."

"Do you even know what part of Alaska you're going to?" Lia asked.

"No. I just found out yesterday I was being banished to the place. Nothing more than that. I guess that's what the escort is for," I said, shrugging my shoulders.

"Escort...now that's interesting," Jeremy said sarcastically.

He patted the spot next to him on the bed, ushering me to sit. Lifting my casted arm onto his lap, he pulled off the black cap, and proceeded to draw a circle with squiggly lines all around it.

I think he was going for a sun, or what he thought resembled a sun. Its long rays extended over half my cast, and I was guessing it was because he wanted me to take a bit of sunshine to Alaska.

He then proceeded to draw orange rimmed glasses on his sun's face, and a huge smile with lines for teeth. Jeremy was definitely more of a Picasso than a Michelangelo.

"Jeremy," Lia glared at him through her narrowed Asian eyes. "You better save me a spot."

"Don't worry. There's lots of room on the back," he grinned slyly. She rolled her eyes, crossing her arms over her chest and slouching back into her seat. "Oh, and could you please pass me the yellow, Lia *dahling*?" he said in a dramatic voice.

She flashed him another wicked glance and reluctantly tossed over the yellow sharpie. He pulled the cap and began to color in his sun.

Lia was next. They switched places and she neatly laid out her choice of pens on the bed behind us, proceeding to draw a rainbow, a multi-colored flower, a butterfly, and her name. Every letter was a different color. Hers was a work of art, compared to Jeremy's kiddy sun and illegible signature.

"Wow. This cast will definitely brighten the whole state of Alaska," I said admiring my newly pimped-out arm.

They both smiled and nodded approvingly, giving each other a high-five.

"So, did you know Alaska is like this ginormous place, one-fifth of the size of the whole United States? You can get lost easily over there. I heard criminal types move there to escape justice...you know, lots of places to hide. So you'd better be careful. And, watch out for the bears, and moose that have babies. They will charge at you if you get too close," Jeremy noted, pressing his glasses back up on his nose.

He must have done some online research. That's what he was good at. At least it showed he really cared.

"I don't know much of anything. But I'm sure I'll be fine. I promise."

"You better call us when you get in, so we know you made it safely," Lia added.

"I will, as soon as I can get to a phone."

"What happened to your cell?" she asked.

"I'm not sure," I said. "It didn't end up with the rest of my things from the crash."

Jeremy turned and gave her a dirty look, and her eyes became saddened.

"I'm so sorry, Emma," she whispered.

"Hey, don't worry about it. I'm sure I'll get a new one." I tried to sound like it didn't bother me, even though it did.

"Do they even have cell phone service in Alaska?" she asked.

"Yes, they do, but not in all areas," Jeremy said, matter-of-factly. The poor boy needed to get a life.

"I wish I could pack you both up in my suitcase and take you with me," I sighed.

"I'd love to come," Jeremy said excitedly. "I've always wanted to try snowboarding, and I've heard Alaska is the place to go."

"Oh please," Lia huffed. "You can't even get both feet on a skateboard, standing still...holding *onto* something."

"Whatever, Lia. You're just jealous of my awesomeness." His bushy eyebrows wiggled up and down.

"We all know, when it comes to sports, you are awesome-*less*," Lia rebutted.

They were just as bad as real siblings, and I actually felt a tiny smile lift on my lips.

"So did you manage to scrounge up all my warm stuff?"

"Yes, but it was a bit unnerving going into your house with no one there." Her gaze flittered away from me and went to Jeremy.

"Yeah, Lia was pretty freaked out," Jeremy chuckled.

"Are you serious, Jeremy? You were *way* more freaked out than I was, you big chicken," she snapped, slapping him on the shoulder. "He made me go in first, and then was glued to my back the whole time, jumping and squealing at every little sound."

"I *never* squealed," Jeremy objected. "But it was a bit uncomfortable."

"We did grab everything warm we could find. We brought your shoes, socks, pajamas, every single long sleeved shirt, jacket, and blue jean you own," Lia said, patting the suitcase with every word.

"We also added some snacks, the camera, and your new electronic reader in your carry-on," Jeremy declared with a wide smile. "Oh, and the picture of your parents is in there too. We had to take it out of the frame because it was metal, and we didn't want the glass to break. It's best not to take anything that might be questionable to the airport. You know how they are these days."

"Thanks guys." Tears filled and stung my eyes again. "I'm gonna miss you *so* much."

"Oh God. We're going to miss you too. What are we going to do without you on our last, crucial year? We're finally going to be seniors," Lia said, her eyes tearing as soon as she saw mine.

21

Jeremy glanced at me, and a single tear grazed his cheek. He quickly turned away and lifted his glasses, wiping his face with his shirt. That was the first time I'd ever seen Jeremy get emotional.

"You guys will be fine. And it won't be forever. I promise to email and send pictures."

"You better," Lia said, wagging her finger at me.

And then, out of nowhere, I was slammed with a sudden euphoric feeling; an unexplainable heat shooting through every cell in my body. My pulse quickened, along with my breath. Tingles pricked my skin. A rush of adrenaline flooded my veins and my surroundings began to haze. I grasped onto the edge of the bed, taking in long, deep breaths.

"Hey, are you okay?" Jeremy asked, scooting over to me, grabbing hold of my shoulders.

"Emma, what's wrong?" Lia called, jumping behind me, pounding my back.

Hello, I'm not choking! I wanted to speak, but I couldn't answer them. It was like all the breath had been sucked out of my lungs.

There was a knock at the door, and we all turned to look.

THREE

AS SOON AS HE STEPPED through the door, my breath seized. "Emma Wise?" the young stranger asked with a crooked grin, combing back thick, dark-brown hair through his fingers. *Was that my escort? Holy hell.*

He looked a little older than me, and had dark, perfect features, with flawless porcelain skin. Long eyelashes framed the brightest hazel eyes I'd ever seen in all of my seventeen years. Dark denim jeans and a fitted, black v-neck sweater adorned his tall frame. His physique was statuesque, but his skin was pale...almost colorless. I assumed it was because he came from Alaska. No sun for half the year. That had to explain it.

I finally caught my breath. "Yes," I exhaled.

He smiled, revealing the whitest, straightest teeth. "I'm Kade Anders, your escort." I noticed that he said 'escort' like he wasn't too sure about the title.

Lia turned to me. Her cheeks were blushed in bright pink, and her almond-shaped eyes were the widest I'd ever seen them. She swallowed hard, and then mouthed the words, *"Oh-my-God-he's-so-hot!"*

I laughed and glanced back at him. His eyes were fastened to mine, and I was immediately bewitched by his beauty. Then, I noticed something in his eyes; something in the way he was looking back at me, like there was a familiarity between us.

He quickly broke eye contact and turned to Jeremy.

Jeremy must have noticed my immaturity and cleared his throat, extra loud.

I had to compose myself. I was acting like a complete idiot, gaping at him like some silly little girl with a kindergarten-crush.

Snap the hell out of it, Emma!

I had to spend the next who-knows-how-many-hours with this guy, and I did *not* want him to think I was immature, which was hard when both of my best friends were seventeen, going on twelve. But that's why I loved them so much.

"So, do you have any type of paperwork to prove you're the escort?" Jeremy asked, staring inquisitively at Kade.

I had a million things swirling through my mind, and knew an escort was coming. I just assumed when the person showed up... I'd follow.

"Right here," Kade answered with a grin. He pulled a paper out from his pocket and handed it to Jeremy.

Jeremy carefully looked over the paper, folded it up, and handed it back to him. He then shuffled over to me and gave me an awkward, one-handed hug.

"So, I guess this is goodbye. Don't forget about us, okay?" his voice was shaky and tears began to well behind his coke-bottle lenses.

"How could I ever forget you two crazies? And I promise to shoot you an email as soon as I get set up." It was taking everything in me to be strong. I was not fond of goodbyes. And I hated leaving everything and everyone I'd ever known behind. My heart was breaking all over again.

Lia leaned in and gave me a soft squeeze. "Looks like you'll be in great hands," she said smiling, her eyes shooting again toward the hot boy at the door.

"I hope so," I whispered. She quickly spun and faced my escort.

"We're leaving our best friend in your hands. She's in a very fragile state right now, so please take really good care of her," she instructed. She looked so tiny, but she was very feisty.

"I promise to take the greatest care of her," Kade answered politely, with a bow of his head.

Lia giggled, winking at me, and then I heard her sob as she turned away. I was hoping she wouldn't have a bi-polar moment like this. She was trying to be strong, but didn't quite make it. My heart was wrenching inside.

"Bye Emma," Lia said bravely, burying her face into Jeremy's shoulder. Jeremy waved at me, and then quickly escorted Lia out of the room. I could tell he wasn't taking it well either. My best friends were leaving, and I didn't know if, or when, I'd ever get to see them again.

Tears dripped down my face, and I was just about to lose it, when my escort headed towards me. I quickly wiped my eyes dry and took in a deep breath.

His powerful smile seemed to pull my sinking heart from its unknown depths of sadness, and place it somewhere a little safer. What kind of magical did this guy have on me? I was usually calm and collected, even when hot guys were around. But this guy was definitely in a league of his own, almost other-worldly.

"Hello, Emma," he spoke in a warm, subtle voice. "Your Aunt Alaine sent me to assist you to your new accommodations. Are you ready?" he asked, holding his hand out to me.

"What?" I was completely distracted by his closeness. His scent was intoxicating; fresh and crisp with hints of sweet, warm spice. I inhaled, becoming high and lightheaded.

"Are you ready to leave?" he politely asked, again.

I mentally slapped myself back into reality...several times.

"Yes. I'm ready," I said grasping his hand.

As soon as we touched...*WHAM!*

An electrical current surged through my veins, and the same euphoric feeling, which I'd felt earlier, shot through me... intensified times ten. Heat rushed through my veins, and my body felt pulled to him, as if we were magnetized. I gasped and he released my hand. As soon as he did, I felt flustered and bewildered. He looked at me. His eyes were wide and filled with confusion.

"What just happened?" I questioned, still feeling a bit woozy. That was the craziest, random, emotional shocker *ever*.

He remained silent, puzzled, gazing down at his hand.

"I don't know," he finally answered. "That's never happened to me before."

Trying to shake it off, I stood up. I pulled my carry-on over my shoulder, took in a deep breath, and flattened my arms down to my sides to avoid his touch. He bent down to pick up my suitcase and offered me his arm, again. I froze, not sure if I should, or shouldn't, take it.

"Shall we try this again?" he asked with the cutest, crooked grin.

I felt my pulse quicken, and then my ginormous, colorfully casted arm came into view and embarrassment painted my cheeks. Jeremy's huge sun with orange-rimmed glasses smiled at us.

Awkward. I mean, it looked like a kindergartner had drawn it.

Kade immediately took notice. "Nice."

I nodded in agreement—not able to form words.

He was very careful not to touch my bare skin, looping his arm through mine. This time there was no shock, but there was still that overwhelming warmth and tingles emanating from his closeness. The cast seemed to be a good conductor.

On our way out, the nurses waved and said goodbye, their eyes glued on Kade. He was cordial and smiled back, making them swoon.

As soon as we exited the main door, a black Cadillac was waiting at the front. The driver came around and opened the rear passenger door. He took my luggage from Kade and placed it in the trunk, but I held on tightly to my carry-on.

Kade motioned for me to enter first. After I slid in, he sat next to me. My body automatically reacted to his proximity in the tight enclosure of the car. I fought internally to keep my mind focused, resisting the urges of my body wanting to slide closer to him, to touch him.

But then, I was temporarily distracted as I noticed someone else, sitting in the front passenger seat. The guy was dressed in a black suit, donning dark-tinted Oakley shades. His face was handsome, but much harder than Kade's. He looked like he was in his late twenties, big and brawny, with broad shoulders and tanned skin. Muscles bulged from his arms, which made his suit look tight and uncomfortable. His hair was black and slicked back; a well-groomed mustache and goatee framed his un-smiling lips. He turned and I smiled at him, but felt awkward when I only received a nod in return.

"That's Malachi. Don't mind him. He's still working on his people skills," Kade chuckled, slapping him on the shoulder. Malachi turned back to Kade, and even though his eyes weren't visible through the darkness of his shades, I could tell by the way his eyebrows were scrunched up, that he was giving him a very evil look. He reminded me of Dwayne "the Rock" Johnson.

"LAX," Malachi instructed to the driver in a deep, intimidating tone.

What was up with the Men in Black escort service?

We rode in silence, except for the radio station playing some oldies. Kade stared out his window, as I constantly tried to fight my body's irresistible urges to get closer to him. It was pure craziness, the things I wanted to do to this complete and total stranger. The scary thing was that I was envisioning it like it was actually happening.

What was going on? Ever since I met him, my emotions wrestled against me. Actually, it started before he even walked through the door.

I'd have to get to the bottom of it later because the car finally came to a stop in front of the Los Angeles Airport.

I was glad when the driver opened the door and let me out, immediately relieving me of the ridiculous pressures my body was putting upon itself. I wondered if Kade was fighting the same urges. Probably not. He didn't show any signs of struggle, or even interest. I mean, why would he? He was gorgeous and I was just, Emma Wise. Besides, he was only *assisting me to my new accommodations,* as he put it.

We walked through the airport which was bustling with travelers. Malachi and Kade were glued to either side of me, acting more like bodyguards than escorts.

All of this attention made me take notice of my surroundings. Maybe it was just my imagination, but then again…maybe not. On the way to our gate, we passed a man leaning against a wall reading a newspaper. There was something odd about him, I just couldn't put my finger on. He was good looking, clean-shaven, had light blonde hair, and was dressed in a dark blue suit with darkly-tinted glasses. He watched us intently as we walked by, then he raised his glasses, and acknowledged Malachi with a subtle nod. As we passed, he rolled up his paper, tucked it under his arm, and walked away.

Strange.

As we continued further down the terminal, another man dressed in a similar suit passed us. He was well over six feet tall and clean-shaven, with dark brown hair, and similar dark shades. He slowed, almost to a stop, as we approached him. He lifted his shades, and gave Malachi the same nod. His gray eyes locked onto mine for a moment, and then he lowered his shades and continued on his way.

Okay. What the hell is going on?

I'd been known for my overly-active imagination, but maybe I was just being paranoid. This could very well be a coincidence. I wanted to say something, but I was too afraid. And even if I tried to make a run for it, I knew I wouldn't get too far. I was under the influence of painkillers, and would probably trip over my own feet and make a big, embarrassing scene. So, I bit my tongue.

I looked at Kade to see if he showed any signs of strangeness by the passing men, but he was preoccupied, pulling our boarding passes from his pocket.

What was becoming of my life? Thoughts of my parents flooded my mind, and I tried hard to hold back the tears burning my eyes.

Soon, I would be leaving the only place I'd ever known, the place where my parents lived and died; traveling hundreds of miles away to an unknown place, where nothing was familiar.

I hadn't even had the chance to mourn the loss of my parents, let alone bury them. Would there even be a burial? Ms. Reed said my Aunt Alaine was going to be taking care of all the arrangements. I hoped she'd include me, and give my parents a proper burial.

My sudden rush of emotions became too overwhelming to keep in. "I need to use the restroom. I'll be right back," I said to Kade, already darting toward the entrance of the ladies room.

"Sure. We'll wait right here," he called after me. A deep look of concern was embedded in his eyes.

I ran into the first available stall, locked the door behind me, and leaned against it for support as I cried. It felt good to cry, like my emotions were bottled up and needed to burst out.

The thought of running away shot through my mind, but then another thought of Malachi chasing me down was terrifying enough to squash it. And, the fact I only had two friends greatly narrowed my hiding places.

The lady over the loud speaker was alerting passengers, gate twenty-eight was about to board. I remembered Kade mentioning that particular gate, so I knew I didn't have much time.

I gathered myself together as best I could, rinsed my face, and glanced in the mirror. My eyes were puffy and my nose was red and shiny. *Great. Now I'm Rudolph.* The make-up was gone, and there was no time to apply any to hide my feelings, which were now plastered all over my face. I took in a deep breath and brushed through my hair with my fingers, covering the scar on my cheek which looked even smaller than before.

As I made my way out of the bathroom, Kade was standing at the exit, smiling. Those warm tingly feelings rushed through my body, abruptly taking the edge off my sadness.

"Hey, are you alright?" His brow was furrowed.

"I'll be fine," I sniffed.

I walked passed him, and as I did, he wrapped his arm around my waist.

"It will be fine, Emma. You'll see. Alaska is amazing, and you'll really like Alaine. She's a wonderful woman," he said warmly.

Right then, I truly believed every word he spoke. His touch did something to me. It comforted me, and made me feel like everything *was* going to be okay.

As we neared Malachi, he dropped his arm from my waist, and I was instantaneously overwhelmed with feelings of sadness and emptiness. He must have felt something too because we both turned to each other as soon as we came apart.

"I'm sorry," he breathed.

He quickly turned to Malachi, who was slowly shaking his head, shooting him that not-so-friendly look, and distanced himself further from me as we neared the gate.

Kade grabbed my luggage and handed the lady our tickets. She tried to make friendly conversation with him, but he just smiled and proceeded down the ramp. I quickly followed him, with Malachi in tow. I was left feeling even more confused than before. My life, body, and emotions were steadily spiraling out of control.

As we entered the plane, Kade placed my bag up into the second row compartment on the left.

"We're in first class?" I asked. I'd never flown first class before.

"Yes, and you can have the window seat." Kade motioned for me to enter first. I smiled, plopping into the roomy, comfortable seat, shoving my carry-on under the seat in front of me. Then, I quickly noticed a problem. There were two seats on each side of the aisle, and three of us.

Malachi and Kade looked at each other. It was a silent stare-down of who'd get the seat next to me.

Oh God, please let it be Kade...

The thought of a trip next to Malachi would be completely

unbearable. He wasn't friendly or talkative, and was big and scary. It would definitely be the worst trip of my life.

"Sorry, man. But, your seat is back there," Kade said, pointing two rows behind us, on the opposite side of the aisle.

"Kade," Malachi spoke in a condescending tone, followed by a very stern look.

"I'll behave," Kade promised. "You better get back there, buddy. You're holding up the line." He patted Malachi on his broad shoulders, then quickly slipped into the seat next to me.

Malachi growled under his breath and proceeded down the aisle, dropping into his aisle seat. A few minutes later we heard more growls and unintelligible words coming from his area. We turned to see a larger-sized woman pointing at the window seat next to him. Malachi did *not* look happy and glared in our direction. I quickly turned around, but Kade just grinned, shooting him a thumbs-up, totally making matters worse.

I hoped to get a chance to talk to him, and shed some light on all the questions darkening my mind. I wanted to know more about the mysterious place which was going to be my new home, and about the aunt who was kept secret from me. But for however long the flight would be, it probably wouldn't be long enough.

FOUR

I T WAS A GRUELING THIRTY minutes before everyone on the plane had taken their seat. The door finally closed, and before we knew it, we were taxiing to the runway.

I'd only taken a few plane rides, and they were just to visit my grandparents in Oregon. Most of our traveling was done on the road. My dad loved road trips, and every year planned a vacation. He'd spend months in advance planning routes, eateries, activities, and accommodations, until there wasn't a moment left unplanned.

I stared blankly out the small window, my heart aching beyond explanation, and watched as our plane took off into the sky. I was leaving everything I'd ever known and loved behind - my city, my friends, my home... everything.

"Hey," Kade whispered. He gently brushed my arm with his fingers, melting a bit of my sorrow.

I turned to him. His hazel eyes bore right through me, as if he knew what I was thinking. He stole my breath for a moment, and then smiled; making my insides quiver. The heaviness in my heart became lighter with his touch. How was that possible? I never thought I'd be able to pull myself from this heavy weight of sadness.

"I'll be fine," I said, turning back toward the window.

"I hope so. I promised your friends to take good care of you," he said softly.

I sighed. I just couldn't see any light at the end of this pitch-black tunnel...except for the small glimmer sitting in the seat next to me. I wondered if I'd ever see him again, after he completed his mission and handed me over to my aunt.

"Can I ask you a question?" I wiped a few stray tears from my cheeks.

"Sure," he answered.

"How come Malachi had to come with you? Why couldn't you have come alone?"

He laughed. "It's for your protection."

"My protection? Why would I need protection?" I questioned.

His face dropped.

"Ummm...I'm not at liberty to say," he said, shifting uneasily in his seat.

"If it concerns me, then I'm *totally* at liberty to know why I'd need protection. Does it have anything to do with those men at the airport?"

He turned to me with narrowed eyes. "What men?" he asked, shocked.

"Those men, in the suits, that kept looking and nodding at Malachi when we passed them."

"You noticed them?"

"Of course I did. How could I not? They were so obvious."

He grinned and shook his head. "You're very perceptive, Emma Wise. I'll give you that. Most people don't notice them at all, but then again... I guess you *aren't* like most people," he added quietly, speaking to himself.

"And, what's that supposed to mean?"

He hesitated. "Those men you saw at the airport aren't bad. They're Watchers," he whispered loudly.

"Watchers? Watchers of what?" I asked a little too loudly.

"Shh..." He placed his finger to his lips, and then turned back to check on Malachi, who looked like he was sleeping. He then turned back to me and leaned in close. "All of your questions will be answered by Alaine. Like I said, I'm not at liberty to speak to you about certain affairs. I've been given a specific job and I must obey it. I'm sorry, Emma." His eyes looked so sad, that I actually felt a tiny bit bad.

"Well, what is your job, exactly?" I questioned.

"To make sure you arrive in Alaska, at your new home, safely."

"Ah. And you've been sworn to silence while transporting your prisoner?"

"Emma, please. I could get into a lot of trouble. I've already said more than I should have, and if Malachi finds out...I-I-," he paused, staring at me with a pleading look.

"Don't worry," I sighed, "You didn't give anything away, and I promise not to ask any more questions." Although I was completely stressed with the lack of answers, I really didn't want to get him into trouble.

"Thank you, Emma," he whispered grasping hold of my hand.

Electrical surges pulsed through my fingers, up my arm, and then the rest of my body. We both gasped. His bright hazel eyes, stricken with shock, locked onto mine, but he didn't let go.

Heat overcame me, my breathing quickened, and my heart pounded wildly. My body pulled towards him. I closed my eyes and tried to fight the urges. I had to keep my mind strong because my body was too weak to reject him.

His hand suddenly left mine, and again, a cold, unsettling feeling took over. I opened my eyes, even more dumbfounded than ever before.

"What the—"

"I'm sorry," he apologized, his eyes carefully studying mine. His knuckles were turning white as he tightly gripped onto the armrests.

"What for?" I breathed.

"I shouldn't have touched you. I thought it was just a freak thing, the first time. I—" he paused, shaking his head in confusion.

"So, you *did* feel something?" I questioned.

"Yes," he admitted, looking forward with a vacant look. "And, I promise it won't happen again." He turned and smiled at me, but his eyes were filled with sadness. I think his words were supposed to benefit me, but they actually felt more hurtful than anything.

I didn't understand all the crazy feelings I was having for Kade. Actually, I was completely baffled. They couldn't be true feelings. They had to be more lustful. *Hello!* I only met the guy a few hours ago.

But there was something there; something happened whenever

we touched. It wasn't natural…it seemed to pull me towards him whenever he was near. I wondered if it was a good thing or bad thing. To me, it felt good, but then again, that could be a bad thing too.

"Whatever," I mumbled. I was a little hurt, but I wasn't going to let it bother me. I wasn't really sure why I'd be hurt in the first place. He was just a guy, who meant absolutely nothing to me.

Kade reclined his seat and closed his eyes, probably pretending like he was tired in order to not talk to me. I reached down for my carry-on and dug through its contents, trying to find something to kill the time.

I found my camera, makeup, and a candy bar.

I picked out the candy bar, placed it on my lap, and then pulled out my electronic reader. Reading was a great way to kill time, and hopefully take my mind to a faraway place.

After shoving my carry-on back under the seat, I lifted the bright, orange reader cover.

The picture of my parents was staring back at me. I paused, studying their smiling faces.

It was taken just before my seventeenth birthday. We'd spent the day at the beach because both my parents had the day off. I'd invited Lia and Jeremy, but only Lia showed. Jeremy was busy that day. Lia snapped the picture, framed it, and gave it to me the next day.

My mom was beautiful. Petite and thin, with long, auburn hair cascading in ringlets down her shoulders. She had the most beautiful green eyes, and always wore the biggest smile on her golden face.

My dad was moderate looking. He had ash blonde hair, which was thinning at the top, and baby blue eyes. He'd always tease me that I got my looks from him, but the truth is...I looked nothing like him.

I did, however, look a little like my mother. We had the same shaped eyes, but hers sparkled like emeralds. Mine were a dull, dirty brown. I always wondered why I was born with brown eyes, when my parents had blue and green. It just wasn't fair.

I gently traced their faces on the photograph. *Drip, drip, drip.* Wet droplets began to fall onto my priceless treasure.

I gasped, quickly hugging it to my chest so my shirt would soak up the tears.

"What's that?" Kade asked in a soft voice. I slowly pulled the picture away, and examined it to make sure it wasn't damaged.

"My parents," I whispered, staring at their happy faces. It didn't even feel like they were gone. It actually felt like I was going on a vacation, and would be home soon to see them. I couldn't begin to rationalize the fact I'd *never* get to see them again. I'd never get the chance to hug them, or tell them I loved them.

"May I see?" He held out his hand, so I handed it to him. He remained silent as he studied it.

"You look happy in this picture," he noted.

"I was."

Gloom and sadness overcame me. Wanting to curl up and die, I brought my knees up to my chest and buried my face into my folded arms. I couldn't help crying. I tried my best to be strong, but the sobs were hard to keep to myself.

Kade's muffled voice caught my ears. He was talking to someone, but I was too far gone into my world of despair.

A few minutes later I felt a blanket drape over my shoulders.

Kade whispered into my ear. "Come now, Emma. You'll get through this. I promise." The warmth in his voice and his touch tugged at me, trying to pull me from the sadness.

I was a mess.

The stewardesses were heading down the aisle with their beverage carts, so I kept my back to the aisle.

"Would you like something to drink?" a lady asked Kade in a sweet voice.

"Just a water for me and...do you happen to have Dr. Pepper?" Kade inquired.

I gasped.

How'd he know I liked Dr. Pepper?

"I'm sorry, I don't," she replied. "But I do have Root Beer, or Coke."

"Root beer, or Coke?" Kade whispered, tapping my back.

"Coke, please," I answered. My brain was on the verge of exploding, and I had an insatiable need for something sweet and carbonated, with loads of caffeine.

I took a deep breath and settled back into my seat. Kade had our drinks in glasses on his tray.

"Your Coke," he said handing it to me.

"Thanks." I was careful to not touch his skin. I didn't realize how thirsty I was. The ice-cold, carbonated, liquid sugar never tasted so good.

"Feeling better?" Kade chuckled.

"Much," I nodded. "I'm sorry."

"For what?" he shot me a strange look.

"For dragging you on my emotional roller-coaster ride. I'm a complete wreck."

He shook his head. "You're much stronger than most people I know. I don't know what it's like to lose a parent, and you've just lost both at once. I think you very much deserve to be a wreck."

He handed back the picture of my parents, so I carefully tucked it back into my carry-on.

"Well, the only thing that seems to be keeping me from falling apart right now is you," I said glancing into his big, bright eyes. It was true and I admitted it, but I just couldn't believe I'd said it aloud.

The cutest grin grew on his face. "Thanks, but..." he paused.

I wasn't in the mood to hear any more negative words, so I smiled, shook my head, and quickly changed the subject.

"So how old are you anyway?" I asked, tipping my cup to get a piece of ice. I wanted to see how much information I could get out of him before he shut me down.

"Um... nineteen." He sounded unsure. "And you're seventeen?"

"Yes. Just turned seventeen. A few days ago, actually," I muttered. "So, do you live in Alaska?"

"I do right now," he answered.

My heart fluttered. *He lived in Alaska!* That was a good thing.

"Were you born there?"

"No."

"Then where are you from?"

He didn't answer but pointed up to the sky with a crooked smile. "Well, that's original," I responded. So he had a sense of humor. "Okay... so, where did you live *before* you moved to Alaska?"

"Midway," he answered.

"Where's that?"

"It's central. I've actually lived in many different places around the world. I've had to move a lot," he answered.

"Army brat?" I questioned.

"Something like that," he shrugged. He was so vague, it was almost maddening.

"So, how long have you known my aunt?"

"About ten years."

"Ten years?" I said much too loudly. Ten years was a very long time to know someone. He must have detailed information about her.

Malachi, loudly and deliberately, cleared his throat. Kade sighed and turned to face him with a wide smile and a wave. I didn't want to look back and see the expression he had on his face, because I knew it wasn't a good one. I also knew that if looks could kill, I'd already be dead...and so would Kade.

Kade turned back and faced me. "I promise you'll get your answers soon."

I knew that meant I needed to stop questioning him.

"Fine. Well, can you tell me if we are flying directly to Alaska, or do we have any other stops?"

"We'll be stopping in Seattle first. From there we will have about twenty minutes before we board our next flight to Anchorage," he answered.

I could see he felt bad and wanted to tell me more, but someone had tied his tongue, and I was guessing it was my aunt. But why? Why did everything have to be kept so secret?

Okay... if no one would talk to me, then I'd try and figure it out myself. I was pretty good at deciphering things. I went over all of the facts and details I'd collected.

First, I was in a horrible accident which took my parents' lives.

Next, I have a lost aunt, who I'd never heard of until yesterday. She comes forward and mysteriously claims guardianship over me, wanting me to move in with her. She must have known about me, but how could she have known about the accident so quickly?

She had to be closely connected somehow. The fact that she'd gotten all the paperwork from the State approved, had a ticket purchased, and sent escorts in less than two days...

I glanced over to Kade who was leaning back in his seat with his eyes closed.

And what was with these escorts? One is unearthly gorgeous, and drives me crazy with his presence and touch, and the other looks like a pissed-off WWE wrestler. They're somehow connected to Watchers and — *Oh my God! My life is starting to feel like a cheap sci-fi flick.* The only things missing were vampires and werewolves. Hmm... Kade sort of looked like a vampire with his pasty white skin.

Oh hell. There goes my ridiculously over-active imagination again. He couldn't be a vampire. He was warm and the sun didn't affect him at all. No sparkles... nothing. I hoped he couldn't read my mind, because if he could, he'd probably have me committed.

My mind started to ache. I don't think I could piece this one together even if I tried. I just hoped I'd get some real answers soon.

I decided to attempt reading, so I opened the bright orange cover to my reader again. A yellow, sticky-note was attached to the screen.

Hey Emma,

Hope you have fun with the reading list. We'll miss you.
Take care of yourself and keep in touch!
Jeremy

Jeremy. I already missed his goofy face.

The first book on the list was, of course, *The Lord of the Rings* by J.R.R. Tolkien. Figures.

I scanned down the rest of the list. The whole first page was of Tolkien and C.S. Lewis. The list seemed never ending. A few were by Shakespeare, which was definitely a gag.

I needed a fun read, something to take my mind on an adventure. I decided to read, *The Lion, the Witch, and the Wardrobe*, by C.S. Lewis. I really enjoyed that one when I was younger. I clicked on it and chapter one loaded onto my screen. I settled back into my seat, wrapping the blanket around me, and began reading...

Once there were four children...

"What's that?" Kade interrupted.

"My reader." I didn't want to get into a conversation again, knowing I could get shut down at any moment, so I kept my eyes on the screen.

"What are you reading?"

"The Lion, the Witch, and the Wardrobe."

"Nice," he said softly.

"Yep," I replied, trying to get past the first line, which I'd already read four times. I could feel his eyes staring, but I didn't want to look. Finally I sighed, turned off the reader, and tucked it back into my carry-on.

"I'm sorry. Have I distracted you?"

"No," I lied. "I just can't focus on anything right now."

"Have you ever been to Alaska, Emma?" he questioned, attempting to make a safe conversation.

"Never, and I'm not really looking forward to it." I exhaled loudly. "I don't care for places where the wildlife eats people.

"I think you'll like it. And, it's better than a place where people are killing people."

"Good point," I agreed. "So what's there to do in Alaska?"

"Well," he said leaning back in his seat, crossing his hands over his chest. "During the winters, we usually go ice fishing, snowmobiling, snowboarding, skiing, ice skating, and sledding. I've been known to make a killer snowman. But the summers are beautiful too. The sun stays out for long periods of time and everything is the greenest green. That's when we do a lot of hiking, river rafting, fishing, boating, and camping. It's a never ending cycle of fun." He turned and winked at me.

"Well I guess… if you put it that way." It actually did sound like fun. Maybe the year I'd have in Alaska wouldn't be too bad after all.

"And what did you do for fun?" he asked.

"Um, mostly go to the malls, shop, watch movies, talk on the phone, text, surf the web, and have sleepovers. You can't really hike in the city and there's no going out after dark. It's a concrete jungle, and wandering alone is forbidden. Sirens from police cars, ambulances, and fire trucks would lull me to sleep at night, and honking horns, people yelling, and passing cars were my morning alarm clock. You get numb to it after a while. But once we moved to the new home near Malibu, it was different. A lot quieter. We did some hiking and fishing on our vacations, but I've never been on skis or a snowboard because my mom didn't like to take road trips during the winter."

"So you've never been on a snowboard? I guess I'll have to teach you," he grinned.

My heart skipped a beat. *Maybe he would be sticking around.*

"So, do you live near my Aunt?" I pressed.

"Yes," he answered. "At the moment, I live in the guest house at the back of her property."

Whoa... He lived closer than I thought.

"That's cool," I tried to say with an even voice, but I didn't want to face him. My cheeks were hot and flustered and were now probably a bright shade of pink.

"Maybe you should get some rest," he said. "We'll be in flight for a few more hours."

"I wish I could." I wanted to rest, but my mind was wide awake.

The stewardess came by to collect the trash, and Kade requested a pillow. She quickly left her spot and returned a few seconds later with two.

"Thank you," he smiled graciously.

She smiled back and sighed softly, her eyes lingering a little too long on him. Boy, would I give a penny for her thoughts. Then again... maybe not.

Kade pressed the button on the armrest between us and lifted it.

My pulse began to race.

He fluffed the pillows and arranged them comfortably on his lap, and then patted them. "Come, Emma. Lie down and get some rest."

My stomach danced with butterflies. "I can't," I breathed.

"I bet you can," he chimed.

"No. I can't," I insisted. I wanted to. I really did. It was completely enticing, but I couldn't bring myself to lie on his lap. I barely knew him, and given the fact I'd never really had a boyfriend before, didn't help. I'd feel majorly awkward, and would not get a second of rest. My insides were already twisted in knots with him just mentioning it.

"Fine," he said with a grin. "We'll do it your way, but it won't be as comfortable." He put the armrest back down, arranging the pillows on it instead. "There… now will you rest? That's the only way you'll be able to heal and build your strength. Alaine will kill me if you arrive weak and tired."

I smiled at his kind gesture, and situated myself comfortably in the chair, laying my head on the pillows. There was no way I'd be able to do this in coach. First class was awesome. And even if I couldn't sleep, I'd at least be able to lie in comfort.

A sudden a surge of warmth cascaded over me, as Kade placed his hand on my forehead. I looked up and his hazel eyes were smiling down at me.

God, he was so handsome.

My heart hammered against my chest as he leaned over. His closeness terminated my breath.

Was he going to kiss me? I'd never been kissed before.

I closed my eyes, feeling his warm breath on my cheek, and then he whispered softly in my ear. "Sleep."

My brain immediately became numb and tingly; my eyes were

overwhelmed with heaviness. I fought to keep them open, but it was a losing battle.

What did he do to me?

"Rest, Emma. I'll be right here when you wake," he whispered.

My eyes were too heavy to keep open, and I soon faded into sleep.

FIVE

"HEY, SLEEPYHEAD. IT'S TIME TO get up," a melodic voice whispered, gently nudging my shoulder.

I slowly opened my eyes and saw the most beautiful face looming above me.

"We've just landed in Seattle."

"Oh, okay." I sat up, trying to straighten my hair with my one good arm. It wasn't a dream. "What happened? I was out cold." I peeked out the window and saw us taxiing to the ramp.

"I told you, you were tired," Kade said with a grin.

"Yeah, I guess you were right."

"How are you feeling?"

I quickly assessed myself, "Good. Actually, I feel awesome, like I slept a whole eight hours."

"Well, that's great to hear because we have to run clear across the terminal to catch our next flight. We're a bit behind schedule."

"Wonderful," I sighed, grabbing my carry-on and placing it on my lap. As soon as the seatbelt light clicked off, Kade jumped up and grabbed my luggage from the overhead compartment. Malachi was quickly up against his back. Kade let me go first, and as soon as they opened the doors, we hurried out.

Although we were running a little behind, we managed to make it through the terminal and to our next gate just as our next flight was boarding. This time I didn't notice if there were any Watchers around. There were way too many people, and most of them turned and looked at us as we walked by. Malachi was extra close, right at my side, and Kade was just a few steps behind.

We immediately boarded our final flight and were seated in the third row of first class. This time, Malachi was in the aisle seat directly across from us, which sucked. Now he'd be able to hear our conversations and keep a close eye on what we were doing. It was uncomfortable to have him there, especially with those mysterious eyes, hidden behind extra-dark shades.

Kade let me have the window seat again. We had another three hours to kill before we reached Anchorage, and this time I wasn't tired. I'd promised myself to keep the conversation simple and legal, whatever that entailed, especially with the extra set of ears across the aisle. I didn't want to find out what would happen if he really became angry.

After we took off, I glanced over to Malachi, who was reclined and seemingly sleeping. Kade's eyes were closed, and he was listening to music on his iPod. He turned to me, opened one eye and smiled.

"Do you need anything?" he asked, tugging out his right ear bud.

"No. I'm good." I seemed to be getting used to Kade's closeness. The intense feelings I had before were dulled, and I assumed it was because we were constantly close to each other.

When dinner was served, I tried to eat as slow as I could to kill the time. After dinner, Kade rented a DVD player with two sets of earphones. We chose from a list of movies, and decided on *Legion*. It was his choice, and I just went along with it.

Malachi refused the device, and reclined his seat with his arms folded over his chest. He was probably going to sleep the next few hours away. I didn't blame him. I wished I could do the same. This time, his companion was a tall, thin businessman tapping away on his laptop.

After the movie, we still had about a half an hour to kill. I didn't feel like reading, and I didn't want to sit in complete silence either.

"So, how are the schools there?" I asked. I knew this *had* to be a safe question. He didn't say anything and flashed me a look of concern. "What? What's wrong?"

"Actually, where you're going, there aren't any schools nearby, so you'll be homeschooled," he mumbled.

"Homeschooled?" I gasped. "You've *got* to be kidding me. I can't be homeschooled my senior year. That's not fair." I was appalled. First, because every homeschooled kid I knew was like super weird and super brainy. And second, I wouldn't make any friends, or get to walk with my class. *Oh my God. This royally sucked.*

"Alaine is a nurse, but she's also a teacher. She's been teaching for the past few years. It won't be that bad," he said in a hushed voice. "And you won't be alone."

Oh great. "What does that mean?"

"Alaine has taken in two other children whose mother passed a few years back. She was Alaine's best friend, and her dying wish was for her to take care of her children. Shortly after Alaine gave her promise, she died. It was pretty tragic."

"Oh," was all I could say. That was a lot to swallow in a few sentences. My Aunt seemed like a good-hearted person. For someone to ask you to take care of their children... that was a huge undertaking. And I guess I was glad I wouldn't be alone. These kids also lost their mother, so they could empathize with me.

"How old are these kids?"

"Courtney's thirteen and Caleb's sixteen," he said with a smirk on his lips, dragging Caleb's name a little too long.

"What? What's wrong with them?"

"Nothing's wrong. They're actually great kids, most of the time. You'll have fun with Courtney...and Caleb. Well, let's just say he'll definitely love you," he chuckled.

"Oh God," I sighed. I was guessing with the lack of teenage girls, and raging hormones, I'd be the prime target of Caleb.

Kade laughed.

"What?" I demanded to know what was wrong.

"Nothing. Seriously. You don't have anything to worry about." His words were *not* reassuring, especially since he was still laughing and had a huge smile plastered on his face.

I let out a deep breathy sigh.

The stewardess announced over the loud speakers that we'd be landing shortly. Finally. I just wanted to get to wherever I needed to go, meet my long-lost Aunt Alaine, and hopefully get some answers.

I glanced out the window and through the dim light saw my new home. Actually, it was just a new place of residence. It would never be home without my parents.

The land was expansive and the scenery was beautifully painted with golden and orange autumn leaves. Mountain tops were brushed with white snow, and large rivers snaked through wide open landscapes.

It was breathtaking from the air, but that was only one view. Getting down to it was another thing. People got lost or eaten in those seemingly beautiful woods, or froze to death on those majestic mountain tops. I'm sure plenty had fallen into those icy rivers or lakes, too. I'd heard some of the horror stories.

I shook my head. *Thanks, Jeremy.*

Then, hundreds of tiny sparkling lights glistened below. It must've been Anchorage, and I was surprised to see more lights than I'd ever expected. The butterflies in my stomach began to do their crazy dance as we made our descent. Kade must have sensed my uneasiness because he leaned over and whispered, "Hey. Don't worry. You'll be alright."

I hoped and prayed he was right. I took in a few deep breaths and tried to settle my nerves. It was the unknown that was making me anxious.

We quickly exited the plane and made our way toward the exit. I began to notice Kade and Malachi acting a bit edgy and paranoid.

They looked uneasy, glancing in all directions, each one glued to my side. Malachi tensed as his cell phone rang.

"Kade, keep an eye on Emma. I'll be right back," he instructed, in a low tone. He was arguing with the person on the other line. It must have been our ride, and it sounded like they were running late.

Kade and I continued slowly, until I noticed a sign to a restroom.

"I'm gonna run into the bathroom," I said, heading toward it.

"But, I—I don't think that's a good idea," he stammered.

"Why? It's right there. And, you can stand outside the door, if that'll make you feel any better. I'll be out *very* quickly. I promise."

"Alright, just hurry," he said nervously, running his hand through his hair.

"Yes, sir." I saluted, to his non-amusement.

The bathroom was surprisingly empty. All the stall doors were wide open, so I decided to snag the middle one. I hung my carry-on on the hook and locked the door. Just as I was about to unbutton my jeans, one of the stall doors squeaked open and then slammed shut, shaking the adjoining stalls. I could have sworn I was the only one in the bathroom. Maybe I was hallucinating, but I didn't hear any footsteps enter either.

And then, I heard the most disturbing sound; a sound that sent a cold shiver up my spine.

"E—mma," a chilling voice hissed. A restless uneasiness shot over me, raising every single hair on my body. "E—mma... Come out and play."

An ice wind blew through the bathroom and all the lights began to flicker. A strong stench began to permeate the room. It smelled like a rotting corpse that had rolled in year-old trash.

What the hell?

I sensed something evil lurking in the bathroom, just outside my stall. My heart hammered frantically against my chest, and I began to feel nauseated.

I wondered if I should peek to see if anything was there, but I was too terrified. What if I saw something horrifying or completely creepy? But, one thing was for sure. I couldn't stay in this stupid stall forever.

I finally convinced myself, and built up enough nerve to take a look. I placed my eye near the crack and glanced around. Suddenly, a dark figure shot across the space in front of me. I stumbled backwards and gasped.

Whatever the hell it was…was fast. Super fast.

Okay. It had to be someone I knew because they knew my name. It was probably a prank, or just someone just trying to scare me. And they were doing a damn great job.

Maybe it was Malachi. He seemed like the type that would do something villainous.

"Kade," I shouted. "Kade!"

He didn't answer.

Where the hell was he? He was supposed to be standing right outside the door.

I waited and listened. No sound or movement was outside. Seconds felt like minutes, and all my senses were on major alert. It was eerily quiet, but the foul odor still saturated the bathroom. I peeked through the crack again and it seemed empty. It appeared to be clear, so I strapped my carry-on over my shoulder.

My cast was solid, and thank God it was on my stronger arm, so it made a fairly good weapon. Jeremy's bright, orange sun smiled at me, but it didn't make me feel any better.

I decided to peek under the stalls, one last time, just to make sure that whatever it was…was really gone. Taking a deep breath, I slowly squatted, bending my head so I could see under the length of the stalls. The left side was clear, and so was the right. I turned my head to check the front.

Bam!

Something slammed against the stall door, knocking me off balance. I fell backward onto the floor, and was met with a dark, horrifying face, staring directly at me. Its eyes were sunken, and black as night. Its skin was a pasty white, with long, black, stringy hair.

It grabbed my leg and yanked me under the stall, dragging me to the middle of the floor. Straddling me, it pressed its large hands on my chest. It paused, glaring at me through cold, evil eyes. Its lips curled back over sharp teeth.

What the hell is it? A vampire?

I threw my casted arm up as hard as I could, whacking it in the face. Its head whipped back a few inches, but its body didn't budge. A deep wicked growl rumbled in its chest as it slowly turned back to face me. Whatever it was…was now totally pissed.

I screamed as it grabbed my arm and flung me across the room. I flew like a rag doll, crashing into one of the sinks, which immediately followed with the sound of bones crushing. Sharp, excruciating pain shot through my chest. I gasped for air, but it came with great difficulty.

The creature shot at me again, knocking me on my back. It wrapped its long, cold fingers around my neck, then bent down and sniffed my face. I was helpless, and in total agony. I shut my eyes tightly as a cold breath brushed my neck.

"You smell, so sweet," the monster hissed. I kept my eyes closed as it inhaled again. "Much too sweet for a nephilim. Your scent confuses me. It's a shame he wants you dead. But, I promise to make it easy. Quick and easy," he whispered in a drawn, wicked tone.

He was going to kill me?

I fought for air, desperately trying to loosen his steeled grip around my neck. But it was locked tight and I was quickly losing consciousness. My limbs became weak and numb while darkness quickly encroached on the edges of my sight.

His grip suddenly loosened.

I immediately sucked in precious air.

I tried to focus through the flickering lights, and noticed two figures slamming each other across the bathroom. They were a blur, and landed with a crash in between one of the stalls.

Something grabbed me from behind, and lifted me from the ground. I was taken bathroom, to an abandoned ticketing booth around the corner.

I kicked and punched, fighting to free myself, despite the searing pain.

"Emma, stop. It's me."

I stopped and turned to my captor. It was Malachi. And for the first time I was actually relieved to see him. His dark shades were off, and beautiful, chocolate brown eyes were focused on me. He didn't look scary. In fact, his eyes were filled with concern.

I continued to fight for breath as agonizing pain shot through my chest.

"What's wrong?" Malachi asked, carefully laying me on the floor.

"It hurts...to breathe." I pushed the words out, trying not to use too much air. Every breath felt like a knife being thrust into my chest.

He placed his hands on my chest and closed his eyes.

"You have a few broken ribs," he said, shaking his head. "Hold still, Emma. And *please*, try not to scream too loud," he said, intently.

I didn't know what he was going to do, but if he told me not to scream, it was probably going to hurt like hell. I braced myself for pain, and shut my eyes. I soon felt heat emanating from his hands, and soon after, a cracking sound followed with...*pain!*

He held his hand over my mouth to muffle my sharp scream. It felt like he'd broken another one of my ribs, but after a few seconds, the pain became bearable and I began to breathe a little easier.

"What'd you do?" I questioned, but he shrugged. "Was it magic?"

"Yeah. I'm a damn good magician," he muttered, with a grin. "We need to leave, now. Can you move?" he asked, raising my head.

"Yeah, I think so." He carefully lifted me to my feet and wrapped his arm around my waist. We paused while he glanced around the corner and sniffed the air.

"What was that thing in the bathroom?" I asked.

He ignored me.

"It's clear... we have to move quickly." He pulled me across the baggage claim area, and out the exit doors, into the cold rain. As soon as we stepped to the curb, a black Hummer came screeching to the front. The front passenger door flew open, and in an instant, Malachi scooped me up and set me on the seat. He slammed the door shut, and then jumped into the back.

"Move it, Dom," he demanded.

The driver hit the gas pedal and screeched out of the parking lot, exiting the airport at speeds close to 100mph.

I fiddled with my seatbelt, which was nearly impossible to buckle with trembling fingers.

Turning to the driver, my breath seized.

Un-freaking-believable.

A young, handsome, fair skinned, guy, with ash-brown hair, and bright green eyes turned and smiled at me. Muscles bulged from his tight, white t-shirt.

"Hey, Emma. I'm Dominic, but *you* can call me Dom," he said with a wink and a smile. Oh boy. This guy looked like he was a player, but he definitely had the looks to back his actions.

"Hey," I responded, finally snapping my seatbelt in.

"Welcome to Alaska," he said, taking his hands off the wheel for a second, and spreading them out.

"Yeah, right," I huffed. If this welcome was any indication of what my life was going to be like... I was in *big* trouble.

A sudden wave of terror struck me. I quickly twisted back to Malachi, and pain shot through my ribs.

"Kade. Where's Kade?" I yelled, almost breathless.

Malachi smiled. "Kade will be fine. Don't worry. He can take care of himself."

"What do you mean? We can't leave him!"

"Oh, don't worry sweetheart. Kade knows his way home," Dominic added, reassuringly.

"Was he the one that rescued me in the bathroom?" I questioned. My voice was shaking as much as the rest of me.

"Yes. And I hope he gets his ass kicked for taking his eyes off of you," Malachi snickered. Dominic laughed as well.

"But he saved my *life.* You can't leave him," I screamed in his defense. "What if he gets killed? Did you see that thing?"

"Like I said, you don't have to worry about Kade, Emma. He'll be just fine," Malachi repeated.

"Oh my God! What the hell is going on?" I shouted, as tears poured down my face. I hated that Malachi was making a joke of Kade fighting with that terrifying creature. It looked evil. Like some sort of demon. What if it hurt him? Or worse... what if it killed him?

"Awe, come on Emma. Don't be like that," Malachi said, reaching over, grasping my shoulder.

"What was that thing?" I questioned, looking deep into his eyes. He didn't respond and looked at the driver, who also kept silent and his eyes on the road. "It was going to kill me, and called me a neph-a-something. What does that mean?"

"Nephilim?" Dominic corrected.

"Yes. That's what it called me. What the hell does that mean?"

I saw Dominic shoot a glance into the rearview mirror at Malachi.

"I- I'm sorry, Emma. But Alaine—" Malachi stuttered.

"Yeah, yeah…I know. Alaine will tell me. But why can't anyone tell me what the hell is going on? I've been living in the dark for the past *two* days. Things have been happening to me that I can't explain. Things are appearing out of nowhere, trying to kill me, and I know you guys have some answers." I was beyond frustrated, and started to hyperventilate.

"I think you need to calm yourself down a bit, Emma," Malachi said, holding his hands up.

"Calm down? How do you expect me to calm down? I was almost killed by a freaking demon creature, and all I want are some *answers*," I bellowed at the top of my lungs. I could feel myself losing it.

"I'm sorry to have to do this to you," he said in a calm voice, placing his hand on my forehead speaking one word. "Sleep."

I quickly felt numb and a sense of déjà vu.

"What did you do to me?" I gasped. My world was quickly fading, and I realized that Kade had done the exact same thing to me on the plane.

Now, that was crossing a personal line, and totally NOT cool!

Heaviness crept over my eyes, until I couldn't keep them open any longer.

SIX

"EMMA. WAKE UP. WE'RE ALMOST there," a familiar voice called through the darkness, gently nudging my arm. Tingles and warmth rushed over me like a warm blanket; a familiar feeling I'd grown accustomed to whenever Kade was near. I slowly peeled my lids open and tried to focus in the darkness.

I was still sitting in the front seat of the Hummer, and we were on a bumpy road. Thick growths of spruce trees lined each side, towering up towards the darkened sky. Kade popped forward from the back seat.

"Hey," he grinned.

"How did you—" I paused and pointed at him, utterly bewildered by his presence.

He wiggled his eyebrows and quickly slunk back into his seat.

Was I dreaming this whole time, or was there actually a demon thing that tried to kill me in the bathroom at the airport? I bent sideways and felt a dull pain in my ribs. The pain was real, so the rest of it had to be. But how did he get here? We left him behind. Maybe they turned around and picked him up while I was asleep.

Wait a minute.

I felt a fire start to burn deep inside when I remembered what Malachi had done.

"Okay, what the hell did you do to me?" I huffed, glancing over to Malachi.

"What do you mean?" he said with a look of innocence on his face.

"You know what I mean. And you did it too," I said, shooting a skeptical look over to Kade. "When you both touched my head and said the word '*sleep*'... in seconds I was out cold – no dreams, nothing – until you woke me up. What is that? What did you do to me?"

"We don't know what you're talking about Emma. That's pure craziness. You were just overly tired and must have overdosed on some of your pain pills," Malachi said incredulously, rolling his eyes. "Actually, I think you were in shock and passed out."

"Well... what about that thing that almost killed me in the bathroom? What was that? It looked like a vampire. Was it...a vampire?"

All three of them burst into laughter.

"There are no such things as vampires, sweetheart," Dominic snickered.

"Then what was it?" I pressed angrily.

They all kept silent. I was livid that they wouldn't respond, so I flipped to face the front, folding my arms over my chest. It was no sense talking or trying to reason with them. They were all keeping to some stupid code-of-silence.

"Kade, your ass is going to be in some deep shit for that bathroom scene," Malachi muttered.

"Whatever, man," Kade replied.

Dominic laughed, and I shook my head, heated with fury.

The next five minutes of bumpy road and silence were hellish.

"We're here," Kade announced with a sigh of relief.

I bet he and Malachi were thrilled that I'd soon be delivered in one piece, and finally out of their hands. I noticed a glowing light above the tree-line ahead. As soon as we rounded a bend, a humongous castle-like mansion towered in the middle of beautifully landscaped property. It looked like it belonged somewhere on the English hillsides, rather than in the middle of Nowheresville, Alaska.

The mansion had two sections. The main section was an immense, three story, cobblestone home. To the right of the main living quarters was a tower made of stone that loomed over the building by a couple of stories. A large metal gate wrapped around the expanse of the property. Flood lights and little black boxes were atop every post. It looked more like a high-society prison yard. I wondered if the fence had electricity running through it. I wouldn't doubt it if it did.

We drove down a cobbled path which came to a round-about. The center was filled with flowers and a large stone fountain. Dominic pulled up to the front of the house where an older, white-haired gentleman in a black suit and bowtie stood, waiting to greet us.

"Good evening, Emma," he said with a wide smile as he opened my door. Wow. He had an English accent. That was pretty awesome.

"Good evening," I replied, with a smile. The cold Alaskan air bit my cheeks, and cut straight through my clothes as I exited the door. Holy heck. It was *freezing*.

"My name is Henry. It's so nice to finally meet you," he said, offering me his arm.

Finally meet me? That was odd. I'd only known I'd been coming here since yesterday.

Henry led me up the steps to the front door which was massive and towering. It looked like it had come straight from a castle, with two angels carved delicately into the wood, adorning each side. The large doors swung open into a grand hallway.

On each side of the hall stood golden pedestals with crystal vases nestled on top, filled with dozens of red roses. A beautiful crystal chandelier greeted us with a warm glow from above. The floors were earth-toned slate, and the walls were painted in a golden-brown color. Everything looked luxurious. My mother would have died if she saw this place. It looked like a palace.

We walked through the hallway into a large open room, which had floors made of white marble. In the center was a mural made of tiny multicolored tiles of the sky, and an angel with outspread wings, bearing a sword. A white marbled stairway with a golden banister led upstairs to the second and third floors.

What did her husband do for a living? Was he a sultan? This was something I wasn't expecting. At best, I thought an extra-large, three story house, moose head hanging on a wall, bear skins on the floor... you know, typical things you'd think an Alaskan would have in their home.

Kade and Malachi entered the room chattering quietly amongst themselves.

"Wait here Emma, I will alert Miss Gray of your arrival," Henry said, disappearing into a hallway tucked just before the staircase.

"Isn't this place awesome?" Kade whispered into my ear. He was so close, my body tingled. I wanted to be mad at him, but my brain had become fogged and I'd suddenly forgotten why.

"Yeah, it's amazing."

I looked up and saw another chandelier, which dwarfed the one in the hall. It was massive, golden, and covered with hundreds of tear-drop crystals. It hung from a large, round skylight made of stained-glass, which pictured a large, red rose in full bloom. From entering the house, I already gathered my aunt liked red roses and was obsessed with angels.

"You'll like it here," Kade assured me again, brushing up against me. His breath was warm against my cheek, sending surges through my veins. Was he trying to use his charm and luring abilities to try and make me feel better? Well...it was working.

"I hope so," I exhaled.

A door snapped shut down the hall and footsteps headed in our direction. Kade immediately took two steps back. My stomach churned, anxious to finally meet my mysterious relative. Henry appeared first and stepped to the side.

As she stepped forward, I gasped, gazing at this beautiful woman standing before me. She was wearing a long, white flowing robe, and had striking resemblances of my mother. They had the same perfect features, only hers were darker. Her skin was like creamy, white porcelain; her hair like dark-brown silk, perfectly curled down her shoulders. Big brown eyes were beaming with joy beneath long, dark eyelashes. Up until now, I thought brown eyes were boring, but she made them look exquisite.

"Emma, I'm so glad you're here," she said with her arms outstretched, approaching me. Hugging me warmly, she then looked down and took my casted arm in her hands with a look of concern. I stood frozen, unsure of what to think, everything became overwhelming.

She stepped back. "I'm so sorry. Please excuse my behavior. I should have introduced myself first. I was just so excited to finally meet you after all these years. My name is Alaine. I'm your mother's half-sister."

"You look a lot like her," I said, fighting back tears that began to sting my eyes.

"I'm so sorry for your loss, Emma. I cannot begin to imagine the pain you are going through, but I can promise you this…I will always be here for you. You are my blood and my last living relative. We will get through this together," she promised, leaning in gently caressing my face. Then she hugged me again tightly, stroking my hair. "It's alright sweetheart."

I hugged her back and sobbed.

It was strange how oddly familiar she felt, like I'd known her all my life. Maybe it was because she reminded me so much of my mother.

"It's very late. I think you should get some sleep. We will talk in the morning," she said softly. "Henry, could you please escort Emma to her room? She must be exhausted."

I glanced over to a large, grandfather clock standing against the wall. It was after midnight. That would explain why she didn't want to talk tonight.

"Yes, madam," Henry replied with a bow of his head.

"Kade, could you please assist Henry, and take Emma's luggage to her room?"

"Of course," Kade chimed, swiping my carry-on from Malachi's hand, and slinging it over his shoulder. My suitcase was already gripped in his other hand.

"And after that, I would like to see you both in my study," she said looking between Malachi and Kade.

They quickly glanced at each other with narrowed looks.

"Emma, I hope you find your room accommodating. If you need anything, please let Henry know."

"I will. Thank you," I answered.

I guess I'd have to wait for answers until tomorrow. It was much too late and I could tell she was tired. I'd leave Kade and Malachi to tell her about my near-death experience, and the creature that almost killed me. I think we all had enough drama for tonight. I felt safe here. Like nothing could get me within the confines of this house, especially with Kade and Malachi nearby.

"This way, Emma," Henry announced, leading me up the stairway. We walked to the third level and took a left, down another hallway. He stopped at the first door on the right, swung it open, and flicked on the light. "After you," he said motioning me to enter.

The room was large, almost the size of my mom and dad's

master suite, and the first thing that hit me were the colors... they reminded me of my room back in California. The setup was almost exact too. It wasn't over the top, like the rest of the house. It was just... normal. The queen sized bed was covered with a fluffy, chocolate-brown bedspread, and the many different shapes and sizes of throw pillows were all welcoming me to jump in.

The furniture was a light blonde wood which made the room feel warm. There was also an attached bathroom, decorated in the same bright colors, and a large walk-in closet. Maybe I spoke too soon. This room was amazing.

"This is all mine?" I asked.

"Yes, Emma. Your aunt decorated it herself."

"Wow. It's... amazing."

Kade bounded in behind me, laid my suitcase on the floor next to the bed, and handed me my carry-on.

"Hey. Thanks, for everything," I said. I didn't want to say anything more because Henry was in the room. I wanted to thank him personally for saving my life, but I guess that too would have to wait.

"No problem. So, I guess I'll see you tomorrow," he muttered, his head slightly tilting to the side.

"I guess," I said, shrugging my shoulders.

"Oh, you will," he laughed. "I'd better get going. Sleep sweet, Emma," he said, lightly brushing my hand with his fingertips. I gasped, trying to catch my breath as the tingles surged through my arm.

Dang him!

I heard him chuckle as he left the room. *What was I going to do with him?* I'd have to wear gloves and a body suit with him around.

Before Henry left, he made sure I knew where the kitchen was - first floor, take a left, and go all the way to the back. Simple enough, but I doubted I'd take a trip to the kitchen tonight.

He then asked if I needed anything, and when I told him I didn't, he excused himself and snapped the door shut behind him.

I was finally alone and an overwhelming feeling of sadness enveloped me.

I walked over to the window and drew back the curtains. The room was obviously facing the back yard, and from what I could see – even in the darkness—it was huge. It was about four football fields long in length and width, and at center was a labyrinth of hedges, surrounded by a well-manicured lawn. I'd have to view it again when the sun was up. It was too dark to get the full picture.

There were lights around the perimeter fence, shining outward into the endless thick of trees. A bright beam of light, which I assumed was coming from the tower, combed the grounds. Wow. This *was* like a high-security prison, but at least I felt protected.

I sucked in a huge breath, and hoped that the creature I'd met tonight wouldn't be intruding or looking for me. I shivered. Just as I was about to close the curtain again, I noticed a small guest house out of the corner of my eye. It was all the way to the right side of the property; a small, quaint, sort of gingerbread looking house. I wondered if that's where Kade was staying. My heart pattered against my chest at the thought.

I didn't know what to think of Kade. He made me wonder if he was really human. I mean, he was gorgeous, had some kind of magical charm that played with my emotions, and dulled my sadness whenever he came around. He was also strong and fast, from what I witnessed in the bathroom.

What really happened in that bathroom after Malachi dragged me out? Kade was obviously alive and seemed unscathed, but what happened to the creature? Did it get away? Did he injure it? Kill it? Another chill of terror shot up my spine.

Everything in my life was one ginormous question, and I knew, if I didn't get most of those questions answered in the morning, my brain just might explode.

A dull pain emanated from my ribs and my head started to throb. I needed a pain pill, but decided to take a shower first. I opened my suitcase and found my warm pajamas, and then noticed my cast. I dug through my carry-on and found a plastic bag, stuck my casted arm into it, and tucked the open parts into the end.

I made my way into the bathroom. Two, lime green towels hung on the rack, and another stack of colorful towels were folded on a shelf. A basket sat on the sink, stocked with shampoo, conditioner, soap, shaving lotion, razors, toothpaste and a new toothbrush. She'd thought of everything.

I pulled back the colorful polka-dotted shower curtain and turned on the water. It was ice cold, like glacier ice. It took a few minutes until it started to get warm, but once it did, I peeled off my clothes and stood under the stream. The hot, steamy water beat down on my head and aching body. It didn't last too long because my right shoulder began to ache from holding my cast out of the water. I quickly washed my hair and scrubbed as best I could.

It felt good to be clean and in my comfortable stretchy pajamas.

Back in the bedroom, I went to the desk and flicked on the small lamp. The laptop looked brand new, and had a cord attached to it that was plugged into the wall. I wondered if it had internet service. It wouldn't hurt to try. I wanted to shoot Lia and Jeremy an email just to let them know that I had arrived safely. Almost. But I wouldn't let them know about the danger. They wouldn't believe me anyway.

As the computer booted up, I walked over to the bed and shoved the decorative pillows to the far side. The computer made a chiming noise. It was ready.

Please have internet service…

I clicked on the internet icon and it immediately popped up.

"*Yes.*"

I quickly signed into my email account. There were two messages waiting from Lia and Jeremy. I clicked on Jeremy's first.

Hey Emma,

I hope you made it to Alaska in one piece. Did you see any bears? Things won't be the same without you here. Please let us know that you arrived safely.

Sincerely,

Jeremy

Sincerely? He was so crazy.

I clicked reply.

Hey Jeremy,

Yes, I made it in one piece, barely, and NO... I didn't see any bears. It was too dark to notice. But you'll be the first to know if I spot one. I'll try and keep Lia's camera with me... just in case.

Well, it's late, and I'm gonna hit the sack. I'll be in touch. I promise. At least this place has internet service.

—Emma

Next, I clicked on Lia's.

Hey Emma!

Oh my gosh. I totally broke down and cried all the way home after we left you at the hospital. I miss you already. So how was your trip? Better yet... how was that hot guy that came to get you? Did you sit by him? Spill the juicy details, okay?

School starts in a few days. Ugh! So wishing you were here. Our senior year is gonna totally suck without you.

Well...my mom's calling me. I have to help with dinner. Call or email when you have the time!

Love ya,

Lia xoxo

Her turn... but I wasn't in any mood to spill, so I kept it short and sweet, like Jeremy's.

Hey Lia,

I made it safely, and they have internet service! I know... Amazing!

Kade was really nice, and yes, I did sit next to him, but he was quiet most of the time. No juicy details to spill...yet.

I miss you guys so much too. I wish you were closer.

I finally met my Aunt. She reminds me so much of my mom, and seems really nice. Oh…and get this… there are NO schools in the area so I'm gonna be HOMESCHOOLED! Yep, I said homeschooled! My senior year is majorly going to suck!

It's really cold here, but the house is huge and beautiful… like mansion beautiful, and in the middle of nowhere. I have my own room, and I promise to take pictures and send them to you soon.

Well, it's late, so I'm gonna hit the sack. I'll email you tomorrow.
Love,
Emma xo

I turned off the laptop, jumped into bed, and tucked myself deep under the warmth of the blanket. My head sank into the soft, fluffy pillow.

Thoughts swirled in my brain over everything that happened over the past days, and then it hit me again; a wave of overwhelming sadness and pain.

What really caused the accident that took my parents' lives? My dad never drove over the speed limit, and was always super cautious, especially when my mom and I were in the car.

I reached for my carry-on at the foot of my bed, to get my reader. After opening it up, I had to blink several times to release the pool of tears which hazed the picture of my parents. I placed it to my heart and hugged it tightly.

I would never see my mom wander into my room, wrap her arms around me, and tell me that everything was going to be fine. If I could only have her back for one more day, to smell the sweet scent of her hair, and have her warm smile melt away my misery. But deep inside, I knew it would never happen. I was left with wonderful memories… and one, solitary picture.

How I wished this was just a horrible nightmare, and when I closed my eyes and opened them again in the morning, it would all be gone.

The constant throb in my head reminded me I was overdue for my next pain pill. Hopefully, it would be strong enough to knock me out. I wanted sleep. I *needed* sleep.

Where was Kade when I needed him? I yearned for his warm touch. He could put me into a deep, restful sleep, so my brain could shut down, even if just for a little while.

I pulled the bottle of pain pills out of the bag and shook two into my palm, but I knew I had to eat something with it. Pills made me nauseated, and the only edible things I had were Skittles and Starburst. *Yuck.* That sounded totally disgusting right now. I needed something with substance, like crackers.

I guess I'd have to head down to the kitchen.

I dried my tears and climbed out of bed. Everyone was probably sleeping, but just in case, at least I looked pretty decent in my cute pajamas. They were black, with bright pink hearts all over.

I slowly cracked open the door and peeked down the hall. The floor was empty and the whole house seemed eerily silent. I quietly headed towards the stairway, and peered down to the lower levels. They were empty as well, so I quickly bounded down the stairs, shivering as soon as my bare feet hit the ice cold marble stairs.

When I reached the bottom, I tried to remember Henry's directions to the kitchen. Down the stairs, take a left, and head all the way back. I followed his instructions, but this was a huge house.

It was dark, but there were a series of night lights guiding the way. I followed the glow down the hall, which opened up into a large, commercial-sized kitchen. The light above the stove was left on, probably for late night wanderers like me.

All the appliances were stainless steel, and the cabinetry was done in a dark cherry wood. The floors were the same earthy slate as the entry. My mother would have loved this dream kitchen.

I ambled over to the large double-door fridge and paused; a little apprehensive about opening it, knowing this wasn't my home. I'd have to get used to it sooner or later, though – at least for the next year. Besides, Henry wouldn't have given me directions if it was off limits.

I sucked in a breath and pulled the door open.

"Hungry?" a voice startled me.

"Holy mother!" I gasped, turning to see Kade sitting on a barstool behind the counter. "You scared the crap out of me. How the heck did you get there?"

"Sorry. I didn't mean to scare you," he apologized. "I usually grab a bite before I head home. I actually came in right after you did."

"You were stalking me?" I asked, with a raised eyebrow.

He paused and grinned. "I guess you could say that. I actually saw you round the corner, and wanted to see why you were sneaking around so late."

"Oh." I instantly blushed.

"By the way…nice PJ's," he said with a large smile.

I could feel my face get flustered, "Thanks." I felt so amazingly lame at that very moment, and had to come up with a question to cover it up.

"So how was your meeting with Alaine?"

"Boring. Malachi briefed her on the trip."

"Oh," I said, feeling a bit uncomfortable.

"Are you looking for something in particular?" he asked.

I hated that he looked so attractive, while I was in my pajamas, with swollen red eyes and nose.

"Are there any crackers? I have to take my pills," I said bashfully, closing the door to the fridge.

He hopped off his stool and made his way over to one of the cupboards.

"Right here. Take your pick," he chimed, opening a cupboard filled with cookies, crackers, and chips.

I walked over and pulled out a box of crackers that were my mom's favorite.

"I just need a few." I opened the bag, and plucked out four. He made his way around to a drawer, pulled out a Ziploc bag and held it open. I dumped the remaining crackers into it, and then he zipped it shut and placed it back on the shelf.

"Thanks," I said.

"No problem."

Kade walked back toward me and leaned in close, nearly pinning me against the counter. His closeness immediately made me dizzy, and sent my world spinning into a state of euphoria. My breath became quick, my pulse was racing, and heat rushed through my veins.

We silently gazed into each other's eyes for a moment. I was completely entrapped. His hazel eyes danced with warmth, and then he smiled at me, instantly making my knees weak.

I quickly shoved a cracker in my mouth and chewed; then another, and another, trying to mask the loud hammering of my heart.

"Are you hungry?" he chuckled, leaning back and looking at me through concerned eyes.

I stared at him with wide eyes and shook my head. *O.M.G.* I was a complete amateur. *Damn it, Emma...pull it together.*

The crackers were making my mouth dry. Like so dry, they were plastered to my teeth and to the roof of my mouth. There was no way in hell I was opening my mouth with him standing in front of me.

Kade grinned and ambled over to the fridge, pulled out two bottles of water, unscrewed the top off one and set it in front of me. I smiled with my lips shut, then quickly gulped the water down. I opened my fist revealing the two pills, and wondered if one would suffice. I hated the nauseated feeling I got from taking pain medication.

"Pain pills?" he asked.

"Yeah. I'm sore and desperately need some sleep, but I really hate the feeling I get when I take them," I sighed, undecided.

"Well, would you like some help getting to sleep?" he asked, raising his brow.

I froze.

I was too embarrassed to say *hell to the yes*. The thought of it made my heart race even faster than before. I looked at him with wide eyes and remained speechless.

"But, if I do help you, you'll have to promise you won't tell your aunt. If she ever found out I was alone with you in your room, *and* put the sleeper on you, she would put *me* to sleep forever… in a shallow grave out back. I'll only agree to it if you ask. And *only* so you can get some sleep. That's it. I can't imagine how hard it must be for you, especially with everything you've been dealing with," he said with a sad sort of grin.

"So that's what it's called? The sleeper?" I questioned.

"Yes."

"It sounds like a wrestling move," I giggled.

"It does, now that you mention it," he said with a wider grin.

"Is it magic?"

"I guess you could call it magic. I've never really thought about it that way," he answered with a tilt to his head.

"Could you do it to yourself?"

"No. Although, sometimes I wish I could," he sighed. "So…do you want my help? Just say the words."

The words were stuck in my throat, but I managed to push *one* out.

"Yes," I exhaled, accompanied with a nod.

"Okay then. I'll be up in a bit. There are eyes everywhere, watching, and I'd be banished in an instant if I were caught sneaking into your room. I happen to know a way in, but you'll have to go up and unlatch your bedroom window," he said, watching me carefully. Maybe he was checking to see if I was really game.

"Sure," I said easily. *Heck yeah, I was game.* I immediately felt heat start to smolder deep inside of me. And then I thought about it. My bedroom window was up three stories high, and I couldn't remember seeing a balcony, or stairs, or any other way to get up.

"Wait. How are you going to get up there?" I questioned.

"Magic," he said with a wink and a grin. "I'll see you soon." He grabbed his water bottle, took a swig, and then headed for the back door.

I had to catch my breath, as I watched him close the door. I clasped my sweaty fingers over my pills, and bounded back down the hallway. My insides brewed with a mixture of excitement and apprehension at the thought of Kade being in my room. I'd never had a boy in my room, except for Jeremy, and technically he didn't count. He was more of a brother than potential boyfriend material.

My feet quickened to the pace of my heart, and soon I found myself racing back down the hallway and back up the stairs. As soon as I reached the top, I leaned over to make sure no one was around or watching. The place was quiet and empty, so I hurried back down the hall, opened my door, and quickly shut and locked it behind me.

I tried to calm myself.

Breathe, Emma. Breathe. And try to act normal. Yeah right. Easier thought than done.

I slowly walked toward the window, and just as I pulled back the curtain and unlatched the window, Kade came swinging in.

"What the… how did you—" I stumbled backwards in awe.

He laughed and turned to latch the window, pulling the curtain shut.

I tried to rationalize how he could have scaled the side of the building, just as fast as I could run up the stairs.

It just… was not right.

He can't be human. Could he? Maybe there was some hidden

ladder, or elevator, or even a rope I failed to see. I'd have to do some inspecting in the morning when there was light. There had to be some kind of logical explanation.

"What took you so long?" he asked, staring at me through narrowed eyes, plopping down at the foot of my bed.

I felt my mouth gaping wide open, so I snapped it shut.

"Who are you? No... *what* are you?" I stammered.

"What do you mean?" he questioned with a sly look in his eyes.

"You know exactly what I mean," I said matching his gaze. "First, you do something to my insides whenever you're near. Second, I saw how fast and strong you were fighting off that creature in the bathroom. And, by the way... thank you, for that. And third, how the heck did you get up here so quick? The only explanation is that you crawled up like a spider, or you flew. So what is it?"

He glanced at me with a crooked grin. "So, you really feel something when I come near you?"

"Huh?" He threw me off, asking me a question to my question. So not fair.

"What exactly happens to you when I come near?" he said, slowly stalking closer to me.

"I don't know. I can't explain it," I said blushing, "but did you hear anything else I said?"

Selective hearing...typical male. Maybe he was human after all, or maybe he was just trying to distract me to keep from answering my question.

"Well, what do *you* think I am?" he asked, stopping inches in front of me.

I had to hold myself together or I was going to faint, and hit the floor with an embarrassing thud. I stepped back and braced myself against the desk.

"I mean, you look human to me, but I've seen you do inhuman things." I waited for him to answer, but he didn't say a word. "Are you a vampire?"

He suddenly burst into laughter. "No. A vampire? You seriously thought I was a vampire?"

"Werewolf?" I asked with a raised eyebrow.

"Emma. You've got to be kidding me. Vampires and Werewolves are so overrated."

"Yes, and that's why I'm asking. You seem to fit into the modern vamp/were category. You're strong, handsome, fast... I seriously have NO clue what you are."

"So, you think I'm handsome?" he asked.

"*Duh.* Even a blind girl could see that," I blurted, quickly realizing what I said. Sometimes I wish I had a plug for my mouth. But a wide smile broke across his face.

"Well, haven't you ever heard of super humans? Those people with extraordinary skills and talents?" he asked.

"Yes, but what you have is totally different. And, what about that thing that attacked me in the bathroom? What was that?"

I finally hit on the thing bothering me most. Kade and Malachi came to "escort" me to Alaska, but in actuality they were protecting me. And I got to see first-hand what they were protecting me against. If it wasn't for them, I'd probably be dead. But then again, ever since I met them, my life had flipped upside down.

He paused, then sighed loudly and had a look of concern in his eyes. The same look he had when we were on the plane. The same look he gave when I'd asked him questions that were too personal.

"I promise I won't say anything. I just want you to answer that one question. I know you won't tell me why I need protection, or why that thing tried to kill me, but can you at least tell me what that creature was?"

He was still hesitating, but I could see him warring within himself.

"Kade… *please*? This is something I deserve to know."

His head suddenly snapped up, his eyes widened, and his lips turned upward into the widest smile I'd seen yet.

"What?" I asked, wondering what was up with his sudden change of emotion.

"That's the first time I've heard you say my name out loud," he said, his face beaming like the sun. "It just sounded so…cool… the way you said it."

"Oh," I exhaled, feeling my cheeks blush, most likely turning a bright shade of red. Was that really the first time I'd said his name? I tried to think back. "I did yell your name when I was being attacked in the bathroom," I admitted.

He smiled, and it was contagious.

"Okay, stop trying to stall," I muttered.

"Sorry. What were we talking about?"

I took a seat on the swivel chair next to my desk and twisted to face him. "I want to know what the creature was that tried to kill me."

"Oh, yeah." His smile disappeared as quickly as it came. "Alright. You win. But remember... I didn't tell you a thing."

"Zip." I mimicked zipping my lips shut.

He sucked in a deep breath and clasped his hands tightly around each other, staring directly at me. "It was a Darkling. The Darkling are pawns, evil assassins, used to do the dirty work of the Fallen. They are the vilest creatures who have ever walked the face of the earth, and they smell like hell because they live underground in sewers, drains, or abandoned dark places. They've been known to feed on anything, and I mean anything."

"The Darkling in the bathroom was sent for you. You were his target. And if the ones who sent him ever learn of his failure, more will be sent until they've confirmed you are dead."

My breath seized.

"There are more of those things? But why? What have I done to make them want to kill me?"

He shook his head. That was a question he wasn't going to answer. It was frustrating, but my brain started firing.

Why? The worst thing I could ever remember doing was in the eighth grade. I lied to my parents, telling them I was going to sleep over at a friend's house, but ended up going to party instead. On the way home, we were pulled over and taken down to the police station, because the driver didn't have a license; she'd taken her parents car without their permission.

The police called my mother, who came in hysterical and crying, and I was grounded for the rest of the year. That's the worst I could think of, and I didn't think it was a good enough reason for anyone to want to kill me.

"Why haven't I ever seen, or heard of a Darkling before?"

"There's a lot that goes on that most are clueless about. There are reasons why humans don't know about the Darkling. They are creatures of the dark and never come out of hiding unless called. And, any human who has ever had the misfortune of running into one... well, they never live to tell about it."

"So, is the Darkling that tried to kill me... dead?"

He paused.

"Yes," he answered.

"Did *you* kill him?" I pressed.

"Yes."

I exhaled, in total shock. "Oh God." I couldn't picture Kade killing that thing. It was terrifyingly strong and fast. "Who sent it?"

He hesitated and looked away, avoiding my gaze.

"Kade, who sent it?"

"Now that's something I'm *definitely* not at liberty to answer. It's much too complicated, and there is just too much involved. It's—" His head dropped, and he pressed his fingers against his temples, shaking his head. "I'm sorry, Emma. I can't. I'm sure Alaine will tell you everything in the morning."

My brain was now in overdrive. More than one person wanted me dead?

"I don't understand. Who wants me dead?" Tears welled in my eyes as I asked those critical words.

"I can't, Emma. I just can't. I'm so sorry," he softly murmured.

"I promise I won't tell anyone."

"If I tell you, I'll be banished for sure, and... and," he paused, and looked up at me, "I wouldn't be able to leave you," he finally admitted. He slumped over burying his face in his hands.

There was complete silence in the room. I stared at him in total disbelief.

"I'm sorry." I replied, giving in. "It's just that I don't think it's fair that I have to wait to get answers, especially when my life is at stake."

"You don't have to worry. I'll make sure you're safe."

He looked up and our eyes locked. His face was glowing, perfect. He looked nineteen, but yet there was something mysterious, hidden deep within his beautiful hazel eyes. It was like looking into the eyes of someone much older, someone who had seen many things.

This beautiful boy saved my life from that horrifying creature, and yet, here he was, sitting in my room. My heart swelled to the point of bursting. I'd never experienced feelings as strong as the ones I'd felt when I was with him. My feelings seemed to go out-of-whack whenever he was near. It was completely baffling. But mixed within the confusion was another feeling. Like somehow, we were destined to find each other, and everything inside of us seemed to be confirming that fact.

But who was he, really? I knew absolutely nothing about him, and by the look of things, I obviously wasn't going to find out anymore tonight. This whole day felt like a horrible nightmare. I was living in a haze of turmoil and bewilderment, and couldn't handle it anymore.

"Could you please just put me to sleep?" I finally said, getting up and walking over toward the bed. I pulled back the covers and crawled in.

"Emma—"

"It's alright. I really need to sleep. I can't deal with everything that's in my head, and right now I'm going way, way over my brain capacity. Please, just put me out and I'll deal with it all tomorrow."

He stood up off the foot of the bed. "Are you sure?" he asked sadly, giving in much too easily.

"I'm sure," I said, mustering a fake smile. He came and sat on the edge of the bed, and tucked the covers around me. "Just promise me one thing."

"And what's that?" he asked.

"That none of those creatures will get me while I'm sleeping."

"Emma, as long as I'm around, you will be safe. I'll be watching, and rest assured... *nothing* will harm you tonight," he promised. His eyes steeled on mine.

"Thank you," I breathed, knowing he meant what he said.

"Thank *you*," he said, returning a half-grin. I could tell he was happy I'd finally stopped asking questions.

"No seriously... Thank you," I whispered. He glanced at me with an inquisitive look. "For saving my life, even though you hardly know me."

He laughed. "I know more about you than you know, Emma Wise," he said with a sly grin.

I wasn't sure what he meant by that, but it made my heart pitter-patter. His closeness wrapped me in a familiar blanket of warmth and peace.

He leaned in, smelling so sweet, so intoxicating. He was so close. Almost too close. His hazel eyes were swimming with compassion. "I promise you, you'll be safe here, and I'll see you in the morning," he whispered.

He raised his hand and gently placed it on my forehead. Electricity shot through me, and I had to fight strong, sudden urge to wrap my arms around him and kiss his beautiful, full lips.

He leaned in, until his warm breath tickled my cheek. He smiled, and whispered that one, wonderful, magical word into my ear. "Sleep."

I suddenly felt peaceful and relaxed, and my eyelids instantly became heavy. His warm lips press against my forehead making me smile.

"Goodnight, Emma. Sleep sweet."

Those were the last words I heard before fading into darkness.

SEVEN

I WOKE IN FOREIGN SURROUNDINGS, dimly lit by a night-light plugged into a corner of the room. The air was chilled, so I pulled my blanket up, snuggling it closer. I glanced over to a little clock set on top the desk and its bright red numbers eerily glowed 7:36am.

For a second I was confused about where I was, but it all came flooding back, like a tidal wave of terror. I'd really hoped these past days were merely a nightmare; I'd wake-up in my own room back in California, my mother calling me down to breakfast, my father already sitting at the table eating his cereal and reading the morning paper. But instead, I was awake and the nightmare was real. I was still alive, but alone in a distant land, with a relative I'd never even known about, and creatures that wanted to kill me.

My mind began stirring, so I decided to shake off the sleep. I stretched, rubbing my eyes, which was a little hard to do with the stupid cast. I turned the colorful appendage and smiled at its quirky artwork, wondering how my best friends were doing back in L.A. I hoped they were missing me as much as I missed them. They'd be starting the new school year in a few days. Senior year... and I was going to miss it all. I was actually looking forward to this year, but not anymore. Homeschooled. *Ugh!*

My broken arm didn't seem nearly as achy as it had been the day before, and I wondered if there was any way the cast could come off sooner. It was so bulky and irritating, making my arm feel claustrophobic.

I stretched and twisted my body in different directions, assessing the rest of my recently battered body. My ribs were still a little tender, but not nearly as sore as they were last night. My stomach raced with acid at the thought of the creature and how it almost killed me. Someone had better give me answers, *today.* I'd get them... one way or another.

I decided to check the abrasions on my stomach and arms, and lifted my shirt to find they were almost completely gone. I rubbed my finger against the scar on my face, but could barely feel it. Amazing. I'd never healed this quickly before.

I finally decided to peel from the warmth of the covers, and ambled towards the window. And then, I suddenly remembered my visit from Kade.

Was it real? Was he really in my room last night? My heart began to thump. I closed my eyes and pictured his gleaming eyes, inches from mine. And then, I snapped myself back into reality.

I pulled back the curtain, surprised to see the same darkness that was there before I went to sleep. It was almost eight in the morning...

Where was the sun? If I were in California, the sun would be out in full force, blinding the eyes of commuters.

Then I remembered something Jeremy mentioned during one of his informative speeches on the Alaskan climate. We were heading to the winter season, where they only had a few hours of daylight. I think he said it was like four or five hours at most. Great.

"Hello dark world. Goodbye sunshine," I mumbled sorrowfully to myself, looking out over the endless expanse of spruce and birch trees. At least autumn's yellow and orange leaves brought some kind of color. Thinking about color, I doubt they had any tanning booths nearby. I doubted they had *anything* nearby.

I sighed and checked the window. It was locked. Kade must have locked it and exited through the main house. That was a gutsy move. I hope he didn't get caught.

Where was my new home, anyway? Alaska was a humongous state. I could be in the interior, on the coast, near the North Pole or somewhere down south? I had no clue. I probably could have known if Malachi hadn't done that sleeper thing on me. So rude! And such was the story of my life.

My *new* life anyway.

I sighed, and finally decided to get ready and see what the new day would drag in for me. More questions, perhaps? It sure wasn't offering a bright, cheerful morning.

I dug through my suitcase and found my favorite jeans, a long sleeved, white shirt, and a purple sweater. I hoped it would be enough layering, as long as I didn't step outside. Then, for sure I'd be a big purple popsicle in a matter of minutes.

Dragging my tired body into the bathroom, I paused at my reflection. The scar on my cheek was almost completely healed. Maybe a bit of magic was rubbing off on me.

I quickly dressed, brushed my teeth, and then decided to head down to the kitchen. My stomach wouldn't stop rumbling and felt a little acidy.

As soon as I stepped out the door...

"Hi!" a cheery voice called from across the hall. There in the hallway, stood a cute girl with bright blue eyes, light brown hair that came down just past her shoulders. She was wearing a very large smile.

"Hi" I replied, returning the smile.

"You must be Emma," she said bouncing towards me. She had on dark blue jeans and a light blue hoodie.

"Yes, and you must be...Courtney?"

"You know my name?" She had a look of thrill in her eyes, which made me giggle. She paused, cocked her head to the side, and placed a finger to her cheek like she was trying to think. "I'll bet Kade told you about me, didn't he?"

"Yes," I said.

"Did he say good things about me, or did he say I was a brat? He always tells people that I'm a brat, but I'm really not." Her eyes narrowed as she waited for my answer.

"He didn't say much about you, but he definitely didn't say you were a brat. He actually said you were pretty cool."

"Really?" Her face lit up and she sighed in relief. "Well that's good. I'm really, really glad you're here. It's been pretty lame not having any other girls around here. I'm going to be fourteen in seven months. Have you met Caleb yet? He's my brother. He's sixteen, but he's *super* boring and lazy. He doesn't like to do anything fun. He just lies around most of the time, and reads, or plays video games."

This girl was a fast talker.

Jeremy was a talker too, so I'd become accustomed to that type of speed. At least she seemed happy. I needed some of that in my life.

"No, I haven't met Caleb yet," I answered.

"Well, he's probably sleeping, anyway. Like I said... he's lazy." She threw her hands up in the air, and rolled her eyes.

And she was entertaining. I grinned.

"So, are you going down for breakfast?" she asked with wide eyes.

"I guess." I wasn't sure what plans were in store for me, and wondered if my Aunt Alaine was up yet.

"Good. I'll go down with you. Today is Thursday, and on Thursdays Miss Lilly makes chocolate chip pancakes. She's the cook and her pancakes are to-die-for."

So, Courtney was hyper, animated, and used her hands to accentuate her words. I could tell she was going to keep me very, very busy, which might actually be a good thing.

We made our way down the stairs and headed toward the kitchen. As soon as we turned the corner, I could smell the sweet aroma of bacon beckoning us. When we entered the kitchen, a stout, round woman, with dark hair tied into a messy bun, turned and faced us.

"Ahh! Hello, Courtney. How are you this fine morning?" She

had some kind of accent, but I couldn't tell which.

"Fine," she chimed. "Miss Lilly, this is Emma. She's living with us now."

"Yes, I know," she said with a warm smile. "Welcome Emma. It's so nice to finally meet you."

"You too," I replied with a smile.

I wasn't sure why everyone was so glad to have *finally* met me. It was like they knew about me for a while. How strange.

Then Kade's words rang through my mind...*I know more about you than you know, Emma Wise...* Did Alaine tell all of them about me? How much did she know? Did my mother keep in touch with her? Unanswered questions kept piling up.

"Well, you both should be heading into the dining room. Breakfast is on the table this morning," she said, shooing us away.

"Thank you," Courtney and I sang in unison.

She grabbed my arm and dragged me toward an adjoining room where echoes of voices and laughter rang out. As soon as we stepped through the doorway, the room fell silent.

"Wow. We sure know how to silence a room. Don't we, Emma?" Courtney announced sarcastically, prancing around to her seat at the far end of the table. She looked at me with wide eyes and patted the open chair next to her. I sucked in a deep breath and proceeded to my seat.

Awkward.

There were two new faces staring at me. Dominic and Malachi were there, but Kade wasn't. That was a bummer.

Each of them nodded as I made my way around the table.

They looked like they were in their early twenties, except for one, who looked closer to my age. All were clean-cut, dressed in jeans and t-shirts, and strikingly handsome. What was up with that? Did Alaine house all the handsome male models of Alaska?

Every eye followed me to my seat, like I was on parade, or some type of oddity. They didn't smile; they just gawked, which made me feel very uncomfortable. I wanted to do a one-eighty and walk right out, but instead I took my seat and turned my chair a little toward Courtney.

As I sat, I heard muffled whispers amongst them.

"Hey, Emma," Malachi greeted in a cool low tone, with a slight nod of his head. He was sitting directly across from me. His shades were off, but he was in cool-guy mode, most likely because the other guys were around. I didn't mind. He'd already shown me his nicer side. I knew he was just a big, grumpy looking, teddy-bear.

"Hey," I said softly.

"Hey, Emma! Remember me?" Dominic called from the far side of the table, waving his arm and wiggling his eyebrows, "The awesome get-away driver?"

"Yes." I smiled and nodded. He chuckled, and then buried his face back into his plate.

"Thomas? Could you *please* pass the pancakes?" Courtney yelled across the table. A blonde guy with longer hair and bright, baby-blue eyes turned and grinned at us.

"Sure princess," he said with sarcasm.

"Thank you," she hollered back.

"Hey Alex, pass this down." Thomas nudged the boy that

looked my age. He had shoulder-length, raven-black hair, dark green eyes, and a pale, handsome face. He glanced at me, picked up the plate and walked it over, setting it down between me and Courtney.

"Thanks, Alex," Courtney turned and offered him a smile.

"Sure thing," he answered with a wink. He glanced at me, spun on his heel, and headed back to his seat.

Courtney stabbed two pancakes and plopped them on my plate, then slathered butter over them and drenched them in syrup. She handed me the plate of bacon, and proceeded to stab her own pancakes. I was tempted to take lots of bacon, but only took three. Three seemed appropriate. I love bacon, but… who doesn't?

"Okay," she whispered. "I'll give you a quick rundown. The one that passed-the-buck is Thomas, which you probably already knew because I yelled his name. He's a trouble maker, like Kade."

The remark made me giggle.

"The guy who brought us the pancakes is Alexander, but he likes to be called Alex. The one across from Thomas is Dominic, and I guess you already know him. If his mouth wasn't full of food, he'd be yakking away."

Dominic turned and gave me a wink, then proceeded to pile food into his mouth.

"And, you've already met Malachi. He's my very favorite." She whispered the last part, and smiled at him with a huge, cheesy smile.

Malachi narrowed his eyes.

She continued, "The only ones missing are Kade and James. James is the oldest and the one that usually takes your aunt on her errands. And, you've obviously met Kade."

"Oh…yes," I said, quickly digging in to my plate.

The odd thing about all of these guys? They looked totally different, but seemed so similar. I couldn't really put my finger on how, but maybe it was because they were all beautiful and perfect. Or seemingly perfect, at least on the outside.

The pancakes were delicious – light and fluffy – and had chocolate chips melted through each bite. It tasted like an extra soft chocolate chip cookie, but it was super rich with the syrup and butter soaked into it. After a few bites I had my sugar-high for the rest of the day.

"Orange juice?" Courtney asked while holding a pitcher over my glass.

"No thanks. I'll just have water," I said. I couldn't put another sugary thing into my mouth.

Malachi jumped from his seat, and returned a few seconds later with a bottle of water. He unscrewed the top, and set it in front of me.

Wow. These guys were well mannered. Most boys I knew wouldn't budge.

"Thanks," I said with a smile. He returned a quick smile, then sat and scraped the remainders on his plate into his mouth.

"Good morning everyone." Henry stepped into the room.

"Morning Henry," they all answered.

He rounded the corner, holding an envelope in his hand. Walking directly to me, he bent down.

"Good morning Emma." he spoke softly, in his awesome English accent.

Everybody stopped and became silent again, staring.

"Good morning Henry."

"Alaine wanted me to give this to you," he said, handing me the envelope.

"Thank you," I smiled.

I wasn't sure what to do with it. Should I wait until I was alone, or should I just open it? What if it was private? If it was private, Henry would have probably told me. I decided to open it. Lifting the flap, I pulled out the letter and began to read.

Dearest Emma,

I am so sorry I cannot be with you this morning. There was an emergency at the medical center and they needed my assistance. I will be back around three, and we will talk then. Until then, please take time to get familiar with your surroundings, but don't wander off the property.

With love,

Alaine

"Who's that from?" Courtney pried.

"My aunt. She had to leave, but she'll be back around three."

"Oh, goody. That means I get to show you around the place. You know... the grand tour," she said with enthusiasm, shoveling the last piece of pancake into her mouth.

"Yeah, that'll be cool." I tried to seem thrilled, but it just seemed like everything that had to do with my new life, was on hold. It was frustrating, and now I had a bunch of hours to kill before I'd get my answers. Well... at least I had Courtney to keep me busy. I'm sure she had a list of things for us to do.

Dizziness overwhelmed me, and that familiar feeling of euphoria blanketed my body. I reached for my water bottle, suddenly feeling hot and flustered. I took a sip, a deep breath, and tried to calm my nerves. Malachi intently watched me, and then the side door swung open.

"Good morning," Kade smiled as he entered the room. He had a sparkle in his eye and a bounce in his step. Seeing his face made every butterfly in my stomach dance with happiness.

Malachi glanced at him and then back to me with an inquisitive, yet unpleasant look in his eyes.

He must have sensed something was going on, since he was with us all day yesterday and saw how flustered I became whenever Kade was close.

I'd have to learn to hide my emotions a lot better because right now, I was wearing them all over my face. It was pretty embarrassing, especially with Malachi's watchful eye.

"What's up guys?" Kade exclaimed.

I felt Malachi's heavy gaze on me, and started to feel anxious. I took a fork-full of the much-too-sweet, chocolate chip pancake and shoved it in my mouth, keeping my eyes on my plate.

The others gave their salutations, while Kade grabbed a chair from the other end of the table, carried it down to our end, and set it down *right* next to me. I felt my face heat up as I glanced at him. That was something impossible to hide.

"Hey, Emma," he said in a soft, sweet tone. My heart skipped another beat until I looked into Malachi's glaring eye.

"Hey, *Kade*," I chimed, hoping it would have some kind of

effect on him. It wasn't fair - the magic he had on me.

He laughed out loud, and I could tell he was thrilled I'd said his name again. I giggled too, but Courtney and Malachi had confused looks on their faces.

"Inside joke," Kade explained.

"Oh. Well, Hi Kade," Courtney said teasingly. "I missed you."

"Why, hello Courtney. I've missed you too. So, what are you up to this morning?" He asked, grabbing a plate and scraping the rest of the pancakes and bacon onto it.

"Nothing much, but I'm glad I'm not the only girl around here anymore," she answered.

"Well, I'll be seeing you guys," Malachi murmured, as he left the table.

If I didn't experience his softer side, I would have been terrified. The others also started to clear the table, heading into the kitchen with their empty plates.

"So, Emma... I see you've grown a tail," Kade said raising his eyebrows, looking toward Courtney, who was busy pouring juice into her glass.

"Mmm-hmm," I hummed.

"What?" Courtney blurted, glancing down towards my backside.

"Courtney you're so dumb. He was talking about *you*," a voice scolded from the kitchen. A tall, lanky boy with golden hair and light blue eyes came around the corner carrying a plate of fruit and toast. He must be Caleb.

There were small similarities between him and Courtney; same shaped face and eyes, but he was just an average boy who'd probably get lost in the crowd at my old school.

"I don't have a tail," she scolded.

"Hello, you *are* the tail," he muttered.

"Shut up, Caleb...I knew that."

"Yeah, right. Why'd you look then?" he countered with a scoff.

"I wasn't. I was..."

"See, just admit it. You're dumb."

"Well, you're...you're ugly." she stuttered.

"Uh, you look like me, so there..." he teased, tossing a grape into his mouth.

"I look nothing like you."

"Whoa, you two. You're not leaving a good impression on Emma," Kade announced, holding a hand up and shaking his head in disapproval.

They both glanced at me.

I'd never had a sibling, but I did have Lia and Jeremy, who could talk some pretty good smack to each other. So, this wasn't something new to me. It was actually entertaining.

"Sorry, Emma," Courtney apologized.

Caleb remained silent, popping another grape into his mouth.

"Don't worry about it. I'm used to it. My best friends do the same thing all the time."

Courtney smiled, took my plate, and got up from the table.

"Let's go Emma," she said, heading toward the kitchen, shooting Caleb an evil eye.

"You guys are leaving me? I just got here, and now I'll be alone... with Caleb?" Kade teased. Caleb rolled his eyes.

"She's giving me the grand tour," I smiled, but my heart ached when he shot me a sad puppy-dog look. *Damn, that was heartbreaking...*

"Well, I guess Courtney beat me too it," he said with a wide grin, biting a piece of bacon. His eyes were greener today, mirroring his fitted green sweater, but there were veins of yellow and brown running through them. I became lost, swimming somewhere within the depths of his eyes when Courtney rudely interrupted.

"*E-mma.* You coming or what?" Her voice dragged, as she stood in the doorway with her arms crossed over her chest.

I smiled at Kade and reluctantly pushed my chair in.

"I better go. So, I'll see you around?"

"You can count on it," he said, holding out his hand. I wanted to touch him so badly, but I also knew that my body would react, and that would be embarrassing... especially with Caleb and Courtney intently watching at us. We needed to behave ourselves, so I offered him my cast instead. I knew his magic, or whatever it was, couldn't penetrate it.

He laughed and took a hold of it.

I turned to Courtney, whose narrowed eyes were fixated on Kade, studying his intentions.

He ignored her by pouring a glass of orange juice.

"Have fun," he chuckled.

"Yeah right. With Courtney?" Caleb taunted. "Emma, you should take a pillow."

"Whatever, loser," Courtney snapped.

I ambled towards Courtney, and looped my arm through hers. "Okay, I'm yours for the next few hours." She smiled and proceeded to drag me away.

EIGHT

"SO WHERE ARE WE GOING?" I asked, hoping to seem excited. She led me back in the front area, which looked more like a hotel lobby.

"Okay," she said, stopping in the center of the exquisite marble floor with the tiled art of the angel and sword. We were facing the staircase. "You already know that the top floor is where we are. We... meaning me, you and Caleb. We're on the left and Caleb's on the right. It has eight bedrooms, four on each side. The other five rooms on our floor are empty." She looked like an airline stewardess going through her motions.

Oh boy. I was getting the *deluxe* tour.

"So where do all the guys sleep?" I questioned, even though I already knew Kade slept in the guest house.

"They all sleep in the cottage out back, but two of them stay in the tower each night. They have shifts. They were all hired by Alaine to keep strangers out. I guess there have been some break-ins in the area, but I don't buy it. The nearest neighbor is like ten miles away. She also said she hired them to make sure we're kept safe from bears and other wildlife, but I haven't seen a bear yet. I've only seen some moose and squirrel, but that's *it*." Her hands were flying around her in frustration.

"Oh," I exhaled. I guess they didn't tell her about the terrifying dark creatures lurking out there, like the one who tried to kill me. And, I was also guessing, if she didn't know already, it wasn't my place to tell her.

She continued. "The second floor is for guests, and totally off limits to us. There are eight bedrooms on that floor too, each with their own bathrooms.

"This floor has the kitchen, dining, library, study and Alaine's master suite. That door on the right, leads into the library and our study where we do our homeschooling," she said with a scrunched up nose. "It's really not too bad. We can actually finish our work in a few hours and get the rest of the day to do whatever we want."

That sounded pretty cool. Better than sitting in classes all day, but I'd still miss being with my friends.

"Down this hall, to the left, is where Alaine's study and master bedroom are. It's huge, like double the size of our rooms, and her bathroom looks like a spa. It's crazy."

"If you walk all the way down the hall, there is the ballroom. That's where Alaine holds all her big, fancy parties. Come, I'll show you," she said, eagerly skipping down the long, fancy hallway.

"Does she have a lot of parties?" I questioned.

"No, not really. Maybe one or two a year," she stated. "But usually kids aren't allowed. The parties are mostly for adults only." Her mouth turned down as she continued down the hall.

I'd seen a few ballrooms in the Hollywood Hills which my mom and dad had listed. They were pretty spectacular, but from what I'd seen so far, this house surpassed the homes I'd ever stepped into. I hoped my aunt wasn't a rich snob. She seemed nice, but then again, I'd only talked with her for about five minutes.

"So what part of Alaska are we in?" I asked.

"We're somewhere near Delta Junction. If you go up from here, you'll see the North Pole. I've been there dozens of times. Mile marker 1422 is down a ways. It's supposedly special because it's the end of the Alaskan Highway. Tourists drive there to take pictures at some lame sign they posted. So, we're kind of in the middle of nowhere. The boonies. There's like miles of nothing but trees surrounding us. And like I said earlier, our nearest neighbor is about ten miles away," she exhaled, with widened eyes.

At least I had some sort of direction now. The area actually had a name I could look up on MapQuest. I knew Jeremy would want to know that. He'd probably try and look me up on Google Earth, but I doubted if he could see my new home out here in Boonieville.

"So how long have you known my aunt?"

"Ummm," she hesitated, stopping and turning toward me. "Practically all my life, I guess. She was my mom's best friend. My mom died of cancer about six years ago, and your aunt took us in," she explained. Her eyes began pooling with tears.

I felt for her, empathized with her. We both shared a similar path; orphaned and taken in by my "Saint" Aunt Alaine.

"I'm sorry," I said resting my hand on her shoulder.

"Thanks. And, I'm sorry about your parents, too. That was a pretty bad accident," she sniffed, wiping away a few stray tears.

"How'd you know...about the accident?"

"Alaine told us. Someone called her while we were eating dinner the other night. Apparently, it was about you and the accident. She was on the phone the rest of the night and early the next day, trying to get everything situated so you could come here."

I sighed and stood in silence for a few seconds, wondering who might have called her. Who knew she was related to my mom if I didn't even know?

"Come on." She grabbed my hand and dragged me back down the hallway.

We entered a large empty room with a ceiling over thirty-feet high. The walls were a rich golden color with elegant, curved sconces evenly placed between white marble pedestals. Each pedestal held a beautiful, life-like statue of an angel, each in a different pose. It was completely breathtaking.

The floor was a golden marble. At the center was a large white marble circle with a mosaic of a single red rose and angel's wings spread out along the sides. Within the mosaic were shimmering golden flakes speckled throughout. It was surrounded by golden tiles that were so shiny you could literally see yourself in them. Above the circle was another huge chandelier, which looked like it belonged in a palace. Thousands of glistening crystals were exquisitely suspended from graceful, golden curved arms. It was literally dazzling. I could only imagine what it looked like on.

"Wow," I exhaled, as Courtney whirled in the center of the floor.

"I know. This place is pretty awesome, huh?"

"I think awesome is an understatement. It's totally exquisite," I slowly walked past the pedestals, studying the intricate details of each angel. They were perfect and beautiful, all resembling gods, with large wings protruding from their backs.

As I came to the end, the last statue caught my attention. I studied the contours of the face, the nose, the defined muscles in the arms and chest, and the shape of the eyes. It was a remarkable resemblance of Kade. I was entranced, my gaze fixed upon this impeccable, oddly familiar statue.

"Boo," Courtney screamed, grabbing my shoulders and scaring the crap out of me.

I jumped, and automatically swung back, whacking her in the shoulder. It was a natural instinct. I couldn't help it.

"Ouch," she laughed, grabbing her arm.

"Sorry," I muttered. "Reflexes." She was lucky it wasn't my casted arm.

"It's alright. At least now I know...don't ever surprise Emma," she grinned, still rubbing her arm. Glancing up at the statue, she said, "You have a crush on him, don't you?"

I felt my face flush with heat, and then attempted to swallow the large lump in my throat before I could answer. "What are you talking about?"

"Kade. You like him. I can tell," she said, her eyes studying me. She'd totally caught me off-guard with the question.

"Why, is that really Kade?" I asked, pointing to the statue, averting her attention from my flustered face.

"Yeah. Your aunt flew someone in from another country...Italy, or some faraway place like that. He was some kind of master stone carver, and his specialty was angels. I guess you've already noticed that your aunt has a major obsession with them."

"Um, yeah. I can totally see that," I whispered, still gawking at the statue. "So, how does she know Kade?"

"Well, Kade and the others moved in right after Alaine's husband passed away. I guess they were hired as security guards or something. Her husband was really rich."

"But Kade actually left us about a year ago. He said he had to go away on some kind of work related deal. I'm glad he's back. He's the most fun."

I laughed, but was curious to what Kade had been doing for the past year. Was his job one that would take him away for long periods of time? Was he in the military?

"So anyway," Courtney interrupted my thoughts, "Alaine asked the carver if he would make one that resembled Kade, and so he did. He's pretty handsome, isn't he?" She turned to watch my reaction.

"Yes, he is very handsome. And *no*, I don't have a crush on him. I don't even know him. I just met him yesterday," I said in a calm and collected tone.

"Haven't you heard of love at first sight?" she giggled, looking back at me.

"Yeah, that's just a myth. It's really more like lust at first sight." I turned and noticed her face was all scrunched up, and then remembered she was only thirteen, homeschooled, and kept away from the general perverted public. "Well, I believe you can't really love someone without truly getting to know them first."

"Yeah, I guess you're right," she said with a sigh. "Well, promise me that I'll be the first to know when it happens."

I rolled my eyes. "Sure," I answered. She smiled and tugged at my arm again.

"I want to show you this amazing place outside next," she said dragging me back down the hallway. "Caleb and I have this super-secret area that no one else knows about. But you have to promise, promise, promise not to tell."

"Okay," I answered.

"Promise," she insisted, with her hands on her hips.

"Alright, I promise. But I'll need to put on something warmer or I'll freeze to death," I stated.

She gave me an exasperated look. "Fine."

"I also need to put a few things away, since we have a lot of time to kill."

We made our way back upstairs, and stopped in front of my room.

"I guess I should clean my room too, so just knock on my door when you're ready," she said before prancing down the hall to her room.

I agreed and began to unpack my suitcase very, very slowly. Everything that could be folded, fit into a single drawer. Two hoodies, two sweaters, and a rain coat hung lonely in one tiny area of the huge walk-in closet. I'd have to get more clothes because that was pretty pathetic.

I made my bed and then emptied my carry-on, shoving the rest of the snacks, my new camera, and my reader in the nightstand drawer. I placed the photograph of my parents on the nightstand next to my bed.

I had to tear my eyes away from their faces. I missed them so much my body began to ache, and my eyes filled and spilled over with tears, all over again. I curled up into a ball on the floor and cried. I knew my parents would have wanted me to be strong. I was trying to be, but it was so hard.

An hour later, I knocked on Courtney's door. When she opened it, I noticed her room was very girly; hot pink and black, but I didn't get to see it all. She grabbed me by the arm and dragged me down the stairs and out the front door. As soon as we stepped outside, the frigid cold air seeped right through my clothes, like I was butt naked.

"Holy heck, it's freezing out here." I shivered, pulling my sweater tightly around me. I quickly tucked my hands into the pockets, which didn't offer any warmth at all. Courtney didn't seem fazed by the cold one bit.

"You have to keep moving. The more you move, the warmer you'll get," she said running along the front of the house. When she reached the end, she disappeared around the side. "Hurry up!"

I picked up my pace and rounded the corner to find her standing, hands on hips, at the entrance of the hedged labyrinth.

From the third floor, the maze didn't look as big, but as I made my way towards it, it was well over ten feet tall.

"Wow, you could really get lost in this thing, huh?" I said, worried.

"Yep," she confirmed. "I actually did get lost the first time I went in. Thank goodness Thomas heard me screaming and found me. Now, I only go in with Caleb. He knows this place by heart. He used to sit in his bedroom and study it, even made drawings so we wouldn't get lost. But I still don't like to come in here alone. It's kind of creepy."

"Well, I'd get pretty creeped out if I went in alone too," I admitted.

"Well, you're with me right now, so let's go." She smiled taking hold of my hand, pulling me into the maze.

"Wait. Do you know where you're going, and how to get out?"

"Of course I do. We come in here almost every day. Well, we used to during the summer. I know the way to, and from, our secret area, by heart."

She guided me left, then left again, then right and left. Before long, I was all turned around. It felt like we were walking in circles, but Courtney kept on like she had a purpose. She finally halted at a corner, pulled apart some of the hedges and stepped inside, completely disappearing into the leaves.

I stood, uncertain, until Courtney's head popped out between the brush.

"Come on, Emma," she urged, and then disappeared again.

I walked closer, pulled the branches apart, and stepped through into a small, hollowed out area. It was pretty cool, a small space about six feet by six feet. A perfect secret place to hideaway from the world.

It reminded me of the *Secret Garden*, and the hidden entrance to a wondrous place. Only this place wasn't too wondrous. It was dirt surrounded with the hedge. I wondered if there were other spots like this within the labyrinth.

"Ready?" she asked.

"Ready for what? Isn't this it?" I asked.

"No, silly." She bent down, moved some dirt away from the ground, revealing a latch, and yanked open a small, wooden door.

"Where does that go?"

"It's a tunnel – a *secret* tunnel – that leads under the fence to the other side. It was already here when we moved in. Caleb found it while we were exploring one day. We're the only two who know about it...and now you, of course. So, you have to promise not to tell anyone."

"I thought you weren't supposed to leave the grounds."

"Well... we've never been in any danger. Ever. There's nothing around here except trees and squirrels. We haven't even encountered a moose yet. Caleb and I do this all the time. We even have a box hidden away on the other side, with some snacks and things inside."

"Really? Well I guess it won't hurt to check it out," I said. "And, I already promised you I wouldn't tell."

"So, you wanna go?" she asked. "We won't stay long. I just want to show you, and then we can come right back. I promise. Please?" she begged, pressing her palms together.

I stared into the dark abyss. I was terrified of the dark, especially after the whole bathroom incident, and also knowing Kade and the others had no clue where we were. But I didn't want Courtney to think I was a scaredy-cat. Plus, I was curious. So, I decided to go, against my better judgment.

"How will we be able to see? It's pitch black down there."

Courtney smiled and reached into some nearby shrubbery, pulling out a large flashlight. She then reached back in and pulled out one more, and waved them both in front of me.

"Don't worry. I've got it covered."

"Are you sure it's safe?" I asked. My stomach started to feel queasy.

"Of course it's safe. Caleb and I go all the time. We'll be quick."

"Alright," I said, giving in. "You go first and I'll follow."

"No problem," she said enthusiastically, practically diving feet first into the dark hole.

I climbed down, slow and steady, having a hard enough time trying to grip with my casted hand. I couldn't afford to fall and end up in a body cast.

I heard a loud thump as Courtney jumped to the ground.

"You're almost down. About ten more steps," she shouted.

"Okay, thanks." My feet finally hit the ground and I turned, her flashlight shining directly in my eyes.

"You're blinding me," I giggled, trying to block the light with my hand.

"Oops, sorry." She directed the beam to the floor and handed me the other one. "Follow me."

She turned and faced her flashlight down a dirt tunnel. It was narrow, dark, and confined; the perfect recipe for claustrophobia. The air was thick and stale from the lack of air flow, and smelled like moldy dirt.

"How far is it to the other side?"

"Not far. Maybe a couple of minutes," she said.

I took in a deep breath. "Alright, let's get going." I knew if we waited any longer, I'd change my mind.

We had to bend forward to fit through the tunnel and it was tight. Both of my arms rubbed against the sides of the walls. Just a few seconds in and I caught myself breathing heavy, and could hear my heart beating loudly. It felt like the whole cave was going to topple in on top of us.

"This tunnel doesn't get any smaller than this, does it?" I was on the verge of hyperventilating.

"Nope. We're almost there."

"Good," I sputtered. "Just hurry and get me out of here."

Courtney giggled, but I seriously couldn't take much more. I didn't do well in tight enclosed spaces.

We pushed forward through the tunnel for around a minute more and came to another little opening like the one that we'd started in. Courtney flashed her light at another ladder which led upward.

"There's a door at the top with a latch that you have to push open. It's not that heavy. Do you want to go first, or do you want me to go?" she asked.

"You go first." I knew with the casted arm, there was no way I could hold on and push a door open.

She started up the ladder and I climbed after her. Her flashlight was tethered to her wrist, dangling, swinging light back and forth through the darkness. It made weird shapes and shadows on the walls. I hated I couldn't see anything behind me, and had an eerie feeling like something was going to grab my leg and yank me down. A wave of chills shot down my spine, so I stayed right on her heels.

She finally stopped and I heard her grunt as she pushed open the small wooden door.

Sunlight and fresh air rushed in. *Thank God!*

Courtney crawled out and offered me her hand. The small exit was carefully hidden between several trees, and camouflaged with leaves and twigs so no one would ever know it was there.

I crawled out and stood in the middle of a spruce forest, just beyond the perimeter fence. I could see the top of the tower, looming in the distance above the tree line. The trees around us were dense; except for the small area we were standing in. It was about ten feet wide all around.

Courtney pulled a medium-sized box out from behind a few other trees, opened it up and took out a blanket which she laid out. Then, she pulled out some water bottles and candy bars and handed me one of each. The water was ice cold and the candy bar was rock hard. I tried to bite into it, but all it did was leave teeth impressions. If I bit down any harder, I'd probably break a tooth, so I decided to push it back into the wrapper and tuck it into my pocket to warm it up a bit.

"So, what do you guys do out here?" I asked. It was a bit unnerving being in a small area, surrounded by trees.

"We usually just hang out. Caleb likes to read. Sometimes I make him play hide-n-seek. I know it's a baby game, but it's super fun out here because we can never find each other," she said with a gleam in her eye. "Do you want to play? Pretty please? Just one quick game?"

"Sure." We still had a few hours to kill anyway. A few games of hide-n-seek would probably help pass the time.

"Okay, I'll count and you hide," she said not so excitedly.

"No. I'll count and you hide," I countered.

"Are you sure?"

"I'm sure."

She smiled widely. "Okay, count to fifty... and no peeking," she exclaimed, running back and forth through the trees.

I pressed my forehead against a tree and started to count, slowly and loudly. "One, two, three, four..." I heard the pattering of footsteps all around me. She was trying to throw me off, but I was pretty good at this. I listened carefully and heard braches snapping to my left. When I finally reached fifty, there was complete silence. "Ready or not... here I come!" I shouted into the trees.

I decided to go with my instincts and go left. I hoped she didn't go too far because I would definitely get lost, and this place was a little too creepy to be alone and lost. My plan was to go in a straight line and peek behind trees, that way I could just turn around and walk straight back.

A dark shadow darted behind one of the trees.

A devilish smile formed on my lips. I was going to be super sneaky, and scare the crap out of her. She kind of deserved it for bringing me out here in this creepy place and begging me play hide-n-seek.

I quietly snuck up to the tree. My plan: jump, scream, and scare.

"Gotcha!" I screamed at the top of my lungs, jumping around to catch her off guard.

I gasped, stumbling backwards. My body began to tremble and my legs suddenly became weak.

It wasn't Courtney.

Two arms wrapped around me, and a large hand clamped over my mouth.

I kicked and punched, but the grip was too tight. It was a man. A very strong man. He wrapped his arm around my throat, but not tight enough to cut off my breathing.

"Please don't scream, Emma," he whispered in my ear. "I'm not going to hurt you. Do you understand?"

It took me a moment to settle down and figure out what he was saying. *Did he just say my name?*

"I won't hurt you. I promise." He assured, relaxing his grip. "I'm going to let you go now, but you need to be quiet. I just want to talk. Understand?"

I nodded, so he released his grip and slowly turned me to face him.

He didn't look anything like that creature in the bathroom. In fact, he wasn't ugly at all. His features were sharp, but mostly hidden under an unkempt beard. His face was a bit thin, like he hadn't eaten in a while, and he stared at me through big, brown, friendly eyes. Scraggly brownish hair fell just below his shoulders. His long chestnut trench coat made him look a bit like a vagrant, but he didn't smell like one. He smelled sweet, like expensive cologne. But what was he doing here? And how did he know my name? I didn't know this man, and never saw his face before.

My pulse started to race again, and panic struck me. Was he evil? I sucked in air to scream, but just as I did, he placed one finger over my mouth.

"Shhh…" he whispered, and my scream fell silent. There was nothing. No sound escaped my lips, no matter how hard I yelled. He seemed to have put some kind of a magic spell on me.

"Emma, I promise I won't hurt you," he whispered. "Just promise me that you won't scream and I'll release your voice," he said in a tired, wary voice.

He hadn't tried to hurt me so far, so I nodded.

He slowly swiped his hand over my mouth, and I gasped, hearing the wind enter my lungs.

"Who are you?" I asked.

"A friend," he whispered, taking hold of my hand. "You've grown into such a beautiful young lady," he said with a glimmer in his eyes.

"Emma? Emma? Where are you?" Courtney shouted from a distance. I looked around, but there were too many trees obstructing her from my sight.

The man grabbed hold of my shoulders. "Emma, you must return to the protection of the property. You shouldn't be out here alone. It's not safe. It's very dangerous, especially for you."

"Why? Why am I in danger?" I questioned. Maybe he could give me some answers.

"*Emma!*" Courtney screamed. She was standing about ten feet away from us, her mouth gaping wide, with a look horror on her face.

"Go, Emma. Get back to safety," the man urged before disappearing into the thick of the trees.

Courtney ran to me and wrapped her arms tightly around my waist.

"Who—who was that?" she sputtered.

"I don't know," I said, trembling. "But he seemed to know *me*."

"Are you okay? Did he hurt you?" she asked, studying my face.

"No. He didn't hurt me. I'm fine, but let's get out of here." If this guy could find me here, how much easier would it be for a Darkling? They were hunters, and this time my protector wasn't here, and had no idea where I was. I shivered, feeling completely vulnerable.

"Yeah, let's get outta here," Courtney urged.

We ran out of the woods and headed back into the tunnel.

NINE

S SOON AS WE CLIMBED up the rickety ladder and exited the dark tunnel back in the confines of the labyrinth, Caleb was standing above us with his arms crossed over his chest. His baby blue eyes were cold and glaring at Courtney.

"What were you thinking?" he barked in a whispered voice.

"What the heck are you talking about?" she returned sassily.

"Emma's not allowed to leave the grounds. It's not safe beyond the gates," he scolded. His eyes shifted to me and then back at Courtney.

Caleb must have known something.

"I - I didn't know. Nobody ever tells me anything," she huffed, with her hands folded across her chest. She glanced at me with a sorrowful look, but didn't mention anything to Caleb about the encounter I'd had on the other side.

I was still trembling inside, squeezing my shaking hands into tight fists. Who was that man, and how did he know my name? How did he find me? Maybe he *was* one of those Watchers? He seemed to be protective and concerned, but why? Why was everyone so concerned for my safety?

I had enough of all these unanswered questions.

I glanced at Caleb, who must have noticed my internal agony, and his eyes suddenly softened.

"Hey, are you alright?" he questioned.

"She's fine. You're fine, aren't you Emma?" Courtney questioned, shooting me a look of *please don't tell*.

"Yeah. I'm fine," I answered, swallowing hard. I knew I'd have to tell somebody about the incident in the forest. This wasn't the sort of thing that was supposed to be kept secret. I wasn't going to be the victim who kept vital information to themselves, and ended up getting into deeper trouble because no one had a clue. I decided I would tell my aunt as soon as I got the chance.

"I'm sorry, Emma. Courtney shouldn't have brought you out here, or taken you to the other side. Alaine arrived home early and she's been looking everywhere for you. Actually, everyone has. When they couldn't find you, I figured Courtney had taken you through the secret tunnel. But, don't worry. I haven't told anyone. I just wanted to make sure you were safe."

"Thanks," I said, gratefully.

His bright, blue eyes returned a wistful, longing gaze. A look Kade warned me about; a look I'd recognized all-too-well in hormonal, teenage males. I was probably the first girl, near his age, he'd encountered in a while. That's what happens when you're starved from others, and homeschooled.

Courtney cleared her throat and glared at Caleb.

"Let's get outta here before they find us. If they find out about the tunnel, our freedom will be history," Caleb said, quickly slipping back out through the branches.

He quickly led us back through the labyrinth. Courtney stayed right at my side, and had a terrified look on her face, but it wasn't her fault. She didn't know there were evil things out there that were trying to kill me. She was just as clueless as I was.

"I'm sorry about your parents," Caleb said softly, glancing over his shoulder.

"Thanks," I replied. "I'm sorry about your mom, too." There was an awkward silence, and I didn't know how else to respond.

"So how was life in the big city?" he asked.

I cleared my throat. "Busy and a lot louder than it is here."

"Our big city is Anchorage. We get to go there once in a while, but it's been a few months since our last visit."

"Wow. That's pretty long," I sighed. "So what do you guys for fun?" I questioned, trying to keep the uncomfortable silence filled.

"Mostly nothing. I usually hang in my room and read or play video games. Sometimes the guys will include us in their outdoor games, but they can get pretty rough. I broke my arm once, playing football with them. Since then, Alaine's forbid us to participate. We usually just sit and watch," he replied, shrugging his shoulders.

"Courtney and I try to get them to play hide-and-seek with us. They don't like it much because we always win. They can never find us when we go into the labyrinth," he said wiggling his eyebrows up and down.

"How did you find that secret area?" I asked.

"Well, we have a lot of extra time," he grumbled. "I just happened to pull some of the hedges apart, and noticed a few places that were hollowed out."

"There are more tunnels?"

"No. Just that one. We've hid snacks, water, and books into each of the others though to help kill the time while they're searching for us. They usually give up after a half-hour or so. Thomas is usually the first to give up."

"Courtney, what do you do for fun?" I asked, surprised she hadn't said a single word so far.

She shrugged, "Not much. Mostly read, or watch movies. Alaine takes us on outings as much as she can, but lately she's been really busy. Sometimes Miss Lilly lets me help make lunch or dinner. She's teaching me how to cook," she said with a half grin.

We finally reached the front of the house, and I was glad. My body was quickly becoming numb and frozen.

Caleb held the door open to let us in, and as soon as we entered the hall, loud voices echoed from the upper levels. I glanced up to see Kade and Thomas rounding the corner of the third floor. As soon as Kade spotted me, he exhaled a deep sigh of relief and smiled. I could hardly suppress the smile of thrill I had when I saw him.

Thomas donned a wide smirk across his face; his blue eyes piercing.

"They're fine. I found them in the labyrinth," Caleb announced proudly.

"I checked the labyrinth...three times," Thomas answered,

glaring at Caleb through narrowed eyes.

"Well, obviously, you didn't check well enough, did you?" Caleb returned smugly, shrugging his shoulders. Thomas mumbled a few unintelligible words through gritted teeth. Kade chuckled, holding a hand to Thomas' chest in a lame attempt to hold him back.

"Emma. Oh, thank God," Alaine called from down the hall. She quickly made her way to me and wrapped her arms around my neck. She did the same to Courtney. "You girls just about gave me a heart attack."

"Sorry," I said sheepishly. "Courtney was giving me the grand tour of the grounds, and took me through the labyrinth."

She quickly glanced at Courtney whose eyes fell to the floor, and a frown curved on her lips.

"Well, I'm just glad you're both safe," she said with her hand on her heart, offering a warm smile. "Come, Emma. I'd like to speak with you now."

I nodded. My insides were dancing, knowing I'd finally get some answers to the questions flooding my mind.

Courtney suddenly gasped and a terrified look shot across her face. She tugged on Caleb's arm and pulled him to the side, whispering something quietly into his ear.

"Is everything alright?" Alaine asked, turning her attention to them.

"Yes," Caleb muttered in a grumpy voice. "Courtney dropped her book somewhere in the labyrinth, and wants me to help her look for it."

"Well, don't be too long," she said with a soft smile, "and I'd like to speak to both of you about your studies after I'm finished with Emma."

"We won't be long. I'm pretty sure I know the area where it dropped," Courtney answered.

That was strange. I didn't remember seeing Courtney with a book. Actually, I was sure she didn't have one.

"Hurry up. Let's go," Caleb grumbled. He briskly walked towards the front door with Courtney in close tow.

"Oh, those two," my aunt sighed, but had a smile on her face.

She wrapped her arm around my shoulder and led me down the corridor to her study. When she swung the door open, I gasped. It was like nothing I'd ever expected. Rows of cherry wood shelves lined the walls, and they were filled with books - hundreds and hundreds of books – of every genre.

The back of the room was dimly lit with old statues and artifacts encased in glass. The room looked like a library or museum, not a study. There were paintings, statues, and photographs of all types of angels; old antique angels from the days of Michelangelo, along with cute, chubby cherubs, and even the modern, more masculine, defined angels with unearthly beauty and large perfect wings.

I slowly walked past all the shelves, examining the books, art, and what looked like ancient relics. It was definitely something only the rich could afford. Some of these things looked like they were dated way back.

After giving me some time to admire her things, she cleared her throat and pulled me from my state of awe.

"Have a seat, Emma," she said pointing to a large, comfortable chair set in front of a desk. She took her seat on the opposite side. "I know you must have a lot of questions."

"Yes," I exhaled loudly.

"Well, let me begin," she said softly. "You are here because we share the same blood. I am one who would never turn my back on family, even if they've never been there for me." Her eyes became saddened and distant.

"I'm sorry," I said sympathetically, not really understanding what she was trying to say.

"No. No," she responded. "You have nothing to be sorry about. Emma, I know I could never replace your mother. She was an extraordinary person, but I want you to know that I will always be here for you," she said with a warm smile. "So, what questions do you have for me? I know you probably have a million."

She was right. There were so many questions turning in my mind...too many, in fact, that I couldn't decide which one to start with. So, I figured the best place to start, was the beginning.

"How did you know about the accident?" I asked, my voice shaking. This was the first thing I wanted to know. Within a day, she'd already called and pulled whatever strings she needed with the State to release me into her custody.

"Well, I make it a point to know what is happening with my family. When both my adoptive parents passed, I was alone. I had no one, and was determined to locate my blood family. I vowed to stay close ever since."

"You were close with my mother?" I questioned.

"Yes. Your mother and I have been in contact ever since you

were born," she admitted.

"But why didn't she ever tell me about you?"

She took in a deep breath. "We all agreed it would be best if I stayed at a distance, only because it would have complicated things. I know everything is very confusing to you right now, but it was the best decision for you at the time. You just have to believe me."

"But why would you being a part of our lives complicate things?" I questioned.

"Let me start from the beginning," she exhaled with a smile.

A sudden bang on the door interrupted us. Both of us turned as the door flew open, and Courtney stood sobbing and hyperventilating, with wide, horror stricken eyes. She was covered in dirt, and had scratches on her face. Her shirt was torn and stretched, and she had twigs and dirt matted in her hair.

"Caleb!" she bellowed. "Caleb was kidnapped! He's going to die... The monster said he'll kill him if you don't give them Emma."

My breath seized, and everything around me began to spin as I processed her words. I turned to Alaine.

"What?" Alaine gasped. "Tell me exactly what happened." She bolted out of her chair and rushed to Courtney's side.

"I—I don't know," she cried. "It was some kind of monster...like a vampire!"

Oh God. They found me! My entire body began to tremble in fear.

"Where?" Alaine pressed, shaking her. "Courtney, where are they?"

Courtney paused, but only for a second.

"We were in the tunnel... in the labyrinth. I forgot to lock the door on the other side when Emma and I came back through, so

Caleb went back with me to do it. When I was climbing down the ladder, something grabbed my leg and yanked me down. It grabbed me by the neck and started choking me, but Caleb jumped down and knocked it away. He told me to run. It's my fault. It's all my fault. I didn't know what to do," Courtney began crying uncontrollably.

"What secret tunnel?" Alaine raised her voice.

"It's in the labyrinth. Caleb found a tunnel in one of the hedges that leads underground, to the other side of the fence," she sobbed.

"Is Caleb still down there?"

"No. The monster took him. He said they'll kill him if you don't give them Emma. He said they will have him at a place called Weeping Rock. If they don't get Emma tonight, Caleb will die!"

"Courtney, I want you to go to your room. I don't want you to leave this house, do you understand?" she said firmly. Courtney nodded.

"Why do they want Emma?"

I froze, and my aunt froze too. She turned to glance at me, taking in a deep breath, and then turned back to Courtney, just as Kade and Thomas rounded the corner.

"What's going on princess?" Thomas asked with a furrowed brow, glancing at Courtney.

"Gather everyone. Quickly. I want you all back here in two minutes," Alaine urged. Kade glanced at me, but all I could do was shake my head.

Kade and Thomas quickly disappeared from the doorway.

"You can go now, Courtney," Alaine said calmly, hugging her and kissing the top of her head. "Caleb will be fine."

Courtney nodded and wiped the tears from her dirty face. She looked at me with a deep sadness in her eyes, and then headed out the door.

I felt horrible for her. I knew she'd trade me for her brother, in an instant, and I didn't blame her. She barely knew me and none of this would've happened if I hadn't come. It just seemed like I was a magnet for terror.

"Emma, I want you to stay here with Courtney. Thomas will stay back and look after you. I will take the others and go get Caleb. We'll bring him back."

"But she just said that if I don't show up, Caleb will die," I protested. I wasn't about to let someone die because of me. That was something I'd never be able to live with.

"Emma," she shook her head, walking up to me.

"It was a Darkling, wasn't it?" I said staring at her with tear filled eyes.

"Yes," she admitted. "And, whoever has sent it, wants you. We don't know how many there are, or what kind of situation we'll be walking into. It's not safe, especially for you."

My breath seized as I remembered my encounter with the stranger on the other side of the fence. "There was a strange man I spoke to on the other side of the gate, who told me the same thing. He warned me that I wasn't safe, and urged me to get back into the perimeter."

"What man?"

"I don't know. He said he was a friend."

She shook her head. "I'm glad it was him and not a Darkling you ran into. And that's why I want you to stay. There are things you aren't aware of. Reasons why those things want to kill you."

"Well, if it's my fate to die... then I'll die, but there's always the chance I won't. I'm not about to sit at home, locked in a room, while you guys are out there risking your lives because of me. I'm going with you, even if I have to run after you," I said stubbornly. The words coming out of my mouth surprised me, just as much as it did her. Her lips turned up into a smile.

"You're so much like your mother," she said taking my face in her hands.

What she was talking about? My mother's personality was completely opposite of mine.

The room suddenly filled. Kade, Thomas, Malachi, Dominic, Alexander, and a slightly older guy, who had to be James, formed a half circle around me and Alaine. Henry stood quietly inside the doorway.

"What's wrong?" Kade asked, his anxious eyes darting between us.

"Caleb's been kidnapped by a Darkling. It attacked him and Courtney in a secret tunnel within the labyrinth. Do any of you know about this tunnel?" she questioned, looking at each one of them.

"No," they said in unison, shaking their heads. I knew they were telling the truth.

"Where is he?" Alexander asked.

"They've taken him to Weeping Rock, and they want Emma in exchange. They've also made a threat to kill Caleb if we don't comply. Get your gear and assemble in the foyer in fifteen minutes. Malachi.

Dominic. Bring the vehicles around front."

"You're not letting her leave, are you?" Kade blurted, stepping forward, pointing at me.

"She's made her choice," Alaine answered. "She will be coming with us. We can discuss this later, Kade. Right now we have to move."

Kade didn't look happy. He shook his head in disappointment and headed out the door with the others.

"Emma, if you're coming with us, I suggest you dress warmly," Alaine suggested with a worried look on her face.

I nodded and quickly left the room, not wanting to stay and debate, in case she changed her mind. I ran most of the way down the hall, and back up the stairs, taking them two at a time. As soon as I hit the third floor and made the turn, Courtney was standing in front of her doorway.

"I'm sorry, Emma," she sobbed, running toward me and hugging me tightly.

"Hey, hey. It's alright. Don't worry about it," I said, patting her back.

"I don't want you to die, Emma. I really don't. I just want my brother back. He's all I have left."

"I'm not gonna to die, and we *will* get your brother back," I said, unsure of my words. "I've seen Kade fight one of those things, and let me tell you... he can kick some major ass. And, I'm sure the others can too."

Her mouth opened as wide as her eyes. "You saw one of those things before? When?" Her words, along with the rest of her, trembled.

She was clearly traumatized by the creature in the tunnel. I didn't blame her, because I was still haunted by my own encounter. Flashes of its pale face, long stringy, raven-black hair, sharp teeth, black sunken eyes, and the stench of its rotted breath horrified me. I could still hear its haunting whisper, calling my name.

"A creature like the one you saw attacked me in the bathroom at the airport. But Kade and Malachi were there to save me."

"Why do they want you?" she asked.

"I don't know. I really don't know," I said, as tears pooled in my eyes.

"Uh-hum," someone interrupted. I turned back and Thomas was standing a few feet behind me. His cologne was overpowering, smelling sweet and crisp. He was handsome, in a California surfer-dude kind of way. His bleach blonde hair was disheveled, covering his ears, and his bright, baby blue eyes held a certain look...the look of a prankster. "I suggest you hurry it up, because they're getting ready to leave. They'll leave you in a second, and won't be sorry they did," he said with a chuckle, thumbing downstairs. He then pivoted and pounced down the stairs.

"Oh crap," I said, wiping my tears. I dashed into my room, but then quickly spun, and headed back to the door. "Courtney, don't worry... they *will* bring Caleb back," I promised. She nodded, and then disappeared into her room, shutting the door behind her. I specifically said *they*, because I wasn't sure if I would be coming back. I wasn't sure of anything anymore.

I made a beeline for my closet and searched for my warmest jacket, but I didn't have one. All I had was a cotton hoodie, and a couple of thin sweaters.

Whatever! They'd have to suffice, and I'd have to layer for warmth. I plucked the last hoodie and a sweater off the hangers, and flung them over my shoulder while I headed for the door. Jeans and converse shoes covered my lower extremities.

I ran down the stairs and as I reached the bottom, Kade suddenly appeared in front of me, catching me off guard. He grabbed my cast and quickly led me to the side.

"What are you doing?" he said in an unhappy tone, staring at me through narrowed eyes.

"What are you talking about?" I returned, giving him an eye.

"You're not coming with us, Emma. It's too dangerous for you out there," he said in a loud whisper. His hazel eyes were piercing, boring an invisible hole through my head and my heart.

I steadied myself. "Oh, yes I am. I have a better chance of surviving with you and the others around me, than I do staying here with Thomas. Those Darkling probably know my aunt would never allow me to go… So what if it's a trap? What if they just happen to show up with reinforcements while you're all gone? I'm as good as *dead*," I said a little louder, with confidence, surprising even myself.

"I don't think they're smart enough," he said.

"Well, it's obvious that someone else is planning for them. How did they know I was in the bathroom at the airport, or in the tunnel in the labyrinth? And, how is Thomas supposed to be able to fight off more than one of those Darkling? Courtney and I are worthless, and so is the rest of the hired help. You'll come back to find a massacre. It seems like they're only after me. If they know I'm not here, then the rest of them might stand a chance of being safe."

I really hadn't given much thought to the whole situation, but the words coming out of my mouth actually made sense. Someone was keeping a close eye on me, and that thought really freaked me out.

Kade's face softened a bit. I was right, and he knew it. He took in a deep breath, exhaled loudly, and shook his head. He still looked a little upset, but I noticed something else, he was concerned... genuinely concerned. And as I did a quick check, the feeling was mutual.

I could tell he wanted to add to the conversation, but everyone had gathered in the middle of the room, each carrying a black duffle bag filled with who-knows-what. Guns, knives, swords? One could only guess what kinds of things were in them. Kade walked over to the others, picked up his own duffle, and swung it over his shoulder.

They were all in uniform: black beanies, black jeans and fitted black t-shirts, worn under black leather coats. They looked like assassins. Beautiful assassins, if there was such a thing. I wondered if that's what they really were. Assassins. It wouldn't surprise me. From what little I saw the night of the bathroom incident, Kade was super-strong and super-fast; unlike anyone I'd ever seen before. But then again, I'd never seen a Darkling either.

The mood instantly changed as Alaine entered the room. She was also dressed in black, but in a very feminine way. Her hair was tied back into a long ponytail, and even though she didn't have any make-up on, her face was luminous. She shot me the same look my mother would give me when she wasn't happy with my decisions, and it made my heart ache, but only for a split second.

"Let's roll," she exclaimed, heading towards the door.

In an instant, we were all on the move.

As soon as we stepped outside, the cold air slammed my face. White haze swirled from my mouth as I exhaled. I quickly attempted to slide my hoodie on, but the skinny sleeve wouldn't fit over my stupid, bulky cast. *Ugh.* It was so frustrating.

Then, warmth suddenly covered me. I turned back as Kade draped his coat over my shoulders. The lingering warmth of his body heat emanated like a heating pad.

"Thanks," I smiled, hugging it around me, breathing in his sweet scent.

"Kade," my Aunt interrupted. Her voice was firm, and for a second I thought she was upset.

"Yes," he answered, taking a step forward.

"I want you to watch over Emma tonight. Guard her with your life. Her safety is your main priority and responsibility this trip, and you *know* how important that is to me," she said glaring at him.

"Yes, ma'am," he said with enthusiasm. I saw a slight grin form on his face and a gleam in his eye.

Inside, my heart fluttered at the thought of him being my bodyguard for the night.

I relaxed a bit, knowing I'd be close to him for the entire trip. I was *his* responsibility, and that made me happy. I had Kade and a small army of bodyguards surrounding me. Maybe, just maybe, I'd have a chance of surviving this night.

Two black Hummers roared up the roundabout. Alaine walked to the first vehicle, opened the front passenger door and slid in. Kade ran over, opened the back door, and motioned for me. All the others piled into the second car, slamming their doors shut. I jumped in and Kade slid in right next to me.

Malachi was our driver. He turned and rolled his eyes when he saw me. He was probably upset I was coming.

"Which way?" Malachi asked.

"Head south. I'll update you as we go," Alaine answered. I sensed her stress rising. Her demeanor and voice were tensed.

"So what's the plan?" Kade asked her.

"The plan is to go in, get Caleb, and get out of there quickly, with everyone alive," she said so matter-of-factly, keeping her head down, rummaging through her bag. Kade sat still with a look of confusion on his face.

That plan of hers wasn't a real plan...it was more of wishful thinking. I could have come up with a plan like that myself.

It looked as if she finally found what she was searching for, and discretely tucked it into her pocket, then craned her neck back to face me.

"Emma, it is imperative you stay put in this car tonight. This vehicle is nearly impenetrable, and the safest place to be where we're going. And, you have to promise me one thing... Never, and I mean NEVER, open the door for anyone, under any circumstance. The Darkling are crafty, and some have been known to shift into other forms. Each of us has our own key. We can get ourselves in if we need to. Do you understand?"

"Am I gonna be alone?" I questioned in a high, fear-filled voice.

"Of course not," she assured, looking over to Kade. "Kade will be with you. And Kade…I'm putting my full faith in you."

"Yes, ma'am," he answered in a distinguished voice. He glanced over to me, and winked. My heart fluttered. I knew I'd be safe, but even if I wasn't, at least I'd be with him.

TEN

"TURN RIGHT, HERE," ALAINE SAID almost a little too late. Malachi made a sharp turn down a narrow, almost hidden, dirt road. The brakes and tires screeched, and everyone was caught off guard. With the sudden turn, Kade's body flew up against mine. I gasped as an immediate electrical surge bolted throughout my entire body, but he quickly pushed himself away.

"That's why they installed that second pedal down there, called a brake," Alaine scolded.

"I'm sorry, but you could have announced the turn a little sooner," Malachi rebutted.

Night had dropped on us like a jaguar upon its prey, and the world outside was now painted in dark black. Neon-green streaks of light danced across the sky. It was the first time I'd witnessed the wondrous aurora borealis. It was awesome, but eerie at the same time.

Jeremy had educated me about how the native Alaskans believed the lights were supposed to be torches from spirits who'd passed on, guiding the feet of newly deceased. Would that be me? Would any of us be one of those whom the lights beckoned?

Dark silhouettes of trees pressed on either side of us, making it impossible to turn the car around. This was definitely a one car road.

My gut was telling me we were getting close. I didn't know how, I just had a feeling. My insides twisted and my heart pounded furiously against my chest, much like a war drum, but far from rhythmic. This beat was frantic and fearful. The rush of fear and adrenaline had me on the edge of my seat, gripping the door handle much too tightly.

Kade must have noticed, and carefully placed his hand upon my cast. I glanced at him, and became lost, swimming in the comfort of his hazel eyes. At that moment, I had a feeling he would do *anything* to protect me.

"There's a fork in the road ahead. Take a left. It's not much further," Alaine announced.

Kade immediately let go of my arm and reached down into the darkness. He brought up his duffle and set it between us, quickly unzipping and searching its contents. I strained to catch a glimpse of what was inside, but everything he extracted was as black as night. Then, I saw a glimmer.

A refraction of light, from the headlights behind us, sparkled on a shimmering piece of metal. It was a blade, a sword, but not too long. It looked dangerously sharp.

He leaned forward, fastening something around his waist, and then sheathed the blade into it. My pulse raced faster than ever.

In the front seat, Alaine was going through her own bag, and attempted to strap something over Malachi's shoulder.

"Ouch," Malachi snapped.

"Oh, come on you big baby," she retorted, flinging one end over his head and fastening it to his side. The belt was filled with large ammo and what looked like... grenades? *Oh my God.* What would they be using *grenades* for? Were they even legal?

I was starting to feel unsure of my decision to come along. This place was the perfect setting for a horror flick, with its dark ominous woods, the blackest of nights, horrifying creatures of death, and terror lurking somewhere in the shadows.

"Why do they want to kill me?" I asked, shocked my thoughts left my lips. I guess it was because it was one huge question that had been wreaking havoc on my mind ever since I had the encounter with the Darkling. It was a lingering, unanswered question pressing on every cell in my being. What had I done to deserve this death sentence?

There was silence for a few moments.

"Malachi, please stop here for a moment," Alaine whispered, resting a hand on his shoulder. Malachi nodded and stopped the Hummer in the middle of the nowhere, and turned off the headlights. He clicked on a dim light so I could see Alaine's face.

The Hummer behind also stopped and turned off their lights, awaiting the next step. Malachi's cell buzzed. It was probably the group behind wondering what was up. Malachi texted them back.

Alaine faced me.

"I know right now you don't feel like there's anything special about you, but you are *very* special, Emma. As you get closer to your eighteenth birthday, there are things that will start to happen to you that you won't understand. Actually, since you've turned seventeen, you're already showing signs of transformation, like how you heal so quickly, which is odd." Her eyes were in deep thought.

"What are you talking about?" Her words completely baffled me. They were like a riddle I couldn't solve. "What's wrong with me?"

She laughed. "There's nothing wrong with you, sweetheart. You are one of a kind."

"In layman's terms, please." I just wanted the straightforward truth, something I could understand.

"Alright Emma. You..." she paused, and I could tell she was weighing her next words. "You are not entirely human. Actually, humanity is the least of your genetic makeup."

I sat there, gaping at her. All I could do was shake my head. I couldn't speak, and had difficulty breathing.

"Your mother is a nephilim, Emma, and your father...well, he was an angel. A Fallen angel."

Every single part of me became numb. I couldn't believe what she was telling me. Fallen angel? Nephilim? *Wait.* The Darkling in the bathroom called me nephilim.

"What is a nephilim?" I managed to push the words out. I needed one question answered at a time.

"A nephilim is a child born of a human and an angel. A half-breed," she answered.

"How is that even possible? I mean, how could I...?" I was speechless.

"It started from your grandmother. She was a mortal woman, and your grandfather was an angel," she explained.

"A Fallen angel?"

"No. Your grandfather was an angel of light. Your *father* was a Fallen angel," she clarified.

This was beyond confusing. "So my father was evil?"

She paused, a look of sadness swept over her face. "Your father was a Fallen angel, but had an... internal struggle. He wanted to be good."

I couldn't believe what she was saying. It felt like I was suddenly thrown into the middle of a twisted dream. My father... a Fallen angel? *Craziness!*

For one thing, my father didn't possess any special powers, supernatural strength, or anything else out of the ordinary. And, he just didn't seem to have that angelic persona about him. He was balding for heaven sakes. Did angels even bald? I'd never seen a single picture of a balding angel. They all had thick, long, beautiful, flowing hair. My dad was just a simple guy, no muscles, and even had a protruding beer belly.

And my mother was half angel? Well, she actually could have been. She was a wonderful, caring person, but still, they both didn't seem to fit the description. To me they seemed completely human. And I should know. I'd lived with them for the past seventeen years.

Next question..."What exactly are Darkling?" I questioned.

"The Darkling were once human. Thousands of years ago, one

man began worshiping the Fallen. He built a temple and a shrine, and offered sacrifices to them. The leaders of the Fallen were pleased with the man, and in turn, took care of him and his family. Word spread, and soon others traveled to the temple, offering their own sacrifices."

"But there were demons, evil spirits who also worshiped the Fallen, who became envious of the relationship between the Fallen and the mortals who worshiped them. In fact, they became so jealous, they invaded the minds of the humans, driving them mad, and sent them into eternal darkness and damnation. The demons also cursed their eyes, so they would never be able to look upon the light of day."

"The Fallen leaders discovered what happened, and gave the mortals a proposition. If they carried out their biddings on earth, in return, they were promised long life, and would be taken care of in the afterlife. The crazed mortals agreed, and became pawns. They hid away in dark places, and over hundreds of years, they mutated, becoming the Darkling. Forever bound to do the evil work of the Fallen under cover of darkness."

I sucked in a long breath. This was all so overwhelming. This wasn't something taught to us in history lessons or Sunday school.

Neither Malachi, nor Kade moved an inch. Their heads remained frozen, staring out of their windows; probably an attempt at giving us some type of privacy.

Alaine continued. "There is a rift in the ranks of the Fallen. Lucian, one of the leaders and second in command, has gone rogue. He and Lucifer had a falling away. Then, on a mission, Lucian's brother was murdered by a nephilim. Though he rightfully deserved death, Lucian swore revenge. He has labeled nephilim as abominations, and has marked every single one for death."

"Were the Fallen responsible for my parent's death?" I questioned.

She hesitated. "Yes. But it wasn't your parents they were after. They were after *you*. Your mother and father were innocent victims."

"Innocent victims? Weren't they targets too?"

"Emma, your parents *were* human."

Her eyes became saddened. There was something deeper to all of this. Ever since the accident, I'd been spiraling further and further down that black hole.

"I don't understand. You just said my mom was a Nephilim."

"Yes," she said softly. "I knew one day it would come to this, I just don't know where to begin."

I could feel my insides twist in tight knots. My eyes began stinging with hot tears. I wasn't sure if I was ready for her answer. I wasn't sure about anything anymore.

"Are you trying to tell me that my parents weren't my *real* parents?"

"They were your parents, Emma. They loved and raised you as their own. But they were not your birth parents. They were human decoys, caring for and hiding you until your eighteenth birthday."

"What?" I exclaimed. I suddenly felt sick to my stomach, and hot tears began streaming down my face. "So my whole life has been a lie?"

"Alaine, I hate to interrupt this moment, but *we're not alone*," Malachi alerted in an urgent tone. We all stared into the darkness, then Malachi clicked on the headlights. About a dozen horrifying creatures stood in the middle of the road ahead of us.

Darkling.

They were all horrifyingly similar...their pasty white skin, black sunken eyes, and dark stringy hair. They looked like a pack of rabid zombies, but these were fully alert and ready for battle.

As soon as the headlights hit their eyes, deafening screams of pain sliced through the air. The Darkling immediately took cover. Some dropped to the ground, scurrying out of the beams, while others dove off the road into the cover of the trees.

All, that is, except one.

The last Darkling standing was huge – more like gigantic. Muscles bulged from the horrific, freak of nature. He stood around ten-feet tall, and wasn't budging. The reason? He had the darkest black goggles hiding his eyes. I guess the big guy wasn't stupid after all.

"Holy shit," Malachi cursed. "Are you guys seeing this? That freaking thing is *crazy*. They must have shot it up with some major steroids. I've never seen anything like it. You, Kade?" Malachi was pumped, excitement gleamed from his face.

"Nope. Never seen anything like that before," Kade answered. His eyes steeled on the creature.

"Should I run it over?" Malachi shot a glance at Alaine, whose eyes were also glued on the Darkling.

"Malachi. Something's wrong," she said, pointing.

In a second, the giant Darkling pulled something from his back. It was large, black, and looked like some type of weapon; a weapon that looked awfully similar to a missile launcher. I'd watched a lot of war movies with my dad, and knew a weapon like that caused death and devastation.

From the moment he pulled the weapon, everything seemed to happen in slow motion. Malachi and Alaine kicked open their doors and dove out of the Hummer. Alaine screamed my name. Kade grabbed my arm and in an instant, I was flung outside, off the road, and rolled into the trees.

Kade jumped over me, grabbing hold of my arm, dragging me on my back away from the Hummer. Then, he threw his body on top of mine, covering my head with his arms.

Boom!

The explosion of the Hummer sent shockwaves through the trees; fiery shrapnel shot everywhere. Flames and smoke bellowed from the wreckage, which had flipped onto its side. I couldn't believe that just a few seconds ago, we were sitting inside, thinking we were safe.

What happened to almost impenetrable?

"Emma. Emma!" Kade yelled, shaking me. My ears were temporarily deafened by the sound of the blast. We were only a few yards from the road, but the trees shielded us from the shards of fiery metal raining down around us.

I looked into Kade's eyes, and noticed that his hazel eyes had gone completely black. It was a bit disturbing, but he looked like he had gone into combat mode.

"Emma, we have to get out of here," he urged. "Are you okay?" His face was close to mine, his warm breath brushed my face.

146

"I'm fine," I said, still taken by the change in his eyes.

Kade's head snapped up as we heard loud noises from the trees around us. He sniffed the air. His head steadied in the direction of the movement, his eyes glaring intently into the darkness.

"We've got to move. I have to get you to safety," he said in a quieted tone. In a split second he was standing, assisting me to my feet, and leading me quickly through the trees. We were hand in hand, running deeper into the darkness of the woods, when I tripped, and my grip released from him. I fell hard to the ground, and when I looked up, Kade was gone. My eyes strained to find him in the darkness, but the only thing I could see was the burning wreckage behind us. Noises echoed all around me.

"*Kade*," I screamed out loud, my pulse racing faster than ever.

I was suddenly scooped off the ground, and cradled in strong arms. I glanced up. I was in Kade's arms, tight and secure. The heat from his chest warmed me to the core. The beating of his heart and the steadiness of his breath relaxed me, as he ran effortlessly through the dark woods.

He finally stopped and carefully set me down behind a large fallen stump.

"Emma. Stay here and stay quiet," he whispered. He sniffed the air around us, his eyes intently gazing towards the glow of the fire. I could hear voices and screams carrying through the woods, but I couldn't pinpoint them. They sounded like they were everywhere.

The sounds of branches cracking alerted us that something was quickly heading in our direction. I knew the Darkling were fast, and they were out there, searching for me.

"Please don't leave me," I begged, grabbing hold of Kade's arm.

"Don't worry, Emma. I won't leave you." He faced me. "Ever."

"Promise?" I whispered.

"I promise," he answered. "It's not safe for you here, though. We need to find the others."

The cracking branches grew louder and louder. Kade pushed me behind him, drew his blade, and took a combative stance. A dark figure shot out of the darkness. Kade swung at it, but it dodged him, flipped over his head, and landed at his back.

"Kade!" Alexander yelled, grabbing hold of Kade's arm to keep him from swinging again.

"Alex. What the hell? Why do you have that stupid mask over your face? I couldn't tell it was you."

Alexander pulled a black ski-mask off his face, and tucked it into his pocket. He then released his grip from Kade.

"Sorry, man. It helps with that damn Darkling stink."

"Where are the others?" Kade asked.

"Kicking some Darkling ass," Alex replied.

"What about Alaine?"

"She's holding her own, as usual. Crap, did you see that monstrous one? That dude looks like he's on steroids. He's gonna be a tough one to take down."

"Yeah, we saw him. We need to get Emma out of these woods. She's easy prey out here."

"Well, the second vehicle is still intact. Dom backed it down the road, maybe a hundred yards. Right now, that's probably the safest place for her to be. At least we can see what's coming from the road."

"I guess. You ready, Emma?" Kade asked, glancing at me.

"As ready as I'll ever be," I replied. My body was trembling with so much fear, I wasn't sure if I wouldn't be able to run.

"Alex, cover her back. I'll take the front. We've got to move quickly."

"Why don't you just carry her? We'll get there faster," Alex questioned.

That was a good question.

"Because if anything comes at us, I'll need to be able to fight. Just watch her back."

It was safer, with two of them on full guard. I just had to pull myself together and do whatever it took to stay alive.

Kade grabbed my cast, and we took off running toward the road. The fire from the Hummer served as our only guide. I tried to keep up, and lifted my feet higher than usual, so I wouldn't trip.

From the corner of my eye I saw something blacker than the dark, shoot towards me.

Wham!

I was struck from the side and thrust through the darkness. I blacked out from the initial impact, but when I regained consciousness, I was tumbling across the cold, rough ground.

A sudden stop against a solid tree stump knocked the wind out of me, and sent excruciating pain through my already injured rib. I scrambled to get to my feet, desperate to get away from whatever it was that attacked me. Kade and Alexander were nowhere in sight.

I tried to run but the pain in my rib was keeping me from moving too fast.

"Kade! Alex!" I screamed, terrified. I knew yelling was a bad idea, because anything could hear me. And I knew it was a Darkling that attacked me. I just prayed that Kade or Alexander would find me first.

There was movement around me, but I couldn't see a thing. And then, I caught whiff of a horrid stench. Something moved again, taunting me from the shadows.

From the corner of my eye, I caught a glimpse of something. I froze trying to focus on the figure. I screamed and covered my face as it shot at me, knocking me to my back. Then there was a heavy pressure on my chest. I yelled in pain as it straddled my injured ribs.

A horrifying pale face, loomed inches from mine. Its eyes were dark as the night, its breath reeked of death, and its head swayed slowly back and forth as it sniffed me.

"Sweet nephilim," it hissed into my ear. I stared into his dark, evil eyes. Saliva dripped from his mouth onto my skin. I wanted to vomit.

A wicked smile grew over his sharp, rotted teeth.

Someone, help me.

I struggled as he wrapped his frigid fingers around my neck, but as soon as he squeezed, he released. His eyes became wide, as if he was shocked, but they never left mine. His back arched and then he let out a piercing screamed.

There was a loud *swoosh* in the air, and in a split second, the Darkling's head was severed from his body, and toppled onto the ground next to mine; its dark eyes, still glaring coldly at me. In a few seconds they turned completely white.

I screamed in horror, trying to get out from under its headless body.

"*Emma.*"

I looked up and saw the most beautiful face lightly illuminated in the darkness.

"Kade," I called to him. Tears streamed down my face.

He stepped closer to me, his blade dripping wet with Darkling blood. He took another step and kicked the body off of me, and then reached down to lift me up.

That was the second time he'd saved my life.

"Are you okay?" he asked, placing his warm hand on the side of my face. I couldn't answer. My heart was pounding so fast I felt like I was going to pass out.

"Hey man, I think she's going into shock." Alexander put his hand on my head like he was trying to feel my temperature.

Kade pulled a small blue vial out of his pouch and unscrewed the lid.

"Drink this Emma," he whispered into my ear. He held the vial up to my lips and I drank.

It was sweet with a bitter aftertaste, but within a few seconds my body stopped trembling, and I felt relaxed and a bit stronger.

"What is that?" I asked.

"A magic brew," he answered, with a sly grin. "I'm sorry that damn bastard got to you. It was my fault."

"It wasn't your fault. That thing came out of nowhere," I replied, but he shook his head.

"Alex, you need to get her back to the car. Emma, he's going to carry you, but I'll be close. I have to check on the others."

"Okay," I agreed.

Kade whisked me up and placed me into Alexander's arms. "Keep her safe, Alex. Guard her with your life," he demanded.

"Don't worry. I've got her."

ELEVEN

I N A FLASH I WAS being carried through the woods, the cold wind whipping across my face. The funny thing, it didn't feel or sound like Alex's feet were hitting the ground. It felt more like we were flying. Everything was a blur, but in a matter of seconds he stopped and we were back on the road.

Alex set me down near the fiery remains of the exploded Hummer, and pulled a sword from his back. It looked like the type of sword King Arthur would have used, but a bit smaller and lighter. The blade was sharp, and looked like it could slice a tree in half with one swing.

Alex grabbed my hand and led me closer to the burning heap of metal.

We stood in the middle of the road, in the light of the fire.

There was a lot of movement within the thick, dark trees. Who, or what, was making the noises? I had no idea. There were no signs of Alaine or the others, but I knew the Darkling were out there; watching, waiting.

I had a strange feeling that something was about to happen, and I was an unarmed target. It was a horrible feeling; a feeling that suddenly made me nauseated.

Where was Kade? He was supposed to protect me.

Alexander's raven-black hair waved lightly in the cool breeze. A single bead of sweat glistened, as it trickled down the side of his face. He sniffed the air, slightly crouched, with his sword gripped tightly in his hand. His eyes were focused, intense, fully blackened and gazing into the darkness, ready for whatever was coming.

The heat of the fire warmed my icy cold skin. Kade's jacket had gotten lost when I was tossed from the Hummer, and my hoodie was a thin layer of worthlessness, leaving me shivering. I slowly inched my way closer to the flame, as close as possible without burning myself. Darkling didn't like the light, so I was pretty sure they wouldn't sneak up behind me.

"I thought we were going to the other Hummer," I whispered.

"We were, but I lost my key. It was probably when I did that awesome somersault over Kade, trying to avoid his blade," he responded without looking back. But I saw his cheek rise with a grin.

"Oh, okay," I whispered again. I didn't know why I was whispering. It's not like it mattered. I guess it was because I didn't want to break his concentration. My life was now in his hands.

But, I liked being in the light anyway. I was starting to hate the darkness and all the terror associated with it. It was better to see what was coming, rather than have it sneak up and kill me. I didn't like those kinds of surprises.

My eyes strained down the dark, dirt road. About a hundred yards away, the faint glimmer of the second Hummer's bumper winked its location to me. The rest remained shielded in the darkness. Hopefully the Darkling wouldn't see it and blow it up too. That was our last mode of transportation.

Alex sniffed the air again, obviously concerned with whatever was lurking in the darkness. His knuckles turned white, as his grip tightened around the handle of his sword.

He then spoke two spine-chilling words.

"They're coming."

A strong smell of death whirled in the wind around me, stinging my nostrils. It was a familiar smell. An evil smell. A smell that alerted me the Darkling were near.

"Emma, whatever you do...don't run," Alex warned. "Stay close and I'll protect you." His words offered little comfort, but I was thankful he was willing to protect me.

"Okay," I whispered in agreement.

Suddenly, a Darkling shot out of the darkness, and in a screaming blur, knocked Alexander backwards. They tumbled to other side of the road and disappeared into the trees. I could hear them fighting, but now I was completely alone, vulnerable, a spotlight in the darkness with no one to protect me.

As I turned, another Darkling stepped into the road. I froze. Its black eyes steeled on mine, and there was nothing I could do. It had me locked, a victim of a rabid monster. Its lips curled, revealing sharp, corroded teeth. I slowly backed toward the opposite side of the road.

Alexander told me not to run, but he wasn't here, and I had no other options. It was run... or die.

The Darkling glared at me... threatening. It move closer and with a snap, it flew at me.

I was thrust backwards, the air completely knocked out of my lungs. I winced as my bare hands were raked over sharp rocks. Pain and helplessness surged through my entire being.

In a blur, a figure flew out of the darkness and kicked the Darkling in the chest. It flew backwards and hit the ground with force, but quickly jumped back to its feet, growling. Kade stood strong to the side of me, locking eyes with it. It suddenly leapt forward, and Kade ran to take him on.

In mid-flight, Kade unsheathed his sword and swung, piercing the blade deep into the Darkling's chest. Its blood-curdling scream sent chills up my spine.

Kade quickly withdrew his blade, grabbed its hair, and swung... detaching its head from its neck. He then casually tossed the severed head into the trees.

I should have closed my eyes, but watching him engaged in battle was both horrifying, and breathtaking. He was my real-life knight in shining armor, determined and unwavering in his responsibility to save my life. My heart felt like it was going to explode right out of my chest.

He turned to face me and paused. Sweat glistened on his brow, his eyes began to soften and changed from pure black, back to hazel.

In a few quick steps he was at my side.

"Are you alright?" he asked.

"I am now."

He reached for my hand and lifted me to my feet. His touch sent a needed warmth through my frozen limbs. I wanted to wrap my arms around him and tell him how thankful I was for saving my life, but I hesitated.

"Where were you?" I asked, almost breathless.

"Trying to find the others, and had to take care of a few Darkling in the woods. But I did have an eye on you the whole time," he assured.

"Did you find Alaine?"

"No, and I couldn't find the others either. Maybe they already went for Caleb."

Alex ambled out of the darkness, wiping his blade on his pants.

"I hate those damn Darkling. Their blood is like freaking tar. It'll take a whole damn day to clean this crap off."

"Quit whining. What'd you kill...*one*? I've already killed three. But then again, who's counting?" Kade jested.

"Obviously you. We'll see who has the most kills by the end of the night."

"You're on," Kade agreed with a wide grin.

"Are you two serious?" They were actually trying to make a game out of this? Did they even care about dying? It seemed like they'd dealt with the Darkling before, like killing them just was a normal routine. Maybe it was. Maybe I was getting worried for nothing.

If I was supposedly three-quarters angel, then why didn't I have any special powers? I was healing fast, but that was about it. I was still humanly slow and very breakable. And if I was breakable, then I could easily die.

I glanced at my cast, smeared with dirt and blood, and suddenly missed my parents, my home, Lia, and Jeremy.

"We've got company," Kade said.

I quickly snapped from my slump, as three Darkling appeared out of the darkness, crouched, slowly stalking towards us. Each carrying some type of terrifying weapon.

Kade immediately stepped in front of me, pushing me behind him. The fire was extremely close to my backside but I didn't budge.

"Emma," Kade spoke.

"Yeah?"

"Stay right here."

That was the second time I was given the command. Did they really think I wanted to run into the darkness alone?

"Okay," I answered. I was frozen with fear anyway. There were three Darkling and three of us, but I was completely worthless.

"Hey Kade," Alex called, readying his sword.

"What?"

"The one with the least amount of kills has to clean the other's blade."

"Deal," Kade answered, crouching, readying for battle.

They were playing 'murder the Darkling', while my sanity was hanging on by a thread. Maybe if I saw it as they did, I could keep what was left of my sanity.

"Count me in," a voice hollered from the darkness. We all turned to see Dominic do a double somersault from the trees. He landed directly in front of Kade and Alex, wielding two smaller, curved blades. They looked thin, but super sharp, and had fresh Darkling blood dripping from them. "So which one of you girls is gonna clean my blade?" His eyebrows rose to Kade and Alex. He then turned and winked at me, making me blush. Dominic had just evened the playing field.

"You wish," Alex huffed. "And, Dom, while you're scrubbing the crap off, my blade will need some extra sharpening as well."

"Dream on, little man. I won't be cleaning your big-ass blades," he sneered.

I was just about to tell them the Darkling were getting closer, when Dominic turned and ran at full force toward them. In one swift, fluid movement, he jumped forward in a perfect spin, effortlessly beheading two Darkling. It was fast, like poetry in motion.

Dominic was a cross between Kade and Malachi. He was over six feet, but was muscular and ripped. He was fair, his features strong and defined, and his eyes were jade green. His clean-cut hair was a light ash color and perfectly disheveled.

Alexander charged after Dominic with abandon and vigor. The last Darkling ducked under Alexander's sword. He pivoted, plunging his blade into Alex's shoulder. Alex wailed and dropped to the ground, trying to remove the blade, but it was just beyond his reach.

Kade charged forward, leapt in the air, and as he came down, he plunged his blade into the Darkling's chest. The Darkling dropped to his knees and took hold of the blade, slowly extracting it. As he did, he glared at Kade and let out a horrifying laugh. Kade stood in front of him with a smirk, and slowly shook his head.

"Hey, Dom. I think he's got too much weight on his shoulders," Kade yelled.

"Well bro, maybe you should help him out," Dominic flung one of his blades to Kade, and in an instant, the Darkling's head was severed, rolling across the ground. Its blackened eyes were still open wide.

I dropped to my knees, lightheaded, until I realized I'd been holding my breath. I'd never witnessed so much death and gore in all my life. This world was macabre. Definitely a world I was not used to. Sure there were murders in L.A., but I'd never *seen* them.

I needed to get my head straight; change my thinking or I wouldn't survive. It was either them, or me. These things were evil and wanted to kill me. They deserved to die. Maybe if I pretended they were the bad guys in Jeremy's video games it would work.

Dominic and Kade assisted Alex over to where I was.

"Take it out," Alex demanded through gritted teeth.

Kade was about to pull the blade from his back when I yelled, "Wait. What if it hit a main artery? He could bleed to death."

"This? This is barely a scrape," Kade answered, yanking the blade from his shoulder.

Alex cringed. "Damn. I thought I had that one," he said, slowly rising to his feet.

"Nope. I got it, and that's four for me," Kade snickered.

"No, no, no. We were starting from scratch. How do we know you killed four?" Dominic rebutted. "So, I'm in the lead with two awesome kills, which everyone had the pleasure of witnessing. Kade, you've got one. And Alex? *Zero*."

"That's bull. I *just* killed one. See his leg right over there?" Alex ranted, pointing to the silhouette of a lifeless Darkling leg. "You saw it, Emma. Right? Emma?"

I didn't respond because I was suddenly distracted by the humongous terror approaching. I pointed, speechless. It was the monster Darkling, heading in our direction.

"Holy shit," Alex shouted.

"Alright, alright. Now, don't go getting your panties in wads. So, the deal is... whoever kills King Kong gets three points," Dominic challenged.

"No. Whoever kills this one, takes it *all*," Kade countered.

They all nodded in silent agreement, and took off toward the Darkling. I was fine with that. I had three deadly assassins protecting me now.

"Emma. Emma." Someone softly called my name. I could barely hear it over the battle cries. I quickly glanced around but saw nothing.

"Emma," the voice called again, this time a little louder.

As I turned, Alaine walked out of the dark trees, but stopped near the edge of the road.

"Emma, come quickly. Come to me," she urged, waving me over. My heart skipped a beat, thrilled to see her alive. I started to run toward her when Kade suddenly jumped in between us. He held his hand up to me.

"Emma, don't move."

I wondered why he wouldn't let me go to her.

Kade faced Alaine and with two quick steps, thrust his blade through the middle of her chest.

She shrieked, grabbing his arms, her eyes wide with confusion and pain.

"What the hell are you doing?" I screamed in horror. I couldn't believe my eyes.

Alaine fell to the ground, gasping for air. I could hear blood gurgling in her throat, as she tried to breathe. I ran to comfort her, but Kade held me back.

"What the hell? Let me *go*. You killed her! Why did you kill her?" I screamed, as hot tears streamed down my face.

"That's not Alaine, Emma."

"What are you talking about?"

"Look at her eyes - they're completely black. And the smell. This is not Alaine. It's a shifter. A Darkling shifter," he repeated, slowly loosening his grip on me.

I fell to my knees, a few feet away from her. It looked like my aunt, an exact replica. But he was right. Her eyes were completely black, and the stench of Darkling wafted heavily in the air around us. If it weren't for that fact, I wouldn't have believed him. It was crazy. Her hair, her features, her clothes... everything was exact. That was terrifying.

"Thank you. I didn't know. I would have gone to her. I could have died," I sobbed.

"You're okay. That's all that matters," he said softly.

Do you think she's okay?" I asked, trembling. "Do you think Alaine is still alive?"

"I don't know," he answered sadly.

The shifter suddenly thrust its hand towards me. I gasped in horror and fell backward, barely avoiding its touch. Kade reached down and lifted me to my feet. He then walked over to the shifter and pulled his blade from its chest, and it let out a blood curdling scream. Within a few seconds it stopped breathing, and I watched its eyes turn from black to white. Then, it slowly shifted back into its true, hideous form. A Darkling.

How deceptive and horrifying. And to think I almost fell for it. I shivered in fear at the thought. That was too close, and now I knew I had to be even more careful and aware of the dangers around me.

Kade turned back to me, wiping his blade. He reached into a pouch on his side, and pulled out a 9mm handgun. I knew exactly what it was because my dad owned one. He'd kept it in a safe in his bedroom, but whenever he cleaned it he'd let me hold it - without the bullets of course. He promised me that one day he'd take me to a shooting range, but that never happened, nor would it ever.

Kade raised my hand, and placed the cold weapon in it. "Just aim for the head or the heart."

I grasped it, worried because I'd never shot a real gun before.

"Thanks... *again*," I said. "It seems like saving me is becoming a habit."

"It's my job," he grinned.

"I thought your job was 'escort'."

"That's part of it, but with you, I think there will be many, many additions to that description," he grinned. I loved his smile. It made me feel like everything was going to turn out alright.

"At least you'll have job security," I smiled.

"Well, just promise me one thing," he said.

"What's that?"

"That you won't go running off with anyone else tonight, except me. Remember, you're *mine* for the evening. My priority," he declared with half smile. "They need my help, so stay put." He smiled, and then ran to help Alex and Dominic.

My heart pattered, and I found myself smiling, despite all that was going on. And it was because of him.

I was in awe watching the three of them battle. They looked as if they were rigged to wires, flying and flipping effortlessly around the giant, chopping at his legs, waist, and arms. But their efforts didn't seem to faze it. It was too heavily protected within its suit of armor. The giant swung back at them with a large, super-sharp blade, but its swings were much slower; easier to read.

Despite his slow swing, if one of those should hit, they'd definitely be in a world of hurt, or worse... dead.

The monster's neck and heart were covered in a steel plate. Those were their vulnerable spots - their kill zones.

Take off the head and they're sure to be dead. That was my new mantra, although I wasn't sure if I'd be able to pull it off.

I wondered why Kade didn't take the head off of the shifter. I turned and stared at its lifeless body, lying on the ground, only feet from me. Maybe shifters were easier to kill. Maybe they didn't need to have their heads taken off.

I heard footsteps running through the bushes to the right of me, and quickly pointed the gun in the direction. My stupid cast made it hard to steady, so I grasped it in my left hand, my clumsy hand. *Dammit.*

Just then, Malachi and Alaine emerged from the darkness.

"Emma," she called, with a wide smile on her face. But, I wasn't going to fall for that trick again. I kept my gun pointed at them.

"Whoa," Malachi exhaled with hands up in the air, stepping back. "Emma, put the gun down. It's us. Use your nose. We smell sweet. Well...then again, Alaine might have a little odor, but that's because she's sweaty and rubbed up against some Darkling," he jested, sniffing around her with a scrunched up nose. Alaine glared at him, and shook her head.

They slowly stepped forward. I sniffed the air, and didn't smell any stench on them, and as they got closer, I could see the whites of their eyes. The shifter had completely black eyes.

I exhaled and lowered the gun. Alaine ran over to me and wrapped me in a tight embrace. She smelled sweet, like a bouquet of roses. Then, I undoubtedly knew it was her.

"I'm so glad you're okay sweetheart," she said, squeezing me tighter.

"Me too," I replied. This felt like a horrible nightmare, but having her close to me helped.

"Damn, that dude's monstrous. And, I thought *my* guns were huge. Well, looks like they need my help," Malachi said, glancing at the Darkling with a gleam in his eyes.

"They can't seem to kill it," I said.

"Well, that's because they're not using the right tools," he said with a wicked grin. He sheathed his blade, and pulled out two grenades from his ammunition belt. He popped the two pins and ran toward the Darkling. "Move it or lose it. And by that...I mean body parts," he yelled in mid-flight.

The others immediately took cover as Malachi sped toward them with two live grenades in his hands. Alaine pulled me to the side of the burning wreckage, and we ducked behind one of the doors.

I had to peek. I wanted to watch the kill of the night. Malachi did a single back-flip in the air, landing on top of the giant's back. He then shoved one of the grenades in the back of his armor at the base of his neck, and the other, somewhere in his backside. Kicking off, he flew through the air, landing a few feet from us. After another leap, he was crouching down between me and Alaine.

The monster Darkling struggled to reach the grenades, but his armor was too bulky.

Bam! A huge explosion had everyone ducking....and *bam!* Another followed immediately after.

Malachi covered our heads as pieces of Darkling rained down, pelting everything around us.

Disgusting.

"Now that's what *I* call going out with a bang," Malachi gloated, standing up beating his chest.

"Better watch out... looks like *your* head's about to explode next," Dominic hollered from the trees.

"Hey, at least I took care of business. You pansies were giving it a massage," Malachi scuffed.

"Whatever," Alexander muttered. "*We* didn't have the grenades."

Alexander, Kade, and Dominic jogged over to us, looking a little battle weary. Kade stood near me, offering an adorable smile.

They all gathered around Alaine, awaiting instructions.

"We need to find James, and head toward Weeping Rock to look for Caleb," Alaine spoke. "I think we've taken care of most of the Darkling, but we've got to be ready for anything. We'll all be going in together, that way Emma will be better protected. So, are you all ready?"

"Yes," they cheered in unison. They sounded like a football team before a big game.

"Let's get Caleb and get the hell out of here," she said. "I saw James heading in that direction earlier. Let's move and hopefully we'll run into him along the way.

TWELVE

KADE GRABBED MY CAST AGAIN, keeping me close. Alaine and Malachi led the way, while Dominic and Alexander took up the rear.

There would probably be a lot more Darkling where we were headed, and I hated the fact I was worthless when it came to fighting. I needed to get this irritating, bulky cast off.

"Hey," I nudged Kade. He turned with raised eyebrows. "Can you cut this thing off?" I raised my casted arm, just as Alaine turned around.

"How does your arm feel, Emma?" she asked.

"It feels fine. Doesn't hurt at all. I'd be better help if the cast was off. At least I could hold the gun properly."

"Have you ever fired a gun before?" Malachi asked in a cocky tone.

"Yes. But not a real one," I responded hesitantly.

He exhaled loudly and Alaine smacked him.

"Malachi, check and see if it's still broken," she said.

He stepped forward and took hold of my casted arm. He closed his eyes, and heat suddenly filled it.

"Nope. It's not broken but there is still some tissue damage. No big deal. I'm sure she can handle it. Right, Emma?"

"Right," I agreed, pulling my cast from his grip.

Alaine nodded. "Come, Emma," she said, taking a knee. I knelt down beside her, and she took my cast, placing it upside-down on her lap. She then pulled a small blade from a hidden pouch attached to her ankle.

That was awesome. Like a secret assassin awesome.

"Don't move," she ordered, with a smile. I held my breath as she proceeded to slice the cast off, like it was a soft stick of butter. In a few seconds, she peeled it from around my arm and handed it to me. She took my wrist and turned it in her hands, pressing it forward and back. "Does it hurt at all?"

"No," I said in complete amazement. Just a few days ago, my arm was broken, twisted, and looked like the only thing holding it together was the skin.

"Well, you've defied death and have healed unbelievably fast. I'd say you're something special," she stated, shaking her head in awe.

"Will I get my powers soon?" I asked.

"Yes, but not until after your eighteenth birthday – your transformation. That's when the nephilim get their gifts, and that's why they are sending the Darkling out to kill them before they turn.

The Darkling sent to kill you probably assumed you were dead, and fled under that assumption."

"How do you know all this information?" I questioned. It was like she was there, watching.

She paused and then it hit me.

"Watchers?" I whispered.

She looked at me with narrowed eyes and turned to Kade, who shrugged his shoulders.

"There will come a time when we can discuss all of this in detail," she said with a smile. "But right now, we've got to move. Time is running out, and they know we're here. We've got to get Caleb out before it's too late."

There was a light tap on my shoulder.

"Emma, would you like me to hold your cast until we get back?" Alexander asked, pulling a knapsack from off his back.

"Sure. That would be great," I said, handing it over. "Thank you, Alex." I was glad he offered to take it. It did have some sentimental value. A reminder of my friends.

"No problem," he said with a smile.

We were on the move, quickly making our way down the darkened road, but the stars looming above, provided us with a dim glow. In California, I'd never noticed the stars before, at least not like this. These were huge and beautiful, like large specks of diamonds sprinkled across the sky.

"Off the road," Alaine urged, in a whispered tone.

There was movement ahead, so we all ducked into the cover of the trees, and stood in silence. I could only hear one sound – the sound of my heart, and it was pounding furiously.

I sucked in slow, deep breaths and closed my eyes, suddenly feeling a warm calmness rush over me. When I opened my eyes again, Kade was standing behind me, inches away, his arms pressed to my sides, pinning me to the tree.

"Just stay with me," he whispered. I nodded.

It took everything within me to keep sane. The warmth of his breath, as he whispered in my ear, sent tingles coursing through my entire body. I tried, with all of my might, to stay focused, but his closeness had my head in a fog.

His scent, though mixed with sweat, was still unbelievably sweet. I tried to hold my breath and keep myself in the present reality. We were on a mission; a mission to find James and save Caleb, who was kidnapped because of me.

Alaine and the others were only feet away, so I had to pull myself together.

"Alex. Dom," Alaine whispered. "There are two Darkling on the road ahead, about fifty yards down. Take them out, as quickly and quietly as possible."

She sounded like a military commander, and as soon as she spoke, they responded. Kade took a step back, putting distance between us, somewhat lifting the enchantment he had on me.

I took in a deep breath.

Alexander and Dominic moved from the back and headed, in complete stealth mode, toward the movement on the road ahead. I tried to focus, but couldn't see a thing. It was pitch black. How could any of them see in this darkness? Did they have some kind of special angel night vision?

If I was supposedly three-quarters angel, then why couldn't I see a thing? At this moment, I felt one-hundred percent human and completely vulnerable. On top of that, I'd still have to wait a whole year for my so-called "angel powers" to kick in.

God, if you can hear me, please give me something to get through this. I'm really not picky. I'll take anything.

Sounds of swords thrashing through the darkness were followed by two distinct thuds, like bowling balls being dropped to the ground. I hoped it was Alex and Dominic who completed their mission, and not the other way around.

"Let's go," Alaine commanded.

Kade grabbed my hand, and we ran down the road, stopping when we neared them. They were safe, except for the two headless Darkling sprawled out on the road.

"The cave should be just ahead," Alaine said, looking through some kind of night vision binoculars. She had this whole covert mission thing down to a science. "It seems clear."

Seems clear? That didn't sound promising. All clear, or even just clear, would have been cool.

My heart started jackhammering, knowing we would be entering the danger zone. I knew the only thing that could settle me was Kade's touch. It did something to me I couldn't explain.

He was intently listening to Alaine's last instructions, where there was mention of the possibility of running into a few of the Fallen. I suddenly grabbed hold of his hand and held it tight.

His head snapped toward me with a look of confusion, but when his eyes met mine, they softened, and he gently tightened his grip. I instantly felt better. Calmer. A soothing power seemed to flow between us.

And then, a familiar clearing of the throat cut through the darkness, like Alaine's knife over my cast. Malachi.

I could feel his piercing gaze, but I wasn't going to let it concern me. I wasn't letting go of Kade. Not now. Not when we were going into a place where I was supposed to be exchanged and possibly executed. Right now, I needed his touch like I needed to breathe, and as long as he was alright with it, I was too.

Everyone's eyes turned to us, and it suddenly went silent. I put my head down and tried to keep a straight, yet terrified, look on my face, which wasn't hard to do. A face that said I didn't care what anyone thought. Kade was assigned to me by Alaine to be my guardian, and I was making sure I wasn't going to lose him.

My facial drama must have worked because when I glanced up, Alaine turned to Malachi and muttered, "Move it."

As they turned, Kade laced his fingers through mine. It felt so natural, so perfect, but also linked us tightly together as he quickly pulled me along with him.

The sound of rushing water was just ahead of us, and the pungent smell of earthy dampness. Alaine didn't speak, but made hand gestures, which everyone seemed to understand but me. Kade pulled me behind him as we slowly waded into the frigid water. I gasped and Malachi immediately turned.

"Shh..." He pressed his finger to his lips.

Loud splashes resounded around us, stopping us dead in our tracks. The group quickly made a tight circle around me.

A painful cry struck nerves in my already trembling body. Dominic suddenly dropped to his knees, gripping an arrow shaft extended from his side.

"Alaine," I screamed.

Oh God. What do I do?

Terrifying growls echoed around us. My instincts went into panic mode as I reached for the gun, but in all the commotion, it was knocked from my grasp and thrown into the river. I dropped down on hands and knees, and desperately searched through the frigid water. I couldn't find it.

I was pulled to my feet as the Darking closely surrounded us. There were at least twenty from what I could see. We were completely outnumbered.

Kade pulled me to his side, but never took his eyes off of the Darkling.

Malachi, Alexander, and Alaine charged forward. Kade turned and grabbed Dominic's arm, assisting him to his feet.

"Damn it hurts," Dominic moaned.

"Hold still," Kade warned. He gripped the arrow shaft and pulled it from his side. Dominic cringed, but took the pain.

"Kade, behind you!" I screamed, watching a figure shoot toward him.

He pushed Dominic away and spun around. Using the same arrow, he thrust it forward, sinking it deep into the eye of an oncoming Darkling. It screamed and dropped, face first, into the water.

That was way too close.

Another bounded toward us, but Kade charged forward and

drop kicked it. It flew backwards and landed with a splash. Kade jumped up, grabbed his sword, and charged after it to finish the job.

I bent down to help Dominic back to his feet.

Wham!

I was slammed from behind, and blacked out for a moment. When I opened my eyes, I was in complete darkness. Cold wind beat against my face. I was dizzy and disoriented, but could tell I was traveling very quickly. Someone had a tight grip around my chest, and a heavy hand clamped over my mouth so I couldn't scream.

It couldn't have been a Darkling because the hand had a sweet, yet smoky smell.

It felt as if we were flying silently through the darkness. Faint echoes of Kade and Dominic yelling my name were quickly diminishing. I was being carried further and further away from them.

I struggled to free myself, but the hold was way too tight. Then my kidnapper whispered one frightful word into my ear.

"Sleep."

Fear gripped my entire being as I quickly felt myself fading.

Soon, darkness blanketed my eyes.

THIRTEEN

ISTANT SCREAMS SNAPPED ME FROM my spelled
sleep. My eyes were blurred, and my head was throbbing.
Wintry air caused my body to shiver in attempt warm
itself, but its efforts were futile. The cold had already seeped deep
into my bones.

I tried to get up, but my feet and arms were tightly fastened
behind me. I was seated on a wooden chair, in a corner of a small
hollowed-out cave. A torch, hanging on the opposite side of the wall,
barely lit the surrounding area.

The walls were glistening with dampness, and the air was thick
and stagnant with a lingering stench of Darkling. Whoever grabbed
me must have been with them, and I was surprised they'd kept me
alive.

The last thing I remembered was being hit from behind, and
then quickly carried away from Kade and the others. They had been

surrounded by Darkling. I just hoped they were okay, and were able to find Caleb.

Footsteps echoed down the corridor. Someone was coming.

I struggled to loosen the ropes binding my wrists, but they were too tight. I was helpless to defend myself, not that I could do much damage anyway.

No matter what, I was going to be strong. I wasn't going to show fear, even though I was terrified. They didn't deserve the pleasure.

The heat of my breath, mixed with the cold air, swirled as it exited my lips. I sat tall, staring at the door, waiting for whatever was going to walk in. My heartbeat quickened as the footsteps drew closer, and an elongated shadow darkened the outside wall.

A tall, dark figure stepped into the room, and then two others followed behind him. They removed large hoods, revealing their faces. I expected to see Darkling, but instead was met by very handsome men.

The one standing in the middle had very dark features. He looked in his mid-thirties and had long black, wavy hair. The others were a bit shorter, but also had dark features, and dark hair. They were tall, over six feet, and well built. Each stared at me for a moment, and sniffed the air like they were confused.

Were these the Fallen?

"Is this the child?" the man in the middle spoke. He exchanged a look of question with the other two.

"Yes," they answered.

"A female? Are you certain?"

"Yes. She bears his mark," one of them answered.

"Why the hell am I here?" I yelled, looking directly at the middle man. He seemed to be the one in charge.

They began laughing.

I wished I had powers. The power to fling fireballs with my eyes, and burn them all to the ground. But instead, all I could do was glare at them.

"Well, well. Isn't she a feisty one," the leader said, staring back at me with a sly grin. He slowly stalked toward me, circling. "It's a shame. You are such a beautiful child." He took my chin in his hand.

"Don't touch me," I said, pulling way.

There was a pause of silence, and then they all erupted into laughter again.

"Let me go," I insisted.

"I'm sorry child, but we cannot do that. Other plans have been made for you," he said. He then turned toward the two who remained by the door. "Where's the other?"

"She got away," one answered, lowering his eyes to the floor.

"How could she have gotten away? Wasn't she near the child?"

"Yes, but she just… vanished. One moment she was there, and the next… she was gone," he explained, baffled.

"She's a nephilim, you *idiots*. Invisibility must be her gift."

"We didn't know. It's the Darkling's job to collect the nephilim, not ours," the other answered.

"It was Lucian who appointed this job to *you*, because the Darkling haven't been able to capture her. So I suggest you leave now and keep searching. This time use your noses," he growled.

"Yes, sir," they answered. The two men pulled their cowls back over their heads and backed out the door.

My head was spinning wildly from their simple conversation.

The man walked over to me after the others left and took a knee at my side.

"What's your name child?" he said in a kind voice.

"Why should you care? You're just going to kill me anyway."

"I'm not the one who wants you dead. I was sent here to make sure that you were delivered. That is all."

"Well, who wants me dead? Is it Lucian?" I asked. I still couldn't believe someone actually wanted to kill me. And not just anyone. Angels. Fallen angels, to be exact. And it was for something I had no control over. I never asked to be born a nephilim or an angel, nor did I have a choice.

He got up off the floor and walked back to the door. I could tell there was something different in his eyes. They looked softer, not so hard and dangerous as they were when he first walked in. Maybe it was because the others weren't here. It seemed as soon as they left, his demeanor changed.

"I'm Emma," I said softly, hopefully playing on his heart-strings...if he had any.

"What?" He turned, his eyes locked on mine.

"My name. It's Emma."

A slight grin grew on his lips as he ran his fingers through his thick black hair, and gazed at me with a puzzled look.

"Well Emma, it's a pleasure to meet you," he said, his eyes steadying on mine. He shook his head and headed back toward me. "I never thought the day would come when I'd meet you. You are quite a rarity. Lucian really doesn't have a clue of what we've captured. If he did... you'd probably be dead, or would have to take a blood oath to become one of his Fallen."

"I - I don't understand what you're talking about," I sighed. I remembered Alaine mentioned Lucian. He was the Fallen angel that had gone rogue, killing all the nephilim in a fit of revenge.

"You are different, Emma. A special breed of angel *and* nephilim. The nephilim have unique and powerful gifts, some of which angels don't possess. Some nephilim are stronger or faster than angels, or have been given multiple gifts. Because of this, they are despised and condemned. In the eyes of the Fallen, the half-breeds are abominations.

"I don't have any special powers," I insisted.

"Not yet child, but you will. Which is why they've tried to kill you before your transformation, which is—"

"On my eighteenth birthday?" I finished his sentence.

"Yes," he answered with an inquisitive look in his eye.

"There is an age old prophecy which tells of one who will be born of an angel and an abomination. A child who will have power greater than the angels. A power that could bring change, and save the earth from destruction. The Fallen don't take kindly to change."

"At the time of your transformation, you will need to choose a side. If you're still alive, that is. If Lucian ever finds out your true origin...it will be a dreadful time. His ultimate goal is to rule, not only the Fallen, but the earth. He's been hiding in the shadows, building his army, waiting. Once he emerges, humankind will experience true evil, firsthand. If they do not submit to him, he will destroy them."

"But let me warn you. Those who have chosen not to join him have died the most unpleasant deaths. Lucian abuses his power, exploiting the innocent, making them suffer in front of others so they will not refuse him. He will take those closest to you and make you watch as he tortures them. He will reach into their chest, pull out their beating heart, and then place it in your hands. He is dangerous. A merciless and murderous leader, with not an ounce of remorse in his pitch-black heart. And he will not relent until you submit to his authority."

His words had frozen me to my core. I shook my head, overwhelmed and ill-fated to this new cursed life.

"Well, let's just hope he doesn't find out," I said. That's all I had to go on. If I had to choose, it was a no-brainer. I'd definitely choose the good side. Why would anyone want to choose the side of a psycho murderer who tortured innocents for his own gain?

I sighed and shook my head in complete disbelief. This was all madness - complete and utter madness. How could I be a super angel who could save the earth, when I couldn't even save myself? I definitely couldn't see it. Not right now, especially being helplessly tied to a chair in the middle of a dark cave.

Overwhelming? That was an understatement. This new life I'd been hurled into was way beyond that. And, why save the earth? No one really cared about the earth anyway, except maybe the tree huggers and environmentalists, which were completely outnumbered by the majority who were destroying it.

When I glanced into his eyes, I could tell he was in deep thought.

"Are *you* an angel?" I asked. I knew it was a stupid question, but I wanted to hear it for myself.

He paused for a moment, looking at me with a raised brow, but didn't speak a word.

"You're one of the Fallen aren't you?"

"Yes," he answered.

"Are you with Lucian?"

"I am, but it doesn't mean I support his reasons or rational. I have my own agendas." He had a look in his eyes. Not evil, but not quite good either.

"So, how do you know so much about me?"

He hesitated again, and then I saw a slight glimmer in his eye.

"I knew your father, a long time ago. He and I were very close. Actually, he was my mentor." He walked closer, and lifted my chin. "You have his eyes."

This information was so inconceivable and so overwhelming, it left me speechless.

He smiled and continued. "I remember the first day he met your mother. He came back to me filled with a joy and excitement I'd never seen in him before. He couldn't stop talking about her - the most wonderful creature ever created."

"When I learned she was a half-breed, a nephilim, I tried to warn him. I told him she wasn't worth risking his life over. But they were star crossed lovers, with a forbidden passion which was doomed from the start. She had charmed him, and he had fallen. The connection between them was strong and unexplainable. His heart had been bonded with hers. He was attracted, like moth to a flame.

He said that when he touched her, it was as if he had been struck by lightning."

My stomach immediately knotted. Everything he was describing - the feelings, the reactions - were the exact same I felt when I was with Kade.

I was just about to ask him a question, when he continued.

"Your father was happiest when he was with her. It's what happens when one is connected through the immortal bond. It's hard to understand, or explain. Something I wished and longed for. Something I still haven't found, to this day." His words were filled with sadness.

"Angels are only allowed to mate with their own kind, those of pure blood. Mating with humans or half-breeds is highly forbidden. Disobey this law, and you will be marked for death. This law is the same for all angels and Fallen." He turned and walked back to the entrance.

His words hurt, and cut deep, like a knife to my heart. I wasn't a pure blood, and if Kade was an angel, which I was almost positive he was, then there was no way we could ever be together. Would we end up as star-crossed lovers, never finding true love, and forbidden to be together because of a stupid law?

And then it hit me. My father had obviously crossed that forbidden line. I was the proof.

"Do you know what happened to my father?" I asked.

"Yes," he answered sadly. "Your father is dead. They murdered him. As soon as the leaders learned of his insubordination, he was immediately taken to the place of execution. I was later told he had been stripped of his wings and slain." He leaned out of the doorway and peered down the corridor, sniffing the air.

I didn't realize his words would have such an effect on me, but they did, and it made my heart ache. Although I never knew my birth father, and actually didn't even know he existed before tonight, I still would have liked to have met him, even if he was a Fallen angel. Alaine said he wanted to be good. He must have been special, and had some kind of goodness in him, for her to fall for him.

"Do you know my mother?" I asked. I needed to know.

"No. I'm sorry. Your father kept everything about her secret from everyone close to him. He wasn't willing to risk our lives, so he never spoke details about her, or their relationship. In case we were ever questioned."

"Oh," I breathed. At least he was admirable.

My hands and feet were throbbing and my fingers were numb. There obviously wasn't enough blood flowing through them, and at the moment, all I could think about was the constant pain.

"Excuse me. Could you please loosen these ties," I asked sweetly." I know I'm going to die, but if possible, I'd like to do it with my limbs intact."

He quickly strode over to me. "I'm sorry," he whispered. He quickly untied the ropes from my hands and feet. Tingling pricks stung my limbs as blood rushed back into the deprived areas. "They will be back soon, so you need to leave quickly."

"What?" *Was he letting me go?*

"Listen to me, Emma. You need to move quickly. Go left, as far as the tunnel will take you. At the end will be a large cavern with a waterfall. Jump down to the pool below and swim beneath the waterfall. There you will enter another cave. Take the tunnel on the right. Remember, it's the *right* tunnel that will lead you out."

"Wait. What about you?" I asked.

This was a place I definitely didn't want to be alone in. I knew there were lots of Darkling out there, and I also knew I wasn't strong enough to defend myself against them.

"I need to stay here and hold them off as long as I can," he said, lifting me from the chair. "Now hurry, Emma. They will be back soon."

"But won't you get into trouble for letting me go? Why are you doing this?" I questioned. My heart began pounding with adrenaline.

"It's a small favor for an old friend. I know he would have done the same for me. Plus, I need a bit of excitement in my life. This past century has been such a bore," he winked.

Century? I shook my head.

He quickly led me to the door and sniffed the air again. "You must go. *Now,*" he spoke with urgency. Pushing me into the corridor, he pointed me in the right direction.

"Thank you," I said, turning and giving him a hug. He hugged me back. "What's your name?"

"Danyel," he answered. "Now run!"

I bolted down the darkened corridor as fast as my feet could carry me. They were still weak and sore from being bound. It was dark, and the few torches attached along the walls offered very limited light. The pounding of my heart was equally as loud as the pounding of my feet as they echoed through the tunnel.

I kept my hands along the walls for balance. My converse shoes were still wet from being in the river, and were rubbing against my ankles, causing sores. But that pain was the least of my worries.

Danyel. His name rang through my mind. He knew my father, and even if he was a member of the Fallen – he saved me.

Loud screams echoed behind me. I paused for a moment and listened. And then I heard a loud voice.

"*Run,* Emma!" The voice resonated down the corridor, as clear as if it were yelling directly into my ear.

Another shot of adrenaline kicked in, and I took off running, twisting and turning down the tunnel. I couldn't hear footsteps, but from what I remembered… I didn't hear any when Kade and Alexander were running through the woods either.

I glanced back over my shoulder and witnessed extended shadows on the wall, which scared the crap out of me. They looked like those freaky shadows in horror movies; the ones where nothing good was attached to the end.

The sound of rushing water was just ahead, and the air abruptly dropped a few degrees. I finally came to the end of the tunnel and stood directly in front of another cave opening. It entered into an underground river. About ten yards away was a drop.

The waterfall.

I stepped forward and gasped as the frigid water rushed over my feet. I waded deeper being careful of the slimy, jagged rocks around me.

I was now knee deep and began to shiver. My limbs suddenly felt numb and like they were dipped in a river of ice.

My teeth clattered loudly against themselves as I slowly made my way toward the edge. I carefully glanced over the waterfall, and suddenly felt woozy. It was at least a fifty foot drop. Danyel made escaping sound so simple.

Yeah…just jump in and swim under the waterfall. Easy peasy. Did he realize how terrifying it was to a mortal? The water below looked dark, eerie, and totally uninviting. What if there were rocks down there? What if I broke a limb, or my neck? What if there were Darkling, or other creatures in the water that could bite me?

A horrible stench suddenly burned my nose. I turned to see two dark figures standing at cavern's opening.

Darkling.

They peered at me through evil, blackened eyes, and grinned through sharp rotted teeth.

"Come child," one hissed.

"Don't you *dare* come near me," I yelled, attempting to sound brave. But my shaky voice failed me.

"We won't hurt you," the other spoke.

"Like hell you won't," I protested.

They inched closer, so I stepped closer to the edge.

"Jagged rocks down there. You'll die if you jump. Break your pretty little neck," one hissed in an evil tone.

They were inching their way closer and closer. Way too close for my comfort. I could smell their hideous odor and it was making me sick. I'd rather jump and die on my own terms than let them capture me.

I was going to do it, but I couldn't let myself think about it. Thinking was bad right now. Really bad. I needed to act before my brain went into rationalization mode, telling me how stupid I was being.

"Don't be foolish child." They suddenly lunged at me.

"Go to hell," I screamed, before taking in a deep breath, closing my eyes, and pushing off the edge.

God help me.

As I dropped over the falls, my stomach tickled with a weightless feeling. In a few seconds I plunged into the deep, frigid waters below. I impulsively wanted to suck air in. It was a natural instinct when submerged into freezing water, but I pinched my nose and held my breath. It felt as if sharp blades were piercing every part me.

As soon as I broke surface, I gasped. My body trembled violently, trying to warm itself as the glacial falls pounded on my head like ice hammers.

At least I was still alive and practically in one piece. I struggled to get my shivering limbs to function and swim. Danyel was right. As I made my way under the falls, I entered another small cavern. A solitary torch lit two tunnels. Right or left. My brain was frozen. I was pretty sure he said to go right. I hoped it was right.

I suddenly heard two loud splashes behind me.

Dammit! When was this nightmare going to end?

Adrenaline kicked in, or whatever was left of it. If it wasn't for that, I'd definitely be an ice angel – or at least, three-quarters of one.

I drug my sub-zero body out of the water. Numb fingers and hands barely managed to pull myself up the rocks. I was so weak and exhausted. I grabbed the torch off the wall, and headed down the right tunnel. I was tempted to set myself on fire just to heat up. It didn't help my clothes were soaking wet, which made it that much harder to move.

My thoughts suddenly went to Kade. I hoped he and the others were safe. Given the horrific circumstances I was in, at least I was alive and free – for now. Pure adrenaline kept my feet moving through the dark tunnel. The faint stench of Darkling carried from the walls.

"Emma!" Someone called from ahead.

I stopped dead in my tracks. My breath ceased. I froze.

Who the hell was that?

I didn't answer and waited. Maybe it was dementia from hypothermia.

There were already two Darkling on my tail. But what if there were more ahead? If there were…I was trapped and totally screwed.

The only weapon I had was the torch, but I was so weak from shivering, I could barely hold it up. Now, more than ever, I wished I had those special powers everyone was talking about. Heck…I'd even take the gun right now!

"Emma," the voice called out again, louder. It was definitely in front of me, and it was male. But it wasn't Kade or the others. It sounded older. I strained to focus down the dark tunnel, but I couldn't see a thing. All I knew was that if I didn't move soon, my muscles would seize.

"Emma. *Move it!*" the voice scolded.

Okay. Whoever it was, they were pretty demanding.

Growls echoed behind me and even more splashes, so I decided to take my chances and run towards the voice.

I ran about ten yards and suddenly saw a figure. I screamed as it reached for me, and swung my torch at it.

"Emma! It's me," he said, catching the torch and steering it to his face. "Your friend from the woods."

It was the bum guy I'd met outside of Alaine's home.

Emotion rushed over me and I fell limp into his arms.

"Emma, you've got to be strong. Just a bit longer," he urged.

He threw me on his back, and I locked my arms around his neck and my legs around his waist. He dropped the torch to the ground and took off running.

He was definitely one of them. Like Kade and the others, because it felt like we were flying.

I couldn't see a thing as we made our way through the pitch-black maze, but I could tell he was traveling super-fast. Cold air whipped against my face as he glided effortlessly through the cavern. I held on tight, my body was frozen to his. And then, I saw a very dim light up ahead.

"Emma, when I put you down, I want you to run. Run and don't look back. Do you understand me?"

"Yes," I answered.

Loud growls echoed down the tunnel. The Darkling were coming.

As soon as we exited, my lungs and nostrils were happy to breathe the clean, fresh air. But my body was extremely numb and fatigued from the cold and constant shivering. The mysterious man took off his long trench coat and wrapped it around me. I hugged it close; his warmth still lingering in it.

"Thank you," I acknowledged. "Who are you?" I wanted to know.

I mean, really. Who the heck was this guy? I'd met him twice, and both times he was looking after me.

"A friend."

"A friend? That's it?"

"Do you need more?" he asked, with a tilt to his head. "Let's just say I'm sort of a guardian."

"So you know Danyel?" Maybe they were working together on the inside.

"Danyel?" His brow furrowed. I took that as a no.

"Never mind. He's the one who helped me escape. He let me go."

"He...let you go?" He said more to himself, but as he did, his eyes softened. "Well, you need to keep going."

"But, wait. Aren't you coming with me?"

"No."

"You're going to make me go out there all alone?"

"You'll be fine, Emma."

"But the Darkling. There's too many of them. You'll be—"

"I'll be fine." He smiled and nodded. He cradled my face in his warm hands. "You can do this. Now go. Run and find the others. They shouldn't be too far away."

I didn't question him. My heart didn't want to leave him to fend off the Darkling alone, but I was much too weak to help him anyway. I wondered how this stranger, my hero, fit into my crazy life. Right now, my mind was reeling with enough crazy crap, like trying to stay alive.

I turned and ran as fast as I could into the trees. A few minutes later, there were loud growls behind me. I quickly dove behind a large stump and turned to peek. My hero was crouched, in attack mode, glaring at the exit of the cave. Two Darkling approached him, flanking him on each side.

He lunged at one of them, whacking it in the face, and tumbled to the ground. With the same fluid motion, he reached for something in his boot and rose to his feet behind the other Darkling. It suddenly screamed, reaching for a blade which had been embedded deep into its back.

The next Darkling charged at my hero, kicking him in the chest, sending him flying backwards, about twenty yards, landing hard against a tree. He groaned, and curled into a ball. He was hurt, and I suddenly felt sick.

The Darkling was on him again, grabbing his arm and flinging him against another tree. He hit hard and dropped limply onto the ground. Three more Darkling exited the cave. I watched in horror as he tried to get up. He was so brave, but I knew he didn't have a chance.

The Darkling quickly surrounded him, sniffing the air in all directions. One bent down, wrapped his grimy fingers around his neck, and slowly lifted him.

"Where's the child?" it hissed.

He didn't answer.

"Speak now or die," it threatened.

I closed my eyes tightly and hoped when I opened them, everything would be gone. But when I opened them again, everything remained the same.

"She's not here. She's *free*," my rescuer yelled. He spit in the Darkling's face and laughed loudly. The Darkling punched him in his gut before throwing him to the ground.

"Take him to Lucian," he motioned to the others.

Lucian? He was here?

Four Darkling reached down and grabbed him, binding his arms behind his back.

I couldn't take it anymore. He risked everything for me. I had to get away, or everything he did for me was in vain. I wasn't about to let that happen.

I slowly backed up, and while their attention was turned to my hero, I ran. I ran deeper and deeper into the woods, getting more and more lost. I didn't know where I was running; I just knew I needed to run as far away from them as I could.

I could barely hear the sound of rushing water. Maybe it was a river. Before I was taken, we were crossing a river. Maybe if I stayed near it, I'd find the others. At least it was some kind of plan.

I quickly maneuvered through the forest, toward the sound of the water, and reached a river. It wasn't large, maybe ten feet wide. My mouth was dry and I was thirsty, so I bent down, cupped the cold water in my hands, and took a sip.

Branches suddenly cracked in the distance.

My head whipped up, listening.

They were coming, and they were close. I knew if I ran they'd catch me.

From what I gathered, they had a great sense of smell. I quickly peeled out of the warmth of my hero's coat and sent it floating down the river, using it as a decoy. Maybe they'd catch its scent and go after it. It was the best I could come up with.

The ground beneath my feet was soft. I bent down and pressed my fingers into cold, thick, squishy mud. I wondered if it would cover my scent. It worked in the movies. What else did I have to lose, besides my life?

I quickly grabbed handfuls of mud and rubbed it all over my face and body – every place that was exposed. Then, I found a small grove of trees near the river and laid flat on my back between them. I figured if they found me, I could fight better on my back, than on my belly. Then I tried to conceal myself, as best I could, by covering my limbs with overgrown brush and fallen leaves.

I was quiet, listening. My breath would be the one thing that would give me away. It was way too fast, and I was having a difficult time slowing it down. I was terrified, lost in the middle of some godforsaken forest, with wicked creatures searching to kill me. I'd definitely need some major therapy after all of this. And that was only *if* I survived.

A strong whiff of Darkling burned my nostrils. Branches cracked all around me, and there were splashes in the river alongside me. They were here. I lay still, trying not to breathe. My heart pounded furiously against my chest wanting to break free and run away. I didn't blame it. I wanted to run too.

I remained motionless as a white face appeared in the darkness above me. Its eyes were reflective, like a cat hunting its prey. It sniffed the air, and took a step closer, pausing inches from where I was lying. I was frozen, petrified.

It bent its head down, a few feet from my face. I closed my eyes; my lungs on the verge of bursting. It inhaled another deep breath.

My heart sounded like a war drum, pounding loud in my ears.

A piercing scream shot through the silence. It was a Darkling downstream.

The Darkling hovering above me, shot up, and took off. They must have picked up the scent of the coat. I sucked in a deep breath. Cold, wonderful air filled my lungs.

Thank you, God!

I remained stay still and silent, until I knew they were gone. But I was too terrified to move, knowing they were still out there hunting for me.

Where was Kade? Where were the others? I'd even settle for Caleb. I hoped they were out there, alive, searching for me.

FOURTEEN

I MUST HAVE FALLEN ASLEEP because warmth blanketed my frozen body. I dreamt I was being whisked away on a soft, white cloud, drifting quietly through the forest, up above the tree line. Nothing could see or hurt me, as long as I was on this cloud.

A bright light began to emanate around me, and then I heard a soft whisper; a familiar whisper calling my name.

"E—mma. E—mma," the voice sang.

I instantly recognized it.

"Mom? Mom," I called.

My mother's face slowly appeared before me, like a hologram, on the edge of the cloud.

"Emma, my sweetheart. I'm so sorry."

"Mom? Where are you?" I cried, trying to push out of the cloud, but it wrapped itself tightly around me.

"Emma, your father and I did our part to watch you grow safely. Now, you need to know the truth. She has all the answers, and will take care of you now," my mother spoke. Her face was solemn, glowing.

"Who? Who are you talking about?"

"She will help you now. She will protect you."

"But, you're my mother. I need you," I cried, as tears streamed from my eyes.

"Yes, sweetheart. You were ours for a time; a wonderful time. But, you must be careful. There are things you don't understand. Dangerous things. Things that are afraid of you, and of what you will become."

"I don't want to become anything. I just want to be with you and dad," I sobbed.

"In time, darling. In time. We will always be with you, watching over you. Always remember that we love you. Your father and I have always, truly loved you, Emma. You've brought so much love and joy into our hearts." Her face slowly began to dissipate, and the white cloud started to change to a dark shade of grey. The warmth disappeared and was replaced with a stinging cold.

"Mom, don't go!" I screamed.

"We love you, Emma. We love you." Their voices trailed off.

"Please don't go. Don't leave me alone. Mom...Dad," I sobbed.

When I woke, I was still on my back in the pitch-black. The heat of my tears trickled down the sides of my face. My mud covered body trembled and ached.

"Emma." A faint voice carried lightly on the night wind.

Oh God. I was losing it.

"Emma."

I froze again, not sure if I should respond. It sounded like Kade, but I wasn't completely sure. I couldn't risk it. Not since I knew they were capable of shifting.

I waited anxiously for a confirmation. There was nothing, except for the gentle sounds of the river, the pounding of my heart, and the howl of the wind through the trees. I slowly sat up. The mud had dried and caked to my skin.

I glanced around, but couldn't see anything. I must have been hearing things.

Then, there was a rustling in the trees ahead. A sudden heat overwhelmed me, and I gasped for breath.

"Kade?" I spoke as quietly as I could. I needed to know. The feeling was too familiar. No one answered. If it wasn't Kade, I was going to be in *big* trouble.

I sat there, terrified and alone, with only the familiar blanket of warmth to comfort me. This feeling only happened when he was around.

"*Kade*," I yelled. My voice killed the silence.

"Emma? Emma, where are you?"

It *was* him! The sound of his voice brought tears to my eyes.

"Kade, I'm over here," I yelled, trying to get to my feet.

Footsteps pounded toward me, and then I saw his face. His hazel eyes beamed in the darkness. His face was as luminous as an angel.

I wanted to run to him and wrap my arms around him, but I was covered in mud. He stopped in front of me, and grinned, not making an attempt to touch me, and I didn't blame him.

"What happened to you?" he chuckled.

"Long story," I huffed. "I never thought I'd find you guys again."

"Hey, I do this for a living. I would've found you, eventually."

"I could feel you. That's why I called out to you," I said, grateful.

"I felt you too, and—"

We were suddenly interrupted by the others.

"Emma, you're *alive*?" Dominic teased, and then stopped with his hands out in front of him. "Whoa, have you been mud wrestling with the Darkling?"

"Haha. Funny," I answered, unamused. "This mud happened to save my life, unlike someone else," I sneered at him, walking towards the river to rinse some of the mud off my face.

"Ooooo…" Alex and Malachi sang out in unison, as they walked toward us.

"Low blow, bro." Alex punched Dominic in the arm.

"Hey, I wasn't the one in charge of her," he scolded, his eyes shot toward Kade. "She was *his* responsibility. I was injured. *I* had an arrow in my side."

Kade's face dropped and became saddened, and my heart suddenly sank deep into my chest. I didn't mean for the insult to include him.

"We were all responsible," Alaine said, appearing out of the darkness. She walked over to me, took me by the hand, and we walked to the river. She bent down, and scooped up water in her hands to help clean the mud off my face.

"I'm so sorry Emma," she whispered.

My stomach churned, begging me to ask her a question. A question that had been burning in my mind. I needed to know.

"Alaine… are you my birth mother?"

She stopped, and there was complete silence. Even the guys fell silent and gaped at us.

She reached for my hand and grasped it tightly in hers. My heart pounded furiously, waiting for her answer.

"Yes, Emma. I am your mother."

I took in a deep breath and couldn't hold back the tears in my eyes. This time, I wasn't sure if they were tears of joy or sadness. Both, I guessed.

"And my father?" I desperately wanted to verify what Danyel had said.

She shook her head with a look of pain in her eyes.

"Your father is dead. He was killed by the Fallen when they found out about us." She swallowed hard, struggling to speak those last few words. A single tear trickled down her cheek. "You would have loved him, Emma, and he would have loved you. I see a lot of him in your eyes," she said softly, holding my face into her hands. She pulled me to her and hugged me tight. "I'm so glad you're safe," she repeated.

She wrapped me in her arms and I hugged her back. Now I knew why Alaine felt so familiar. She was my birth mother.

"Hey, Emma. How did you get free?" Dominic questioned, interrupting our moment. "The last thing I remember... you were standing right by me, and the next, you were gone."

"Someone grabbed me. I don't know who it was, but it definitely wasn't a Darkling, and it put the sleeper on me."

"Whoa. Looks like someone needs an ass-whoopin'," Dominic huffed, smacking Kade on the arm. "Right?"

"Right," Kade agreed, but his eyes looked distant. I wondered what he was thinking.

"Hey. I'm ready to give an ass whoopin'. Bring it," Alex hyped, raising his sword above his head.

"Boys, please. Let Emma finish," Alaine said. They all turned to me.

"Well, I woke up in a cave, bound to a chair, when three Fallen came in. One of them questioned the others, asking them where the *other* nephilim was. They didn't know, so he sent them back out to search. When they left, the leader started talking to me. He told me I was part of some ancient prophecy, and also said he was a friend of my father. Then, he let me go."

Alaine gasped. I could tell by the look in her eyes, I'd struck something. "Did he give you a name?" she asked.

"Danyel."

Alaine turned and stared blankly into nothingness. "Danyel," she whispered loudly.

"Do you know him?" I asked.

"Danyel was your father's best friend. His partner. I'd never met him, but your father talked a lot about him."

"Yeah, that's what he said. But he wasn't the only one who helped me escape. There was another, and I'm certain he was an angel too. I met him before, when I was with Courtney outside of the property. Tonight, he was there again. He carried me out of the tunnel, and told me to run and find you. He fought the Darkling so I could get away, but he was outnumbered and captured."

"Did he say who he was?" Alaine asked.

"No. He just said he was a friend."

"He must have known your father," she said softly.

"I heard the Darkling say they were taking him to Lucian. We have to save him. He risked his life so I could get away. We can't let him be killed. Him and Danyel."

She closed her eyes and exhaled deeply, then got up and turned to the others.

"If Emma is right, and Lucian *is* here, we need to be extra careful. We don't know how many Fallen are with him. Our main priority is to find Caleb and James and get out." She glanced over to me. "If we do find Danyel and the other, along the way, then we will try and save them too. But I will not risk our lives for them."

"But, they risked their lives for me," I cried.

"And so are they," she said pointing to Dominic, Malachi, Alexander, and Kade. As soon as I turned and looked into each of their eyes, I knew she was right. They had already risked so much for me. The thought of any of them dying because of me, made me sick inside.

"It's a pleasure, Emma," Kade assured.

"Yeah...and it helps that we actually like you. Well, mostly," Malachi smirked, and then grinned.

"Yeah, a cute thing like you is definitely worth dying for," Dominic said with a wink.

"Yeah, me too, Emma. Ditto what they all just said," Alex agreed.

"Thank you so much," I said, overwhelmed. I hardly knew them, but knew they would fight to protect me. They already had.

"We need to get moving," Alaine said, placing her hand on my shoulder. "And we will do whatever it takes to make sure everyone gets out safely. But we can't make any promises, especially knowing Lucian is there."

"Why would Lucian be here?" I questioned.

"He probably has nothing better to do than torture and watch others die," Malachi responded. He was probably right, and the thought made me ill.

"Emma, do you think you could get us back into the cave?" Alaine asked.

"I think so. I remember running from that direction – right of the river. So, as long as we head that way, we should find it," I instructed.

"Dom, I want you to keep a hand on Emma at all times. Don't you dare let her out of your site," Alaine ordered.

Kade's head snapped up, his eyes narrowed on her. He looked as if he was about to say something when she held up her hand. "I'm sorry Kade, but I really need you to cover them, since Dom is injured."

"That's bullshit," Kade cursed under his breath.

"Easy, big guy. You don't have to worry. I'll take really good care of her," Dominic teased. He walked up to me, tied a loop knot with a rope around my arm and fastened it to his. "This time, you won't be pulling a Houdini. If they try and take you, they'll be getting a bonus," he laughed.

Dominic was strong, tall, and handsome. Muscles bulged from his tight black shirt; his handsome, defined face was covered in sweat and dirt. His green eyes gleamed in the dark. Any girl would probably die to be this close to him, but for some reason I wasn't feeling anything.

Not the way I did when Kade was near. Maybe it was because we were surrounded by things that wanted to kill us.

I glanced at Kade and shrugged my shoulders, shooting him a look of 'sorry'. He closed his eyes and shook his head in frustration.

Dominic made matters worse. "Hey man. No hard feelings. She's not your girl anyway."

"You got that right," Alaine butted in. "She's off limits to all of you, and don't you forget it," she said, pointing her finger angrily at each of them.

I watched Kade's expression and saw a glint of sadness; his face mirroring the shooting pain in my heart as she spoke those harsh words. I was off limits, and I knew it. I didn't want anyone, especially Kade, to have a mark of death on their heads because of me.

"Let's go – and *quietly*," Alaine commanded. She led the group with Malachi at her side. Alexander and Kade fell behind me and Dominic.

Something sticking out of the ground tripped me, but Dominic caught me before I hit the ground. The rope actually worked. He pulled me back up, like a fish on the end of a hook.

"See. It works," he smiled. I rolled my eyes.

As we started to walk again, he grasped hold my hand. His hand was large, and his grip was tight.

"Excuse me, but you're squeezing the feeling right out of my hand."

"Oh, sorry," he said, loosening his grip. He probably didn't know his own strength.

We continued through the dark forest. The air was even colder now, and my blood wasn't ready for this kind of cold. Plus, my clothes were still damp, and I was shivering to the core. The only thing I could think about was Kade's warming touch. It seemed to work when he came within a certain distance, or touched me.

Alaine held up her hand, but I didn't see it and bumped into the back of Malachi. He felt like a brick wall. I bounced back and stumbled into Kade's arms.

He caught me, carefully lifting me upright, and in the process, an instant surge of warmth filled my body. I gasped.

"Thank you," I said.

"Anytime," he answered. As soon as his touch left me, I became cold, and started shivering again. Why didn't it happen when I touched anyone else?

"Hey, Emma. I hope you'll be getting your powers soon, because you're a bit clumsy," Dominic teased.

"Thanks," I huffed.

"Watch out, Dom. When she transforms, she'll probably give you a good ass beating," Malachi said, coming to my defense.

"I'd love to see that," Alexander laughed.

"Enough," Alaine scolded. "Emma, is that the way into the cave?" She pointed to a small clearing just beyond the trees.

It was a lot darker now, but I noticed the area my nameless hero had his run-in with the Darkling. Hidden under a thick overgrowth of brush was where we had exited the cave. I couldn't believe we were returning to this horrible place.

"Yeah, that's it. There's a long tunnel that leads to a cavern under a waterfall. But we'd have to find a way to get up. There's no way to climb."

"Waterfall? That's not a problem," Dominic whispered in my ear.

Yeah, sure. It didn't seem like anything was a problem for them. I was the one that seemed to bring enough problems for everyone. Mom and Dad would still be alive. Caleb, Danyel, and my nameless rescuer would be free, and we wouldn't be running around in some God forsaken forest, avoiding Darkling and Fallen angels.

Before my emotions became too overwhelming, we were on the move. Dominic pulled me close, and wrapped his arm around my waist.

"Dude, let her breathe," Kade blurted.

"Relax man. She's my responsibility now, and this time she's not getting away. Just watch our back."

I heard Kade exhale and mutter a series of unintelligible words.

"Before we enter... Malachi, go ahead and make sure the way is clear. We'll have to move quickly. Dom, has your injury recovered enough to carry Emma?"

"Ribs fine, just a little tender."

"I can carry Emma, if you can't," Alexander butted in. They all turned and glared at him. "Just saying."

"She's not a freaking bag of potatoes," Kade scolded.

"I didn't say she was. What's your problem? Why are you getting all huffy?" Alexander asked, turning to face him.

"It's nothing," Kade said through gritted teeth.

"Whoa," Dominic said with raised hands.

"Would you guys knock it off?" Alaine came back and stood in the middle of them. "I said this once, and I'm going to only say it once more. Emma is off limits. If I catch any of you trying to make a play for her... you're history. Period." She turned and walked away. "Dominic, carry Emma. End of discussion."

The three sneered at each other, but Dominic's lips turned up into a wide smile. He'd won. Even in the dark, I could see Kade's face turn red. I'd never seen him upset before, but he still looked handsome, regardless. He glanced at me and I gave him a smile, then he turned and walked away. Alexander went after Kade. He patted his shoulder and whispered something I couldn't hear.

"Let's move." Alaine waved for everyone to follow her. I didn't even realize Malachi was gone, and in a split second was whisked up into Dominic's arms. I wrapped my arms around his neck as we took off, literally flying through the tunnel. I focused on the only thing I could hear, the quick and steady beating of Dominic's heart. After a few minutes, we stopped at the waterfall.

Dominic kept me tight in his arms. "Now that wasn't too bad, was it?" he admitted. His warm breath tickled my ear.

I shook my head, and quickly released my arms from around his neck. "You can put me down now, thanks."

"Yeah, sure," he said, setting me down carefully, but our arms were still fastened together with the rope. Everyone was accounted for, except Malachi. Maybe he tried to find a way up.

Then, as soon as I processed the thought, a rope ladder dropped down from the top of the falls.

What the heck?

Alaine was the first to wade into the water and swim for it. She quickly climbed a few rungs and then motioned for the rest of us to follow.

"Climb on my back," Dominic said. I was about to jump on, when Kade came up from behind me, put his hands on either side of my waist and effortlessly lifted me up. His touch made me tingle, as it always did. I turned and he smiled at me, making my heart skip a beat.

As Dominic waded into the water, I fastened my arms and legs around him. I was already freezing. I groaned in pain as the frigid water froze me to the core. My body quickly became a trembling mess.

"Hey, you okay back there?" Dominic asked.

"Yeah, just freezing to death," I responded through clattering teeth.

"I'll get you outta the water in a few. Hold on," he said.

A few? In a few, my body temperature would drop drastically, and I could get hypothermia and die.

I tried to urge warmth through myself, but it was too damn cold. Warmth was not a word in my dictionary right now.

We made it to the waterfall, and things went from bad to worse. Ice water hammered down on our heads.

Dominic grabbed hold of the rope ladder. "Hold on, Emma," he said turning back. I tightened my grip as best I could.

As he started to climb out of the water, my body felt extra heavy, like tons of lead weights were hanging from my appendages. My hands and fingers were numb, and my arms and legs were extremely tired. The trembling didn't help, and made me extra weak. The rope was unsteady; swaying every which way as Dominic quickly climbed up. I tried to hold on as tightly as I could, and fought to keep my grip on him, but the constant, frigid water beating down on me was taking its toll.

We were halfway up when my arms suddenly gave. I slipped from Dominic's neck, and fell backward. My right arm, which was still tied to Dominic's, jerked me to a halt. I heard him curse after catching himself from falling. I was dangling, halfway up the falls. Dominic's rope saved me again.

"*Emma,*" Kade shouted. I looked down. He was below us, battling his way up the ladder. He finally got close enough to reach my legs, and pulled them to rest on top of his shoulders. Even his touch wasn't enough to warm me now. I needed to get out, quick. Dominic climbed quickly with one arm, and Kade stayed right behind him, resting me on his shoulders. I was too weak to do anything but keep my balance and try not to fall.

When we finally reached the top, Dominic pulled me up, and I collapsed.

Alaine's voice was muffled. "Get her to dry ground, quick! Someone look for wood to start a fire."

I was scooped up while someone pulled my wet hoodie off. I opened my eyes. It was Dominic. As soon as I was on the ground, I felt the rope release from my arm.

"We need to get her warm, or she'll go into shock." Alaine's voice was frantic.

I struggled to speak, but managed to say one word. One crucial word.

"Kade."

"What was that sweetheart?" Alaine bent down, putting her ear to my lips.

"I need... Kade," I breathed.

She paused. Her brow furrowed and her eyes had a deep look of concern, and then a knowing.

I felt myself fading in and out of consciousness.

"Kade," she yelled.

I couldn't keep my eyes open. They shut tight, my body violently trembling from the cold, and there was nothing I could do to stop it. Seconds felt like an eternity of suffering. Then suddenly, I was lifted from the ground and warmth rushed throughout my entire body.

I opened my eyes, and Kade's beautiful face was inches from mine; his hazel eyes beaming as he held me tight in his arms. He'd taken his shirt off, making our connection even stronger. The shivering slowly started to subside. Warmth from his touch cascaded in waves over me. I was in heaven. If I could, I would stay right here, in his arms, forever. I closed my eyes, hugging him closer, not caring what anyone thought or said, and he hugged me back.

"You'll be alright now," he whispered, quietly in my ear. "I need you to drink some of this," he said, placing the same blue flask to my lips.

I drank and then snuggled closer to him, burying my face into his bare chest. His scent took me on a high I didn't want to come back from, and as the magical brew made its way through my system, I began to feel even more warmth and strength.

A voice broke the silence.

"There are no Darkling in sight, and no signs of James or Caleb,"

Malachi reported, returning from his reconnaissance mission.

"James has to be here...unless—" She paused, and I knew she was worried he was injured or dead. "This place should be crawling with Darkling."

"Maybe, James took them all out," Alex added.

"He's good, but not that good," Malachi answered.

"No, they're still here. Somewhere. I can smell them. They've probably gathered somewhere, and are waiting. They won't leave, knowing Emma and I are here. I'm almost certain Lucian is present because he wants to be the one to destroy the last of the nephilim," Alaine noted.

"The *last*?" I shrieked.

"Yes. That's what I was informed. They've hunted and killed every other nephilim, and now...we are all that's left. That's probably why Lucian is here. He wants to make sure we are destroyed," she sighed. "That's why it was imperative you were brought to me as quickly as possible. I'm so sorry you were dragged into all of this, Emma."

"It's not your fault," I replied.

So that was it. We were *supposedly* the last of the nephilim. The rest – slaughtered in the name of revenge. It made me sick. How did one have the power to put a death sentence on others who weren't even given a choice? They were born nephilim, they didn't choose it. And then I remembered something my mother told me about. The Holocaust. *Millions* of innocents were gathered and slaughtered. They weren't given a choice or a voice. All because one evil man *thought* they were inferior.

I hoped I would survive this night and live to see eighteen. Then hopefully, if the prophecy was right, I'd help to make a difference.

"I want Emma to stay here. I can't afford for her to come with us. It's too risky, especially if Lucian finds out who or what she really is."

I was *not* going to be separated from them again. Kade's touch was already making me stronger. The shivering was already down to where I could manage it, and even though I was weak, I could dig deep and pull myself through.

"Absolutely not," I said, turning to Alaine. "You can't leave me here. I'm going with you, whether you like it or not."

"Chip off the old block. Huh, Alaine?" Dominic laughed, nudging her arm. She turned and shot him an evil eye, shaking her head.

"And one more thing," I said, since I was on a roll.

"What's that?" she sighed.

"I get to stay with Kade for the rest of this mission."

Her eyes were weary, and although I knew she disapproved, she consented.

"Fine, but I'm only allowing it because you're still too weak," she said in a motherly tone.

Thank God. I needed Kade's touch to keep me alive. It was mysterious and unexplainable, but it was his touch alone, which kept me from death. There was no one else who could offer me that. It was clear Alaine knew it, too. I could see it in her eyes. She saw in us, what she had with my father, and it scared her.

"I'll carry you as long as you need to," Kade said, loud enough so the rest could hear.

"Oh. So, now you're all rainbows and daisies?" Dominic snickered.

Kade turned and gave him a wink.

I wrapped my arms around his neck and smiled, knowing I was getting stronger every second we were touching. His life force was healing mine.

FIFTEEN

WE STARTED INTO THE DARKENED tunnel; the very one I ran out of not too long ago, being chased by the Darkling. Malachi stripped a torch from the wall, while wielding a sword in the other. The rest also had their weapons drawn, except Kade, who had me. I laid my head on his chest and listened to the steady beat of his heart. Warmth radiated from him like a heating pad.

"I know they're here," Alaine whispered, "I can feel them. We need to be extra careful, and be prepared for an attack."

"I can walk," I whispered to Kade.

He shook his head. "I'll put you down when I have to. Until then...rest up."

I didn't argue. I wanted to stay wrapped in his strong arms as long as possible.

Alexander grabbed Kade's shoulders and peered over at me.

"Don't worry guys. I've got your back," he said with a wink.

"Thanks man," Kade said with a grin.

"Yeah, thanks Alex," I said with a wide smile.

"And I've got *his* back," Dominic added, smacking Alex's shoulders really hard.

"Whatever dude. Get your own back," Alex smirked, shrugging Dominic's hands off of him.

I giggled and closed my eyes, tightening my arms around Kade's neck, and pressed in as close as I could. As I did, I could hear his heart beat a little faster, and it made me smile.

The faint stench of the Darkling hung in the stale air as we moved quietly through the tunnel. We passed several empty rooms and stopped every once in a while to listen.

Every second I was with Kade, the stronger and stronger I became. Maybe it had something to do with my *special* gift, to heal quickly? But, there was a definite connection between us. I knew if it wasn't for his touch, I'd still be suffering from hypothermia...or dead.

I thought about Jeremy and Lia, and wondered what they'd think if I told them about my new life. I knew they wouldn't believe me, and Jeremy would probably give me some long lecture on lying.

"What's so funny?" Kade asked. I didn't realize I'd laughed out loud.

"Oh, sorry. I was thinking about my friends, and how they'd never believe any of this."

"The ones I met at the hospital?"

"Yes, Lia and Jeremy. I forgot you'd met them."

"They seemed really nice. I could tell they care a lot for you."

"They do. They're just as bad as my parents."

My parents. Mentioning them was like pouring a gallon of salt on an opened wound.

"I'm so sorry," Kade whispered.

"Thanks. I'll be fine."

"Hey, do you guys smell that?" Malachi stopped, sniffing the air. In a few seconds, it hit. A nostril burning stench. Darkling. They had to be close.

There was a small hollowed out cave about ten yards back, so we backtracked and piled in. Malachi put out his torch, and we waited in the dark.

"How many do you think there are?" Dominic whispered.

"I don't know, but we'll find out soon," Malachi answered. "Ready?"

"Are you kidding? We were born ready," Dominic answered, in a loud whisper.

"Hey Dom, I bet I get more kills than you." Alexander threw out another challenge.

"Whatever, little man. You're on," Dominic replied.

"Pffffft... Well, whatever you have in brawn, you lack in brains."

"Would you two shut-up?" Alaine scolded. "They'll come in here and kill all of us, while you two are yapping away."

"Alaine...shhhhh. You're making more noise than both of us," Dominic whispered loudly.

Alaine sighed and they began laughing quietly.

Were angels really this immature, or was it just our angels?

Wicked cackles echoed down the corridor.

Alexander pointed to himself and made a motion he was going. Dominic gave him the "cut throat" sign and pointed to himself. While they were playing their little game of charades, Malachi and Alaine slipped out. Within seconds they were back.

"Now, that's how you take care of business. Fast and furious," Malachi teased.

"Wha—?" Dominic squeaked.

"Move," Alaine scolded.

As we made our way down the corridor, we dodged the carnage left by Malachi and Alaine. Three heads, three bodies. Which head belonged to which? No one would ever know.

I should have been freaking out, running around and losing my mind, but I'd already seen too much. I was either becoming numb, or slowly becoming used to my new life.

What was I thinking? This whole damn thing was a nightmare. My life had become one huge, living nightmare.

Welcome to your new life, Emma. Instead of "good night, sleep tight, don't let the bed bugs bite", it was "make sure your doors and windows are bolted shut, or the Darkling and Fallen angels will come out and kill you!"

Oh God. I was talking to myself in my own mind. That was a sure sign I was definitely *losing it*. But, since I was on a roll, I figured I'd give myself a pep talk.

No pansying out. Fight till the death, and definitely...no crying. If I should get caught and tortured... then everything I just said goes out the door.

Alright...I was fine with that.

My heart started to beat wildly because it knew we were headed into the lion's den. I knew if I ran into Danyel again, he'd definitely *not* be happy to see me...him *and* my nameless rescuer. If we were all captured or killed, then everything they did would have been in vain. That would suck. Completely.

"You can let me down now," I whispered to Kade. As much as I wanted to stay in his arms, I knew we'd have a better chance if he could fight.

"Don't worry. I've got you," he whispered back.

"I know. But I'm fine now. Much stronger, thanks to you. I think you can protect me a lot easier if I was out of your hands." He hesitated, his lips turned up into a smile, and then he carefully set me down.

My legs were still weak, but strong enough to run or kick something if I had to. And then, something was running at us. Malachi pushed Alaine backward and swung. Who or whatever it was stopped and caught Malachi's hand in mid-flight.

"Swing happy?" he asked.

"James, where the hell have you been?" Malachi blurted.

"Undercover," James replied. "I know where they have Caleb. He's fine, but terrified. And..." he paused and faced Alaine.

"And what?" she asked.

"Alaine, I think you'd better brace yourself," he said, with a furrowed brow, and a deep look of concern in his eyes.

"What is it James?" She pressed, with a deep look of concern.

James paused and then glanced at the others.

"James, tell me," Alaine demanded. "What is it?"

He inhaled then steeled his eyes on her. "It's Samuel. He's alive and... he's here."

There were gasps of confusion, and then everyone froze. Alaine stood still, gaping at James, dissecting his words. She was speechless, and began shaking her head.

"Alaine?" James asked, waiting for a response.

Her wide eyes began to pool with tears. "No, no, no. It can't be him. You're wrong," she stammered. "It had to have been someone else."

James grabbed her by the shoulders and steadied her. "Alaine, it *was* Samuel. I'm certain of it. I saw him with my own eyes. I didn't believe it at first, but one of them even said his name. Lucian has captured him and Danyel. They're pretty messed up, and I have a feeling they're going to kill them soon."

"James. Don't you dare lie to me. Don't you tell me he's alive, when he's been dead for the past seventeen years."

"I don't understand it, Alaine, but I am *not* lying to you. I would never joke about that," James assured.

"How? How could this happen? I don't understand..." Alaine's face went pale. She grabbed hold of James, and then fell to her knees, sobbing.

I stood there, confused, watching Alaine crumble to pieces. Kade stepped next to me and grabbed a hold of my hand. I looked at him, baffled.

"Who's Samuel?" I asked.

Alaine turned and looked at me. Tears streamed down her cheeks. "Emma. Samuel is your father."

I froze. My brain tried hard to process her words.

"I thought he was dead?"

"He was. I thought he was. They told me he was murdered." She stared blankly through me, shaking her head. I wasn't sure how to feel, but my heart was breaking for her.

What was I supposed to do? How could I console her?

"Where are they?" Malachi asked James.

"About two-hundred yards down, in a large cavern off a small tunnel to the left. There are three Fallen and eight Darkling. They're alive, but barely. The Darkling are torturing them while the Fallen sit and watch."

James looked to be the oldest of the bunch, maybe mid-to-late-thirties, with clean-cut, dirty blonde hair. He was around six-foot, muscular like Kade and Alexander, but not massive like Dominic or Malachi. His face was handsome and flawless like the others, but he had sharper, more mature features.

"James. Are you certain? Are you one hundred percent positive it was Samuel?" Alaine pressed.

"I'm *positive*, Alaine," he assured, looking directly into her eyes.

"What do we do?" Alaine gasped and grasped her heart. This was the first time I'd seen her lose her composure. Her eyes had a blank, lost look in them. She'd led them with confidence up until now, and at the mention of Samuel, she melted into a worthless mess.

She looked so weak and hopeless, so I walked over and hugged her. She wrapped her arms tightly around me and pulled me close. "I thought he was dead. They told me he was dead," she repeated.

James and Malachi each laid a hand on her. Kade and the others just stood back, and watched quietly.

"We should be doing something?" I urged, pulling back from her. "They need our help."

"Three Fallen? And Lucian is one of them?" Malachi questioned.

"Yes," James answered.

"Holy crap," Dominic barked. The rest mumbled expletives under their breath.

Our strong unit was crumbling. This couldn't be happening.

"We need to go," I urged Alaine. I needed to do something to shake her out of her funk. And then it hit me…

"Mom," I said, shaking her. "Mom!"

Her eyes snapped up at me, at first with a look of shock, and then with a tiny glimmer of hope. A smile formed on the edges of her lips, and her hands softly cradled the side of my face.

"Since the day you were taken from my arms, I dreamt of this moment."

It took her hands in mine. "We need a plan," I said, pronouncing each word slowly.

Alaine wiped her face, closed her eyes, and took in a long deep breath.

"Yes," she agreed. "I'm sorry. My behavior was inappropriate and unprofessional. It-It's just been so long. It's like he's back from the dead."

"Well he won't be, if we don't rescue him," I urged, pulling her up to her feet.

"Emma's right. We have to do something, or they'll die," James agreed.

"Lucien must know we're here, and he'll be ready," she said.

"Why is everyone so afraid of Lucian?" I questioned.

"Lucian is one of the oldest members of the Fallen. He's been around since the beginning. Since the *fall*. He was Lucifer's right hand man and commander of his army; that is...until they had their own falling away. Lucian is one of the strongest, most cunning angels alive. He was the one who issued the decree to kill *all* nephilim."

"Which is why we need to get Alaine and Emma out of here," Malachi urged.

"I agree." Kade stepped forward.

"I hope you all know this is a suicide mission," Alexander said, stepping forward.

"Hey... Go *big* or go *home*, bro," Dominic said with a little too much enthusiasm.

"Wait," I butted in. "I think I might have a plan. It's risky, but I'm willing to do it." They all went silent and stared, which I took as an 'okay'. So I shared my plan.

"No. There has to be another way." Kade crossed his arms in front of his chest and shook his head.

"I think it's a damn great idea," Dominic countered, winking at me. Kade shot him an evil look. "Hey, what else do we have? I think we'll have a shot. If it doesn't work... then we'll all die together. I'm in." Dominic stuck his hand out in the middle of everyone.

Malachi and James slapped their hands on top of his, and then Alexander and I followed. Kade and Alaine hesitated. I knew it was because they were protective of me, and afraid for my safety. I looked at them both and nodded. I tried giving a look of confidence; a look that said I was all in, and I believed in my plan. It worked. Alaine slowly placed her hand on mine, squeezed gently, and wrapped her free hand around my shoulder.

"It could work," she said, turning to Kade.

Kade shook his head. "I just want you all to know that I don't agree with this. I'm only going along because I won't turn my back on my friends," he said, reluctantly placing his hand on top.

It was done. The plan was sealed. We all huddled in a group hug, not knowing if we'd see each other again.

I closed my eyes and pictured my parents smiling at me. Then I thought of Lia and Jeremy, sleeping snuggly in their beds, with nothing to worry about except chores and the new school year... Senior year. The things I took for granted.

Here I was, risking my life to save a boy I didn't even know, and my angel father and his best friend – neither of whom I knew existed until today - from supernatural beings who wanted me dead.

I sighed, taking in a deep breath. Then, I turned and took my first step toward my destiny, and whatever fate had planned for me tonight.

SIXTEEN

I HEADED DOWN THE DARK tunnel alone, while the others stayed behind, and prayed my plan would work. It seemed like a great plan at the time, but as I began my quest alone, I started to second-guess myself.

The best that could happen? We rescue Caleb, Danyel, my father—Samuel, who was hopefully my rescuer. I had a feeling that Samuel was my rescuer. He did have the same dark-brown eyes I did, but his face was totally covered with an unkempt beard, so I couldn't really tell what he looked like. But there was something deep inside of me, a tiny feeling which told me he was my father. I smiled at the thought.

I just hoped if my plan didn't work... I'd die quickly.

I could tell I was getting close because the stench of the Darkling was almost unbearable. It was a stink I'd never get used to. It made me gag and my eyes water.

Faint moans followed by cheers and laughter, echoed through the tunnel sending a chill down my spine. My pulse started to race, my stomach twisted in the tightest of knots, and my legs started to feel weak and wobbly.

"Come on, Emma. Hold it together," I whispered to myself.

I couldn't give up. I couldn't go back. Peoples' lives were at stake, and sadly entrusted in my feeble, un-transformed hands.

Another torch, ten yards away, lit the tunnel off to the left.

Footsteps, scuffling along the dirt ground headed in my direction.

What do I do?

Then Dominic's words "go big, or go home" rang through my head.

I really, really wanted to go home, but I didn't think knocking my mud covered converse shoes together three times was magical enough to send me there. But heck, this all seemed like some twisted fairytale anyway, so I decided to try it. I closed my eyes and quickly clicked my heels together. One...Two...Three...

I opened my eyes.

Crap!

Whatever. It was worth a try. But, I wasn't Dorothy, and instead of a witch and flying monkeys, I had a murderous Fallen angel and Darkling. Heck, I'd take flying monkeys over the Darkling any day!

I gathered myself, took in a deep breath, and trudged toward the oncoming evil lurking around the corner. As soon as I took the turn, a Darkling halted in its tracks, his black eyes locked onto mine. Its white, creepy face loomed back and forth, sniffing the air, trying to figure out what it had just run into.

"Take me to your leader," I demanded, crossing my arms over my chest.

He paused, stepping closer to me, continuing to sniff the air. His eyes suddenly narrowed, like he finally figured out who I was. An evil, horrifying laugh rumbled in his throat.

I became terrified, but tried my best not to show it. There was one thing I was really good at when I was scared, and that was running my mouth. So I blurted out a snarky remark.

"Damn, you stink. And you're freaking ugly. Poor God must have hurt his back trying to bend and scrape the bottom of the crap barrel to create you."

That must have *really* pissed him off, because he lunged forward and grabbed my arms tightly. I tried to fight him off, but he hurled me to the ground, knocking the wind out of me. He then grabbed my right arm and dragged me over the dirt and rocks. Pain throbbed where it was broken a few days ago. I held my breath, trying to keep my mind off of it.

We were soon at a large wooden door. The Darkling kept a firm grip on me, while it pulled it open.

As soon as the door swung open, I gasped. My rescuer was lying on the ground, face down. He looked unconscious, or dead, and it suddenly made my stomach turn.

Was he my father?

And then I saw Danyel, curled up, grasping his side, trying to raise himself from the floor. Both he and my hero's shirts were torn off, and they were covered with lacerations, bruises, and blood.

My heart hammered. If they could do that kind of damage to

them, what could they do to me? But I couldn't think about that right now. I had to keep focused.

I did a quick scan of the room, and what we were up against. There were seven Darkling standing against the right side of the room, and three others who looked like they could be the Fallen. I suddenly recognized two of them. They were the ones who were with Danyel. The ones he sent out to find Alaine.

One was standing over Danyel, beating him with a club that had some kind of spikes attached to it. The second one was standing against the wall, next to an older man who was seated in a large wooden chair. He had to be Lucian.

Caleb was bound and gagged in a chair at the far corner of the cave. He was filthy, and his clothes shredded. He looked up at me; his wide blue eyes were filled with horror. I knew the feeling. I tried to squeeze out a smile, to offer him some kind of hope, but my own hope was barely hanging on by a thread.

"Ahhh. So, what has the demon dragged in?" the older gentleman asked, looking at me with a wicked grin.

"A nephilim," the Darkling hissed.

"So this is the child? The one that keeps getting away?" His words were soft, but sharp. He rose from his seat as the Darkling dragged me closer.

Lucian didn't look strong or God-like as the others had built him up to be. He was about as tall as the others, and didn't seem muscular at all. His hair was white, clean-cut, and drawn back, which made him look regal and wise, and he didn't have one single wrinkle on his face. He was actually sort of good looking... for a super old guy.

He knelt in front of me, raised his hand, and softly swept his fingers across my cheek.

"What is your name, child?"

"Why do you care?" I said, pulling away from his touch.

He laughed.

"What would make you think I wouldn't?" he questioned, carefully watching me with a glint in his eye. He motioned for the Darkling to release me, and as soon as he did, I got up and ran over to Caleb.

"Why did you take him? He's just a human boy," I said, untying Caleb's ropes. Inside I was trembling, fumbling with the knots.

"So if he's a *human* boy, then what does that make you?" He asked, toying with me.

I didn't care if he was the oldest, strongest, and wisest of all the Fallen angels. He wanted me dead, and he killed my parents. I hated him. I hated him with every cell in my being.

I finally freed Caleb but he remained glued to his seat. His hands twisted around the red marks left by the ropes.

"I don't know what I am. I thought I was human, until one of your demon pawns called me a nephilim," I barked.

Lucian laughed and the rest of the room erupted, mimicking him.

I began to burn with rage, but I needed to keep my cool. "I've heard that you're one of the leaders of the Fallen. Is that true?"

He grinned, and slowly answered, "Yes. That is true."

"Then I have a question for you."

"Go ahead. Speak child," he said inquisitively.

"How can you tell if someone is *spawned* of an angel?"

He gazed at me with a look of wonder, and a wide smile grew across his face. I think he was amused. Good. My plan was taking effect. My mother always said I could command a room. I was pretty witty, sarcastic, and usually quick with my words, when I wanted to be.

"I like this one," he said, turning to the others. "I've never had such pleasure speaking to a nephilim, in all my years."

"Well, maybe that's because you murder them before they even have a chance. And how do you even know that I *am* one of those things?" I asked. The more questions I asked, the more his attention would be on me, and away from anyone else in the room.

He walked towards me, while the others in the room watched intently. I glanced at Danyel, and he slowly shook his head in disagreement. His eyes narrowed, and then I remembered what he said... Lucian didn't know who I really was, and if he ever found out... *oh crap.*

My heart began to pound as Lucian spoke, inching closer and closer to me.

"Well child, first of all, angels have a distinct smell. A fragrance that is sweet, pleasant, and purely angelic." He was now a few feet away, and took in a deep breath. "And you, child... have a particularly sweet smell." He paused, and I held my breath. "Secondly, if you are a nephilim, you will bear the mark of the angel you were spawned from."

"Well, I don't have any marks. Not even a birthmark, so you're wrong about that," I said with confidence. I knew for a fact I didn't have a birthmark. I was sure of it.

"The mark will be hidden, just under your hairline, on the back of your neck," he informed in an easy tone. He was now inches from me. "If you were a pure blood, your mark would be on the back of your right ear." He softly brushed the hair away from my ear and it sent a shiver down my spine.

"I do have a scar on my neck, but it was from an accident I had as a kid. I fell off of my bike and gashed it," I explained.

"May I see your scar?" he inquired. His eyes were glowering and I realized I didn't have a choice.

I glanced back at Danyel, who shut his eyes. It was too late. My mother told me the story about the scar, but I never remembered the event. What if it was a mark? Would he really be able to tell if I was something other than a nephilim? I didn't want to start a fight, so I slowly pulled up my hair to let him look.

There was complete silence as Lucian traced his finger along the scar on the back of my neck.

"This is no scar. This *is* your mark," he stated, in a cold, chiding tone.

I dropped my hair and turned around. His eyes were fastened to the Fallen near Danyel.

"Bring him to me," he ordered, pointing to my motionless rescuer.

The Fallen grabbed his leg and dragged him over to Lucian. He moaned, slightly moving his head.

He was alive.

Lucian kicked him over so he could view the back of his right ear. He lifted his thick brown hair and studied the mark. He made a quick motion with his head to the other angels, and turned to me, his eyes steeled on mine.

"Come child," he demanded. I stepped forward, my legs trembling. "Have you seen your mark?"

"You mean my scar?" I corrected.

He glared at me in exasperation.

"Tell me this. Why does he bear a mark, identical to yours? Did he happen to fall off the same bike?"

I stepped closer and glanced at the mark behind my hero's ear. It was the shape of an "X" with a small diamond in the center. It also had an arrow going through it, from right to left. The left part of the arrow had a point, and the right had a small circle on the end.

I never really looked at my mark. It was nearly impossible, given the location. But if it looked like his, it was definitely not a scar. Something must have stumped Lucian, because he had a bewildered look in his eye, as he studied the mark behind my hero's ear.

The Fallen standing near him spoke. "Lucian, there is no doubt that she bears Samuel's mark, but she also bears another below it. It almost looks like—"

"Quiet!" Lucian roared.

Oh shit. I wondered what they were talking about? I reached back to feel my mark, but my neck was smooth.

All breath in me seized, but the Fallen had just confirmed my deepest question. My rescuer *was* Samuel. Samuel *was* my father.

Lucians head snapped up. He glared at the other Fallen, and his face suddenly became hard; brows tightened, teeth clenched. He turned to me, and with a quick blink of his eyes... they changed, becoming black as night.

I was now, officially terrified.

Where the hell are they?

No sooner than I thought those words, both Fallen on both sides of Lucian were skewered with Dominic's swords. The one standing over Samuel, pulled the sword from his side. The other dropped motionless. His went right through his heart.

A deep, horrifying growl rumbled from Lucian's throat. He slowly backed to the far corner of the room.

I thought he was some great warrior?

Dominic rushed through the door with Malachi, Kade, Alexander, and James right behind him. Dominic headed toward the Fallen on the ground, pulled the sword from his heart, and severed his head. In seconds the Fallen burned to a pile of ash. That was completely shocking.

Malachi attacked the second. He was injured, but still strong. I could tell he was a warrior, because he was quick, dodging Malachi's attempts. Their clanging swords echoed through the cave. Dominic jumped in to help him.

I turned and witnessed Kade, Alex, and James taking out the Darkling one by one, quickly and with precision. My plan worked. I had turned the attention of the room to me so that the others could come in and catch the enemy off-guard. Thank God they came when they did. If they waited any longer, Lucian would have killed me himself.

In the heat of the battle, I grabbed Caleb by the arm, and ran for the door. As soon as we stepped out, Alaine was there. She grabbed Caleb and hugged him tightly, then grabbed me and pulled me into their huddle.

"You're safe. Oh thank God, you're safe." Her words trembled as she spoke.

"Dammit! That's gonna leave a mark," Dominic yelled. Blood spewed from a large open wound on his arm. Malachi came up from behind the second Fallen angel and... *Bam!*

Blood and brain matter splattered all over Dominic.

"What the hell?" Dominic griped, wiping the blood and grime off his face.

Another deep, evil growl rumbled from Lucian.

"I hope you remember this night, because the next time you see me, you will all die." He spread his arms out to his sides and magically, the most beautiful, silky black wings appeared from his back. Hidden wings?

I was beside myself, gazing upon this being; a wonder I'd only read about, or seen in the movies. All this time I thought angel's wings were white. Maybe his were black because he was Fallen. Whatever it was, it was beyond amazing.

His wings spread out, and they were enormous, around twenty-feet from tip to tip. One solitary flap sent a gust of wind swirling throughout the cavern. Lucian was now hovering weightlessly above the ground. The nice looking white-haired man now looked evil, powerful, and completely God-like.

Dominic, Malachi, and James immediately dove to the ground, and in a split-second, with another flap of his wings, Lucian shot out the doorway like a bullet.

Alaine pushed me and Caleb to the ground, diving on top of us.

I suddenly felt dizzy and everything around me became a blur. It was like I was enclosed in a water bubble, but didn't dare move.

Pieces of rock crumbled like sand, as Lucian's wings skimmed the sides of the cavern walls above us. If we didn't hit the ground, he would have easily taken off our heads.

As soon as Lucian left, Dominic started his griping.

"Are you telling me you had that gun the whole time?" Dominic snapped at Malachi. "Dude, you could have saved me a scar."

"Hey, if I used it sooner, I would have wasted bullets. Reloading takes time. One shot, one kill. So quit whining you big baby," Malachi rebutted, tucking the gun back in the holster on his hip.

"Hey, Dom. I killed *three* Darkling, and you killed *one* Fallen. Guess who's cleaning my blade tonight?" Alex teased holding his bloodied sword in the air.

"Bull... One Fallen is easily worth five Darkling. Darkling are easy kills. Angels take more skill, as you can see," he said, pointing to his bloody appendage.

"No way. I could have taken out that Fallen without getting a single scratch. You're losing it, bro. Those bulging muscles are slowing you down."

"Yeah, whatever. I can take *you* out without getting a scratch," Dominic snapped back at Alex.

"Okay! If you all don't want to die tonight, then I suggest we get the hell out of here," Alaine yelled. She stumbled and grabbed onto my arm, like she was weak.

"Are you okay?" I asked.

"I'll be fine. I just need a few minutes," she said with a smile.

She must have used her power to make us invisible to Lucian, and using that power made her weak. At least, it seemed like a pretty decent explanation.

"Malachi, you take Samuel. James, I need you to assist Danyel. Dominic, you take Caleb, and Kade – I'll let you take Emma. Now let's get out of here."

"Hop on little man, but watch the injury," Dominic said to Caleb, bending down so he could climb on his back. Samuel was still unconscious, so Malachi threw him over his shoulder. Danyel was hanging on, but barely. James wrapped his arm around his waist to assist him.

Kade sheathed his sword and walked over to me with a grin. A single bead of sweat trickled down the side of his face. Damn, he was handsome.

"You ready?" he asked, turning his back to me.

"Yes," I whispered, but my heart screamed it. I hopped on his back, wrapped my arms around his neck, and locked my legs around his waist. The surges of warmth were there, but I invited them, hugging him even tighter. He gripped tightly to my arms. I laid my head on his back and inhaled his sweet scent, glad he was alive. Glad we all were alive and leaving together, with the additions of Danyel and Samuel...my father.

Before I could think another thought, we were flying, out of the cave and back into the woods, weaving through the darkness. How could they maneuver so fast without seeing a thing? I wondered if I'd be able to see in the dark when I transformed.

I wouldn't worry about that right now. Right now I wanted to snuggle deep into Kade's neck, and that's exactly what I did. He rubbed my arms and pulled me tighter to him. I closed my eyes and envisioned us alone, in eternal bliss. But that's all it ever would be. A vision.

A few minutes later we were back on the road. The fires of the vehicle that exploded had dwindled and almost burned out.

"Everybody in," James urged.

There was no hesitation. Everyone knew what they had to do. They opened the back and loaded Samuel and Danyel in. Alaine and James climbed in with them. Malachi jumped in the driver's seat, and Dominic was shotgun. Me, Kade, Alexander, and Caleb squished in the backseat.

Malachi kept the lights off, but as soon as the last door shut, he threw the car in reverse and hit the gas. He suddenly slammed on the brakes; we all flew forward and to the side, as the Hummer did a one-eighty spin.

"*Malachi*," Alaine and a few others scolded.

"Sorry," he replied, in a not-so-apologetic tone. He threw the car into drive and sped off.

"Alaine, where are we going?" Malachi asked.

"To the bunker," she replied.

"Bunker? Why aren't we going back to the house?" I immediately questioned, turning back to Alaine.

"Because the house and property are protected by an invisible barrier, a barrier which Fallen cannot pass. Samuel and Danyel will not be able to enter, unless that barrier is removed. If we do that, we'd put everyone else at a huge risk, especially since Lucian is out for revenge. He'll stop at nothing now, until we are all dead."

"James and I will be staying at the bunker with them. I want you to return to the house with the others."

"No way. I've already been orphaned once, and I'm not going to let it happen all over again," I insisted.

Her face was weary, and covered with dirt and sweat.

I waited for a rebuttal, and nothing came.

"We will discuss it when we arrive, but I will not risk your safety. I suggest you get some sleep. We have a long drive ahead of us."

I was beyond exhausted. Everyone was. Caleb, on my left, had already passed out and was snoring. We were human after all, or at least I was, for now. Kade turned to face me, but I couldn't see his expression in the dark. He reached for my hand and laced his fingers through mine. It felt right. Perfect. I laid my head on his shoulder and soon fell fast asleep.

SEVENTEEN

"EMMA. WE'RE HERE," KADE GENTLY nudged me awake. I'd totally lost my bearings, but smiled as my eyes focused on his smiling face.

We were parked in some kind of extra-large concrete garage; every wall was sealed and I couldn't figure out how we'd gotten in. We exited the Hummer and walked toward one of the walls, everyone except Samuel, who was being carried by James. Alaine pressed a spot on the wall, and suddenly a portion of the concrete began to rise.

Whoa. That was some major high tech stuff.

"Let's go," she urged.

Everyone followed her through a long narrow hallway that led downward about one-hundred yards, and at the end was a large metal door. She punched in a code, on a small black pad on the wall, and then pushed the door open.

We entered a large open room, beautifully furnished. The walls were painted in a light sand color. To the right, was a full kitchen made of stainless steel and cherry wood, which was stocked with everything imaginable. To the left, was a large seating area with a huge plasma screen TV attached to the wall. At the back, were three large rooms, and I could see a bathroom attached to each.

"This is a bunker?" I whispered to Kade in shock. This looked like some kind of model home.

He nodded and whispered back, "Yeah, Alaine had it built several years ago, in case anything like this happened."

"James, could you please take Samuel into the first room and lay him on the bed. Danyel, you can have the next room over. Feel free to use the bathroom to wash up. There are clean clothes and towels in the drawers. Hopefully you can find something that fits."

"Thank you for your kindness, Alaine. You and your boys," Danyel replied with a bow of his head.

"You're very welcome," she said with a weak smile. Alaine looked drained. "Emma, you can take the last room." I guess she was letting me stay.

"Thanks," I said.

She smiled, then turned and followed Samuel into the room and shut the door behind her.

"I need to get a hold of Thomas," Malachi said shuffling into the kitchen. Dominic and Alexander plopped down on the couches in the seating area. Caleb grabbed one of the cushions and hit the floor, snoring as soon as his head went down. Malachi dug into his pocket and pulled out his cell phone.

"Damn. No service," he huffed.

"Just use the TV. It's one of those smart ones, and it's connected outside, to the internet. Alaine spared no expense," Alexander advised from the couch.

Dominic turned on the TV, and within in a few minutes, Thomas popped up on the large screen, looking like he was right in the room with us.

"Hey, where the heck are you guys?" he asked. "Did everyone make it?"

"We're in the bunker," Malachi answered. "And everyone is accounted for."

"Mission accomplished. Sweet," Thomas said, holding a thumbs-up.

"Barely. We've got some serious stories to share. For starters, we picked up two extras. Which is why we're here," Malachi added.

"Who?"

"Danyel and...*Samuel*," Malachi answered, stressing Samuel's name.

"Samuel? Alaine's Samuel?" Thomas asked completely dumb-founded.

"Yep. Long story... We'll give you the whole scoop later," Malachi confirmed.

"So how was babysitting?" Alexander asked Thomas with a laugh.

"Not too bad. I actually got *some* action. Two Darkling were lurking around the grounds, along the outer fence. I caught them on the camera, so I snuck up behind them. I got one right in the back. When I was pulling out my sword, the other one got away. They were probably on recon. Checking to see who stayed back. So... is anyone coming back to the house?"

"Alaine is sending Kade, Dom, and Alex back with Caleb. She'll be staying back to keep the barrier intact," Malachi answered. "How's Courtney?"

"Sound asleep."

"Stay alert, and keep an eye out for more Darkling. We rained on Lucian's parade tonight, and he's beyond pissed. Said he's gonna kill all of us... you included," Dominic jested.

"Awesome," Thomas answered, nodding his head with a smile.

I whispered to Kade, "I thought the Darkling can't get in because of the barrier."

"The barrier can only keep the Fallen out. That's why they send the Darkling."

"Oh," I sighed. That was scary.

"Well, hurry up. I'm getting bored over here," Thomas laughed.

"Bored? Well, I've got something that'll keep you busy *all* night," Dominic said, wiggling his eyebrows.

"I'm afraid to ask," Thomas chuckled.

"Get your gloves on little lady, our weapons need some major cleaning. We'll be home soon," he said twiddling his fingers at the camera.

"Whatever, dude," Thomas sneered, and then disconnected. Everyone laughed.

"Come on, little man. We're taking you home," Dominic said, nudging Caleb with his foot.

Caleb groaned, and slowly peeled himself off the floor, his eyes a bright shade of red. Dominic and Alexander made their way to the door.

"Bye, Emma," each said as they left. I waved goodbye.

"I'd better go," Kade said, running his hand through his hair.

"Yeah," I said, and my heart twisted.

"I'll see you soon," he said with a grin. He smiled and walked toward the others.

"See you soon," I replied.

"I'll walk you guys out," Malachi said, assisting a wobbly Caleb. I watched them leave, and as soon as the door snapped shut... I was alone.

I stood there, feeling completely lost. Like I'd just woken from a nightmare and everything around me was different. Changed. The only thing that seemed *real* was me, and I was even beginning to question that.

I glanced down at myself. My shirt, jeans, shoes... were all covered in mud. A sudden rush of overwhelming emotion flooded over me, taking me over the top. Maybe over-exhaustion, or the fact that I'd survived death several times this night. Hot tears pooled in my eyes, so I turned and headed to my room. I needed to sleep, and this time... I definitely wouldn't need any help.

"Hey, Emma."

I gasped as I heard Kade's voice and turned back. He stood at the door, holding it open with one hand. "You did good tonight. You were very brave, and should be proud of yourself," he said with a nod of appreciation.

A tear escaped my eye and slid down my cheek.

"Thank you," I breathed. Suddenly, an overwhelming, unexplainable feeling swept over me. I found myself running into his arms and hugging him tightly, not caring how he'd respond. But, he wrapped his arms around me and hugged back.

I looked up at his handsome face, and he gently brushed the tears flowing from my eyes. He pressed his soft, warm lips against my forehead. I closed my eyes and inhaled. His sweet scent made me dizzy. His fingers traced the lines of my face, and then slowly, carefully, he lifted my chin. I froze. My breath seized as he leaned in closer and closer.

"Kade!" A voice snapped.

My emotions whiplashed and I was rapidly yanked from heaven. We both turned our heads to find Alaine standing in the doorway, glaring at us.

Aww crap.

As soon as Kade's arms left me, all the good feelings left too.

"I'm sorry," he whispered.

"Don't be. I'm not," I admitted, smiling back at him.

He grinned and turned to Alaine.

"Kade, I'll see you tomorrow," Alaine said, in a not-so-friendly tone.

"Alright," he said, with a sad nod. "Bye, Emma."

"Bye," I replied, watching him leave for the second time.

"Emma, why don't you go and get cleaned up. I'd like you to come to the room when you're finished. Samuel is awake and we'd like to speak to you."

"Okay," I answered, but my thoughts were still lingering on Kade.

I slipped into my room and locked the door behind me. I opened the drawers and found some shirts and sweatpants in different sizes, and even found some underwear that fit.

I balled up the clothes and headed for the bathroom. I paused inside, not recognizing my reflection in the mirror. It was scary, how different I looked. I quickly peeled out of my mud-caked clothes and threw them in the hamper.

Turning on the water, I waited until steam began rising, then stepped in. Chills shot through my body, as the hot water collided with my cold limbs.

I was still in shock over what had become of my life. First the death of my parents, and on top of that...the Darkling, Fallen angels, nephilim, Alaine, Samuel, Kade...and here I was, stuck somewhere in the middle. I still didn't understand who or what I really was, and right now, it was way too overwhelming to begin to try. I curled up into a ball on the shower floor and cried, letting the hot water beat down on my aching body. It felt good to cry, especially with no one around.

I couldn't explain the feelings I was having, knowing that I'd be in the same room with my birth mother and father, who never existed in my world until a few hours ago. Maybe it was apprehension, maybe it was nerves, but it had my stomach in knots.

I'd also forgotten, for just a moment, I'd had a cast on this morning. Now it was off, and my arm was fine, aside from a minor ache. That was a miracle in itself. I could recall a flash of what it looked like – completely broken. I hoped the same healing ability could heal the rest of my aching body. Even my hair and toenails felt as if they were aching.

I finally pulled myself up, grabbed the shampoo, lathered and rinsed twice, just to make sure the mud caked into my scalp was gone. Conditioner was next, so I glopped a large amount in my palm and rubbed it through my hair. It smelled yummy, like ripe green apples.

I finished my shower and quickly dressed, ready to meet my birth parents, together, for the first time. As I opened the door, my stomach filled with slam-dancing butterflies and my pulse took off like a racehorse.

Standing outside their door, I knocked.

"Come in, Emma," Alaine called.

My heart hammered as my fingers touched the cold, brass knob and slowly turned.

As I stepped in, the room was dimly lit by a small lamp next to the bedside, and smelled of sweet soap. Samuel wasn't on the bed, but the bathroom door was shut.

"Come, take a seat," Alaine motioned for me to sit in one of two chairs positioned next to the bed.

I took a seat and became nervous; my knee bounced restlessly up and down, my hands clasped tightly around each other. Then, the bathroom door opened. My breath hitched as Samuel stepped out. He was almost unrecognizable – clean-shaven and hair neatly pulled back into a tight ponytail. His face was luminous, and much younger. His large, brown eyes gleamed as he looked up and noticed me.

"Emma," he spoke with smile.

"Hi," I replied, nervous as hell.

He took a step and doubled-over, grasping his side. Alaine rushed over and helped him back to the bed.

"Lie down," she ordered, fluffing his pillows.

"You don't need to tend to me, Alaine. I'm more than capable," he insisted.

"Still stubborn, after all these years," Alaine teased, but they both shared a smile. Samuel scooted back up on the bed, while Alaine took a seat next to me. She grabbed my hand and held it tightly.

"Emma, this is Samuel...your father," she replied.

I didn't know what to say. We had already given our salutations twice before, but those times, he was introduced as a friend.

I gazed into his smiling eyes.

"I'm sorry I didn't tell you sooner. I was afraid you wouldn't have believed me," he said in a sorrowful tone.

"Well, you're right about that. I wouldn't have. When we first met, I thought you were just some crazy bum."

Samuel rolled with laughter, and then grabbed his chest and started moaning.

"You'd better take it easy, Samuel. They broke and bruised nearly every one of your ribs," Alaine stated.

"You should call Malachi. He's good at fixing broken ribs," I advised, wondering why they hadn't thought about it.

"And how would you know that?" Alaine questioned. She and Samuel stared intently at me.

"Um, because when I met that Darkling at the airport, I broke a rib and he fixed it."

Alaine gasped, horrified at my statement. "Well, he and Kade failed to mention that part of your trip to me. I'll deal with them later," she fumed.

"Please don't," I begged. "They saved me. Kade warned me not to go into the bathroom, but I was stubborn. I mean... how could I know there were things that wanted to kill me? But he saved me. He kicked that Darkling's ass, while Malachi pulled me out, and healed my ribs. They did their job. They kept me safe. So please don't be mad at them."

Alaine sighed, and turned to Samuel.

"She's a lot like you. Stubborn and strong willed," Samuel chuckled.

"But she's also like you...daring and fearless," she said. "I can't believe we're all here, together. It's like a dream come true."

"It is," Samuel agreed. "This *is* a dream come true."

I felt a little awkward and uncomfortable. They were staring at each other with goo-goo eyes.

Alaine looked young. Like in her mid-twenties, but I knew she was much older. I guess being half-angel slowed the aging process. Samuel looked a little older than her, maybe early thirties, but they were beautiful together. I didn't know how I would fit in, but in my heart I knew I did, somehow.

Alaine took hold of Samuel's hand and sobbed.

"I thought you were dead, Samuel. I thought the Fallen had killed you. Why didn't you come to me?" Tears streamed down her face.

"I'm so sorry, Alaine. I didn't want to put you in more jeopardy than you already were. They took me to be executed on Montem Mortis, the Mount of Death. They severed my wings, and stabbed me through the chest, then pushed me off and left me for dead. But somehow, miraculously, they missed... my heart was still beating. I managed to muster enough strength to pull myself into a cave, where I stayed until I was strong enough to leave. If they knew I was still alive, they would have come, not only for me, but everyone dear to me."

"Well, it was hell and a constant battle anyway. The Midway sent the Guardians when they thought you were dead. They've been watching over me, and saved my life on many occasions. When David died, I moved them to the house," she sobbed.

"I'm sorry about David. I know how much you loved him."

"Yes," she paused, "But you didn't even give me a choice. I could have been with you all those years."

"But I could have never afforded you all of this," he said.

"All of this? The house, the stuff...it means *nothing*. This," she said resting her hand on her heart, "means everything. And it's been broken, ever since I heard of your death."

"I'm so sorry, Alaine," Samuel said, leaning over and pulling her into his embrace.

I stayed still and silent, looking down, giving them their moment.

"Emma," Alaine whispered, after a few minutes.

"Hmmm?" I looked up to both sets of eyes steeled on mine.

"I'm so glad you're here. I thought I'd lost you forever. My heart has known and felt the greatest agony. The loss of a soul mate, and an only child. It is something I would never wish on my worst enemy. But today, you were both were given back to me. A miracle. You have no idea. This *is* a dream come true." Tears streamed from her eyes.

I swallowed hard, trying to release a huge lump that had formed in my throat. I felt for her. We both had lost everything, but were given something in return. Love... and family.

This was the beginning of my new life. A life I never knew existed. A life I really wasn't ready for.

"*Alaine!*" a voice yelled, pounding on the door. There was loud commotion, and lots of shuffling outside the room. Alaine jumped from her seat, grabbed a gun from the dresser, and headed for the door. Samuel jumped from the bed and was at her side in a second.

She swung it open.

Malachi was standing with Caleb limp in his arms, covered in blood. Alaine dropped her gun and cradled him in hers.

"What happened?" she screamed, laying him on the bed. She felt his neck for a pulse.

"They were attacked by the Fallen," he informed. "They know where we are. It's just a matter of time before they find a way in."

"Where are the others?" she asked.

"In the room outside. Battered, but alive."

Alaine quickly checked Caleb's vitals.

"Caleb's alive, but barely," she said trembling, ripping his shirt off. James grabbed the medical bag and ran to assist her.

I quickly made my way to the door. I had to see for myself that Kade was alright. Alexander and Dominic were sitting at the dining table covered in dirt and blood. They looked like they'd just survived another war. But barely.

"Where's Kade?" I asked, scanning the room.

"He went to Midway for help," Malachi answered.

"Midway?"

"The place where Guardians are given assignments. The place

where we came from," Dominic said, pulling a shard of metal from his arm. "Kade wanted to go. It's the only chance we have of survival. Plus, he's the fastest and knows ways of getting there without being detected. Hopefully he'll get back in time with reinforcements."

I stood there, numb, and looked around me.

My world was spiraling out of control.

In one room, Alaine and James were trying to save Caleb's life, while Samuel and Malachi looked on. In another, Dominic and Alexander were tending to their injuries, bloody and weak. Kade was alone, somewhere out there, where rogue Fallen were on a mission of death and destruction. And now, we were trapped and helpless in an underground bunker. There was nowhere to run, and nowhere to hide.

God help us.

A HIDDEN WINGS POEM
BY AMBER MCCALLISTER

Once the light touched me, I unknowingly changed everything
I was loved beyond comprehension
I was cherished to the heights of Heaven
I was treasured by family and strangers alike

Blind to my identity, I lived the life I was given
Love filled my senses
Hope permeated my heart
Happiness ruled my spirit

Darkness overtook me
Love was savagely ripped away
Hope fade into nothingness
Bleak eternity stared me in the face

I could now see what was once hidden
Light amid dark
Hope amid despair
Love amid hate

Beauty among ashes began to take form
On beautiful wings hope came to me

Enveloped by pure and endless passion, it breathed life back into me
I was given a new life - the one I was meant to live

Heart-wrenching battles and fierce struggles came my way
They tore at my heart breaking it into pieces
Yet my hope never failed to put my heart back together again
I was tested for a reason
I was put on trial to see if I was worthy

With more determination than I could ever remember
I walked this path of pain and discovery
My heart guided me – keeping me steady and sure-footed
I had to believe that it would not steer me wrong

When at least an end was in sight, I paused
Unsure if I should let my heart rejoice
The scars I bear will remind me of who I am
The One who cannot escape what is coming

Not without fear, I resolutely accepted my destiny
I transformed into something too beautiful to describe
One teeming with life, love, and purpose
Though my future was too brilliant for me to behold
I knew it was mine and I was forever in its embrace

While my struggles may be over, my heart still longs
Will happiness truly be mine?

Does eternity sing a song of promise or lament of my loss?

My desire burns within me and passion floods my soul

Until the end, I will fight for my hope, my love, my mate

KEEP READING FOR THE
NEXT INSTALLMENT IN
THE HIDDEN WINGS
SERIES!

ANSWERS
LIE IN
UNRAVELING
SECRETS
OF THE
PAST.

DESCENT

A HIDDEN WINGS NOVELLA

FROM BESTSELLING AUTHOR

CAMEO RENAE

ANSWERS
LIE IN
UNRAVELING
SECRETS
OF THE
PAST.

DESCENT

A HIDDEN WINGS NOVELLA

Descent is dedicated to all the READERS who asked to know more
about the characters. After writing this, I've fallen in
love with them even more. Thank you!

I'd also like to thank those who helped me make it shine:
KARLA MATHIS BOSTIC, KIMBERLY ROYALS BELDEN,
HEATHER ADAMS, AND SARAH DAVIS
(my *awesome* publisher). You all are my rock stars!

To ALL THE PAGES THAT HELPED PROMOTE, and to
DERINDA LOVE of Young Adult & Teen Readers, AMBER
GARCIA, and CHRISTY LYNN FOSTER
for helping with its launch.

And last but not least. To my STREET TEAM…for being there for
me, encouraging me, reading, and sharing my stories…
I love you all!

PROLOGUE

L UCIFER. HIS VOICE WAS LIKE the softest of velvet and the sweetest of honey, filling the Heavens with the most glorious melodies. His music reverberated through every cell of your being; filling, lulling, and entrancing you with his song and worship.

Because of this, he was praised by all that surrounded him. But, it would also be that constant praise which allowed pride to seep into the tiniest crevices of his heart. Pride slowly turned to jealousy. Jealousy turned to hate, and it was that hate which began to alter and callous his once pure heart.

As time endured, Lucifer's pride, his jealousy, his hate, and finally his deceit... led to THE FALL.

ONE

SAMUEL'S BEGINNING
SAMUEL

I WAS GIVEN A CHOICE and it was the most difficult, life altering decision one could ever make. Right or wrong. Life or death. Good or evil. At the time, I was so wrapped up in the deception that I didn't realize how much that one choice would throw my whole existence into a spiraling decline. But in the end, it was my decision, and my consequence.

After centuries of war and death, I wished I was given one more chance. A chance to rewind and do it all over again. It should have been an easy decision but my heart was torn.

We were told that if we chose to stay in Heaven we would be bound under the laws of one Supreme Being, and be slaves for all eternity. If we left, we'd be free to do whatever we wanted, whenever we wanted.

Or so I thought. That was the ultimate deception.

I was a young angel. Not young in human years, but young in immortal years, and I still had much to learn. Lucifer was given leadership and authority to train up the younger to become the next worshipers. But, something happened. Something which was never intended. The very one whom God had chosen and saw fit to give charge over a third of his angels, was secretly and deceitfully plotting against him. One by one he turned the hearts and minds of the angels against their creator.

I was one of those third entrusted in his care.

Each one of us had slowly become brainwashed believing the sweet, yet forked tongue of our leader. Why should we have had any cause to doubt him? He was placed in the highest regard by the Almighty himself.

He subliminally and constantly fed us his twisted truths; that we were slaves, and would be for all of eternity; that our very existence was to feed the selfish desires of one almighty being, when we ourselves were all powerful and immortal.

God knew of his treachery, and allowed each immortal to choose. A simple choice. A choice to stay, or to leave with Lucifer.

After each decided, those that chose Lucifer were immediately cast out of Heaven and banished for all eternity.

A third of the angels fell with Lucifer that day, and as we fell our beautiful white wings caught fire and scorched black. Even after the healing they remained black. As dark as the heart of whom we fell with. Changed forever. Just as our entire reason for existence had.

We were now banished to live in the most uninhabitable region existing, the Underworld, which was filled with nothing but sweltering heat and stench. There was no life in this God forsaken place. The ground was parched and sulfur rose from large cracks steaming from the molten lava, which flowed below. This was our new home. Our Hell.

The majority of the first part of the century, after the Fall, was spent tunneling and building an underground empire for us and Lucifer to reside in. It was miles deep, but surprisingly they did come upon a hollow cavern which had water running deep, deep underground. It was much cooler than any other area in the Underworld, so Lucifer claimed the area as his dwelling.

Lucifer's dwelling was built in a way where it was nearly impossible to access, unless you were a member of the Fallen, or given authority. There were five levels of Hell, and each level was guarded by the fiercest, most horrifying creatures imaginable. Lucifer gathered and even birthed some of these creatures from the fiery pit of Hell.

This made it nearly impossible to gain access to him. Anyone who attempted to travel through the levels…failed, and met their demise in the most horrific ways imaginable.

We thought that after the fall, our existence, our life, would have changed for the better. We thought we would be free, and could do as we wished. We were never more wrong.

We now had a new leader. A leader who craved more power and dominion than that of our creator. A leader whose heart turned so dark, so black, and so calloused, which turned us into slaves and warriors fighting a senseless war against our brothers. Those who fell with Lucifer and chose not to abide by his rules were immediately executed. So we did what we needed to, just to stay alive.

For hundreds of years we fought against Heaven's angels. We fought for power. We fought for human souls; we fought for dominion over the earth. We were never free.

Each in authority was given one member to mentor. I was given a young angel named Danyel.

Danyel wasn't much younger than I, but he lacked most of the skills which were necessary to stay alive in battle. I took him under my wing and taught him everything I knew. Skills picked up and mastered, along with knowledge I had gained which kept me alive these past centuries.

Danyel and I were companions, but through the many years of fighting together, he had also become my best friend, and even more so, like a brother to me. We fought side by side, defeating and accomplishing every task given to us, and had become a force to reckon with.

For centuries we fought, but began to wonder what it was all for. Hundreds of angels died, and for what?

Power?

But we kept our conversations to ourselves. Never letting them linger for fear of being executed. So, we continued to fight the senseless war hoping that one day it would all end, and we could finally find some peace.

But it wasn't peace that finally found me. It was something much greater. Something I never expected or anticipated. I found happiness for the first time in a very long time, and that was the day I met Alaine.

The Fallen were given permission to roam the mortal world freely, but I despised it almost as much as the Underworld. Most humans in my eyes were but mere cockroaches, scattering about with no real purpose. I, and the rest of the Angels, questioned why God had chosen to create them. They were just another flawed creation. Most of their leaders were evil and deceptive, and the majority of the populations followed like sheep being led to slaughter.

I had waited, anticipating the day I would witness their destruction. But, as the cockroaches, they somehow managed to survive.

Lucian, one of Lucifer's closest allies, was given charge over all his affairs. He was nearly as old as Lucifer and was powerful, ruthless, and had no problem dealing death to all he felt worthy... or even unworthy.

He was swift to carry out executions and handed mercy to none. But slowly, as the years passed, and just as Lucifer...Lucian's heart began to grow dark and cold.

Because of Lucian's high ranking position, pride slowly began to seep into his heart. Pride eventually turned to jealousy, and jealousy into hate. And it was that hate which began to build a wedge of disloyalty, distrust, and betrayal between him and Lucifer.

Finally, one unsuspecting day, Lucian stood up to Lucifer and blasphemed him. He abandoned the Underworld, taking hundreds of Fallen with him. Fallen whose loyalties had now turned towards Lucian.

But, I also remember the look in Lucifer's eyes as they blazed with fire. Blazed with a deep seeded hatred and revenge. I knew, deep inside, that he would not allow Lucian to get away with such treacheries, but he surprised us all when he let him leave. Alive.

We all knew it wouldn't be long before Lucifer would have his revenge.

But, let's back up just a bit...to my beginning.

My name is Samuel, and I was born a Pureblood Angel. My father and mother still reside in Heaven, and I...well, it's obvious that I had chosen to become one of the Fallen.

It has been a few centuries since the Fall, and over that long course of time I had become a fully trained and high ranking warrior in the Fallen's army. My days and nights are mostly spent in very remote areas within the mortal world. I hate the Underworld. Most of the Fallen choose to stay there, because Lucifer keeps them well stocked with food and strong drink, but I can never handle the smell or the heat.

Most of the Fallen stay away from the mortal world, unless they are called, because of its many temptations, and their hatred for the cockroaches.

What does God see in them anyway?

He should have destroyed them in the beginning, the day they fell in the Garden.

He should have destroyed us all.

There was one law. One binding law for both Angels and Fallen alike. None were to mate with the mortals. If they did and were caught, they would immediately be executed. If the mortal female became impregnated, they would also be hunted and killed.

There were always those few Fallen who willingly chose to defy the law, and some who didn't get caught. Thus, the Nephilim were born. Halfbreed children born to mortal mothers and immortal fathers. Because they were half immortal, each Nephilim was born with a gift, released on their eighteenth birthday. Until the transformation, they were completely human. But after, they became part of the immortal world, and easier to track because of their scent. Angels have a sweet unique scent that they use to identify each other. The Fallen had the same scent but it had a strong smoky smell along with it.

Most Nephilim children had no knowledge of who or what they really were, and didn't understand the transformation. When their gift came, some abused it, but most kept it secret. Even that didn't work, because most were found and executed by Lucian and his league of Fallen.

TWO

ALAINE'S BEGINNING

I T WAS A BRIGHT MOONLIT night as Jane Wilder sat near the river, just down from her new home, dreaming up ways of how she'd like to spend her twenty-first birthday. This was her new favorite spot to escape from the rest of the world, breathe the fresh air, and relax under the canopy of the moon and stars.

She'd just finished the tedious task of unpacking, having recently moved from the city to her new home out in the Oregon country. It wasn't too far from the rest of civilization, but far enough to seem distant, which was ideal for her.

Jane twisted a ribbon in her silky brown hair, letting it fall behind her. She closed her chocolate brown eyes, and let all other senses take over. The sound of the rushing water and the air stirring through the tall grass made her muscles loosen, and the stresses melt away. The cool night breeze blew gently, kissing her delicate skin, sending a shiver through her.

She took in a breath of the fresh, crisp air, and smelled the many fragrances of wild flowers surrounding her, and then gently lay back into a blanket of tall, feathery grass. She almost fell asleep, when the breezes picked up and delivered a chilly gust. It woke her just enough to hear a rustling in the grass behind her.

Jane slowly peeled her eyes open and saw a bright golden light appear out of nowhere. She gasped and immediately sat up, and then her breath seized as she turned around to witness an amazing sight. She thought she was dreaming, for behind her, stood the most beautiful stranger. She swore she saw white wings fold behind him, but when she blinked again...they were gone. She must have been hallucinating.

He was tall and muscular; his body, perfectly proportioned. His golden hair fell like waves of silk down his shoulders. His skin glowed in a golden haze around him. His eyes were dark brown, but had a golden ring around them. His features were strong and sharp, and looked as if they were chiseled by God himself. He was too perfect. A masterpiece, and much too beautiful to be human.

Jane's immediate emotion was fear, but the longer she gazed into his eyes, an overwhelming sense of tranquility washed over her. A sense of knowing that she was safe with him, even though she had no clue who he was. His presence was like a warm blanket, enveloping her, wrapping her in a wonderful, seductive magic.

He stepped forward, slowly holding his hand out to her, and she didn't hesitate. Jane automatically stood to her feet and stepped toward him. As soon as she took hold of his hand, the world around her melted away.

She was lost, in complete and total ecstasy. His breathe, his smell, his touch, completely intoxicated her. She was drunk with his presence, dizzy, but yet every part of her was alive and tingled in excitement.

The ethereal visitor laid her down in the grass. He knew it was against the law, but the attraction to this mortal was too much for him to withhold. He was taken by her, and Jane was completely taken by him, both having never experienced such feelings before.

That night the stranger romanced her by the river. His touch melted every part of her body. His breath made her world spin. His kiss was unyielding, hot and deep, sending electricity buzzing through her entire body.

She would have never given in so fast to lustful desires. Never. It wasn't like her. But, there was something so magnetizing about him that she could not resist.

The next morning, the bright sun greeted Jane's tired eyes. She was alone, still lying down by the river, her mind still lost in a fog. She wondered how she could still be there, but as sure as the river flowed, it all came rushing back to her.

The stranger.

The lust.

The unimaginable things they did out in the open.

Her clothes were still on, and for a moment she wondered if it was all just a dream. But there was something that seemed so real.

His face. She couldn't shake the face of the stranger, which was now imbedded, into her memory. A beautiful face with no name.

She closed her eyes and as she did, she suddenly felt dizzy and nauseous.

She headed back to the house, and decided to lay down for a bit, thinking it was just a passing feeling. Maybe it was just the beginning of a cold. But those feelings only grew worse.

Jane didn't tell anyone about her one-night stand with the stranger, because no one would believe her anyway. Having a one-night stand was something she was completely against, and besides, she didn't want anyone to know, especially her parents, who were esteemed members of their church.

A few weeks passed and Jane's symptoms became worse. She learned that whatever happened down by the river was definitely not a dream, and that the beautiful stranger had left her with a gift. An unwelcomed gift.

Jane was pregnant.

But what Jane didn't realize what that this gift was from an immortal. A Pureblooded Angel, and it was his seed that grew quickly within her womb. Her child would be a Nephilim. A Halfbreed. Half human and half angel, and right now, these were dangerous times to be in.

There were different jobs for each Angel. Some were worshipers, some warriors, some Guardians. Most of the Guardians were sent to a place called the Midway.

The Midway was a point resting just between Heaven and Earth. A place where Heaven dispatched Guardian Angels out on specific assignments, and where Guardians were transported through portholes which would open up into different locations all over the earth; points of entry which would take them closest to their commissions.

It was necessary for the Guardians to use the portholes because they didn't have wings. They were to blend in with the mortal society, and remain hidden from those they were guarding. But sometimes, human contact was necessary, as was the case with Jane.

One specific Guardian was sent to Jane, but this Guardian was not sent from the Midway. She was sent from Jane's admirer, on a very secretive assignment. None knew of her assignment, except one, her mate. But he also didn't know the details.

The Guardian's name was Khelsey, one of a handful of female Guardians. She was breathtakingly beautiful, and stood around six feet tall. She was lean, toned, and had the silkiest golden hair which fell down her back. Her eyes sparkled like the brightest sapphires.

But Khelsey wasn't only beautiful, she was a skilled warrior, and could fight right alongside the best of her male counterparts. Her assignment was to watch and protect Jane while she carried the Nephilim child, and to give her comfort.

A few select others were sent out on a mission to find the most desirable and deserving home for the child to be raised, and not a single word was to be breathed about the birth, because it would put Jane and her child in grave danger.

You see, it is law in both Heaven and Hell, which states that all Angels are to mate solely with those of their kind. Purebloods.

Mating with mortals was strictly forbidden, and cause for immediate execution.

There was an evil order of Fallen Angels who despised the Nephilim.

So, it was imperative that Jane remained hidden.

Jane told her family and friends that she was taking an extended vacation, and would be in a remote area where she would not be in contact with them for a few months. They believed her because Jane loved to be away from the hustle and bustle of the city life. Ever since she was little, the woods or places of quiet and solitude were her sanctuary.

Khelsey escorted Jane to a secret location set up by Jane's mysterious one-night stand. It was a cabin hidden deep within a wooded forest where they would stay for the next eight weeks. The inside of the cabin was beautiful, and all open except for the bathroom. The furnishings were very pricy, and done in earth tones. The bed was a large queen-size and was very comfortable. Khelsey had a comfortable extra-long twin at the other end of the room. She needed to be close, just in case of an emergency. The kitchen was well stocked with everything they would need for the upcoming weeks ahead.

It was much more beautiful than Jane's normal home, and much more luxurious. Her benefactor must have been very wealthy.

Khelsey and Jane quickly became close companions. They spent many hours talking about life, and how completely different their two worlds were. But Jane didn't hear more than she needed to. She was still clueless about the stranger who came to her that night. All she knew was that he was an immortal, and probably ranked somewhere high in the hierarchy. That's why he had to remain secret.

Khelsey learned a lot about her new mortal friend, and felt a deep compassion, knowing the difficult course which lay ahead for her. She knew she would have to give up the child who grew within her womb, and not by choice. It was a necessity to keep it alive.

Jane cried a lot, and it was difficult for Khelsey to try and console her. Mortal females were very emotional during pregnancy, and Khelsey found herself put in an uncomfortable position when Jane hammered her for questions about the baby's father. But Khelsey was sworn to silence and didn't break her vow.

Jane knew that the child in her belly was a Halfbreed, and she wasn't prepared for what was to come. The child grew at an astounding rate, and within two months she was already at full term and ready to give birth.

As time drew closer to the delivery, a midwife was sent along with one assistant. The assistant was the one who would escort the child to its new family immediately after the birth.

The inside of the cabin was carefully sterilized, and everyone was prepared for the birthing. It was a cold September night and the moon was full. The wind whistled through the cracks in the windows making the cabin seem a bit eerie.

Jane lay on her bed, while the midwife wiped the sweat from her brow.

"You can do it Jane. Push!" the midwife said, lifting her forward.

Jane moaned loudly and pushed with all her might, and then fell back exhausted onto her pillow.

"Jane. You're strong. I know you can do this. You'll just have to push a little longer," Khelsey urged, holding tightly to one of her hands.

Jane strained as she pushed again, screaming to release the child. After an hour of hard labor, the baby was finally born.

"It's a girl," the midwife announced. She held the child, wrapped tightly in a blanket, out to her.

"Oh, she's beautiful, Jane," Khelsey gasped. She stood and caught a glimpse of the child's beautiful porcelain face, rosy cheeks, and bright red lips. Her hair was a soft brown.

"Would you like to hold her, to say your last good-bye?" the midwife asked Jane.

Jane closed her eyes, and shook her head. She turned her back to the midwife and the room immediately filled with her sobs. Khelsey rushed back to her side to try and comfort her, but nothing at this moment would be able to console her breaking heart.

Jane knew she couldn't bear to look into the eyes of the child she couldn't keep. The child she could never speak of. The child she carried in her womb over these past months, and would soon be taken away from her, never to be seen or heard of again.

The child had to be taken from her and hidden away so that they both could live, especially with the dark and evil powers lurking about.

The midwife glanced at Khelsey.

"It's alright. Go ahead and take the child," Khelsey said softly to the midwife.

The midwife carefully handed the beautiful baby girl to her assistant, who wrapped another warm blanket around the child. She turned, nodded at Khelsey, and then disappeared into the night.

It was over.

The child was gone, and Jane would have to come to terms with what had happened. She would have to keep reminding herself that her child was going to live a wonderful life, a safe life, but also a life of never knowing who her real mother was and of her true descent.

A thundering boom shook the cabin and a horrible stench began to consume the air.

"Damn it!" Khelsey immediately knew what was happening. She jumped up and reached for her weapon, her trusted sword. The same sword she'd used throughout many battles. It had become a part of her, moving as fluently as one of her own limbs.

It was a gift, given by her father who was a highly respected warrior in the Angel's army. When he noticed how naturally his daughter fought and defended those she loved, he had the sword created and fashioned specifically for her.

Khelsey was one of the best of her kind, and thus, the reason she was assigned to this particular mission. She was sent to protect Jane and her baby, and would defend them at all costs.

Khelsey knew what stalked them outside was very evil. An evil she hated, despised, and had fought against many times before. This evil had come for one purpose and one purpose alone. To kill Jane and her newborn child.

"Shhhhhh," Khelsey whispered, placing her finger over her mouth as she headed for the window. A dark shadow passed across it and she froze. She made a motion to the midwife, who quickly turned off all the lights. "Take Jane out the back. There should be another Guardian waiting. They'll need to take to the air, because the Darkling are out there."

The midwife nodded. She already knew what to do. She and her assistant were also immortals. Angels in disguise within the mortal world. She ran over to Jane and threw a blanket around her.

"We need to leave, dear," she urged.

"What's out there?" Jane whispered, wiping her tears, and instantly pulling herself from her sorrow.

"Darkling," the midwife answered.

"Darkling?"

"Yes, a terrible evil sent to kill you. We must leave at once," she urged.

Jane's heart began to hammer against her chest. Her breath quickened, and she suddenly felt faint.

The midwife took hold of her and led her quickly and quietly to a chair at the back of the room. She pushed the chair off of a circular rug, and then kicked the rug away. Under it was a secret trap door. She quickly yanked it open and urged Jane to get in.

"Is it safe?" Jane whispered, her eyes wide with terror, staring into the darkness below.

The midwife shrugged, "I don't know, but there are Watchers and a Guardian outside who will help us. Khelsey will give us time, but we have to move now."

Jane glanced over to Khelsey with a deep look of concern.

"Are you going to be okay?"

Khelsey nodded. "Don't worry. I've got your back."

"Thank you," Jane whispered.

Khelsey nodded. "Take care of yourself, Jane," she responded with a smile.

Jane nodded, and the midwife nudged her.

Jane jumped down into the dark hole first, and then the midwife followed right behind her. As soon as they were gone Khelsey ran over, shut and locked the hatch, and quickly covered it over with the rug and the chair. She then made her way back toward the door.

Footsteps scuffled around outside. Khelsey quietly stepped toward the window to catch a glimpse. The stench of the Darkling seeped right through every crack, burning her nostrils. It was a smell of death and rot she could never get used to. She grasped her sword, hoping there were only a few. She'd managed to slay a few on her own, but right now, the main thing was to keep them away from Jane as long as possible, and hopefully to kill them all in the process.

Khelsey had no fear. She was used to battle, and this was just another one. The only difference was that this time she was alone. She usually had a partner.

Loud steps pounded letting her know they were right outside.

BAM!!!

They struck the door.

She knew they could kick it in with no problem, so she stood to the side and gripped her sword tightly.

BAM!!!

Suddenly, the door came flying right off the hinges crashing into the back wall.

A Darkling rushed in, and as it took a second step into the room, Khelsey swung her sword and removed his head. It came down with a thud, and rolled across the floor. Thick tar-like blood splattered everywhere. Two more charged in, bigger than the last. They must have sent the smaller one first, knowing it would be a casualty of war.

The second Darkling was over six feet tall and muscular. Its head was huge and its arms were bulging with muscles. Its eyes were black and evil, its razor sharp teeth were bared and dripping with hate. Its pasty white face sniffed the air, and his eyes snapped to Khelsey as he caught her scent.

Khelsey held her ground as the Darkling charged. She swung her sword and sliced his arm, but he continued and struck her chest with a great force. She flew backward crashing hard onto the ground. She struggled for breath as it charged at her again. It leapt into the air, a small dagger targeted at her heart.

It dropped, about to land on her chest, but at the last second she twisted sideways, and the blade plunged into the floor, missing her by inches.

The third Darkling was the largest and most grotesque. Its face was hideously disfigured, like it had been bashed in, sliced, and burned during previous battles. One eye hung halfway down its face and was a whitish color. But its body was massive and bulging with unnatural muscles and huge veins which were on the verge of exploding.

It went around sniffing the room, trying to catch the scent of the others. It stopped at the chair, hunched over, and let out a beastly laugh as it pushed the chair away. It found their scent, and Khelsey knew she needed to divert its attention. It was much too soon.

She kicked away from the Darkling who struggled to release its blade from the floor, and jumped up, charging at the third Darkling. She swung her sword, but it dodged the blade with ease, and kicked her in her gut sending her sailing backward. This time the bed caught her fall.

The third Darkling roared. "They've escaped! Go out back."

The second stood and nodded.

Khelsey had fought many Darkling before, but these seemed like a different breed. They were a lot bigger, stronger, and a bit smarter than the others she'd come across during her years of contact with them.

As the second Darkling started for the door, Khelsey aimed and threw her sword at it. Her aim was precise, and before the Darkling had a chance to step out the door, her blade swiftly took its head off. Its eyes were still wide open with confusion as its head rolled out the door, and its body dropped to the ground with a thud.

The last Darkling snarled, deep and terrifying, and then withdrew a weapon hidden within its chest. It was a longer curved dagger, and its razor sharp blade gleamed in the darkness, seeking its next victim.

Khelsey knew she didn't have a chance without her sword. It was much too far from her reach, and even if she tried to make a dash for it, the Darkling was much closer.

Its eyes were locked on its target, dark and dangerous, and filled with hate as it made its way toward her. But Khelsey showed no fear. She jumped up and ran to meet him head on, in hope that she could knock his weapon free.

But the Darkling was much too strong. It reached out with its long arm, and wrapped its fingers around her throat, and flung her across the room like a rag doll. She hit the wall with such great force that it cracked the side of the cabin, making the wood split and splinters fly everywhere.

Khelsey gasped, trying to catch her breath, but before she could get up the Darkling knocked her back again, and straddled her. She fought the monster with all her might, but its weight and strength pinned her down tight. There was nothing she could do to get it off, but she still continuously fought with whatever strength she had left within her.

The evil monster atop her showed no mercy. It bashed and slammed her repeatedly with its huge fists, until she was barely conscious. She was helpless against this creature, and knew that her time was coming to an end. But even then, she glared at the creature and spat in its face. The Darkling laughed and placed the sharp blade to her throat.

"You will die in vain. We will kill the girl and the abomination."

"GO. TO. HELL!" Khelsey yelled.

She then shut her eyes and frantically searched for her one true love, for his face in the recesses of her mind. She wanted to find him, and have his beautiful smile and his face, be the last thing she saw before she passed. She found his face, and in the midst of the horror...she smiled.

"Too late," it snarled.

Those were the Darkling's last words. The last words Khelsey would ever hear. She then felt pressure of the blade, as the Darkling pressed it to her throat and sliced.

THREE

ESCAPING DANGER

"GO! QUICKLY!" THE MIDWIFE URGED, as she pushed Jane through the darkness. They could hear Khelsey battling with the Darkling above, and knew the creatures had made it inside. They needed to hurry before they found out where they had escaped.

On hands and knees they scurried toward a dim exit light. The ground was soggy from the rain that had fallen over the past couple of days. The air was stagnant and smelled of mold and earth. Jane winced as her hands sunk into conditions she couldn't let her mind rest on. Cobwebs caught her face, but she pushed through and kept on. She knew she had to pull herself together if she wanted to live.

She crawled as quickly as she could, not knowing what waited for them on the outside.

A few feet before the exit, the midwife flew forward grabbing Jane's mouth to keep her from screaming, and then quickly pulled her to the side behind a plank.

"Shhhhhh," she whispered into Jane's ear.

Terrified, Jane's eyes widened with fear, and focused on the exit. A strong foul odor, which they encountered in the house, began to permeate the area, burning their eyes and nostrils. Suddenly, a pale white face appeared at the exit. It was sniffing the air, and they heard a loud rumbling in its throat.

Darkling.

Jane gasped at the horror. Eyes as black as the night searched the darkness and a horrifying growl resounded as its face locked onto them.

What Jane didn't know, was that the Darkling had exceptional night vision. She wanted to scream, but she was frozen with fear. In one swift movement, the midwife pushed her out of the way, and lunged toward the creature, knocking it backwards away from the exit.

"Run, Jane!" she screamed, as they tumbled into the woods.

Jane was frozen with fear, but quickly pulled the pieces of herself together and dashed through the exit. As soon as she abandoned the dark confines beneath the cottage, something flew at her. She dove out of the way as a body collided into the side of the house, landing with a thud a few feet from her.

Her heart hammered against her chest, her pulse raced, and her eyes snapped open, wide with fright.

Something moved in the distance, and she watched as the midwife rose to her feet wearing a large smile and a look of satisfaction on her face.

Jane glanced back at the body lying next to her, unconscious. It was the Darkling.

A tall, dark haired man came out of the woods and stood behind the midwife. He was handsome, and tall, with dark features and dark brown hair.

He started walking toward Jane, offering his hand. "I'm here to take you to safety, Jane." His voice was low and kind. Jane started to move toward him, and just as she took a few steps, the midwife screamed and started running toward them.

Suddenly, there was a swishing sound, and just as Jane blinked, an arrow plunged through the middle of the man's chest.

The midwife wailed, running over to him. She must have known him because she threw her body over his and wept.

"JANE, RUN!" The midwife turned to Jane, as tears flowed down her face. Another arrow whizzed past her head and stuck into the side of a tree.

Jane ran aimlessly into the dark woods, terrified, not having a clue of where she was headed. The woods were ominous and she was panic-stricken, thinking of what she might encounter behind any one of the trees in the dark forest. She swore she could hear something behind her, but she kept on, never turning back, running as fast as her feet could carry her.

The ground was still wet, and it was too late before she noticed a sharp moss covered rock jetting out from the ground. She tripped over it and flew forward, hitting the ground.

Jane struggled to get back to her feet when she was snatched and whisked upward into the air. She screamed and struggled, but her captor held her tightly in his arms, and took off, soaring high into the dark vast sky.

After a few moments, Jane gave in. She was much too high in the air to keep struggling.

"Are you finished?" a low voice questioned. "I'm not going to hurt you. I'm here to help you." The voice sounded vaguely familiar, and warmth suddenly wrapped around her. A warmth she'd felt only once before in her life.

Her captor gently turned her, cradling her in his arms. Jane froze as she came face to face with the man who haunted her dreams. The face she saw every time she closed her eyes. The mysterious stranger who was the father of her child.

He flew higher and higher into the air making Jane's stomach twist.

"Who are you?" Jane asked, staring at his beautiful face. His eyes kept focused into the darkness.

"Yesterday, I was your lover. Today, I am your savior," he said with a sad sort of grin. "I'm sorry I've put you in so much danger. I didn't mean for this to happen to you, but I have vowed, as long as I have breath, to make certain of your safety and the safety of our child."

"I know what you are," Jane said.

"Does it frighten you?"

"No. You don't frighten me. Khelsey told me that you are a compassionate, chivalrous, chieftain of sorts. But I have one question."

"I hope it is a question I can answer," he said.

"Why did you come to me? That night by the river?" she asked.

His brow creased and his eyes pondered.

"I noticed you. There was never another mortal, in all of my many years, which I have taken notice of. My emotions became fragile and unprotected, the first time I laid my eyes on you.

You were alone down by the river, only a few days earlier. You were lying in the grass as I passed over. You looked as if you were asleep, but it was your beauty that drew me closer. It drew me in, like a moth to a flame. A forbidden desire with a deadly consequence. But I couldn't resist.

I came to you that night with intentions of only speaking with you. But the moment we made contact, I became a victim under your spell. Never, in all of my years, have I felt such closeness to another."

Jane was speechless, because the feelings he was describing, was the same she felt. She never believed in love at first sight, but there was something about him that was entrancing, magical. A feeling that made her want to be with him, even now, as he held her so close.

"You didn't tell me your name," she said.

It's best for you and the child that it stays that way."

"Why? I don't understand why this is all happening," Jane said, getting very emotional. Her eyes filled with tears.

"None of this was supposed to happen, Jane. It's my fault and I take full responsibility. That's why I sent Khelsey to you, and the others. The child will be well taken care of, and always under my watchful eye."

Jane exhaled and nodded. There wasn't much more she could do. She was at his mercy now if she wanted to live.

"Where are you taking me?"

"Somewhere safe, where evil cannot find you. And, right now, the further you are from the child, the better."

Jane wrapped her arms around his neck as he flew her far and away to safety.

Jane was kept safe for a few years, and when certain she was clear from being hunted, she never saw, or heard of, her beautiful stranger again.

Eventually, she married a mortal man, and together they had a beautiful daughter. But Jane never forgot of her first child. She was always on her mind and in her heart.

FOUR

SPECIAL DELIVERY

I T WAS UNDER THE COVER of darkness and with the help of
the Watchers, that Jane's newborn child could be delivered
safely during the middle of the night. The midwife's assistant,
also an immortal, took extra precautions to make sure they weren't
followed.

They didn't travel far, and ended up in another small town in
Oregon, with a family who was privately seeking to adopt a child. It
was a young couple, thoroughly investigated, and approved worthy
for the adoption. They were the most perfect candidates for this
precious gift, and anxiously awaited the arrival of their new addition.

The transaction was made between private parties, and the
paperwork had already been approved. It was fairly easy for
immortals to manipulate the simple minded humans.

It was 1:11 on that cold September 20th, morning. The doorbell rang on 2121 Serendipity Drive, waking its inhabitants.

Mrs. Gray nudged her husband and fell back to sleep. She assumed it must have been their senile neighbor on her constant search for her stray cat.

Mr. Gray stumbled down the stairs in his robe. His dirty blonde hair was disheveled, and his eyes were heavy with sleep. But as soon as he opened the door, and the assistant placed the tiny bundle into his arms, his sapphire eyes popped open, and a large smile grew on his lips. He was silent for a few moments, staring at the beautiful child sleeping in the comfort of his arms.

Mr. Gray gaped at the assistant.

"Would you like to come inside?" he asked, but his eyes shifted back to the baby.

"I'm sorry, Mr. Gray, but I really must be going. I have another deadline to attend to," she replied.

"Is...Is this?" he asked, stuttering, glancing up to the deliverer and back down to the sleeping baby.

"It's a girl, Mr. Gray. And, congratulations," she said with a smile and a nod. "Please give my congratulations to Mrs. Gray as well. The paperwork is already in order. All we ask is that you take great care of her."

"Oh, we will. And, thank you, Miss...?" he paused, reaching his hand out to shake hers.

"Abigail. Abigail Reed," she said, shaking his hand.

"Thank you, Miss Reed," he said.

She smiled, knowing that the child would be in the best possible care with the Gray's. Then she gave him a nod, and left.

Mr. Gray quietly shut the door behind him. Butterflies turned in his stomach. He wanted to scream and wake his wife, but he didn't want to wake the baby. His excitement bubbled over as he started up the stairs to their bedroom.

As soon as he entered the room he flicked on the light.

"Sam. Get up," he whispered loudly.

"Jared, please turn the light off," his wife grumbled, pulling the pillow over her head.

"Sam, get up," he urged in a quiet tone. She moaned. "Samantha. I reeeeeally need for you to open your eyes right now. I have the most amazing surprise for you."

Samantha pushed the pillow off her face and peeled her heavy eyes open. As soon as she saw the bundle cradled in her husband's arms, she shot up. Her brown eyes grew wide and she gasped, throwing both of her hands over her mouth.

Her husband nodded, and tears immediately began to flow from her eyes.

She pushed off the bed and hurried over to them. Jared pushed back a little piece of fabric, which was covering the precious tiny face. She looked like a little doll. Her porcelain white skin was so smooth, and she had the longest eyelashes, and the softest brown hair. Her lips and cheeks were lightly dusted in pink.

"Samantha. Meet your daughter," Jared said, placing the baby in her arms.

She lovingly cradled the child in her arms, and then leaned down and gently pressed her lips to her tiny forehead.

"Welcome home, our sweet Alaine," she whispered quietly. "You will never be without love in this home." She then turned to her husband and smiled, and he wrapped his arms around his new family.

"Alaine Gray," he whispered. "That has a really nice ring to it."

FIVE

GROWING UP

LAINE GREW UP IN A loving home. Her parents treated her as if she was their own, and she never went without anything. They vowed never to keep secrets from her, and when she was old enough, they told her that she was adopted. But that never really mattered in the Gray household. There were always more than enough hugs, kisses, laughter, and a fair share of discipline to go around.

But there was one major detail that her parents were unaware of, and that was just how different Alaine really was. Different because half of the blood which flowed through her veins was that of an immortal - a Pureblood Angel.

Alaine would continue to live a normal mortal life until she reached the age of eighteen.

When a Nephilim child reaches eighteen, a transformation occurs. A change deep within which awakens the immortal part of their being. The part which was lying dormant, and as it awakens, it bestows a special gift unto its host.

Each gift was rare and unique to the Nephilim it was given, and also different from those of the Angels. Angels are very powerful and have certain kinds of magic, but some of the Nephilim powers were known to supersede those of their pureblooded fathers. This was because each Nephilim possessed only one great power or magic, and one alone, which magnified its ability.

The day before Alaine's eighteenth birthday was as normal as any other day. Her friends were planning a party after school the next day to celebrate, and all the way home, she was excited. This would be her first party away from her parents, and one that they approved of.

"Hey mom," she called out, dropping her books on the kitchen table.

"Hi sweetheart," Mrs. Gray chimed. She walked over and gave Alaine a hug. "How was school?"

"Boring as usual," Alaine huffed.

"Well, go get changed and do your homework, while I finish cooking," she said, scooting her off upstairs.

As soon as Alaine opened the door to her bedroom and stepped inside, she sensed something was different. An unfamiliar but sweet fragrance enveloped her. It was a scent she had never smelled before, but the more she inhaled it, the more it made her feel calm and happy, and a sense of peace buzzed within her. It was the strangest, most wonderful feeling.

She then noticed a tiny golden box sitting on top of her pillow. She walked over to it and held it in her hand. The same scent that had permeated the room strongly perfumed the box. Alaine carefully pulled open the cover, and her eyes sparkled as she saw the beautiful gift inside. A necklace. A delicate golden chain which held a teardrop shaped stone pendant. It was reddish with tiny veins of yellow and green running through it.

"Mom?" Alaine called downstairs.

"Yes?" she answered.

"Thank you for the beautiful necklace!"

There was silence for a few moments, and then Alaine heard her mom's footsteps prancing up the stairs.

"What necklace?" she questioned, peeking her head into the room.

"This necklace," Alaine said, holding it up. "It's beautiful. Thank you so much!"

Mrs. Gray shook her head, her brow crinkled in confusion. "Honey, I didn't give you that necklace. Where did you get it?"

"It was sitting on top of my pillow. Are you sure you didn't—?" Alaine asked again, thinking her mom was joking, but the look on her face clearly stated that this was definitely not a joke. She was positively baffled. "Well, do you know who gave it to me?"

"I'm not sure, and am almost certain your father didn't get it for you. And there haven't been any visitors today. I'd know because I didn't leave the house all day," Mrs. Gray noted. "It is a beautiful necklace. I've never seen anything like it. Well, maybe your father did get it for you, and wanted to surprise you. Sometimes he can be sneaky. We'll ask him when he gets home."

Alaine nodded and smiled as her mom gave her a kiss on the head, and then sauntered back down the stairs to finish dinner.

She sat at the edge of the bed and held the box in her fingers, examining it, wondering if there was anything that would give away its benefactor. She pulled out the small cushion from which the necklace rested, and her stomach twisted at the sight of a delicate golden-flaked paper, folded exactly to fit at the bottom of the box. She carefully removed it and as she did, the same sweet scent began to waft from it as she began to unfold, what looked like a letter.

It was handwritten in the most beautiful cursive she'd ever seen. Her stomach twisted with excitement and apprehension as she read the first three words.

My dearest Alaine,

I am so sorry that I have never had the pleasure of meeting my beautiful daughter in person. Please know this. I have always kept a watchful eye over you. Now that you will become eighteen, I wanted to present you with this gift. It is a small token of my love, on the day before your transformation.

Do not be afraid of your gift, and as much possible, keep it secret. Human minds will never be able to comprehend it, and human hearts will be envious. One day, I will send someone to explain, but until then, remain steadfast to your own heart and discernments. They will, at most times, steer you in the right direction.

The adornment is a Bloodstone of Christ, one of the rarest and most sacred of all amulets known to both men and Angels. This stone will give its wearer protection, power, and health. Wear it always my daughter, for there are many evils that abound in your world.

There is a small mark on the back of your neck, which is the mark of your descent. Keep it hidden, especially from those who ask. Knowledge of this mark could lead to death.

My wish is that fate will one day bring us together, for it has been a weighted burden upon my heart. There are many troubling and perplexing circumstances which have kept the distance between us, but always know this... I love you, and have always loved you, my beautiful Alaine.

Keep safe,

Your Father

Alaine sat on the edge of her bed and read the letter over and over countless times, to the point that it became embedded within her heart and mind. It was so simple, yet filled with so many complexities.

Her fingers brushed the back of her neck in search of the mark he spoke of. She wondered why a mark of descent could lead to death, but she couldn't question something she could never find answers to. Her mother mentioned a strange birthmark there, but it was very small, and easily concealed by her hair, so she'd never given it a second thought. Now, she would be sure to keep it secret.

Why, after all of these years had her real father chosen to make contact with her?

How could he have known where she lived or knew her name, without any type of contact? But the biggest question that reeled in her mind was that of the transformation. What kind of transformation? This one question would drive her crazy with wonder.

Alaine loved the Gray's with all of her heart. They raised her like she was one of their own, and she trusted them completely. But there was a feeling, deep inside of her, which was telling her that she shouldn't share the contents of this letter with them. That this letter was to remain a secret between her and her blood father, whoever he was.

Plus, Alaine knew her mother well. She knew if she let her mom read the letter, she would freak out, and cops would probably be involved. That was something Alaine didn't want to deal with, especially on her eighteenth birthday.

Up until this moment, her birth parents were merely a passing thought. Alaine did wonder who they were, and what they looked like, but her thoughts never lingered because of the love the Gray's had given her. But now, after reading this letter, they would be all she could think of.

When Mr. Gray came home that evening, he confirmed the necklace wasn't from him, and assumed it was from one of her friends. Alaine nodded in agreement, although she already knew the truth.

That night she locked her windows tight, and pulled the curtains shut. She wasn't sure if her father had actually delivered the box himself, or if someone else delivered it for him. But, the thought of someone entering her room, without her permission, made her feel uneasy.

Alaine tossed and turned and sleep did not find her easy that last night before her eighteenth birthday. Questions bombarded her mind. Questions she had no answers to, or how to find them.

She took the delicate necklace from the box, and held it in the palm of her hand, staring at the stone as if something magical were to happen. She wondered if it was, in fact, a real Bloodstone. An amulet of power and protection from the days of Christ.

She closed her hand over it, and as she did she felt warmth encompass her. Her muscles loosened, her brain became numb, and her eyes became heavy. In a matter of minutes, she fell fast asleep.

The next day was just as normal as any other, and she didn't feel any different. Alaine got dressed, ate breakfast, went to school, came home, and quickly finished her homework. Throughout the entire day, her mind would not let her rest, and kept her wondering about the mysterious letter and her even more mysterious birth father.

Her best friend Jessica had planned a small birthday party at her house, so Alaine dashed up to her room to change. She finally decided on a pair of new blue jeans, a white t-shirt, and a black long-sleeved sweater.

She stared at her reflection in the mirror as she brushed her long, silky, brown hair, and wondered if she looked anything like her birth parents. Alaine was stunning. Her dark features accentuated her flawless porcelain skin, and long lashes framed her beautiful chocolate-brown eyes.

"Alaine! Jessica is here!" Mrs. Gray called upstairs, popping her from her thoughts.

It was 7:00pm on a Friday night, when Alaine jumped into Jessica's car and headed to her house to celebrate her eighteenth birthday party. The town they lived in was very small, and their school was private, so there weren't many who attended. It was just a few friends, some food and drinks, clusters of balloons with streamers, and a homemade cake baked by Jessica herself.

There were exactly twelve in attendance, and of the twelve were four boys. None of which were boyfriend material. One of them was Jessica's cousin Wesley, and the other three were his friends... geeky, band boys who looked awkward just standing.

The party helped keep Alaine's mind occupied. She wanted to share her letter with someone, but the warning kept her from doing it. She knew if she told her friends, word would spread like wildfire, and that was something she definitely didn't want to happen. She felt alone with this new information. The transformation was so unclear, and Alaine had to fight to keep her mind in the party.

But another detail, which Alaine had no clue about, was that her transformation would happen at the exact time of her birth, which was 11:23 pm.

As time ticked on, and the party crawled towards its eminent death, its partiers also looked the same. It was only ten o'clock but some were yawning, and one girl had already passed out on the couch. The boys were huddled in the corner talking about god knows what.

"Hey, why don't we ditch this joint and go to the cemetery! Maybe we can spot some ghosts if we're lucky," Wesley blurted.

"YEAH!" the guys cheered in unison. They all jumped up and were revving to go.

"Are you crazy?" Jessica scolded. "That's the dumbest idea I've ever heard! This is Alaine's party, and she doesn't want to go to some creepy cemetery to look for stupid ghosts." She spun on her heel and glared at Alaine. "Right, Alaine?"

But, Alaine actually thought it was an awesome idea. Things of the paranormal intrigued her ever since she was a small child, and right now, being in a cemetery, on an adventure of sorts, was much better than sitting in a boring house.

"Right, Alaine?" Jessica grumbled. Her foot tapped loudly, waiting for her answer.

"I don't know... it might be kinda fun," Alaine mumbled, shrugging her shoulders.

"See, Jessica! Alaine's much cooler than you! It's her birthday and she wants to have some fun, and I'm sorry to tell you this, but your party sucks," Wesley countered.

Jessica glared at him, crossing both arms over her chest. "Fine. But, I'm not getting out of the car."

"Good. You'll scare the ghosts away, anyway," Wesley jested.

By the time everyone loaded in the cars and drove to the cemetery it was nearly 11:00 pm The group had now whittled down to seven members. Four boys and three girls, including Jessica, who technically didn't count because she was too chicken to leave the car.

Susan, another classmate of theirs, agreed to tag along. She was a quiet girl who mostly kept to herself, but seemed equally excited about the adventure. Wide coke-bottle glasses covered her pretty blue-gray eyes. Her dull blonde hair was pulled back into a loose ponytail. She was wearing baggy jeans and an oversized forest green sweatshirt with a picture of a cat on the front. She probably owned one, because stray pieces of pet dander clung desperately to her.

Wesley led the six of them into the cemetery with a single flashlight. The boys treaded loudly together, making ghost sounds and trying to scare each other. Alaine and Susan trailed closely behind.

This was one of the older cemeteries in the area. The ground was covered with old dried leaves, and a wall of towering Fir and Alder trees surrounded the outer part of the grounds. It seemed like a sad place, which had been long forgotten.

A quiet eeriness blanketed the area except for the soft wind stirring the leaves on the ground and rustling through the trees. The moon was almost at its fullest and the stars sparkled like bright diamonds. There were a few dark clouds spread out across the midnight sky, which seemed to add to the eeriness, along with a thin layer of mist which covered the earth.

The breeze was chilled and sent a shiver up my spine, just as much as the creepy, gray tombstones jetting from the earth.

Wesley led the group to the center of the cemetery, where a large rectangular tombstone rested. Lying over that tomb was a beautiful stone carving of an angel. It was so detailed. Its arms were outstretched, hugging the tomb. Its face was hidden, resting within the nook of its other arm, mourning the loss of whoever had passed inside. Gorgeous wings were folded behind its back. Alaine couldn't take her eyes off of it. It was the most beautiful, yet sorrowful, thing she'd ever seen.

The group sat in a circle in the middle of the cemetery, just in front of the tombstone, and Wesley began sharing his ghost stories. Everyone seemed completely captivated. Susan even jumped a few times, and squeezed Alaine's arm, but Alaine's thoughts lingered elsewhere. Little did she know that time was slowly ticking toward her transformation.

It was 11:20pm, when a loud howling echoed from the darkness of trees in the distance, halting Wesley's next story. Every head shot towards the dark trees. Suddenly, the quiet was filled with the most horrifying growls. Suddenly, four sets of yellow eyes appeared in the darkness.

Wolves.

There was talk in town of a pack of rabid wolves running wild in the area, but they hadn't been caught. They were killing small farm animals and even attacked a few kids.

One of the boys jumped up and sprinted towards the car, and as he did the wolves bounded out of the woods rushing towards them.

The rest of the boys jumped up and screamed, darting toward the cars.

The wolves were massive but very agile as they raced across the grounds.

Alaine sprang up and bolted for the car, but paused when she heard a high-pitched scream behind her. Susan had fallen and was crawling around on all fours, desperately running her hands over the ground in search of her glasses.

She had to make a choice. Run for her life, or go back and help her. Alaine chose the second, because there was no way she'd leave Susan, knowing she'd be torn to shreds.

In an instant, Alaine felt a heat on her chest, and when she looked down her Bloodstone amulet was glowing bright red. A sense of strength rushed through her as she grasped it in her fingers. After a quick exhale, she raced back towards Susan. When she reached her, the wolves were only twenty yards away.

11:23pm.

A sudden pain shot through Alaine's midsection, dropping her to the ground. It echoed through every nerve in her body, incapacitating her. Her limbs felt like she was being poked with hot needles, all at once. Her head was pounding, feeling like it was on the verge of exploding. She writhed in pain, a pain she'd never experienced before.

"Alaine!" Susan screamed, grabbing hold of her arm. "Alaine!"

A scorching heat initiated from the top of her head, and surged downwards. But as soon as it hit her feet, it stopped. The pain immediately disappeared, and everything around her started to become fuzzy, like she was looking at the world through ripples of water.

Susan was hysterical. Screaming and crying and shaking Alaine's arm.

Then something happened. Something strange. The wolves stopped dead in their tracks a few yards away and sniffed the air and ground around them, as if they were searching.

Alaine and Susan froze, bewildered by their sudden pause of movement. She slowly stood and helped a nearly blind Susan to her feet, and pulled her back to the car.

"My glasses! I need my glasses! I can't see, and my parents will kill me because they're expensive," Susan bawled.

Alaine sighed and took in a deep breath. They were nearly ten feet from the car.

"Get back to the car, and I'll get your glasses," she said, pushing Susan forward. As soon as she let go of her, Jessica's wide eyes snapped to Susan.

"Susan!" she wailed. She reached over and threw the door open. Susan jumped in, and slammed it shut, quickly locking it.

The wolves ran right past Alaine and bounded after Susan, jumping on the side of the car, making it rock back and forth. Alaine could hear the girls screaming inside.

Why didn't the wolves attack her? She was standing right there, out in the open!

She turned and started running back toward the tombstone. A glimmer of light on the grass led her to Susan's glasses. She reached down and picked them up, feeling a bit dizzy. She nearly fainted when she heard a voice. It sounded like it was coming from the tombstone.

"Alaine," the voice called softly.

Alaine didn't know what to think, but the wolves had caught her scent and were heading straight back towards her.

"Alaine, don't be afraid. Your father sent me. Hurry!" A pretty girl appeared from behind the statue. She was about Alaine's age, but had long red hair and green eyes. Alaine ran toward her, and they both ducked behind the stone.

"Who are you?" Alaine asked.

"My name is Aurora. Hurry, come," she said sweetly, motioning Alaine to come. Alaine followed her to the opposite side of the statue, and as she did, Aurora started to blow behind her.

"What are you doing?" Alaine asked.

"Removing your scent," she replied. "How are you feeling?"

Alaine paused. "Dizzy, and everything is hazy. What's happening to me?"

"Your transformation. At the exact time of your birth, Nephilim are given a gift. It is only revealed after the transformation. You, Alaine, have been given the gift of invisibility."

Alaine gawked at Aurora.

"What the heck is a Nephilim, and what are you talking about?"

"A Nephilim is a Halfbreed. Half human, half angel. Alaine, your birth mother was a mortal female, but your father is an immortal. He is an Angel."

Alaine closed her eyes and shook her head. She figured that this was just a dream and she would wake up in her bed soon.

"Why do you think the wolves stopped before they reached you? You were invisible to them. The only reason why they couldn't see your friend was because she was touching you. Didn't you notice that when you let go of her, your other friend took notice of her?"

"But how can you see me if I'm invisible?"

"I have a special gift. One that can see one's aura, even if invisible. That's why your father sent me, even though he didn't know what your gift would be. He wanted to make sure, in case no one else could find you, I would still be able to find you by your aura."

Alaine was confounded. This all seemed like some crazy, twisted dream.

"I didn't think Angels existed."

"Oh, but they do, Alaine. I'm an Angel," Aurora whispered. In a split second, two large white wings expanded behind Aurora's back. They were the most beautiful things Alaine had ever laid her eyes on. She gasped, and almost fell backward, but Aurora caught her arm.

"How? What?" Alaine was confounded.

"You were born at eleven twenty-three in the evening, eighteen years ago. Because of dangerous situations, immediately after your birth you were taken from your birth mother, and delivered to the

Gray's. Understand that it had to be that way. Your birth mother never intended to give you up, but it was necessary for your safety."

"A--are th-they still alive?" Alaine stuttered.

"Yes, and you have a half-sister who is completely human," Aurora confessed.

Alaine couldn't believe it. This news was overwhelming, but suddenly her chest felt heat again.

"The wolves are coming," Aurora alerted. "Quick, jump on my back. Your friends are waiting. I'll take you to them."

"Won't they see you?" Alaine asked.

"Don't worry. I'm practiced at remaining hidden to humans," she giggled.

Alaine jumped up onto Aurora's back, and they took off into the sky. She watched the wolves circle the tombstone, snapping and howling. They'd escaped just in time.

Aurora flew Alaine to a patch of trees on the opposite side of the cemetery. She set her down quietly. She was across the parking lot, and the wolves were still near the center tombstone. All of her friends' eyes were locked in their direction. The boys, along with Jessica and Susan were frantically calling Alaine's name.

"Alaine, keep safe. Your father has also left you another gift. A garment, which has been placed in your closet to protect you if evil should come. If the Bloodstone ever glows, or you feel afraid, put it on. It contains magic," she said.

She was just about to take off again when Alaine grabbed her arm. "Wait! What's his name?"

"I am not allowed to speak his name, but I will tell you this. Your birth mother's name was Jane Wilder. She still resides in the area."

"In Oregon?"

Aurora nodded.

Alaine gasped. She couldn't believe it. All this time, her birth mother lived in the same state and she had no idea! And, she also had a half-sister that she knew nothing about.

"You must go," Aurora urged. Before Alaine could answer, she flapped her wings and shot off into the air. "Quickly, Alaine! Return to your friends," her voice carried before disappearing into the night.

"Alaine! Alaine!" Jessica screamed out of a small crack in her window, desperately calling her lost friend.

Loud howls, growls, and snapping of teeth made the girls heads snap back to the other car. Two wolves had jumped onto the boy's car, and their horrified screams could be heard loud and clear through the closed windows. Wesley had started the car, but was waiting for the girls to leave first.

Alaine dashed across the narrow road towards Jessica's car. She glanced at the reflection in the window, and immediately noticed that she wasn't there. The street light and trees behind her were, but not her.

She *was* invisible!

Alaine took a few deep breaths and slowly watched her reflection slowly reappear.

"Jessica!" Alaine screamed, pounding on the window, making both girls inside jump and scream. Susan dove toward her and quickly unlocked the door. Alaine shoved in and slammed the door behind her.

"Where the hell were you?" Jessica scolded.

"I went back for Susan's glasses."

"You scared the hell out of us! I was calling you. I thought something horrible had happened," she yelled. She was visibly upset. Tears streamed from her red eyes, and she was trembling.

"I'm sorry. I was there. But it's dark, and I was trying to hide from the wolves. I used the trees as cover." Alaine tried to make sense of it all, but there was no way of explaining what had happened.

"Whatever, Alaine! You could have been killed! I told you this was a stupid idea!" Alaine kept quiet as Jessica started the car. Just as she pulled away a wolf jumped in front of them. She slammed on the breaks and pounded the horn. "Damn you, stupid wolf!" she hollered, glaring at it. She punched the gas petal, screeching forward nearly running it over. Wesley and the boys followed close behind.

Alaine handed Susan her glasses, and she thanked her, sobbing and also shaking.

The night of Alaine's eighteenth birthday would be a night they would never forget.

Alaine had NO answers to what had just happened, but knew that she needed to keep quiet about her encounter with Aurora. She had so many secrets, she wanted to burst. Her body was trembling from a mixture of fear, excitement, and finally getting a few answers.

Nephilim. The word terrified yet excited Alaine. She glanced back down to the Bloodstone amulet which was no longer glowing or heated, and twisted it in her fingers. Such a strange little stone.

DESCENT

Jessica dropped Susan off at home first, and on the way to drop Alaine off there was an awkward silence. When they pulled up in front of Alaine's home, she thanked Jessica for throwing her the party, and then quickly ran into the comfort of her home. She bounced up the stairs to her room, and held her breath before opening her closet door.

In the middle of her clothes hung a long white bag, which stuck out like a sore thumb amongst her dark color-coordinated area. She yanked it from its spot and laid it on her bed, quickly unzipping it. Her jaw dropped as her eyes fastened onto the garment.

It was a tight black leather suit, which looked like it was made for some kind of superhero. Like Cat Woman or Bat Girl. She ran her fingers down the material, and as she did she felt electricity run through them. Tingles started from her fingertips, ran up her hand and continued up her arm. She quickly pulled back, confused from the reaction.

There was a small note attached to the neck.

If you ever doubt or fear the dark, put this on. It is Vestimentum Angelorum, a garment of the Angels. It has magical powers which will be activated once joined with its wearer, and will help keep you safe when I am unable.

Alaine thankfully never had to use the suit until she was older. Questions still remained unanswered, but she now always felt like she was protected. By whom, she never knew, but she always felt a watchful eye over her.

There was a deep hatred which continued to grow for the Nephilim. It wasn't necessarily from the Otherworlds, but from a few Fallen who had gone rogue. Because some of the Halfbreeds possessed greater powers then them, these few had become envious, labeling them as abominations. It was then that the trouble started.

After Lucian's subversive parting with Lucifer, he dispatched a small company of five warriors to seek out the Nephilim and bring them back so he could witness their powers for himself. His closest ally led the hunt. They found one of them, but what they didn't realize was that this particular Nephilim had been given the gift of superior strength. He never tired, and his skin was like iron.

Lucian's band could not hold him, and he fought back, killing four of them. One barely escaped and returned to Lucian. When Lucian was informed of his best friend's death, a deep hatred took root in his already blackened heart. It quickly grew and spread through his being like an incurable sickness.

He'd already despised the Nephilim, but now he wanted every last one of them dead. He called for the Darkling, evil pawns used to carry out wicked, malicious orders. The Darkling did the biddings of the Fallen in exchange for immortality. They were sent out into the cover of night with one order... to seek out the Nephilim, and kill them before their transformations. Those that had made it past transformation were handled differently. The Darkling would merely seek them out, and then send the Fallen in to finish the job, which was done while they slept.

Alaine's gift allowed her to survive beyond many others. The Darkling could never find that which they could never see. But, she was also well protected without her knowledge. Things happened around her that she was unaware of. Her life was saved many times, and it was because she had favor in high places.

SIX

FIRST ENCOUNTER
SAMUEL

THE DAY I MET ALAINE was as fresh in my mind as the morning dew on a blade of grass. Danyel and I were on break from an ongoing war, and I decided to take a chance and head into the human cities to blend with the mortals. It was something I somewhat enjoyed. Being lost in their world with little care. Just to observe their many ways, and wondering why God chose to create them.

I don't know why, but that day I was drawn to the city of Portland, Oregon. I sat outside of a small café, had a cup of coffee, and entertained myself watching the innumerable expressions of the passing crowds. Signs of joy, gloom, grief, hate, tension, weariness, love, and even those who seemed completely emotionless.

I was suddenly captivated by a couple on the opposite side of the highway. The female had run from one direction, straight into the male's arms. He swung her around in a tight embrace, and it ended in a passionate kiss. It was then I began to ponder how these mortals found their mates. Was it merely an inkling, or were they drawn to each other?

But, just as these thoughts entered my mind, something caught me off guard. A sudden sensation which sent my emotions reeling in all directions. Confusion, exhilaration, euphoria. They heated me to my core. My chest tightened, and as I turned, a young female was standing next to me. Her eyes were wide with confusion. I tried, but was unable to strip my eyes from her. This mortal was near perfection. She was fair and petite. Her dark brown eyes had mesmerized me. I was an immortal. A Fallen Angel under her spell. Bewitched by her beauty.

"Hello," I whispered.

She did not utter a word, but another mortal female tugged at her arm.

"Alaine. Let's go," she whispered. She took her arm and tugged her away from me, through the doors of the café. As the distance between us grew larger, the immense feelings began to dissipate.

Alaine. The enchantress had a name. A name which echoed through my entire being, secretly calling out to her. I wanted to be near her. Wanted to know every detail about her.

But one question pressed on my mind. Was she truly mortal?

I'd never before experienced such erratic emotions, but had heard countless stories of them. Through the centuries, when a

Pureblood found their mate, an instant awareness and connection was made between the kindred spirits.

With a touch, a strong connection and mutual bond was formed, linking the two together...forever. This binding was so strong that whenever they were apart, each heart ached for the other, longing to be joined once again.

I wanted to follow after her, but instead I stayed put and battled my emotions, waiting and hoping she would return. Had she experienced the same feelings I had? Her wide eyes told me that we had shared something.

But those things left unexplained would haunt me. I couldn't let her disappear without first discovering who she really was. If she were mortal, I would be crushed. But how could feelings so strong lead to someone who was so forbidden? She had to be more. Maybe she was a Pureblood, like me. Maybe she was also on assignment. Maybe she was a Guardian.

I would stay until I found out.

ALAINE

I'd recently celebrated my 22nd birthday, and was on break from college, studying to become a nurse. Both of my parents were battling their own separate medical illnesses, and I wanted to learn how to better care for them, and give back a little for all the years they helped me.

DESCENT

A colleague of mine, Krystal Kross, wanted to take me to a fairly new café that she'd heard about. They supposedly served some *killer* coffee and sandwiches, so I was game.

As we walked toward the entrance I noticed a young man sitting by himself at one of the two tables outside, observing the people passing by. He had slightly wavy, dark-brown hair which was a bit shorter on the sides than it was on top, and was all drawn back. From the side, his features were strong and masculine, and his skin was slightly tanned. Muscles were well defined on his arms, and I could only think they were equally proportioned throughout his tall, lean frame. He was definitely a beautiful specimen.

A light smirk formed his face as he watched a couple embrace across the street. He had a cup of coffee set in front of him which steam was still escaping from.

As we walked closer to him I suddenly felt a heat flash throughout my body. My world became a blur, and tingles pricked my skin. I felt strange. Like every part of my being was being drawn towards this stranger, and before I knew it, I was standing a few feet away from him. Staring, but I couldn't seem to pull myself away.

I watched the expression on his face change as his head turned, and the most beautiful, big-brown eyes met mine. His eyes showed a look of confoundment; mimicking the look I felt I'd had.

I was completely entranced by him. He felt so familiar, but yet was completely unfamiliar. His face seemed to be glowing with an unearthly beauty, and the area around him seemed to have a strong gravitational force, almost magnetic, beckoning me, pulling me closer.

Krystal squeezed my arm, snapping me from my reverie.

"Alaine. Let's go," she urged, giving me a crazy look.

I had to will myself to leave. Fight to keep my head straight, but my feet were anchored, not wanting to move from its current place of bliss.

But my mind finally won, and as we departed from his presence, my body began to unbend, and feel a little more at ease.

What the hell was happening to me?

That first encounter left both Samuel and Alaine disconcerted. Samuel wrestled with the decision to stay and see if he could find out more about Alaine, or just leave and forget about her, although he doubted leaving would be so easy.

Alaine, on the other hand, fought her inner turmoil to return to the stranger outside. She'd never experienced such impulsive internal cravings, and it all happened without a touch, and without an inkling of who he was. It was as if her body longed to be near him.

The inside of café started to feel small, suffocating, almost like it was closing in on her. Her mind was lost in a cloud, and her thoughts were floating. Everything around her seemed dull and faded, and her mind was fixed on one thing. Him. The stranger who was sitting outside. Alone.

Her thoughts made her insides twist with excitement and apprehension. Should she go to him? Alaine was desperate to find answers. She needed to know who he was, so despite her normal behavior, she excused her friend and started toward him.

As she neared the exit, her stomach twisted with a million butterflies. Heat rushed through her and her legs became weak and shaky. She took in another deep breath and continued. Her hand touched the door, the only obstruction between them, and as soon as she pushed it open, tingles immediately pricked her skin.

The air around them was humming with electricity. The closer she drew to him, the vibrations became stronger. Like a silent yet beautiful song, entrancing and luring one heart towards the other.

His head snapped back to her, and his beautiful brown eyes flashed with a bit of excitement, pleasure, and confusion. She paused at the doorway. Their eyes steeled on one another.

He lifted his hand out to her, and without hesitation, she took it. Instantly... time froze, and the world around them faded away. Now, only they remained. Two left in their own existence, sharing one unfamiliar connection. The attraction was undeniable. It was magical. One string tugging on two hearts, magically binding them together...forever.

SEVEN

PASSION
SAMUEL

AFTER OUR FIRST ENCOUNTER, MY mind would not allow me to stray from Alaine for too long. I was unfocused, even in battle, and became thankful and indebted to Danyel, who managed to save me from more than a few near death situations.

I was completely spellbound. Everything about Alaine possessed, captivated, and seduced me. Her presence, her smell, her touch. It was like a drug. She was a substance of which my body craved, and I experienced withdrawals whenever there was distance between us.

But my worst fears were realized when I learned that Alaine was not a Pureblood. She was a Nephilim, a Halfbreed, which made our relationship completely forbidden within the laws of the Otherworlds. The worlds above and below which held every single Pureblood accountable. A law which was clear and precise. Purebloods were only allowed to mate with Purebloods. Any breeding among the mortals was considered immoral and highly forbidden. If caught, both mortal and immortal were immediately sought after and executed, along with any illegitimate children. The Nephilim.

We were damned from the start, and our hearts were the ones that had led us astray. But how could feelings so strong, so sure, and so mutual, be so forbidden?

It was confounding, the fact that she was only a Halfbreed, but we shared a connection which should have been given exclusively to immortal Purebloods, who were destined to live out the rest of their lives together. A bond transcending all time. A bond which could not be broken, unless one was killed. But even in death, a part of them would remain forever imbedded in the heart of their mate.

If Alaine and I consummated our bond we would be breaking the law, and this law had one consequence. Death.

I was shocked to learn that she was a Nephilim, because it was rare to see one survive in these dark days, especially past their transformation. That was because they were now being hunted and killed by Lucian and his murderous buffoons.

But it was Alaine's gift of invisibility which kept her alive through the years when evil was sent to kill her. With her amulet she was able to recognize when evil was near, and mastered her gift to escape death countless times.

Angels have a distinct fragrance, sweet and perfumed, and also have a heightened sense of smell that they use to identify each other.

The Fallen have a very similar aroma, but it became tainted the day of The Fall. That peculiar smoky aroma set them apart from their Heavenly counterparts, making them easier to identify.

Everything was seemingly perfect in my life, despite the fact it all had to be kept secret, but there was also Danyel, my best friend and companion, who I had to contend with. He continually asked me questions about my disappearances, and I hated the fact I had to conceal so many truths from him.

I did confess that I had met someone, but I never revealed her name. This way, if he were ever questioned, he would remain innocent. He instantly knew she wasn't a Pureblood, because if she was, he would have already been introduced to her.

I kept Alaine completely secret, being careful and sure of her safety.

Danyel was completely opposed to our relationship, because he knew that if it continued, it would eventually end in death. But he also noticed a change in me. A positive change that happened the moment I touched her. I was not my own anymore. Alaine had possessed a part of me, and I, a part of her.

The day I laid eyes on her I noticed she radiated a beautiful aura, which since transferred to me. Danyel said he could see it in my eyes, how complete and content I had become. She changed me, and for the better.

Danyel admitted he was a bit jealous, and longed to find his mate and the same happiness I had gained with Alaine. I hoped, for his sake, that he would too.

But, from now on I would be fighting a completely different battle. A battle to keep Alaine safe. It would be a most difficult task, but one that I was ready for.

ALAINE

The day I laid eyes on Samuel, my life changed forever. Something strange happened that day at the café. Some kind of universal connection, which couldn't be explained. Samuel said it was a type of bonding which only happens between Purebloods, but I wasn't a pureblood, and thus, the bonding completely baffled us.

I learned a lot about Samuel from all the time we spent together. He told me about Angels, about the Fall, and about his enduring existence. I was entirely captivated by his wondrous stories and the fact that he was a Fallen Angel and experienced warrior.

But now, this beautiful, magical being, was with me. There was something so enchanting about him. He was affectionate and warm, not anything I expected one of the Fallen to be. I treasured his friendship, his devotion, and his passion.

I shared the stories of my youth, about my parents, even the note left by my birth father, and the visitation of the angel that night in the cemetery. They weren't nearly as fascinating as his, but he seemed absorbed and attentive to every detail.

I told him about the mark on the back of my neck, and that I was told never to reveal it to anyone. He completely understood and never questioned me about it, allowing me to keep it secret. This simple act made my trust and love for him grow even more.

But, Samuel was still under the hand of Lucifer, and needed to leave me for lengths at a time, to go back to his Fallen world and missions. He didn't want to leave, but he had to, as not to draw attention. While he was gone my thoughts remained with him, hoping and wishing he would keep safe. At night my dreams were filled with his face, and his smile. His scent always lingered around me, comforting, filling me with warmth until his return.

Samuel was deeply concerned for my safety, but I was just as deeply concerned for his. We took our relationship very slow, but our friendship grew and blossomed into something beautiful. Something strong. Something the two of us could not deny or anyone could ever destroy.

I wanted to be with him, and even though the stakes were high, I was willing to risk it all. How could you deny someone love, when that love is so real, so pure, and so absolute. I had found my soul mate. The one I wanted to spend the rest of my existence with, no matter what the cost.

Despite the law, which forbade them to be together, Samuel and Alaine continued their relationship. Being in each other's presence was not only something they wanted, it was something they needed.

One night under a full moon and a twinkling diamond sky, Samuel and Alaine cuddled under a large willow tree, discussing his recent battle and her nursing classes. Alaine was wrapped tightly in the circle of his arms, and electricity buzzed all around them.

Samuel paused and gazed into Alaine's eyes. His gaze was alluring.

"I love you," he whispered. He leaned over and pressed his lips to her forehead.

She smiled and breathed him in. Her chocolate eyes sparkled. "I love you too."

He softly brushed his fingers down her cheek, and then slowly raised her chin, pressing his full lips against hers. His kiss was soft, tender, but then deepened the more he tasted.

His taste was also sweet, enticing her, luring her deeper into his paradise.

In an instant they were lost. Lost in an eternal ecstasy which made them weak. Carnal desires roared within them, yearning, thirsting for more.

The seduction of the bond could not be held back any longer.

Covered only by the dark sky, emotions took over all reason. Their bodies blazed with a fiery passion as two bodies became one. Each tangled in the other's web of ecstasy.

At their eclipse, Samuel unfolded the most beautiful black wings from his back, and wrapped Alaine protectively in the warmth of his embrace. While she slept, he carefully studied every detail of her face. He knew at that moment that there was no one he could ever love more, and it was her love in return which gave purpose to his existence.

EIGHT

THE GIFT
ALAINE

ONE NIGHT OF PASSION LED TO
A MOST UNEXPECTED GIFT.
ALAINE WAS PREGNANT.

I STARTED TO FEEL SICK the day after Samuel and I spent the night out under the stars, but it was much too soon for symptoms of morning sickness so I didn't even give it a thought. After a few more days of feeling nauseous and throwing up, I decided to head down to the local drugstore and buy a test… just to humor myself. I was completely caught by surprise when the results came in. It was something I never expected.

POSITIVE!

Oh, that's when my world began spinning. I was completely terrified, but also delighted because I was carrying Samuel's child. I couldn't wait for him to return from his mission so I could share the news, but I wondered what he would think about it. I knew he would be very distressed, knowing the situation we were already in.

He was troubled a lot lately, and very careful of where we traveled, especially together. I know he wanted to keep me safe, but I hated that our relationship had to remain so secret, and was so forbidden. If other immortals found out that we were together and now having a child, we would be a huge target. I knew this fact was going to weigh heavy on his heart.

SAMUEL

I came back from war, and was given the news that Alaine was with child. I was happy because Alaine was glowing and seemed to be happy, but disconcerted because this child she was carrying would not be able to remain in our care.

We were bringing an innocent child into our world, filled with death and despair.

What was even more troublesome was an age old prophecy of the Fallen. This prophecy foretold the birth of a child, a child born of a Pureblood and a Halfbreed, who would bring change to the Otherworlds.

I realized that this prophecy was of our unborn child. If any of the Fallen discovered the child, it would mean inescapable danger and death for all of us. If the child survived, it would eventually have to learn to fight, or risk capture and become a slave to the evil of immoral hearts.

My heart ached knowing I had to tell Alaine she wouldn't be able to keep the child. To ensure its survival it needed to be hidden away with a good mortal family. A couple who would raise the child as their own until the day of transformation.

The maturation of an immortal child within the womb was much more rapid than those of the mortals. Alaine and I needed to discuss arrangements for this child soon, and I knew it was going to be a dreadful task.

That evening, Samuel took Alaine to their secret place under the willow tree. He carefully explained to her that she would not be able to keep the child, and needed to find someone suitable to raise the child immediately after birth.

Samuel's heart ached as he listened to the uncontrollable sobs of his love. Alaine was completely heartbroken, but already had a knowing deep inside that if their child had any chance of living a normal life, it would have to be away from them.

She finally gathered herself so she could think straight, and then it hit her. Alaine knew exactly who she wanted to raise their child. There was only one choice. ONE ALONE. And she prayed that this couple would say yes.

Those many years back... the night of Alaine's eighteenth birthday when the Angel told her that her birth mother was still alive and living in her area, Alaine started to do some research on her own.

She eventually found her mother, who had kept her maiden name Jane Wilder. But Alaine waited until she was out from the Gray's home, and in college, before she made contact. She first sent a letter, but after getting no response, she decided to take a drive to the address that she was given.

Alaine learned that Jane's husband had left her and their daughter about five years before. She also learned that Jane had been diagnosed with cancer and was battling to stay alive. She was staying in a nursing home, a few miles away.

Alaine was apprehensive to meet her at first, not knowing if she would be accepted, but she had to at least see her before she passed away.

When Alaine peeked into Jane's room, her heart dropped. She looked like an old woman, so thin and pale, and was attached to many wires. Her hair had fallen out, probably due the chemo treatments, but Jane's eyes were closed.

Alaine slowly stepped into her room, and with each step, her heart beat faster and faster. She started to second guess herself, and just as she was about to turn around, Jane's eyes opened.

"Hello," Jane breathed weakly. "Are you looking for someone?"

"Um. Yes. I. I'm looking for Jane Wilder," Alaine stuttered.

Jane smiled. "I'm Jane Wilder. Do I know you?"

Alaine paused, swallowing hard. "Yes...and no."

When she saw Jane's brow crease she knew she had to tell her, even though she was terrified of rejection. Alaine walked up to Jane and carefully rested her hand on hers.

"Mrs. Wilder, my name is Alaine Gray. I am your daughter."

Jane's eyes widened in total confusion. She began to shake her head, but as she looked into Alaine's eyes, she began to weep.

"How did you find me?"

"Well…it's kind of a complicated story. On my eighteenth birthday, an Angel named Aurora once told me about you and my birth father. She gave me your name and said that you were in the area. I did some research online and found out where you lived."

Jane shook her head, but after a few moments, took hold of Alaine's arm and pulled her closer and embraced her. She wept, and apologized for having to give her up, and prayed that she had a wonderful life.

Alaine thanked her for making the right decision, and shared stories of her childhood, and all of her wonderful memories growing up with the Gray's.

A few hours later a teenage girl came walking in, and paused when she saw Alaine.

Her skin was flawless, the color of cream, and her features were very petite. Long auburn hair curled down her shoulders, and her eyes were a bright green. She was beautiful. Alaine introduced herself, and found out that her name was Victoria. This was her half-sister.

Victoria walked over to Jane and gave her a kiss on the forehead, and then put some fresh flowers in a vase, which sat in front of her. Victoria seemed happy to learn that she had an older sister. Alaine noticed a lot of similarities between her and Victoria. Although Alaine had chocolate brown hair and eyes, they had the same shaped eyes and smile.

Alaine made sure to visit daily, and Jane enjoyed talking with and listening to Alaine's stories about growing up.

But it wasn't long before the cancer ravaged Jane's weak body, and it soon came to the point where she could no longer talk. Alaine still came, sat next to her bedside, and told her happy stories of her youth. Within a few weeks, Jane was gone.

Alaine was devastated, but also glad she was given the chance to have met and talked with her birth mother before she passed, and also relieved that she and Jane had a chance to make amends.

After their mother passed, Alaine and Victoria kept in close contact. Alaine helped her with whatever she needed to finish her last year of high school, and after graduation, paid for her courses to study Real Estate. That was something Victoria wanted to do, because her boyfriend's parents were in real estate and they had become very wealthy.

During their times together, Alaine opened her heart to Victoria. She told her about the note, the bloodstone, and the secret world of the Angels who roamed the earth.

Victoria swore to never tell a soul, and Alaine believed her. She knew her sister had a pure heart, and she was finally glad to share her secret with someone. Victoria shared about her childhood and how her father left them when he found out her mother was sick. He wasn't a very nice man, so Victoria was glad when he left.

Now, Victoria was 20 years old, and engaged to her high-school sweetheart, Christian Wise. Their wedding was a month away, and Alaine was in a predicament. She now had to ask Victoria if she would be willing to raise her child. This was not an easy thing to ask someone to do, to raise a child who was not their own.

Alaine worried over how she was going to present them with the news.

How could she explain that she was only pregnant for a few months, and then would be giving birth?

What if they said no?

If Victoria and Christian didn't want her child, Alaine had no other plans and had no clue of what she would do.

The thought of her child being with family would make the loss a bit easier, and Alaine knew that Victoria and Christian would make perfect parents. The downside was that she and Samuel would have to remain completely out of their lives to ensure their safety.

Alaine called Victoria and set up meeting with her and her fiancé Christian a few days later. Samuel was away, so she would have to do this herself, but she wanted to prepare them as much in advance as she could. She just hoped and prayed that they would accept her offer. Her most precious gift.

When the day arrived, Alaine's stomach churned, twisting and turning in knots. Christian and Victoria met her at a small café in town. They greeted each other, and then Alaine led them to a private booth in the back corner.

Victoria was gorgeous in just a simple white top and blue jeans. Her bright green eyes lit up when she saw Alaine, and a smile widened on her flawless, porcelain face. Christian was not too bad looking either. He had ash-blond hair, which was neatly cut, and baby blue eyes. They both looked so in love, so thrilled to just be in each other's presence.

They both sat across from Alaine, and Victoria knew immediately that something was up.

"Hey, is everything okay?" Victoria questioned.

"Yes. Everything's fine. I just need to ask you both a serious question."

Victoria and Christian glanced at each other and then both sets of eyes steeled on Alaine. Alaine's pulse raced and her stomach twisted.

"Have you ever discussed or considered having children?" Alaine asked.

Their faces dropped, and Victoria glanced over to Christian.

Christian took hold of her hand, and then turned to Alaine. "We have discussed it, but I have a medical condition which makes me unable to have children. But we have discussed our options, and were thinking that maybe we'd adopt in the future. But that's a few years down the line. We'd like to travel a bit first, and spend some married time alone before we take the plunge and raise a child." Christian grinned and wrapped his arm around Victoria.

Alaine's heart sank. She was quiet, feeling horrible for thinking of asking them to carry such a heavy load. They had already made plans that didn't include a child. But then again, maybe if they were given the option...?

"Alaine, what is it? What did you want to ask us?" Victoria said softly.

Alaine paused and gazed lovingly into her sister's eyes.

"I'm pregnant." Alaine's eyes immediately started to fill with tears.

Victoria gasped, and held both hands over her mouth. Her eyes started to pool as she looked at Alaine.

"Oh, Alaine, I'm---" Victoria didn't know how to respond, not knowing if this news was good or bad.

"I can't keep the baby," she sobbed. "I asked you both to meet me here to see if maybe you'd be willing to care for it."

"Like adopt?" Christian breathed with a look of confusion on his face.

"Yes," Alaine sniffed. She grabbed a napkin and dabbed the wet away, trying to compose herself.

"When is your due date?" he questioned.

"I'm not sure, but it would be in about three months."

"Three months?" Victoria inhaled, looking at Alaine's belly. "You don't even look like you're pregnant."

"It's complicated," was all Alaine could say as she looked into Victoria's eyes. Victoria nodded, knowing the secrets that her sister had shared with her. She knew this child would be different. Special.

She turned to Christian and they shared a silent stare. There were no words, but each was speaking very loud and clear to the other. With simultaneous nods, they turned back to Alaine. Christian wrapped his arm around Victoria.

"We'll do it" she chimed, smiling widely. "We'll adopt your baby."

Alaine's head snapped up to their smiling faces. She began to weep, but stood up and hugged them both tightly.

"Do you know if it's a boy or a girl yet?" she asked.

"No." Alaine shook her head. "Do you want me to tell you if I find out?"

"No! I want it to be a surprise!" Victoria squealed.

"So what steps do we need to take?" Christian asked.

"I'll have an attorney draw everything up, and have them come and meet you. You won't have to worry about anything. I will take care of all the expenses, and I'll also keep in touch and give you all the details."

"Alright," Christian said facing Victoria. "Honey, we're gonna have a baby!" Victoria threw her arms around his neck, and pressed her lips to his, giving him a loud smack.

They were happy. Truly happy. Alaine smiled inside and out, knowing that they were going to be the ones to raise the precious child growing in her womb. But, she would have to explain to Victoria that she would not be able to see her again after the child was born. It was much too dangerous, and Alaine didn't want to put any of their lives in danger.

NINE

EMMA'S BIRTH

THE FEW MONTHS OF PREGNANCY were hard, and Samuel and Alaine watched her belly grow bigger every day, until it was just about time. Samuel took care of all the arrangements and had her secretly brought to a place just outside of the city.

It was a recently closed medical facility which had moved to a bigger location a few miles down the road. But for now, this place was abandoned and awaiting renovations, and a perfect place for Alaine to have the child.

It was late one afternoon when Alaine felt a shooting pain in her abdomen. She doubled over and moaned.

"I think it's time," she breathed to Samuel.

Samuel ran to her side, helped her to a chair, and then grabbed her phone and dialed.

"She's ready. Meet us in twenty minutes." He hung up the phone and assisted Alaine to the door. But first he stopped, stepped out and smelled the air.

"Let's go." The air was clear, so he quickly led her out to the car and assisted her in. She moaned again, grabbing her abdomen.

"Samuel. Hurry. I think this baby wants out now." In a flash he was opening the driver's door and shoving in.

They reached the location in less than twenty minutes. Samuel drove the car behind the building, and parked near the back door. He got out and sniffed the air again. It seemed to be clear. Just then, a man in a dark suit popped out of the darkness, making Alaine jump.

Were they caught?

The man walked up to Samuel and they shared a few words. After a few minutes, they shook hands and the man turned and walked away. Samuel rushed over to the car, and opened Alaine's door.

"Who was that?" she questioned.

"A Watcher. There are a few of them out there. Friends of mine. They'll be keeping a close eye outside to make sure we don't have any unwanted visitors."

Alaine exhaled a deep breath. There was still so much she needed to learn about this new world. Another sharp pain shot through her, and she groaned. Samuel whisked her up in his arms and carried her inside. He took her to a small room and laid her on the bed in the corner. The room was white and smelled sterile, and everything was already set up for her to give birth.

A few minutes later two ladies walked in, both beautiful, and both looked to be in their early thirties. Alaine suspected they were Angels because they looked too perfect, and had that wonderful sweet scent.

"Alaine, it's so nice to see you again," the first woman said, walking towards her. "My name is Laura. I am your midwife, same as I was for your mother."

Alaine's eyes widened. "My mother?"

"Yes. I was there the day you were born, and so was Abigail. She was the one who delivered you safely to the Gray's." The midwife turned to her assistant who smiled.

Alaine froze. Her brain was smoking, trying to process that information. They didn't look too much older than she was, and they were there for her birth? Whoa. That was crazy.

"Hi Alaine. I'm Abigail Reed." The assistant headed to shake her hand, but as Alaine held out hers, another sharp pain surged through her belly. She screamed through gritted teeth, sending everyone to their places.

"I'd say this baby wants out," Laura noted. She put on her gloves, while Abigail set up the baby's area.

Samuel came around and took Alaine by the hand.

"It's going to be alright, Alaine. Just breathe. Everything will be alright," he whispered into her ear.

It was a long few hours of labor, but after one last push, the baby was born.

"It's a girl!" Laura announced. She handed her over to Abigail to clean her up.

Samuel leaned over and wrapped Alaine in his arms. She wept and wept, and he held her tight, whispering how proud he was, and how much he loved her.

After cleaning the baby, Abigail wrapped her in a blanket and walked her over to Samuel and Alaine.

"Would you like to hold her?"

Alaine lifted her arms toward the bundle and brought her to her chest. She gasped, and the tears continuously flowed down her face.

She was perfect, and so tiny. Her little nose was so sweet, her lips were bright pink and perfectly shaped, and her little cheeks looked like they were brushed with pink blush. Her eyelids fluttered, and for a split second, she smiled.

Alaine looked at Samuel. She could tell he was torn.

Alaine put her nose down to her little head and breathed in her scent. She smelled so sweet. She was sweet in every way imaginable.

"She's beautiful, just like her mother," Samuel whispered. He wrapped his arms around Alaine and the baby, and then leaned over and kissed his daughter on the cheek. She scrunched her little nose, and for a moment there was laughter. For a moment, they were a real family. But, that moment was not going to last long, and everyone in the room knew it.

They were interrupted by one of the Watchers, who came to the door. He motioned for Samuel to come, and they quickly disappeared into the hall.

Alaine could hear their murmurs echoing off the walls, but she couldn't take her eyes off of her beautiful daughter. She studied the details of her soft face. So amazingly perfect.

But when her heart should have been happy, it started to break when she realized she had to give her away.

Samuel came back in with a deep furrow in his brow. He eyes looked concerned, but as soon as he laid them on Alaine, he smiled. "I'm sorry Alaine. We need to say goodbye."

"Are we in danger?"

"No. It's just a precaution. The Watchers spotted one of the Fallen a few miles away."

Laura gasped and immediately went to Alaine's side and held out her hands to take the child. Alaine's world suddenly became hazy. She ran this day in her mind over and over, but was still not prepared for it. This was something she could never prepare for. Her heart felt like it was shattering into a million pieces.

She glanced down at her newborn daughter through tear-filled eyes.

This precious, sleeping, baby girl had no idea of the events going on around her; no idea she was in danger, or that her mother's heart was breaking. She had no clue that she was going to be whisked away in a few moments to a new set of parents.

Alaine whispered softly in her ear. "I love you so much my precious daughter, more than every single breath I breathe, more than life itself. I'm so sorry. I wish I could keep you, but always remember that I will be here should you ever need me."

Alaine's eyes flooded with tears. She kissed her precious daughter on the forehead, breathed in her scent, and handed her over to the midwife.

She carried the child to Samuel, and placed her in his arms. His eyes sparkled as he stared at his daughter's beautiful face. He leaned down and pressed his lips on her cheek, whispered something into her little ear. Then, he gave her one last kiss goodbye.

Abigail headed toward them, and Samuel carefully handed her the child. She turned one last time to Alaine, but Alaine was curled up, sobbing. Her heart was breaking, her body aching.

Samuel sadly gave Abigail a nod, so she quickly took the baby---so innocent, so oblivious to the dangers of the dark world around her---and fled into the night.

The next few months were very difficult for both Samuel and Alaine. Alaine was hard to console at first, but it was Samuel's constant love and commitment which helped to pull her together.

Although their daughter was now in the loving care of Victoria and Christian, there could be no physical contact and very limited correspondence. This was to assure that the Fallen would have no leads or connections to the Wise family, and keep them safe.

But Abigail Reed did find out the name she was given. Her name was Emma. Emma Wise. The day Alaine learned Emma's name, it took residence in her heart and mind, and there wasn't a day that went by that she didn't think about her.

Her heart ached knowing she would miss watching her grow, cutting her first tooth, taking her first step, and saying her first word. But if all that heartache meant that Emma would be safe, then it was worth it.

TEN

THE TRAGEDY
SAMUEL

M Y INNER VOICE WAS WARNING me that someone had found out about my relationship with Alaine. I just hoped with all my being that they didn't find out about Emma.

I had no doubt that Alaine could take care of herself, especially with her gift of invisibility. I taught her everything I knew about Angels and the Fallen, and how to recognize the signs when either was near. That gave her an edge, and a fighting chance of survival.

But our daughter was helpless. There was no way any mortal who surrounded her could win a battle with an Immortal, or live to tell about it.

But I was curious. Why would they send two of their best to collect me? I wasn't afraid to die. Death had no sting, especially to many of the Fallen who wished for it.

I no longer wished for death.

I had finally found happiness, and found the one my heart had been searching for my entire existence. The one I wanted to share the rest of my eternity with...regardless if we were star-crossed lovers sharing one forbidden love.

"Samuel." My thoughts were broken as Abaddon spoke my name.

I nodded and let them take me.

We entered the porthole into the Underworld, a place I never pleasured in returning to. Desolate. Dry. Dead. The ground was parched, and steam rose from large crevices within its surface. Not one sign of life. A colorless, foul, cursed world, much like most of the hearts that dwelt here.

Although I was one of the Fallen, I preferred to stay in the mortal world as to not become too accustomed to this one. Regret of past decisions was a heavy weight to bear, and I was doomed to spend an eternity carrying it.

As Abaddon and Apollyon flew me east towards Montem Mortis, the Mount of Death, I realized I was in grave danger. This was the place traitors and those who disregarded the laws, were brought for execution.

I couldn't help but notice the corpses of all my Fallen brothers on the rocks below. Bones of some I knew personally. Some who stood up against this senseless war and wanted it to end. They were executed because of it. This leadership was tyrannical: wanting to make war when there was no cause for one.

Humans had a choice. It was something given to them. We, on the other hand, did not.

We soared higher, to the top of the mountain.

Alaine.

Emma.

Their names filled my heart as we drew closer, giving me strength and some kind of hope to hold on to.

We landed on a small area at the top where the dirt had become blackened from all of the previous blood spilled. Lucian was waiting. His white hair was drawn back, and his wings were folded behind his back, which meant that whatever was going to happen, wasn't going to take long.

Abaddon walked toward him and bowed, showing his allegiance. "We've brought Samuel."

Apollyon stepped behind me and whispered something so soft, at first I thought it was the wind. "I've heard about your mortal love. I also have one. Trust my sword."

Were my ears deceiving me? How could he have known about Alaine? I turned my head to the side and he gave the slightest nod. Apollyon was a master swordsman. The best I'd ever come across or had seen in battle. He was so quick, so precise, and each one of his swings was deliberate and fatal, never missing its target.

Lucian's eyes fixed on me, pitch black, with evil intentions. But I wasn't afraid of him. Yes, he was an ancient, almost as old as Lucifer, but other than that he was no different from any of us. He was just handed his leadership and authority.

I could sense his intentions, and they were evil.

Immortals could die one of two ways. Take off the head, or pierce the heart.

If my arms weren't bound, I would have fought him till the death. But with my arms secured tightly behind me, there wasn't much I could do. I couldn't fly, because if I called my wings, they would tear my arms off. The only thing I could do was trust in a whisper. It was all I had.

I steeled my eyes on Lucian, and he gave me a wicked grin.

I suddenly envisioned my sword in my hand, slicing the smirk off his face, then his head. I would smile as I watched it fall face-first into the dirt, hopefully hitting a rock on the way down. Then, I would rip out his heart, just to be certain of his death. That would be a beautiful sight.

I usually had a nice disposition, but I was still a Fallen Angel. One that most didn't mess with.

"So, you are Samuel?" Lucian huffed. He still had a smirk on his face.

Samuel stood still, firm, and said nothing.

I've received word that you've been keeping intimate company with a mortal. Is this true?"

"Where did you come by this information?" Samuel questioned.

"That does not concern you!" Lucian growled. "Don't you know that breeding with the mortal insects is forbidden?"

"Yes, and that should not concern you," Samuel smirked.

"Oh, but it does. Lucifer has placed me in charge of the Fallen, and I will make sure they do not breed and create bastard abominations, and future enemies to us."

Samuel's heart began to fill with hate for Lucian as he thought about his Alaine, and their beautiful daughter Emma. They were the furthest things from abominations.

"I have done nothing wrong," Samuel said in defense, and with all honesty.

"Well, I'm here to make sure of that."

Samuel glared at him.

Samuel knew that Lucian had brought him here for one purpose and one purpose alone. Execution. And he wasn't going to leave until it was carried out. Once brought to Montem Mortis, you never returned. That was Lucian's way. Guilty or innocent, it didn't matter. Each visitor met their fate, and he was there as a maniacal spectator.

Lucian spoke one word, and Samuel knew it was the beginning of the end.

"Abaddon."

Samuel stood tall and closed his eyes. His thoughts went to his Alaine. His love. His world. The pain might be bearable if he could keep his mind on her. She gave him strength.

He said a silent prayer. A prayer to a God who had long forgotten him. A God he had forsaken many centuries ago. A prayer not for himself, but for Alaine and Emma. A prayer to keep them safe.

Abaddon stepped forward and reached for his sword.

"Let me do this," Apollyon said, taking a step toward him.

A large smile formed on Lucian's lips, and he nodded. Abaddon stepped behind Samuel and recalled the bind, letting Samuel's arms free, but then quickly placed the bind on his legs.

"Wings!" Lucian roared.

Apollyon nodded to Samuel, so he called out his wings.

Calling out ones wings was as simple as a thought, which releases a magical connection between the host and his winged appendage.

In a moment, the most beautiful black wings spread across Samuel's back. Wings that had aided him through the centuries. Wings that had taken him to safety, and helped him fight and defeat his enemies.

Apollyon nodded again and Samuel shut his eyes tight, knowing what was to come. Pain. His mind searched for Alaine. He needed to find her face.

Abaddon took hold of his left wing and stretched it out. With one quick swish, Apollyon swung his sword, severing it from Samuel's back. Samuel fell to his knees, pain surged through his body. His wings were a vital part of him.

Before he had a chance to catch his breath...Swish! His other wing was severed.

Abaddon threw them off the side of the mountain as if they were trash.

Samuel's pain was excruciating, like nothing he had ever endured before. But he found Alaine, in his mind's eye. He saw her beautiful face and the warmth in her big, brown eyes smiling at him.

"I love you," he whispered with a smile on his face.

"Stand him up," Lucian yelled. Abaddon assisted Samuel to his feet. Blood poured from his open wounds, down his back, and started to cover the ground around him.

Samuel opened his eyes and smiled.

"What makes you smile when death is near?"

"Love. Love makes me smile, and is something you can never take from me. Something you could never kill, and something that will never die. It is something I have found, and will keep until my last breath, and it will rest with me for all eternity."

Samuel's happiness made Lucian furious. "Kill him," he roared

Apollyon raised his sword, and then thrust it into Samuel's chest. Samuel dropped. His legs gave out and the world around him started to fade. Soon his body fell limp to the ground. Lifeless.

Lucian knew that Apollyon had never missed his target. Not once, so he never doubted that Samuel was dead.

"Toss him over the side and let's be rid of him."

Abaddon recalled the bind from Samuel's legs, and dragged him to the edge of the mountain. He then lifted him over his head, and dropped him down the side, to the razor sharp rocks below.

ALAINE

As soon as Samuel kissed me goodbye and disappeared into the night sky, my heart began to ache for him. I knew he needed to go away, and he'd done so every few months for almost a year now, but it was never easy.

I figured the best and easiest way would be to sleep.

My sleep would always be sweet because every time I closed my eyes he was there, in my dreams. I never knew how long he was going to be away. Days, weeks, months? Each day harder than the next, and longer than the day before. It was the dead time, the time spent awake, which was the hardest.

I turned off my light and wrapped the blanket around me, wishing it were his strong arms. I was just about to shut my eyes when I noticed how extra dark it seemed outside. Like the moon and stars weren't there.

In the distance I heard dogs barking. But these were not simple barks, they were more territorial. I waited, listening, and a few minutes later a dog yelped loudly like it was in pain.

I jumped from the covers and pulled back the curtain, just enough to peek out the window. My chest started to feel heated, and when I glanced down, the bloodstone around my neck started glowing bright red, which meant danger was near.

A shadow, darker than the night, shot across the window. I gasped, stumbling backwards, and then caught a sweet, yet smoky scent in the breeze.

Fallen.

They were here.

And then my heart sank in a horrifying realization. If they were here for me, then what would happen to Samuel? I hoped he was okay. I hoped they didn't find out about us.

Then my thoughts shot to Emma, hoping she was safe. I hope they didn't know about her or where she was.

There was a loud bang downstairs.

I needed to get out. Quick.

I grabbed my perfume and sprayed it all over the room to mask my smell, and then ran to my closet and locked the door from the inside. Samuel had rigged it for extra protection, even though a door wouldn't keep the Fallen out for long.

He had also installed a secret door, with three different sets of tunnels which all connected, but each one led to a different exit.

Taking a deep breath, I tied my hair back into a ponytail, and grabbed the magical black-leather suit my Immortal father had given me. I wanted to put it on, but there was no time. The bloodstone was getting hotter and brighter. I also didn't want to use my invisibility so soon, because the longer I used it, the weaker I became, and I needed as much strength as I could to get away.

I squeezed into the small trap door and before closing it I sprayed the closet again, and then locked it quietly behind me. I was now in complete darkness, and the only light was that from the bloodstone glowing red around my neck, making everything seem eerie.

From the outside, you would never know there was a trap door there.

As I made my way down the narrow tunnel, I could hear footsteps hammering above me, and then a loud crash as if they kicked in a door. My heart hammered against the walls of my chest, and I prayed that the spray would conceal my scent long enough for me to get out.

But now, the question was which exit to take. If I took the exit out the front, I could run into the trees across the street, and then on to the undercover car parked a few blocks away. Samuel had thought of everything. Every detail in case this day ever came. I doubted it would, but now I was glad he had prepared me. He'd been around for hundreds of years, knowing that anything could happen at any moment.

I climbed through the dark tunnel and went to the back of the house first to check the wind. It was blowing away from me, and toward the back of the house, so it would carry the scent of the spray. I just hoped they would pick it up, and not my own. I gripped bottle in my hand, took in a deep breath, and sprayed as much of the perfume as I could. I then doubled back, and checked the front of the house.

It appeared to be clear, but the Fallen could be anywhere. I sniffed the air, but the smell of the perfume was much too overpowering.

Shaking, I concentrated on my gift. Soon everything around me became a translucent haze, and I knew that I was now invisible to them. I pushed out and focused on one tree across the street, and ran as fast as I could to it.

As soon as I reached it I heard movement behind me, and then a stench filled the air, burning my nostrils.

Darkling.

Whoever sent them, really wanted to find me, and now I was surrounded. One of the Fallen was soaring above me searching the surrounding area. His black wings were outstretched, shining in the moonlight, searching the surrounding area. Further off in the distance another one was circling.

The Darkling had entered the house, and I could hear things crashing inside. They were trashing the place. There was no way I could return, and no way to make it to the car. It was too late, and no one else was on the road in the area. I would stick out like a sore thumb.

I needed to find a safe place to hide.

I felt heat burn my chest and caught my gasp.

A Darkling stood feet away from me, sniffing the air around it. It was onto my scent, but confused because it couldn't see me.

If I moved, he might hear me, but if I stayed, it would run right into me.

I held my breath and started to take a step toward the street. I knew that I could run faster on the pavement, and could avoid tripping over any rocks or twisting my ankle in any holes if I went through the trees.

There was a low, guttural growl behind me. I turned back, and the Darkling was now a few inches away. It took another deep breath, like it had figured out something was there. I quickly ducked, as it swung is sharp claws at the air where I was standing.

HOLY HELL! That was way too close!

It looked bewildered, like it thought it was going to hit something, but didn't.

I could feel myself getting weaker. My gift was making me tired, and I didn't know how much longer I could hold it. I quickly shuffled to the road on hands and knees, and as soon as I hit the pavement, I jumped up and ran. Ran as fast as I could in my bare feet. I didn't know where I was going, but I took off down the street sprinting for my life.

One of the Fallen swooped right down in front of me, making me jump and fall backward, but he obviously didn't see me because he did the same thing a few yards away, scouring the area. I jumped back up and continued running.

A few blocks away lived an old couple, the Mercers, who I visited frequently. They were friends of my parents, so I would take them baked treats as often as I could. They had two Rottweilers named Bill and Ted, and every time I visited, I'd bring each of them a raw steak. They adored me, but they *hated* everyone else.

The Mercers built them a large sized doghouse, a lot bigger than those two mutts were, and even put soft dog beds in it. I asked them why, because the dogs preferred to sleep in the grass, but they said it was because Bill and Ted were their babies, and they wanted them to have a place to sleep in case it rained or became cold. I understood, even though their babies could rip the limbs off of anyone with one bite.

That was the only place I could think of which would be safe enough to hide. Bill and Ted's doghouse. Plus, I would have the added protection of the two meanest dogs on the planet. As I ran, my body began to tremble. I was getting weaker and weaker. This was the longest I'd ever called my gift, and I didn't know how much longer I could stay invisible.

I pushed. Pushed with everything I had left in me, and finally made it to the Mercers front yard. I collapsed on the grass, and when everything became clear, I knew I had become visible again.

The gift had weakened me to the point that I couldn't stand. My legs were like Jell-O, so I pulled myself with my arms, digging every last ounce of strength I had left in me to survive. I was running on pure adrenaline now.

Bill and Ted saw me crawling in the grass and immediately began barking ferociously. They didn't know it was me, and were just protecting their territory.

"Bill! Ted! Shut-up you stupid dogs!" I snapped.

As I got close enough for them to see me and catch my scent, they stopped and began jumping up and down, like they usually did in expectation of a treat.

But I didn't stop. I couldn't. I knew the Fallen must have heard the dogs, and would be here soon, so I pulled myself past them, into the doghouse, and tucked myself into a corner.

Bill and Ted followed me, and began licking my face. I tried to push them away, but suddenly a deep growl rumbled from Ted.

He took off outside snarling and snapping like rabid, bloodthirsty beast. Bill followed behind, furious at whom or whatever had entered their property.

If I didn't know these dogs I would have been completely terrified. They were huge and scary, and I prayed that these dogs would be my saving grace. Hopefully the Fallen would think that no one would dare enter these beasts lair.

Samuel. My thoughts went to him. I hoped and prayed that he was safe, and that he would return to me.

Right now, if they found me, I was helpless to fight back. There was nothing I could do, and nowhere to run. I was too weak and exhausted, and needed sleep to rejuvenate. With rest...Immortals heal, but I was only half Immortal, so I needed a lot extra.

I curled up in the corner and shut my eyes. Even with my two guard dogs outside barking loud enough to wake the dead, the world around me faded to black, and I fell fast asleep.

ELEVEN

THE AWAKENING

S AMUEL'S BODY LAID LIFELESS ON Montem Mortis for three whole days.

But then something happened. Something magical. Something that Lucian had not expected. His eyes fluttered behind his eyelids, showing signs of life.

Samuel was alive!

Apollyon had pierced his chest, but missed his heart. You see, there is only one area around the heart in which his sword could have entered, and it needed to be precise. A few millimeters in one direction or the other would have resulted in death.

Trust my sword. Those were his words.

Apollyon had been secretly practicing and mastering the skill which could injure, but not kill. So close to the heart, that onlookers would think it fatal. And then, when he applied a little pressure to the heart with the inserted blade, he could stop the heart from beating for a few moments, causing the victim to appear dead, when in actuality it was as if they were being put into a coma.

He saved Samuel's life.

Samuel slowly peeled his eyelids open, and every cell in his Immortal body began to scream out in anguish. One arm, both legs, and multiple ribs and backbones were broken. Lacerations and bruises from the fall down the sharp, rocky mountain covered his body. His back felt ablaze, open and bleeding where they had severed his wings.

His wings could grow back, as long as he was still alive. But growing back a full set could take months. Being stuck in the Underworld, where time was much slower than in the mortal world, would mean years of being away from Alaine.

Samuel tried to move, but experienced a pain so excruciating he almost passed out. He needed to find a place to heal, a place to rest, but that was easier thought than done. He was halfway up a steep mountain, covered with razor sharp rocks, and badly injured with no wings.

But still, the first thing on his mind was Alaine. He wondered if they sent someone after her, and if she made it out safely. It was the thought of her, and seeing her again, that gave him hope; despite the pain he decided to keep trying.

Inch by painful inch, Samuel willed his broken body to move. He needed to find shelter, and knew it would be nearly impossible in this Hellhole. But as he pulled himself over the rocky terrain, he noticed something. Tiny white stones carved into the shape of arrows, which could only be seen if one was close enough to the ground. They were set six inches apart from one another, and all seemed to be leading in one direction.

Samuel hoped it wasn't leading him to danger, but there was something inside of him which told him otherwise. Someone had taken the time to carefully carve these stones, and then deliberately and specifically place each one in an area which was the easiest to travel.

He painstakingly pulled himself over razor sharp rocks, following the stone arrows around a rocky bend. They were leading him to a small opening in the side of the mountain. The jagged entrance was barely wide enough for a man to fit, but the top of the entrance had a large stone jetting out, so no one above would ever know it was there.

This was going to be the most difficult task he'd ever had to face: to squeeze through the small hole with two gaping wounds on his back, and a broken body.

Samuel was starting to black out. He was dehydrated, and the heat was getting to him. He knew it would be hell to survive without food or water. His lips were cracked, and his mouth and throat were so dry it felt like sandpaper when he tried to swallow whatever little saliva he had left.

But he'd have to worry about that later. Right now he needed to focus on getting inside that cave before he was noticed.

SAMUEL

I thought I was dead. I thought I'd never see the light of day again, but I was wrong. Apollyon saved my life. I just hoped that one day I'd be able to return the favor.

I had been through my share of injuries, but this pain was nearly unbearable. I knew both my legs were broken, along with multiple ribs, and my left arm was bent abnormally. I was covered in bruises and lacerations. If I hadn't been so brutally battered, or lost my wings, my body would have been able to heal much faster. But because of these massive injuries, the healing would take some time. I would need to rest, and I would eventually need to find food and water.

I prepared myself mentally, and thought on the only things that gave me strength. Alaine and Emma. They were the only two in my life who made the suffering worthwhile, and it was only because of them, that I promised to survive and make it back to the mortal world to look after them.

As much as it would break my heart, I knew I would never be able to return to Alaine, or tell her that I was alive, knowing she would risk everything to be with me. That was something I wasn't willing to do: to put her life in greater danger because I was in it. It was obvious that Lucian had a deep seeded hatred for the Nephilim, and if he found out that I was back in the picture... the thought was beyond horrific.

But this was in hope that Alaine was still alive. I wouldn't allow my mind to think otherwise. In my mind she was safe, and had escaped all danger that came her way. She knew what to do. She knew how to get away. If I had an ounce of faith left in me, it would be in her.

The only way I could get into the cave was sideways, because the entrance was shaped like an oval. I'd have to keep my back on the less jagged side.

I propped myself up as close as I could to the entrance, and stuck my arms inside. I then put my head in, and pulled, twisting my body to the side. I gasped for breath. My broken body screamed with a stabbing pain. The top of my chest was pressed up against one edge, and I braced my arms against the inside walls of the cave to pull the rest of my body through. I took in a deep breath and focused. I exhaled and pulled. Pulled with all my might.

The sharp rocks tore into my skin, but I couldn't stop. I gritted my teeth in pure anguish, and squeezed my broken ribs through.

Halfway...but the pain.

I felt warmth run down my back. My wounds had been torn open again.

I began to black out, and knew I needed to pull myself all the way inside.

My legs were broken so I couldn't put any kind of weight on them. My arm was also broken near the wrist, but I could still use the strongest part, above the elbow to help pull me through.

I took in another deep breath and pulled. With all my might I pulled the rest of my body through the dark hole. The torturous pain from my broken legs, combined with the burning agony from my opened wounds was unrelenting.

My world went black.

DESCENT

When I came to, I was confused, but the pain quickly reminded me exactly where I was and what had happened. I rolled to the side to let what little light there was, shine in on the inside of the cave.

It was a perfect squared area which measured about twenty-feet by twenty-feet.

As my eyes began to focus I started to think I was hallucinating. At the back corner of the cave was a small bed laid out on the ground, which had a pillow and blanket folded atop. To the side of it was a large wooden crate, and next to that were five extra-large skins, which were used to hold drink. They looked as if they were filled. I needed to drink, and I hoped there was strong drink in one, to help numb the pain.

Now, the daunting task of dragging myself twenty feet across the cave floor, and then getting my broken limbs onto the bed. It would have been impossible if the thirst didn't drive me there.

The journey across the cave was torturous and prolonged. My teeth were gritted so hard I thought they would break, but even with greatest difficulty, I finally made it.

I rolled onto the bed which was soft, and much nicer than the rocky floor, and I wondered who my saving grace was. Was it Apollyon?

I reached for the first skin and opened it. It was water and as soon as it touched my lips, it brought me back to life. I drank and drank, wetting my parched mouth and throat.

I then lifted the lid to the crate sitting next to me, and found that it was filled with food. Bread, dried meat, dried fruit; things which would not spoil easily and enough to get me through the healing.

There was a small note folded on the top:

If you are reading this, Congratulations on surviving and finding the cave. You should be supplied with enough food and drink until you heal. The darkest skin holds the strongest drink. Drink, rest, and leave as soon as you can.

It wasn't signed, so there was no way I would be able to find out who had saved me. I just hoped that if they were ever put in this position, that they would be given the same grace.

I knew the only way I could leave this wretched place would be with my wings. The porthole was much too far, and the Underworld was completely barren, which made being seen almost eminent. I couldn't risk it. I'd be confined to the cave for however long it would take to regrow my wings.

I just hoped, with every ounce of hope left within my broken body that Alaine was okay.

ALAINE

I woke to loud snoring and stench of the two huge mutts curled up next to me. Bill and Ted had saved my life, and kept me warm throughout the night. For that, I would be forever grateful.

The sun was blaring, and it seemed to be a beautiful Saturday morning. The world outside was seemingly peaceful. I was hoping that last night was a just dream, but if it really were, I'd be in my own bed and not in a smelly doghouse.

Samuel told me that the Fallen didn't like to be out during the day, that they preferred doing their evil deeds under cover of darkness, away from mortal eyes. Regardless, I decided to wait another hour before crawling out from my cover. The air was clear of any dangerous smells, and the neighborhood started stirring.

I quickly and cautiously made my way back home, threw a few necessities in a suitcase, and left in the car Samuel specifically bought in case of an emergency, just like this. I knew I would have to leave this place and never return. Someone had found out about me, so now, I needed to be extra careful.

Samuel told me that if anything ever happened, and we were somehow separated, that he would find me. I could never believe he could be killed, and knew that if he could find me once, he could find me again, especially now that we were connected.

I wondered where I could run. I needed a place to hide, and a place to reside that would be difficult for the Fallen to find me. The only place I could think of would be a city, bustling with lots of people and lots of smells. A place one could easily get lost.

Maybe a place a little closer to Emma. Not too close of course. I would never interfere with her new life, or risk it, but I wanted to be near, in case she should ever need me.

So it was decided. I was moving to Los Angeles.

SAMUEL

Minutes felt like hours, hours felt like days, and days like an eternity. I was a prisoner, bound to the cave until I was fully healed. With each passing day my wounds healed, bones mended, and wings grew until they were almost strong enough to fly. On the cave wall, I had marked seventy-seven days. Seventy-seven days of pain, loneliness, and despair. Seventy-seven days of trying to survive the darkness of this tiny hole in the Underworld, a literal Hellhole.

I planned to make my escape when the sun was at its peak. That was when the surface was sweltering and at its hottest, and when the Fallen usually took underground into the depths of Hell. The sun never really went down in the Underworld, but because it was desolate and barren, it was the most dismal place to be.

I would need to get to the porthole as quickly as possible. I just hoped that my new wings would be able to carry me swiftly. I summoned them a few times each day to stretch and strengthen them. They were even more impressive, shiny black and stronger than ever, and seemed to be very strong. Outstretched, they were glorious, and barely fit within the confines of the cave.

I felt the need to take to the air and had to fight the urges. Wings were meant to fly, but I had to suppress mine for the time being. Soon, they would carry me to safety. Soon they would fly me to the porthole, and back to the world of Alaine and Emma.

TWELVE

GUARDIANS
ALAINE

I T HAD BEEN TEN MONTHS and I still hadn't heard a word from Samuel. My worst fear was that he was dead, but I kept pushing that thought out of my mind. I just hoped that he would be able to find me.

There was no way I could have left a note for him, because the Fallen would have intercepted it.

He'd been away before, for lengths at a time, and I was aware of the time differences between the mortal world and the Otherworlds. All I could do was to wait it out, and hope for the best.

I stayed in a small apartment, and spent most of my time working the night shift at a nearby hospital. It kept me busy and helped keep my mind off of Samuel. By the time I came home, I was exhausted. As soon as I showered, had something to eat, and my head hit the pillow... I fell fast asleep. But I never minded sleep, because I dreamt of him.

Days dragged on and on, and before I knew it two years had flown by. Two years and no word from Samuel. I started to doubt. I started to think that he wasn't ever going to come back for me.

One morning, as I sat in a small café, I was approached by a girl. She was staring at me like she knew me. I quickly took a glance behind me, but there was no one else there. Her eyes were bright green and she wore a huge smile on her lips. She had silky red hair, which was pulled back into a long braid, and she was wearing a short white sundress.

"Alaine," she spoke softly, "do you remember me?"

I shook my head. "I'm sorry. Who are you?" There was something familiar about her, but I just couldn't put my finger on it.

"I was the one who saved you from the wolves in the cemetery, on your eighteenth birthday. I'm Aurora. Remember?"

I gasped. That moment in time seemed so long ago, so much like a dream, and I often wondered if it was. "How did you find me?

"You have Watchers. Not all the time. Just when you need it, and from afar. They keep you safe while you sleep."

"Am I in danger?" I glanced around, but there didn't seem to be anyone else, and the air was only sweet with her scent.

"Not right now. But I've been sent with news." Aurora's eyes became saddened, and she took a seat across of me.

"Is Emma okay?" That was the first thing I could think of.

"Yes. No one has found out, or knows of the child except for a few who have been sworn to silence. I am here to give you news of Samuel."

My breath seized as soon as she spoke his name. I swallowed hard, my pulse racing, hoping that she wouldn't give me any bad news.

"Is he hurt?"

"No," she breathed.

I sighed in relief. "Oh my! Thank goodness!"

"No, Alaine," she took my hand in hers, "Samuel is dead."

My world froze, and at that moment, a part of me died. I felt my eyes heat with tears. I looked into her eyes again, and they were deeply burdened and concerned for me.

"What happened?" I needed to hear the truth for myself. I needed to make sure that this wasn't a hoax or just a horrible dream.

"We heard from a source that they found out about his relationship with you, which is forbidden in the Otherworlds. A few of the Fallen members captured him, and took him into the Underworld. He was taken to one of their leaders and immediately executed. We weren't given the details. I'm so sorry, Alaine. I'm never prepared to deliver bad news."

I couldn't be true. I'd waited all this time, praying and hoping to feel that wonderful buzz of electricity, and turn to see his face, smiling, having found me once again. It was that hope which drove me to get up each morning, which kept me moving, and believing that we would be together again.

Death.

Finality.

With a few words, Samuel had been stripped from my life…
forever.

Aurora came to deliver the tragic message, but also said that the
Midway would be sending me Guardians. I didn't know what that
really meant, but I didn't really care either. I was in complete and
total shock, and grief-stricken over losing my one true love.

That night, after it all sunk in… I cried. I cried so hard that my
entire body ached. I cried until I couldn't cry anymore. I wanted to
sleep and let it all pass away. I took a strong sleeping pill and after
hours of sobbing, fell fast asleep.

It was a few days before I pulled myself out of despondency.
Emma was still out there, and part of Samuel still lived in her. There
would come a time when she would need me. A time when she
would transform and would have questions. I needed to be prepared
for whatever the future would bring.

I buried myself in work and took every overtime shift I could,
but after years had passed, something I never thought would happen,
happened.

I met a mortal man who seemed to be compatible with me, and
his name was David. He was compassionate, funny, and I enjoyed
his company. He worked for a while at the hospital, but I later found
out that he didn't need to work, because he had an abundance of
wealth handed down to him. David just enjoyed helping others, and
wanted to feel like he could earn his own way if he needed to.

Alaine and David became close friends, but never more than that, because her heart was still so guarded. She knew David wanted more out of their relationship, but deep inside there was still a deep love for Samuel. After all this time, she still loved him, and knew she always would. But she and Samuel were doomed from the very beginning, and it was their love for each other which killed him.

Alaine knew Samuel would want her to be happy. So finally, after years of being alone, she decided to give love another shot.

David and Alaine were married, and he moved them to his beautiful home in Alaska. It was far from the city, but Alaine loved it. It gave her a place to breathe.

There was a beautiful hedged labyrinth at the back of the house, along with a small cottage. During the summers, beautiful wild flowers bloomed everywhere, and during the winter, everything was covered in a glittery white. It was a magical place.

Alaine never had need of anything, because David took the best care of her, and made sure she was happy. After all those years of pain and sorrow, she had finally found some joy.

But that happiness only lasted a few years. Soon, fate stepped in and David became ill with a disease that quickly consumed his body, and there was no known cure. Over the next few months, Alaine cared for David, and was there with him when he breathed his last breath. His passing left her alone again, grieving another tragic loss.

But there were cautious eyes watching Alaine. Her mysterious father, the one whom she'd never met, had set up an invisible barrier around her home without her knowledge. It was a barrier of protection which the Fallen could not pass.

He'd heard that Lucian was on the loose and had separated himself from Lucifer, taking a small part of his army with him. Because one of the Nephilim killed Lucian's ally, he put a mark of death on every single head. Now, Alaine and Emma were in grave danger.

But just when Alaine thought that the worst had passed, something else unexpected happened. One of her closest friends called her one evening, having been diagnosed with stage-four cancer. She was told she had less than a month to live, and had two small children. Caleb, age ten, and Courtney, age seven.

She asked Alaine, that when she passed, if she could take care of her children. Alaine remembered how hard it was for her to ask Victoria and Christian to take her child, so she knew there was no way she would be able to turn down her dying friend's wish.

So, even though it was a difficult decision, and knowing the dangerous and dark world they would become a part of, she gave her friend her word.

Alaine helped her friend through her pain, and tried to make her as comfortable as possible. She was also there, and held her hand as she took her last breath. She died in peace knowing her children were safe.

Alaine now had two mortal children in her care. She didn't have to worry much about Emma, because she was still young, human, and nearly impossible to find. The immortal side of her wouldn't present itself until she neared her eighteenth birthday.

DESCENT

Because of Lucian's murderous plot against the Nephilim, and now with two mortal children in her care, the Midway sent Alaine six Guardians. They were the best of the best, and their names were James, Dominic, Malachi, Kade, Thomas, and Alexander.

James, the eldest, was Alaine's personal Guardian, and eventually became her assistant. The others were sent for extra protection, because most of the Nephilim had already been slaughtered.

The Guardians were shocked that the Midway sent so many to aid Alaine. Having more than one Guardian was unheard of, so they suspected that someone in the higher ranks was looking out for her.

SAMUEL

I finally made it back to the mortal world, and after years of searching, I learned that Alaine had married a mortal man named David and they had moved to Alaska. By the time I made it to Alaska, I found out that he had passed away, and she now had six Guardians residing with her, along with two mortal children.

She must have been in danger to have so many Guardians, and I vowed to stay on the outskirts to try and take care of any intruders. I knew that if I went to Alaine, the risk would be too great. So I stayed away, hidden in the shadows, but never too far.

I traveled back and forth between Los Angeles and Alaska for a while, and looked in on both Alaine and Emma.

Emma was growing up so fast, and was so beautiful. Christian and Victoria adored her, and were very protective which made me happy. I kept my distance, but still kept an eye out for any of the rogue Fallen.

One night, as I walked down their street, my nose began to burn with the strong smell of Darkling. I found one a few blocks away, wandering in the darkness. I wasn't sure if it was searching for her, but I killed it anyway.

It had been too close to Emma. I swore to protect her at all costs, to protect both of them until my last breath.

THIRTEEN

BRINGING EMMA HOME
ALAINE

SIX YEARS LATER...

I T WAS THE MIDDLE OF the night when I received the most horrifying call. A call that brought my worst nightmare to life.

Emma was in an accident, and Christian and Victoria were killed. I was completely devastated, knowing my sister and her husband were dead.

I didn't know the exact details, but I had a huge suspicion that the Fallen had something to do with it. All I knew was that Emma had survived, but she was badly injured and now all alone in a hospital in Los Angeles.

Her Guardian was keeping a close watch, but I needed to bring her here to be with me. I needed to bring her home, as quickly as possible, so I could keep her safe.

I was on the phone all night making important phone calls to specific people who would be critical in her safe return. One of them, an immortal with high influence in the mortal world, was Abigail Reed.

She was highly involved in the legal system, and was there for both mine and Emma's birth. She agreed to wrap up the Guardianship paperwork and make sure Emma would be legally set to travel to Alaska. She even agreed to go and visit her herself, and deliver the news.

There couldn't be one holdback, because now, time was as important as life or death.

Even though Emma's Guardian was already there, I sent another to assist him. The Midway also sent Watchers to make sure that there were no Fallen or Darkling along the way. They wouldn't have to worry too much during the day, but there would be a moment when they would be out in the darkness, and that's when evil usually showed itself.

I stayed up all night and made sure everything was in place. Tickets, escorts, the drivers…hopefully this would be an easy mission. Those watching and guarding over her were the best at what they did.

Morning came too soon, and all I could think about was Emma lying alone, injured, and wondering what happened to her parents. I wished I could have jumped on a plane and met her there, but everything had a proper time and purpose.

The wait for her to arrive had my stomach in knots. I didn't know how to explain everything to her, or even where to begin. I guess I'd have to deal with each question as it came. I made her a promise. A promise that I would always be here if she should ever need me, and now I was going to keep that promise. I would spend the rest of my life protecting her.

It was nearly midnight when Henry, my butler, came to my study to alert me of Emma's arrival. My heart began to race and my hands began to sweat. I was excited, yet anxious, at the thought of seeing her for the first time since her birth. I didn't know how I, or she, was going to react, but every part of me began to tremble.

I had to hold the walls for support as we made our way down the hall.

Would she accept me? Or would she hate me for giving her up, and then bringing her into this dark world which she never knew existed?

Henry stepped out of the way, and as soon as I came around the corner and looked into her eyes, I felt nothing but a mother's love for her daughter.

She was beautiful, beyond what I could have ever imagined. I saw strong resemblances of both Samuel and I, but she was a mixture of the best parts of us. So grown up, but still so young and vulnerable. My heart swelled a thousand times as I looked into her weary eyes, filled with so much pain and despair. She'd been through so much.

I wanted to heal her sadness right then and there, but I knew that wasn't going to happen anytime soon. So instead, I headed toward her with open arms.

"Emma, I'm so glad you're here," I said, walking up to her and hugging her tightly. I then looked down and noticed her casted arm, and took it into my hands, concerned and overwhelmed by what had happened to her.

She didn't move, but stood still and silent.

I realized that I was probably overstepping my boundaries, and stepped back. "I'm so sorry. Please excuse my behavior. I should have introduced myself first. I was just so excited to finally meet you after all these years. My name is Alaine. I'm your mother's half-sister."

"You look a lot like her," she said softly. Her eyes welled with tears.

"I'm so sorry for your loss, Emma. I cannot begin to imagine the pain you are going through, but I can promise you this, I will always be here for you. You are my blood and my last living relative. We will get through this together." I made her that promise, and knew that it was one I would keep.

I couldn't help but wrap my arms around her again, and was surprised when she hugged me back and cried. "It's alright sweetheart. It's very late. I think you should get some sleep. We will talk in the morning," I said, softly.

There was a deep sadness in her eyes. A sadness that I could not ease. She had just lost everyone she had ever loved, and left the only home she'd ever known. She probably had friends she left behind, and I knew she had many questions.

But I also saw in her eyes that she was weary and needed rest. It was after midnight.

"Henry, could you please escort Emma to her room? She must be exhausted."

"Yes, madam," Henry replied with a bow of his head.

We'd have lots of time to talk, and tomorrow would be a new day.

Staring into her deep brown eyes reminded me so much of Samuel, and my heart ached at the thought of him. She had no clue who I was, or of her descent, but I knew deep inside that she would become something great. It was within her. Hidden for now, but it was there.

All I needed to do was to stay focused, and keep us alive until her greatness was revealed. At least I had her back. Our daughter. She was the only thing I had left of Samuel, and she was here…with me. And now, I would spend the rest of my life fighting for her.

ABOUT CAMEO:

 Cameo Renae was born in San Francisco, raised in Maui, Hawaii, and recently moved with her husband and children to Alaska.

She's a daydreamer, a caffeine and peppermint addict, loves to laugh, loves to read, and loves to escape reality. One of her greatest joys is creating fantasy worlds filled with adventure and romance, and sharing it with others.

One day she hopes to find her own magic wardrobe, and ride away on her magical unicorn. Until then...she'll keep writing.

WWW.CAMEORENAE.COM

CPSIA information can be obtained at www.ICGtesting.com
Printed in the USA
BVOW02s1506211115

428026BV00001B/22/P

9 781939 769213